Born in the UK, **Becky Wicks** has suffered interminable wanderlust from an early age. She's lived and worked all over the world, from London to Dubai, Sydney, Bali, NYC and Amsterdam. She's written for the likes of *GQ*, *Hello!*, *Fabulous* and *Time Out*, a host of YA romance, plus three travel memoirs—*Burqalicious*, *Balilicious* and *Latinalicious* (HarperCollins, Australia). Now she blends travel with romance for Mills & Boon and loves every minute! Tweet her @bex_wicks and subscribe at beckywicks.com.

Emily Forbes is an award-winning author of Medical Romance for Mills & Boon. She has written over twenty-five books and has twice been a finalist in the Australian Romantic Book of the Year Award, which she won in 2013 for her novel *Sydney Harbour Hospital: Bella's Wishlist*. You can get in touch with Emily at emilyforbes@internode.on.net, or visit her website at emily-forbesauthor.com.

FALLING AGAIN FOR THE ANIMAL WHISPERER

BECKY WICKS

RESCUING THE PARAMEDIC'S HEART

EMILY FORBES

MILLS & BOON

First Published in Great Britain 2021
by Mills & Boon, an imprint of HarperCollins*Publishers*
1 London Bridge Street, London, SE1 9GF

Falling Again for the Animal Whisperer © 2021 by Becky Wicks

Rescuing the Paramedic's Heart © 2021 by Emily Forbes

ISBN: 978-0-263-29755-3

MIX
Paper from
responsible sources
FSC® C007454

This book is produced from independently certified FSC™ paper
to ensure responsible forest management.
For more information visit www.harpercollins.co.uk/green.

Printed and bound in Spain
by CPI, Barcelona

FALLING AGAIN FOR THE ANIMAL WHISPERER

BECKY WICKS

MILLS & BOON

To all the medical staff out there
who have worked even more tirelessly and selflessly
during the COVID-19 outbreak.
Sending you thanks and love.

CHAPTER ONE

'TEMPERATURE, RESPIRATION—BOTH PERFECT. This is exactly the news we want this morning, little one.' Jodie Everleigh set their four-legged patient as straight as she could on the table in front of them. Marlow was a lot wrigglier than he had been when his owner had brought him in yesterday, which was a good sign.

The poor little Labrador puppy had been in the West Bow Vet Hospital overnight on a drip, thanks to vomiting inexplicably on his owner's kitchen floor for four days.

'He's finally eating well too,' her partner Aileen told her, easing into the exam room with two cups of coffee.

Jodie took her caffeine fix, black as usual, and watched as Aileen ruffled the pup's soft golden fur around his ears, prompting him to try and lick her face from the table.

'Did I tell you how grateful I am that you're as good at knowing when I need coffee as you are with the animals?' she told her, noting the rain start up again over Edinburgh's glum-looking streets out the window. Aileen gave her the thumbs up over the puppy and Jodie smiled, stifling a yawn. They'd built this practice together from the ground up, and their staff had become her second family.

'If he keeps his breakfast down without any vomiting, we might get to send him home this afternoon,' she said, checking the schedule quickly on the iPad on the wall. 'I'll check on our kitten Simba back there. Mark will be in at noon, so he'll do the dog booster vaccinations and...'

'Anika can do the rabbit nail clip if you have to pick Emmie up from the stables,' Aileen finished.

'She might have to,' Jodie replied, thinking back in slight dismay to this morning's argument with her daughter Emmie. She'd promised to go riding with her but she'd been so busy she'd forgotten, and Emmie had run to her father, citing her a bad mother. She knew Emmie didn't mean it. She was just an impassioned pre-teen whose body was changing as fast as her opinion on who was the better parent.

Ethan probably had been, lately, she mused. Her ex-husband had a new girlfriend, Saskia, who seemed to have boundless energy as well as a love of horses. While Jodie was happy for her ex-husband, it didn't escape her how she herself seemed to live for work and not much else lately—but what was she supposed to do? She was a single mother, and she'd worked damn hard to provide Emmie and herself with the life they both loved here.

Jodie's phone buzzed. Her father. 'Hey, Dad, sorry I've not called this week. I've been swamped—'

'Jodie, I'm afraid it's not good news. Are you sitting down?'

'Oh, God, what?' She dropped heavily to the swivel chair behind the desk and braced herself. 'It's not Mum, is it?'

Her dad sounded frazzled, tired. 'Mum's fine. It's my brother...your uncle Casper.'

'Casper?'

'He died last night, Jodie. He had a heart attack on the estate at Everleigh…' Her father trailed off, seemingly trying to compose himself. Her heart was thudding suddenly, like that of a rabbit kicking its way through her ribcage. Uncle Casper was *dead*?

Her palm turned sweaty around the phone. She hadn't seen Casper in years, not since her wedding, but he'd been a staple in her life all through her childhood. She'd pretty much grown up on his estate around his veterinary practice and horses in Dorset. 'Dad, I'm so sorry,' she managed.

'The funeral is on Friday. Cole called me with the news.'

Her head was spinning harder now, making it hard to breathe. 'Cole Crawford called you?'

She felt glued to her swivel seat. 'He didn't call me,' she found herself saying, and then wondered why she was surprised. Why the hell would Cole Crawford call her? He hadn't called her in twelve years, not since he'd announced, right before they'd been due to leave for Edinburgh, *together*, that he wouldn't be joining her there.

Her father relayed the funeral details and she only half heard them.

Already the memories were flooding her brain like tidal waves—her funny, witty, wealthy, horse-mad uncle Casper was dead, and Cole, her first love, her first everything, had called her father with the news, which meant he was probably still working at Casper's estate.

She hung up, thoughts reeling.

She could still see Cole's face as clear as day. The way it had changed from that of an eleven-year-old boy to a nineteen-year-old man over endless long summers in Dorset. She'd lived for them, the same way he'd seemed to live only for Casper's horses when they'd first met. His compassion for the animals had rubbed off on her and led her to where she was today.

She could see the look in Cole's brown, soulful eyes at fifteen years old, kissing her for the first time. Sixteen years old, telling her he loved her. And then… nineteen years old, telling her he wouldn't be going to Edinburgh with her, to vet school, like they'd planned. Before that moment, when he'd destroyed *all* their future plans together, she'd assumed she'd met the love of her life.

She'd begged to know what had happened, why he was changing his mind about vet school, and Edinburgh, and her. She'd never got any answers.

The last thing she wanted to do, she realised, was see Cole Crawford again.

CHAPTER TWO

THE RAIN WAS sheeting down in hard diagonal slashes as Cole steered the Land Rover down the single-track country road. The puddles reared up around the wheels, sending vertical mudslides up the sides, right up to the windows. February in Dorset was always like this but the daffodils were poking their heads up already.

'Spring's here, somewhere,' he muttered to Ziggy, eyes on the road. 'We have to see how this one goes without Casper, huh?'

His faithful Border collie and respected veterinary assistant lolled his tongue out on the passenger seat beside him. Ziggy had been travelling these roads, doing the house calls with him, ever since he was a pup. Cole was grateful for his company today.

He'd kept himself to himself and the animals more than usual, he supposed, since Casper's death. He still didn't know if he'd processed it. Casper's heart had simply given up, right there on the spot. He'd been seventy-two years old and fighting fit, or so everyone had thought.

'You never know when it's coming,' he said out loud over the steering wheel. Ziggy looked at him blankly. And then, out of nowhere, Jodie was back in his mind.

He'd been getting these 'hits' of her since he'd called

her father with the news. He knew they'd both be at the funeral and the thought of seeing her face up close, twelve years after he'd broken things off with her, wasn't sitting too well at all. Not that she didn't have a beautiful face…but the last time he'd seen it she'd been crushed and furious. She'd looked at him like he was ripping her heart out from her chest with a meat hook and later the absence of her had left him feeling just as hollow.

Jodie.

He'd be saying her name again a lot in a matter of days, talking to her face to face, looking straight into those eyes. All the shades of blue, warm like the ocean in summer. They'd been like anchors to him once. They'd probably be as cold as ice now, he thought wryly, considering how he'd left things. They'd been through so much. He'd been through more than she knew without her…although he was sure getting married and having a kid had kept her more than busy.

Life had been tough for him before Jodie had entered his life in a riot of city girl attitude, aged eleven, the same as him. His parents' berry farm, Thistles, was struggling back then and he'd known things were very wrong even before his father had been locked away for tax evasion. Most fathers didn't welcome their sons home at the end of the day with a bottle of whisky and two fists to use on a kid's face. He'd never told anyone. The guy had been a waste of space right up to the day he'd died, six months after he'd got out of jail. Jodie had been gone by then, pregnant, on the verge of getting married.

Ziggy barked as he swerved to avoid a pothole and he hit the gas harder. 'I've got it, buddy.'

The cow was waiting in agony at Rob Briar's dairy

farm; this rain wouldn't stop him hurrying, but images of Jodie were coming thick and fast, threatening to break his focus. The photo of her in the wedding dress had killed him—some posh politician's son had swept her off her high-heeled feet. It was his own fault he'd lost her, but pregnant and married after six months of college? Crazy.

He could still hear Casper telling him the news. *'Jodie's pregnant. She met a Scotsman up there, it seems pretty serious. She's going to marry him.'*

She'd always been his. Even when he'd broken things off for her own safety, he'd stupidly assumed she'd be his again when he'd figured out how to handle things at home, or at least created a safe environment to bring her back to. He'd used to love the way Jodie Everleigh took him by surprise, but a wedding and a baby at nineteen…he'd never expected *that*.

Twelve years earlier

'So, are you excited, Cole? It's going to be an adventure. Did you see the rooms are all ready for us in Waverleigh House? It's the best student house in Edinburgh.'

Jodie went on and on, babbling excitedly the way she did, and Cole felt the ball of angst fill his stomach like a lead balloon.

She was about to leave Everleigh again. They were sitting on the hay bales outside the stables, waiting for her car. In minutes it would pull up on the gravel and take her to the train station, and he still hadn't been able to tell her what had happened.

He'd been putting his news off all weekend. How could he crush her by telling her he couldn't come to Edinburgh, or university, because of his father? She didn't even know how violent the man really was; he'd been locked up for the last four and a half years, the whole time they'd been an item.

She knew he was serving time for tax evasion, but no one knew about the physical abuse he and his mother had endured before that.

Jodie was still talking, one leg draped over his lap in her jeans, resting against his shoulder. Their fingers were laced together. He'd never said it, he wasn't so great with words, but he didn't think he'd ever fit with anyone the way he fitted with Jodie.

Suddenly, she was frowning at him, trying to read him. 'What's wrong? You've been weird all weekend.'

'Jodie.' He swallowed, extracting himself from her and pulling his knees up to his chest. Her bags were at their feet. Everleigh's driveway was still empty but the sky was darkening above them, almost like the heavens were preparing for his fate. He drew a long breath, rammed his hands in his hair. 'I'm not coming with you to Edinburgh. I'm sorry.'

Jodie laughed. 'Very funny. As if you could live without me…' She leaned in to kiss him again but he turned his face away.

He said nothing, racking his brain as to how to explain it without sounding weak and pathetic. He knew he should have stood up to his father's violence years ago, but when they'd locked him up, he'd been so relieved to finally be free of him that he'd lost himself in Jodie, finally.

He hadn't thought about when he'd be released, or that he might get out early and come home even angrier than before. He hadn't predicted his own mother would welcome him back so eagerly either, but she'd always been even weaker around the man than *him*.

'Cole?' The colour had drained from Jodie's face. She blinked at him. 'You're serious. You're not coming?'

'I can't, Jodie.'

She pursed her lips, stepped back and crossed her arms, then uncrossed them quickly, flustered. 'Why? Cole, you already have a place. I thought we were doing this together. I know it's all a big change but, come on, it's the Royal School of Veterinary Studies, it's the best. And we can come back down here whenever we want for the weekends and holidays…'

When his father would be waiting to mess them both up. 'No. Listen to me, Jodie, it's not the right time.'

Cole had already been accused of turning his father back to drink. Funny, that. There had been no alcohol in the house when he'd come home from prison via the pub, steaming drunk.

Now there were beer cans all over the living room and Cole had spent the whole weekend hiding the bruise on his right thigh from Jodie. It had throbbed for hours after the TV had crashed into him, then shattered on the floor tiles. Luckily his mother had been out. All Cole had done was explain that his place in Edinburgh was set in stone, and he was leaving with Jodie at the end of the month.

His father had been quick to stomp on his plans as much as the broken television: *'I need you here around the farm. How dare you think you can just leave without earning your keep?'* He'd already pulled the funding reserved for his studies. His callous actions made Cole's teeth start to grind all over again.

'What's going on?' Jodie's blue eyes were imploring. He should just tell her.

But he'd already been over this with himself. If he

told Jodie, she would storm over to his house and confront his father, and he couldn't put her in the line of fire
like that. She might also ask her rich dad or Casper to
help, which of course they would, and his father would
go crazy if anyone tried to pull him away from here
now.

Jodie had no clue the abuse people suffered whenever
his dad got angry. He'd never told *anyone*.

'Tell anyone and I'll kill you,' his dad would rage,
seconds after landing a punch on him, or throwing him
against a wall, or sending a bottle flying at his head
from across the kitchen. The TV was nothing, he'd done
worse than that before over the years. What if he struck
out at Jodie now he was home? The thought made him
go cold.

'Maybe I'll defer a year, I don't know,' he said now.
In the distance a horse let out a whinny.

'I'll defer a year too, then,' she shot back.

Dammit. He should have known she would say that.
'No, Jodie.'

She looked at him in defiance. 'Well, I'm not going
without you.'

'You have to go, Jodie, it's all you've talked about
for years.'

'It's all *we've* talked about for years. We were going
to study together, and then come back here, work on the
rescue centre, more horses like Mustang. What's happened?' She reached for his face. Tears were pooling
in her eyes now and it almost broke him. 'Cole, what's
happened?'

'Nothing,' he lied.

'I love you,' she said. Her eyes said she expected to
hear the truth.

He just shook his head.

'Talk to me.' Jodie gripped his hair either side of his head, drew him closer. He could feel her hands shaking. 'Talk to me. I just told you I love you. Why won't you say it back?'

Because if I do, I won't be able to let you go. The voice in his head was raging. He loved her so much it hurt but he had to put her safety first, and her education. She wanted to go to vet school so badly, she was so excited. He wouldn't let her risk all that just to be with him in the mess he'd created. He had to stay here for a while at least, keep his mother safe, figure out his next steps.

'You don't love me? You don't want to be with me? Is *that* why you're pulling out of coming to Edinburgh?' Confusion flooded Jodie's eyes. Cole fought not to press his thumbs to the tears streaming down her cheeks but he dug his nails into his palms and forced himself not to move. He'd crack the moment he touched her. Jodie deserved better than this.

'I'm sorry,' he said, forcing his eyes to the floor. 'We're going in different directions.'

'What? I don't understand what's happening, Cole!'

The car's headlights behind her turned her trembling body into a silhouette and he felt the loss of her overwhelm him instantly. He almost reached for her again. He almost told her that of course he loved her, that he was trying to *protect* her. But maybe it was better this way. She wouldn't stay for anyone who didn't want her. She'd be safer and the further away she was from here and him the better.

The silence was excruciating. The car pulled up and the driver rolled the window down. 'Train station, love?'

Jodie lowered her voice, eyes glistening. 'You waited all weekend to break up with me right at the last minute?' She sounded angry now, fuming, humiliated. He focused on his breathing, tried to stay cool. 'I can't believe this,' she hissed.

'I'm sorry.'

Jodie started scrambling for her bags. He jumped down and went to help her but she shoved at his chest, forcing him back onto the hay bale with a strength that surprised him. 'No!'

She flung the car door open and launched herself into the back seat, slamming it after her. 'You know where I'll be when you come to your senses,' she said through the window. 'And if you don't, it's your loss, Cole Crawford.'

CHAPTER THREE

'THIS WEATHER! Is it always like this here?' Emmie looked affronted in the passenger seat and Jodie almost let out a laugh.

They were somewhere on a rural road between Weymouth and Dorchester, but things looked different from how she remembered. There were more sheds, more farms, more cottages between the villages, out in the sticks. There was definitely more rain.

'It's not like this in the summertime,' she told her daughter, which was true. 'You should see the flowers here usually, all around the ditches. There's yellow flag, great willowherb, meadowsweet, purple loosestrife...' She listed a bunch that Cole had told her the names of once.

Emmie wrinkled her nose at the snowflakes that were now flurrying down on the windows instead of rain. She clearly didn't care about the flowers, and was already missing her horse, Saxon.

Up ahead, the traffic had almost ground to a halt. Jodie glanced at the clock on the dashboard. The funeral was in two hours. They were just a few miles from the estate but if it didn't clear up, they might be late.

'We're going to be late,' Emmie announced unnecessarily, pulling out her phone for the hundredth time. Seconds later she moaned, 'Mum, there's no signal here.'

'It'll come back,' Jodie told her, hoping it was true. She had to call into West Bow soon and make sure things were OK. She was full of butterflies. Scowling at the snow, she knew she could tell herself the butterflies were because of so many things, but who was she kidding? She was about to see Cole again. The thought had left her tossing and turning all night in the hotel bed.

A tractor crawled up alongside them, urging her further towards the roadside. The snow was coming down heavier now. It was almost a blizzard. With despair she noticed the signal must have died on her phone too and messed up the GPS. The map had sent them down a wrong one-way road.

'Dammit,' she cursed in frustration, swiping her scarf over her shoulder with her loose hair. She needed to go back, but there was nowhere to turn.

Emmie rolled her eyes. 'Way to go, Mum.'

Jodie's stomach was in knots. She didn't even have the energy to tell Emmie not to be so rude. She already knew her daughter didn't want to be here, but with Ethan and his girlfriend going away for a long weekend she'd had no choice but to take Emmie out of school and bring her.

'This is the worst day ever,' Emmie grumbled, tapping in vain at her phone screen. 'We could have spent this weekend riding Saxon! I didn't even know your uncle Casper.'

'Actually, you did meet Casper once,' Jodie said, distracted. 'You were just very small, that's all. In fact, you hadn't even been born.'

'Gross!'

Emmie had been a tiny bulge in her wedding gown the

last time she'd seen Casper. He had tried to seem happy for her the whole time, but she'd known deep down he hadn't been. She'd caught her uncle looking between her and Ethan, like he was trying and failing to spot the same kind of connection he'd often commented on between herself and Cole. He'd always thought of Cole like the son he'd never had. He'd also watched them fall madly in love. She guessed her uncle had always assumed it would be her and Cole having a baby together, eventually. Not that she could ever regret having had Emmie.

Averting her eyes back to the road, she recalled the moment she'd pulled up the pregnancy test to find the tiny blue line. It had been a signal that her life was about to change once again.

She'd still been heartbroken over Cole ending their relationship when the accident had happened. Had it been vodka or tequila she and Ethan had been glugging like water when they'd ended up in bed, blurring the lines of their friendship and setting the life-changing chain of events in motion? She couldn't even remember now.

Ethan's father had been on the verge of being re-elected for the fourth time—everyone had known who the Labour MP was, and everyone had known his son, too. The election had already been a roller-coaster for the whole family. Ethan had been under huge pressure to stay out of the limelight, not to screw up his studies, or his life. It was the reason he'd been drowning his own sorrows alongside her behind the closed doors of their shared student flat that night.

Jodie hadn't ever come under quite that much pressure. If anything, perfection to her busy screenwriting, jet-setting parents was having her out of their hair for seven years while she completed her degree. But she'd *wanted* to complete her studies to the best of her ability; vet school had been her dream for as long as she could remember.

When she'd discovered she was pregnant—from the one night in her life she hadn't used contraception—neither she nor Ethan had wanted to abandon their studies. But they'd refused to abort the baby.

'You'll live to regret it, if you have this baby,' her mother had said.

But she'd stood her ground. She'd known she'd live to regret it if she *didn't.*

Ethan had been supportive, but they'd both known they couldn't study *and* raise a child with no help.

It had come as a surprise when their parents had joined forces and offered to finance a home and childcare so they could finish their degrees and keep the baby…with one small caveat from Ethan's father. They had to marry. A twenty-year-old son with a baby out of wedlock would not have looked good on an MP's campaign trail.

Looking back, she knew she should never have agreed to such a ludicrous suggestion. She was still ashamed of how she'd bowed in submission, but she'd cared for Ethan more than for herself at the time, she supposed. She had been lost, naive and still grieving for Cole. Ethan had been her good friend; appeasing their families had also been making the best of a bad situation. They'd been sure they could make it work and divorce quietly a few years later. What was a marriage certificate anyway? Just a piece of paper.

To this day, only their families and closest friends knew the deal they'd struck. For a second she wondered if Cole had ever questioned her marrying Ethan so young; or wished things had worked out between *them.*

Don't be ridiculous, she scolded herself. *He didn't*

try to contact you once after breaking up with you! He never even tried to come to Edinburgh in the end. Why would he care if you got married...or divorced?

Jodie reached for her coffee cup, before remembering it had been empty for almost three hours. She was so far from home already—there was no going back.

It's only two nights, she told herself, trying to stay calm as she slowed the car a metre behind the tractor. She'd booked them into The Ship Inn—a fifteenth-century hotel a mile from Everleigh Estate. Even the thought of staying in the same area as Cole Crawford for the weekend was making her feel queasy.

'So, was Casper married?' Emmie asked now.

'Nope,' she said, squinting through the snow. 'Some people said he was married to his horses.'

'Who will be looking after them now he's gone?'

'I assume he has staff,' she answered, though she had been wondering herself how the inheritance would be split and what would become of Everleigh. No one had mentioned his will yet, which surprised her. Her father would have said something surely, if he knew.

The snow was coming down even thicker now, huge white blobs battling with the windshield wipers. The sat-nav still wasn't working properly and she was about ready to crack when eventually, after crawling the Peugeot along like a caterpillar, she found a place ahead to turn around.

They'd only just made it past a rickety cattle grid when the car engine spluttered to a stop.

The snow shouldn't make him too late, Cole thought. The Land Rover had got them through worse than this. He only worried for the people on their way to the funeral. Over five hundred attendees were supposed to be showing up at two p.m. *Including Jodie.*

Ziggy started barking manically over the radio. Frowning, he slowed the vehicle, feeling the tyres crunch on the fresh snow. Ziggy never barked unless he was alerting him to danger.

Then he saw the silver car through the blizzard. It was almost invisible, the windshield covering fast with snow. Clearly the wipers weren't working.

'They must have broken down,' he said to Ziggy.

He steered the Land Rover past the car and noted two figures in the front. He wasn't sure, but he thought he could make out a woman and a young girl. Jumping out into the blizzard, his boots made fresh dents in the tyre marks as he strode to the back and pulled his tow rope from the boot.

A woman was standing in the snow now.

'The engine just died,' she called out, squinting through the flurry. He pulled his hat down against the snow and held up the tow rope.

He couldn't see her face but she was standing half-sheltered by the open car door. He fought a smile at her tight denim jeans tucked into unscuffed, too-clean brown leather boots. She clearly wasn't from around here.

Cole was at the car door in seconds, peering around her at the kid first, checking she was OK. Her long blonde hair looked freshly brushed and she commanded his gaze with big restless ocean-blue eyes. She was what…ten? Eleven?

'Can you help us, please? We're late to a funeral,' the woman said from the confines of a giant red woollen scarf. He pushed his hat up and stepped back to look at her. Her eyes grew round, just as his throat grew tight. 'Cole?'

Jodie.

Her face was as white as the snow, or maybe more ashen. Damn, he thought, taking her all in up close with the snow settling on her hair. Here she was, right in front of him, out of the blue. The kid...was her daughter, he realised now.

He was half smiling again, more out of shock than anything, but he only realised this when he met Jodie's narrowed eyes. Ice-blue, just like the last time she'd looked at him, pleading for answers. He tried not to let on the whirlwind in his brain that had replaced all regular cognitive behaviour. 'Cole...can you just help us?'

Her voice was trembling slightly as she shut the door. She almost caught her sweater sleeve in it and he heard her tut in annoyance. She was nervous, agitated, like a cornered deer with nowhere to run.

Age hadn't changed her much, he noted. He'd feigned indifference back then but the first time he'd laid eyes on her she'd been the most exotic thing he'd ever seen, and she'd seemed disarmingly unaware of how pretty she was. It was like Casper had invited a rare creature onto the estate that, for once, he'd had no clue what to do with.

The young kid wound the window down, and stuck her head out. 'You know this man, Mum?'

'One second, sweetheart.'

He heard Jodie suck in a breath as she followed him to the back of the car. She was hugging her arms around herself against the cold or the shock of seeing him sooner than expected, maybe both.

She opened her mouth to speak but a motorcyclist slipped past their vehicles and sped off too fast. The action sent a cold slushy shower of muddy water over them and Jodie shrieked.

He dropped the tow rope and reached for her at the same time as she stumbled against him. In a second he was holding her too tightly at the side of the road. Some protective impulse had kicked in, like the time he'd yanked her from Mustang's path. The new rescue horse could have mown her down if he hadn't seen it coming and jumped the fence.

'Cole,' she whispered shakily against him. Her palms were pressed flat against his chest over his jacket. She drew long, slow, deep breaths under his chin like she was struggling for air. A long-extinguished fire began to smoke from the depths of his core as his fingers scrunched into a tumble of soft, damp hair that made the past fly back in a heartbeat.

It was maybe three…four long seconds before she pulled back from him, swiping in vain at her muddy jeans, avoiding his eyes. She was soaked and so was he, not that he'd noticed till now. Time was unwinding. Her honey-brown waves were springing into curls, like her hair always had when it had got wet.

He found his voice, adjusted his hat. 'You'll dry off.'

'It's not like I'm not always covered in mud, whenever I'm around you,' she replied. Then she scowled to herself, like she'd sworn she wouldn't remind herself, or him, of anything to do with their past. He was sure they *both* knew that wasn't going to be easy, but then she *was* only staying a couple of days at most so how hard would it be just to stay out of each other's way?

Right after he got her out of this mess.

The towing interface came out easily from its compartment in the back. He could almost feel Jodie's eyes appraising his muddy boots and jacket from behind him as he screwed it in place. He caught her daughter's gaze in the wing mirror.

So this was Ethan Sanders's daughter. Ethan was an equine dental vet. Cole had looked him up years ago in a moment of curiosity, right after he'd come home from his last stint in Sri Lanka and broken things off with Diyana. Jodie didn't know about Diyana. He assumed not anyway, unless Casper had mentioned it.

As much as it had pained him over the years, he was glad Jodie had married someone who'd gone on to be successful. It wasn't his business, but he wondered why their marriage had ended.

His heart was like a wild horse throwing a fit in his chest now. That…*thing*…whatever it was between him and Jodie that he'd felt the first time he'd kissed her had thrown him off guard. He'd felt something reconnecting the second he'd pulled her head under his chin again; two live wires fusing back together.

He caught himself. It was all in his head. She was getting to him already. 'We should go, Jodie. We both have somewhere to be. Attach this to the back of your car.'

She took the rope he held out to her and he watched her drag a hand nervously through her long hair. 'The funeral, will we make it on time? Emmie and I still have to get to The Ship Inn, we need to change…'

'Forget that.' He made for the Land Rover with the other end of the tow rope, wiping his snowy hands on his jeans. 'No time. You'll just have to come with me.'

CHAPTER FOUR

THE REST OF the day was a blur to Jodie. Five hundred expected guests had become three hundred after the church ceremony and burial because of the weather. There were still more people than she'd ever seen in the huge farmhouse.

The kitchen was as she remembered it, as warm and inviting as ever, with its dark wooden beams laden with pots and pans and the fire blazing in the hearth. Cole, however, sent a chill right through her.

He'd changed into a navy-blue suit and tie. She couldn't help noticing the aristocratic cut of an expert tailor, which surprised her somewhat as it spoke of a man with money. Lots of it. To anyone else the suit would highlight his chiselled features, piercing brown eyes and shrewd mind, but to her, the whole look hid the real him. Cole might have money now but he was anything but a suit and business guy.

Jodie looked away. She didn't know him any more, and she didn't particularly want to, but she'd bet her last banknote his life was a revolving door of mud and mayhem and horses and avoiding small talk...or any kind of talk, she thought in a flicker of fresh irritation at how he'd ended things with her.

'It's good to see you, Crawford.' Her father, with

his freshly shaven jaw set in stern contemplation, was resting one hand on the end of the marble centre island. From his seat on one of the bar stools, Cole nodded bluntly at the obvious lie. Her father had never approved of him—he'd once remarked that Cole had his head in the clouds and would never be able to support her.

'I know you were close to my brother, Crawford,' her father continued. 'I hear he pulled some strings to get you a scholarship in London after you ducked out of going to Edinburgh with Jodie?'

Jodie felt her cheeks blaze at the dig on her behalf, and she hid behind a bite of her puff pastry canapé. If this was her father's way of reprimanding Cole for treating her poorly he didn't have to, especially not today of all days. Although she couldn't deny that she *was* interested to hear what he'd say.

'That's correct.' Cole seemed unfazed by the dig. Maybe he hadn't even noticed it. He reached a hand down to pet Ziggy. 'I owe a lot to Casper. I worked hard for him but you're right, his contacts in London helped with my scholarship. I also trained here at Everleigh in the summers, when I wasn't in Sri Lanka. And I came right back after I graduated. That was always the plan.'

Her father was nodding politely but Jodie felt the bad blood simmer in her veins again. How dared he talk about his 'plan' with Casper when he'd pulled the plans they'd made together right out from under her? Also...*he'd been in Sri Lanka?* What on earth had taken him there?

'This was always more of a home to me than Thistles. Casper was kind of a father figure to me, I'm sure you know that.' Cole reached for the bowl of peanuts on the counter. He scooped a handful into his mouth and she heard them crunch, feeling his eyes on her. Was he thinking she looked different now? Better or worse?

Why should she care?

'I was sorry to hear about Jack,' her dad continued, and Cole frowned, filling the space with even more awkwardness. She knew Cole's father had never even met her dad. The only time she'd seen Jack herself had been when the cops had dragged him off in handcuffs. They'd been fourteen, summer had just begun, and she'd followed the sound of the sirens across the adjoining fields to Thistles.

Cole had held her back at the gate. Jack had been blind drunk, struggling with the authorities. He'd ended up serving time for tax evasion, something about stashing funds in a foreign account. She'd never got the details. Cole wouldn't talk about it, not that he'd ever talked about his dad a lot *before* he'd been arrested either. Or any of his family. He really had just seemed to live for his horses.

'How did he die?' she asked now, feeling slightly guilty that she hadn't called him when she'd heard about Jack passing away.

Cole met her eyes. 'He was taking a leak into the River Stour. Guess he didn't realise where the edge was.'

'He *drowned*?' Jodie felt terrible. Cole just nodded, his face not giving anything away.

'And your mother?' she pressed, cursing the fact that her mouth was asking questions when she'd told her mind not to care about his life at all. His mother had always been sweet to her. She had been a quiet, meek little thing, wouldn't say boo to a goose. 'How is she?'

'Loving life, thank you,' Cole said. His face softened slightly 'After my dad was found dead she lived here at

Everleigh for a few months. Then she met a guy called Darren at the organic market. They run a mixed farm of arable, sheep and beef now down in Puddletown.'

'That sounds nice for her and…Darren, was it?' her father said, feigning interest. Jodie had almost forgotten he was there, but she felt her mouth twitch in spite of her mood. Her dad wouldn't know a dairy heifer from a chocolate milkshake and he had little interest in farmers, or anything they stood for. Casper had had chickens, pigs and horses, a sprawling estate and a successful veterinary practice in the countryside. Michael Everleigh had accolades and trophies and first-class tickets to movie premieres.

Her mother, Vivian, was the other half of their successful screenwriting duo and the three of them had lived in Greenwich since she was born. The Everleigh brothers couldn't have been more different if they'd tried. Looking at her father now, Jodie realised he hadn't *disliked* Cole. He'd just never really understood him. Not like *she* did…or thought she had, once.

From the second she'd met Cole she'd been fascinated, even though he'd shown no real interest in her that first summer. His indifference had only fascinated her more because he hadn't been like the boys at her school. She could still recall the moment she'd first laid eyes on his wild black, untamed curls and muddy jeans.

Cole had rescued wild horses with Casper and ridden them bareback, barefoot. He'd had zero interest in TV or any other gadgets but he'd known how to drive a tractor and milk a goat. He'd liked reading big, wordy books by writers like Tolstoy, Hemingway and Shakespeare, which she'd thought odd because he'd never had too many words to share himself. And he'd spent most of his nights in the stables, turning pages, tuning in to the horses.

His quietness had made him observant of everything, especially around the animals. She'd seen the proof many times that he'd had a real gift for picking up on the tiniest shifts in their behaviour and demeanour. He'd made countless diagnoses out on calls and around the estate way before Casper had even made any examinations.

To Jodie he'd been a mystery. A welcome distraction from the fact that she'd been deposited with her uncle Casper purely so her parents could get rid of her for the summer. He was a still a mystery now, she mused, noting how his new short beard lined his lips—lips she'd once kissed hungrily, lazily, desperately, in every way possible, for hours on end.

Cole's phone buzzed. 'It's the solicitor,' he told them after a moment. 'I bet she can't make it through this snow to read the will.'

'Shame, that, seeing as *no* one knows what my brother put in that will yet,' her dad grumbled. 'I'm probably the allocated executor,' he continued, 'and I really have to leave right after this.'

Jodie met Cole's eyes, wincing at her father's words. He clearly expected to have inherited the estate, being Casper's only sibling. Yet he was still putting his work schedule first.

'Excuse me a moment,' Cole said. He slid off his school and moved to the corner of the kitchen by the copper sink. Jodie watched Ziggy pad after him, wishing she wasn't still so sucked in by his infuriating handsomeness. Cole's commanding bone structure and the nose that ended bluntly instead of in a point gave him as much character as his new beard. His whole persona spoke of a life outdoors in the elements, and she shivered in the warm kitchen, recalling the feeling back at the car of being in his arms again.

She'd wanted to feel repulsed, but she'd stuck to him like a magnet for far longer than necessary. It had felt like that, at least.

His conversation seemed to last a while. She kept one eye on Emmie, who was chatting to a young boy about her age over by the roaring fireplace. But whenever she glanced at him, Cole seemed to be watching her, nodding, as if his conversation involved her somehow. Or maybe he was simply appraising this new, older version of someone he'd once known so well, the same as she was doing with him.

Had he ever thought about her when he'd been studying in London, instead of Edinburgh? Or in Sri Lanka? She'd never been anywhere that exotic.

Where else in the world had he been while she and Ethan had been rained into an Edinburgh townhouse, surrounded by nappies and baby toys? They'd had childcare and assistance, thanks to their parents, but their lives hadn't exactly been like most students' lives for the seven years they'd worked on their degrees.

Not that Cole was entirely to blame for her pregnancy...it could just as easily have been *his* child she'd conceived, she supposed. Even though they'd always been careful. She'd only been off the Pill a couple of months when she'd slept with Ethan and they'd both been so incredibly drunk it was a miracle they'd even figured out what went where.

Cole caught her eyes again. Annoyed, she averted her gaze and reached for another canapé. All the times they'd had sex on this property, they'd 'christened' pretty much every room. It had been by far the best sex of her life. She suddenly felt hot in her tight black dress. She didn't want to find anything attractive about Cole but it was like asking a toddler not to like ice cream.

Jodie watched Cole pull on his plaid jacket and a thick woollen scarf.

Finally off the phone, she expected him to try and sneak off unseen, just him and his dog. Instead, he signalled for her to follow him outside into the snow.

The log cabin on the path towards the stables must have been at least fifteen feet long. It was sheltered by swaying oaks and sycamores, a peaceful oasis made entirely of thick knotted tree trunks and weathered oak panels. Jodie pulled her jacket tighter around her black lace dress as Cole led them to a stop outside the window.

'This wasn't here before,' she observed, as the snow swirled around them and settled on the cherry trees in the garden. 'Wasn't this just a field?'

'Yes,' he said. 'I built it here because of the trees. Gives me more privacy.'

'You built it yourself?'

He laughed softly. 'I had some help. We took reclaimed steel sash windows from at least five different projects in the area. Would've gone to waste otherwise.'

'Good to hear you're such an eco-warrior,' she quipped, aware that her nerves around him were making her prickly. He'd done a good job. The place had clearly cost a lot of money, humble as it appeared.

'I work out the back; we had another consultation space built with access right onto the paddocks.'

'What do you do here exactly?'

'Behavioural therapy, with horses mostly. People come to me with all kinds of animals. They just started showing up at the main house and it got a little much. So we began redirecting them here.'

'Behavioural therapy, huh?' Jodie was letting it all sink in. It shouldn't surprise her that people sought Cole out. He was better at reading animals than any vet she'd ever met.

A light inside the cabin illuminated a fireplace as they passed a window. She made out a comfy-looking long couch and a sheepskin rug. The shelves around the fireplace were piled with books. Tolstoy, Hemingway, Shakespeare... All the classics he'd always been buried in, still within reach. No TV.

She wouldn't say it out loud, but they both knew Cole had built this cabin just where they'd imagined 'their retreat' would be. Her stomach churned as he led her onwards, but she couldn't help stopping by the snow-covered stone benches laid out in a semi-circle around one side of the firepit. They'd put cushions over those in the summer, years ago.

'Casper always loved that fire pit,' she said.

Cole stopped beside her in the snow, sighing in nostalgia. 'He did.'

They were both silent for a moment, remembering her uncle. He'd been the king of toasting marshmallows. 'It's so strange, being here without him,' she said quietly, swallowing a lump in her throat.

'Tell me about it.' Cole eyed her sideways. She noticed his fingers twitching at his sides before he shoved them in his pockets. 'We need to talk, Jodie.'

Discomfort crossed his handsome features, making her heart start to thrum. She swallowed again, a mix of tears and nerves. Of course they needed to talk. They both knew they had unresolved issues.

'What about?' she said anyway. She'd let him start

with an apology. He owed her that much for the stone-cold silence that had tormented her like a ghost, after he'd watched her drive off in that taxi. She'd told him to come and find her when he came to his senses, but he never had.

He was looking at her now the way he'd looked at her before, she realised, when he'd delivered the most terrible news. She felt a little queasy. 'Let's go somewhere warmer,' he suggested.

At the heavy wooden doors to the stables Cole ushered her inside away from the elements and pressed a booted foot to the door behind them, closing it with a bang. The wind reached through the gap beneath like icy fingers, blowing at a half-empty hay net on the wall.

Jodie's teeth began to chatter as the sweet, damp smell of grass and ammonia rattled her memory bank. They'd sheltered from a summer storm in here once, and had made love against the creaking fences of empty stalls, and behind hay bales, even on the seat of the old rusting tractor. The rain on the corrugated iron roof had been like a barrage of deafening bullets, concealing their moans of pleasure.

'So...you wanted to talk,' she said, wishing the memories weren't so vivid in his presence.

Cole's deep brown eyes narrowed, forcing his brows to meet beneath his hat. Saying nothing, he uncoiled his scarf. Before she could refuse he looped the thick, black woollen warmth of it around her neck and she prayed he wouldn't hear her heart thudding wildly in the silence.

'Come,' he said. 'There's someone who wants to see you.'

He led her along the gated stalls. There was a horse in each one, but he stopped at the second to last in line.

Jodie almost teared up again at the sight of their horse. 'Mustang is still here?'

'Where else would he be?'

Cole lifted the bar at the stall door. The top half was pinned back by an iron hook and the huge black stallion stopped his graceful grazing on a pile of sweet grass to look at her. He was older and slower now, Jodie noticed with a pang… The horse, not Cole.

Cole was bigger and stronger and broader and he filled her with as much apprehension as ever. She watched him in the lowlight, holding out his palm, letting Mustang snuffle him.

Damn him for looking so good next to a horse. The only thing hotter was watching him tame one. He looked good with a beard, she mused again before she could remind herself not to think such things. She knew the coarse hairs along his jaw hid a small scar on his chin. He'd said he'd got it slipping on seaweed, foraging for winkles one summer when he was ten.

'He remembers you,' Cole told her, without looking away from Mustang.

'I'm sure he does.' Jodie followed him into the stall. She'd always been in awe of their relationship—Cole had brought Mustang to the estate from a government enclosure, after he'd been herded with a pack of wild horses to make way for agricultural land. Mustang had been bucking wild when he'd arrived. Cole had been the only one able to get close.

Mustang took a step towards her with his head bowed. 'Hey, sweet thing,' she said with affection. 'Remember how you came at me like a five-hundred-kilogram Doberman the first time I crawled into your pen? Cole had to jump in front of me to stop you.'

'Jodie.' He stood up straighter then leaned pensively

against the fence looking at her like he meant business. Her stomach did another somersault. 'The solicitor said Casper made me executor of the will.'

She blinked at him. 'You?'

'We can schedule a meeting to go over the details but there's something you should know about the inheritance. It's only fair to tell you, too, now that I know myself.'

Jodie stared at him blankly and continued running a hand absently along Mustang's soft mane. She supposed making Cole executor of the will made sense: he'd been like a son to Casper. But she couldn't imagine why she'd inherited anything; she hadn't seen or spoken to her uncle in a long time, aside from the odd Christmas card. Anything to do with him or Everleigh had just reminded her of Cole.

'Jodie, he's left you fifty percent.'

Her hand froze. Surely he couldn't mean what she thought he meant. The estate was worth millions. She made a squeaking noise before her words came out right: 'Fifty percent...of what?'

Cole shook his head, extended his arm and gestured around them. 'This, Jodie. Half of Everleigh, half of the estate.'

Half of the estate? She shook her head numbly. It was a moment before she could speak.

'Well...what about the other half?' she managed, pulling her arms around herself. This was crazy. What would her father say?

Cole took off his hat and dragged a hand through his hair, like he didn't know what to say, and suddenly she knew.

'You?' Jodie almost laughed in shock, and stumbled over a pile of straw.

'Equal shares,' he confirmed, putting a hand on her elbow to steady her. 'This is as much of a surprise to me as it is to you. I thought he'd leave everything to your dad; his only brother.'

Jodie's throat was dry. She buried her face lower into his scarf, struggling to comprehend what was happening. The soft, warm wool smelled like Cole, like comfort and cologne…and pain and rejection.

She crossed to the fence beside him, leaned against it for support. 'This is nuts… I mean, what am I supposed to do here? What does he want me to do with half of Everleigh?'

Cole shrugged. 'Work on it with me?'

'With you?' Jodie almost laughed again. The idea was preposterous. 'Cole, we haven't spoken in the last twelve years; we wouldn't even be speaking now if Casper hadn't died.'

'I know. Jodie, I'm as shocked as you are, but it's what he wanted.'

She shook her head as Mustang snuffled on the hay at their feet. 'Well, he didn't think it through. I have a life in Scotland now, Cole, so I'll have to sell my half.'

'You can't,' he said simply, standing taller and exiting the stall. She stopped at the gate behind him and crossed her arms.

'What do you mean, I can't sell? It's my half. I appreciate it, I really do, it's…life-changing. But I can't work here with you at Everleigh.'

'I know we have history.' He sounded almost regretful now and she felt sick again, just remembering how many nights she'd cried herself to sleep waiting for the call from him that had never come. 'We've both done things that hurt the other…'

'What did I do to hurt *you*, exactly?' Jodie was

genuinely baffled. He'd left her so broken it had taken months, maybe even years to reassemble the shattered fragments of her former self. Cole said nothing, his mouth becoming a thin line. It dawned on her what he'd meant.

'Do you mean getting married and having a baby? Did I hurt you by moving on with my life?' she said incredulously.

Cole eyebrows furrowed. 'It was only six months after we broke up, Jodie.'

She was absolutely furious now. How *dared* he? 'What's timing got to do with it? Your timing wasn't great either, breaking up with me right as we were meant to move to Edinburgh together! You never contacted me again, Cole! You never even told me what had changed between us.'

She reined her emotions back quickly before they could get the better of her. A simmering fury was coursing through her bloodstream as she faced him head on. He had no idea what she'd been through with Ethan either, wearing a ring, walking down the aisle for the whispering media just to appease his father and keep the public in high regard of all his damned political aspirations.

Mustang shuffled a few steps further away, as if sensing a storm brewing. 'I'm definitely selling my share,' she reiterated. 'I can tell you that already.'

Cole pursed his lips at the floor. 'I thought you'd say that.'

Jodie bristled. 'Well, considering our history, can you blame me for not throwing a party?'

He ran a hand across his chin. 'Jodie, Casper had it written into the will that you can't sell your half for a year.'

'What?' She felt like he'd tasered her.

'The will stipulates that you have to come back here as often as you can during that year, a minimum of three days each time. We're to maintain the property and assets together. Then, if after a year, you still want to sell, you're free to do so.'

She shook her head, totally shocked.

'It's what Casper wanted.'

'Th-this is unreal,' she stuttered. 'Why? I mean, why did he want both of us here? This is your home, not mine.'

Cole just shrugged again. 'It was your home too, once.'

Her phone buzzed on silent mode in her pocket. Grateful for the interruption, she swiped to answer it and walked towards the stable exit. Her heart was beating like a drum.

'It's Meg at The Ship Inn,' chirped the voice down the phone. 'Our heating's out, honey. Is there any way you can stay at Everleigh tonight?'

Jodie drew a sharp breath as she heard Cole bolt the gate to Mustang's stall. *What would go wrong next?*

'I don't know if that's a good idea,' she heard herself say. The urge to get as far away from Cole as possible, to process all this new information was imperative if she wasn't going to spontaneously combust, but the wind was howling outside and the snow was settling thick and heavy. Escape was looking less likely with every passing second.

CHAPTER FIVE

'HOW MANY ANIMALS do you see a day?' Emmie asked. She was sitting on his swivel chair in a vivid blue T-shirt. Cole didn't recognise the picture of the band on the front of it.

'About twenty, give or take, between the team,' he told her, lifting the German shepherd's ears one by one and shining the light around the tufts of fur. The dog wasn't scratching like he'd been before, and was much calmer.

'Twenty? That's probably more than my mum sees at West Bow in a day, and she works *all* the time. You know she has her own practice? I'm surprised she's even taking one day off from it. What's wrong with this dog?'

So many questions, he thought in amusement. 'Otitis,' he said.

Emmie raised her eyebrows. 'Sounds like the name of an indie band.'

'It's a pretty common ear infection in dogs, actually.'

Cole hadn't invited Jodie's daughter into the surgery but she'd appeared of her own accord an hour ago. She seemed to be interested in learning about the place and what they did at a countryside veterinary practice.

He didn't mind the company. She seemed like a bright, intelligent kid and it was still strange being here without Casper. He just hoped there wouldn't be any emergencies. The unprecedented amount of snow still falling was punching as many holes in Everleigh's schedule as Casper's sudden absence, and the news about his and Jodie's shared inheritance had shaken him. He hadn't known a thing about Casper's decision till the solicitor had called, and from the look on Jodie's face last night she hadn't expected it either.

'My team usually handles appointments like this,' he told his curious new assistant. 'Dacey's the dermatologist and Vinny's the small animal practitioner. They'll be here soon if they can get through the snow.'

'So, what do *you* do here?'

'A mix of things. I do the house calls for livestock mostly. And the animal therapy.'

'Animal therapy?' Emmie's eyes were as round and blue as Jodie's, he thought again. He wondered if she knew anything about her mother's former boyfriends, or how uncomfortable Jodie was clearly finding it being back here. Jodie seemed like a great mother, from what he'd seen so far. Last night she'd left him in the stables to find Emmie and tell her they might have to stay a few more days to sort some things out.

When he'd stepped back into the house they'd been chatting by the fire in the kitchen. Emmie had seemed relatively unfazed, whatever her mother had told her, though Jodie had made an effort to stay away from him before the live-in housekeeper, Evie, had shown her to her room.

'What's animal therapy?' Emmie queried now, drumming a pen on the desk. 'Is that…like, emotional support for animals?'

'That's a good way to put it. It's about being part vet, part detective, part therapist. People come to me with their animal problems, and then I help the animals with their people problems. Pass me that stethoscope, will you?'

The door creaked open. 'There you are!' Jodie poked her head in. She visibly tensed in the doorway at the sight of them together. He noticed his bulky black scarf over her arm and couldn't ignore the way his jaw clenched at her sudden appearance.

She'd looked pretty good in his scarf last night, like old times. She'd looked infuriatingly good in the black lace dress too. In fact, Jodie's presence on the estate was undoing him quietly. What with laying Casper to rest, and Jodie unearthing so many other things at the same time, he'd been lucky to catch a couple of hours' sleep before his wake-up call at five a.m. And then there was Blaze's imminent arrival.

'Cole was just telling me about how he's part vet, part detective, part therapist,' Emmie said. 'I saw the manège and the stables when we drove in. Do people bring the big animals here, to you?'

'Depends how big we're talking,' he said with a straight face. 'I haven't seen an elephant in a while.'

'An elephant?'

'We had a lot of those in Sri Lanka.'

'Emmie, Cole's trying to work,' Jodie interjected, one hand still on the door handle. 'Let's go.'

'I don't mind Emmie being here,' he told her.

Cole ran the stethoscope over the German shepherd's chest and ribs in a final check-up before release. When he glanced up, Jodie was watching him as intently as Emmie was. She seemed to remember she was holding his scarf and went about hanging it on a hook on the wall.

It was the wrong place for it now, he thought, appreciating her pert backside in her jeans. He kept it on the hook by the kitchen door, but he wasn't going to tell her that. Her being here, staying in the house, was kind of strange, but he liked the way she was retracing old steps, like the spirit of the Jodie who'd been here before.

She looked good with a few more pounds on her—curves and curls had always been his 'type'. Not that he'd had too many relationships, only Jodie and Diyana in Sri Lanka. He wondered if Jodie would ask him about Sri Lanka.

'How many horses do you have here?' Emmie asked.

'You're into horses, huh?'

'She's mad about horses,' Jodie answered.

'My horse Saxon is seven, we keep him on a farm a few miles from home. Mum used to come riding with us more, but she's usually too busy these days.'

Jodie looked uncomfortable and he detected a small rift for the first time.

He nodded. 'Well, we have eight here already on the estate, and more space than that beyond the gates. You're both welcome to ride while you're here,' he said. 'Kids come in and ride them at weekends. We're on a bit of a hiatus with that now because of our change in circumstances, but seeing as you're here…' He glanced at Jodie before continuing and she looked at him gratefully.

'There's room for more rescues too, when they start coming in,' he added, 'We were working on creating a safe space for mistreated animals.'

Emmie sat up straighter on the chair. 'Here? You'd have a rescue centre here?'

'Sure, why not? It's something your mum and I thought about setting up a long time ago, when we were kids.'

'Really?' Emmie looked thrilled.

'There are a lot of people who own horses who shouldn't, Emmie,' he continued. 'Others have accidents, or they can't live where they used to. Blaze is just one of them. He'll be arriving this morning, so you'll meet him.'

Jodie stepped further into the room. 'Blaze?'

'He was found running loose after a fire took out his enclosure.'

'That's awful. How hurt was he?'

'He's pretty messed up.'

Emmie was looking between them in interest. 'Hey, Emmie, meet me out by the stables in five,' Cole said, seeing the discomfort on Jodie's face. He felt bad for a second. Maybe he shouldn't have mentioned anything they'd planned together once, in front of the child she'd had with another guy, but it was the truth after all. He'd messed up all hopes of him and Jodie setting up the rescue centre here together when he'd broken things off, but if she *was* going to be spending more time here for a while, she'd see him going ahead with it, whether she sold her half eventually or not. There was no way he was stopping now. The horses needed him. He'd made too many promises.

'I have a job for you,' he told Emmie. 'So wrap up warm.'

She pulled a face. 'It's not mucking out, is it?'

'No.'

'Can I ride?'

'Not now.' He took the German shepherd's file and ushered her off the chair. 'Maybe later,' he added, dropping into the seat as she sprang from it. 'We'll all go out if the snow clears. It's better at sunset anyway.'

Emmie slipped past Jodie in the doorway and he

slid his coffee flask across the desk, peered inside. *Empty, dammit.*

'Cole?' Jodie had shut the door. She stopped in front of the desk and he studied her boots on the floor tiles. The tension swirled up between them like dust from freshly swept hay as he marked the file and gave the dog the all-clear for pick-up.

'Cole. This rescue centre…'

'It's not fully planned out yet,' he said, putting his pen down. 'You know how things work around here.'

She bit her lip for a second. 'Not any more I don't. You didn't exactly go out of your way to involve me till now.'

He cleared his throat. He supposed he deserved that. 'We thought we'd start with Blaze, see how things go. It could be good for the place in the long term. We finalised the agreements just days before Casper…' He trailed off. Jodie's face softened suddenly.

'I understand, Cole.'

'I couldn't pull out of this after he died, Jodie.'

'I told you, I understand.'

He knew she understood his loyalty to Casper, but he could see the inner conflict at work behind her eyes already. Jodie had decided on the spot to sell her half of the property, right as Blaze was about to arrive and the rescue plan they'd devised together long ago was coming somewhat into fruition.

Would she still sell? He entertained the notion of her changing her mind, then stopped himself. She had spelled it out loud and clear last night. She might not be wearing a wedding ring any more but she had a life in Scotland and a practice of her own, and a daughter settled in school. Why would she want anything to do with Everleigh—or him—any more?

'So, Blaze was running loose?' She rested a butt cheek on the desk, folded her arms.

'A kid found him out on the heath a while ago; he's a skewbald, chestnut and white, but he was almost black from third- and fourth-degree burns. He's lost about fifteen percent of his body weight and he still won't eat.'

'Unbelievable.'

'Someone knew to call me. The horse had nowhere to go. The owner doesn't want him back, not in this state, he's traumatised. We've been keeping him up at Honeybrook till his wounds healed enough so he could travel.'

'A skewbald that was almost black,' she echoed, glowering at the floor.

'I promised the kid who found him I'd try my best. I need time. I need him here. I thought the training might be good for me too. Maybe a project like this will help take people's minds off…'

'Losing Casper. I know.'

Cole swallowed back the lump in his throat, picking up the pen and tapping it on the desk to fill the silence. He didn't trust his voice now. Casper's death was the reason Jodie was back here. He'd barely had time to process what it might mean for him, or her, going forward, but he couldn't stop thinking about the night Casper had stopped him going to Jodie, after his father had died. Jodie didn't know; he'd never told her. Only Casper had known.

Twelve years earlier…

Cole took the notebook from his satchel and sat down on the hay bale. Resting it on top of his hardcover copy of Hemingway's *For Whom the Bell Tolls*, he got out his pen and tuned his ears to the soft patter of rain on the corrugated iron.

He'd come to the stables for peace, like he always did when his mind got too loud, but pushing back into the warmth of his hood against the bales he struggled with what to say on paper.

He couldn't call Jodie now, he didn't trust his mouth not to betray him.

He'd known something was different, though, when he'd first walked into the surgery with the backpack and an overnight train ticket, and a vague idea of how to find her when he got to the student campus. The air had felt thicker even before Casper took one look at him and said, 'Don't go to her now. Jodie's pregnant. She met a Scotsman up there, and it seems pretty serious. She's going to marry him.'

Jodie was having some guy's baby at nineteen, just months into vet school? It had to have been a mistake, surely?

But she was *marrying* him…so maybe she was really in love. He felt bile in his throat at the thought.

Either way, he couldn't go and knock on her door and ask for a second chance now. That would be too much for him to handle. Seeing Jodie like that, with someone else's baby inside her… Hell, no. Maybe he should write down everything he would have said in person, and send it in a letter.

April 15th
Jodie,
What can I say? I was going to come to Edinburgh this weekend to try and talk to you. I wanted to show you how much I love you. I never

stopped loving you. I was about to get on the train but Casper told me not to, because you're pregnant and engaged. It feels like I just lost you all over again, this time for ever.

My dad's dead, Jodie. He drowned. They just pulled him out of a river, so he can't hurt you, or us, any more. When he got out of jail I didn't want him getting anywhere near you, or Mum. I guess this is a good time to admit he beat the hell out of me for years before he got locked up for tax evasion. I didn't mean to push you this far away, but I thought I was saving you from the misery of it all.

You saw him drunk that night the police came, and you saw me messed up lots of times, but he did worse things than that. He threatened to hurt the animals, and Mum, and you if I ever told anyone about him.

I told myself when I broke up with you that I was doing the right thing. I thought I was saving you from worrying about me, or getting yourself involved in any of my family's mess. I knew you would confront him and put yourself in danger for me—you're just like that and I love you for it. I wanted you to go and do better things with your life than wait around for me, at least for now. But now you're having a baby!

I wish I'd talked to you about all this before I lost you. Maybe we could have figured something out together. I will always love you and, God, I will miss you, but more than that I want you to be happy.

Yours...

Mustang's soft muzzle against his shoulder brought him back to the moment.

Yours...

Yours what?
Yours for ever? Yours not any more? Yours truly?
He'd told her the truth after all. He wondered if she'd guessed *some* of what had been going on in his home, seeing as he'd never taken her back there. Or maybe he'd hidden it so well that this news would be a complete shock, but surely she would understand he'd never wanted to darken her light with the details.

Reading over it again, he realised he could have told her more in the letter, like how all the cuts on his neck that time weren't from crawling under barbed wire, chasing a chicken, like he'd said, but from blocking the glass table after his father had hurled it at him from across the living room.

There had been countless times he'd lied to Jodie to protect her. Pretending to her that he hadn't wanted her in his life any more had been only one of them, even if it had been the biggest lie of all.

A dog's bark told him someone was passing the kennels. Cole gathered his hat and the notebook, and halfway towards the house he decided he wouldn't send the letter. It wasn't fair to do it now she'd found happiness with someone else.

Over dinner he changed his mind.

In the morning, he sealed the letter with an old-fashioned wax stamp in Casper's study. It looked final, meaningful...ominous.

Kicking his boots up on the desk he wielded the pen and then realised he didn't have an address. He *would* send it...but he'd have to get the exact address from Casper first.

One week later, he slipped the unaddressed envelope into a box, where the sight of it couldn't cause his stomach to twist into knots. What would a pregnant woman do with that information anyway? What right did he have to contact Jodie with his excuses now that she was happy, with a good man taking care of her? He should have told her sooner, instead of being such a coward.

She hadn't contacted him herself anyway, and she would have heard about his father by now, surely. She probably wanted nothing more to do with him.

Weeks turned into months and the excuses kept on coming, until eventually the letter went nowhere, and Cole went on with his life without Jodie.

'Have you ever worked a snow blower before?' Cole asked Emmie, wheeling the giant lawnmower-type machine from the shed onto the snowy gravel.

'Not exactly.'

'Well, it's as good a time as any to learn. We need this pathway clear before Blaze arrives. We have other clients who'll need to get in with their animals, too. It's a pretty important job, are you up for it?'

Emmie shrugged, pushing her freshly brushed hair over her shoulder. 'I don't know. Maybe.'

'Less enthusiasm, please. We try to keep things cool around here,' he teased, and Jodie watched as Emmie bit back a smile.

It was interesting, watching their interactions. Emmie was sometimes difficult, but he seemed to know instinctively how to handle her. She supposed his intuition was a big part of what had clearly made him so successful. Casper's financial help had been a boost, but no more than strapping a firework onto a rocket ship.

She wondered if he'd ever thought about having kids of his own, or whether he'd met anyone else after their break-up. She hadn't asked him anything about his life after her. She hadn't exactly had much time yet, but then again she almost didn't want to know. She was emotional enough already and sleep hadn't come for her last night till well after three a.m.

Damn Cole for looking so sexy, she thought yet again as he yanked the starter motor and the snow blower spluttered to life in front of them. He tossed her his coffee flask and put a gloved hand over Emmie's to guide her as she started to wheel the juddering machine over the thick white snow that had piled up by the stable entrance. 'Finish up around here, then you can start around the cabin, yes?'

'Yes, sir, whatever you say.' Emmie mock saluted him, but Jodie could tell she was enjoying herself. Together they watched her set off up the path, blowing snow happily into smaller piles at the sides of the road.

'A woman on a mission,' she commented, mostly to herself.

'I can see where she gets that from.' Cole grinned. 'If she wants to ride later, she'll work for it, like *we* both had to.'

Jodie stifled a laugh, even as discomfort settled in at his proximity now they were alone. Usually she'd be concerned about her daughter operating machinery she'd never used, but Cole oozed confidence in everything he did and it seemed to be rubbing off on Emmie like it had her once.

There was something about Everleigh that had always made her feel quite safe. Good energy in the air, she realised, even though Casper wasn't here. It didn't mean she'd be uprooting herself to make a base here, though. Far from it.

They'd be meeting with the solicitor, Ms Tanner, as soon as she could make it to discuss the options. Jodie was hoping there would be a way around the caveat. Coming all the way back down here so often, as Casper had stipulated, would be hugely inconvenient for everyone, especially Emmie.

And me, she thought, eyeing Cole.

Her insides shifted, thinking about the rescue horse and his plans for starting a rescue centre here. The horses needed Cole and his own special way of dealing with their physical and emotional needs. If she sold her share to someone else, they might not have as much enthusiasm for his…methods. They wouldn't have a clue what Everleigh meant to him either.

Not your problem, she reminded herself.

'Casper made you work for everything,' Cole remembered out loud, catching her eye from under another woolly hat and taking the coffee flask she'd forgotten she was holding. 'You hated it at first, but you still got up at five a.m. when there was something important to do.'

'The coffee always helped,' she admitted as Emmie shrieked in delight again up ahead.

'Black, no milk, no sugar.'

'I'm surprised you remember how I like my coffee,' she replied. 'It seemed a lot to me like you wanted to forget everything about me.'

He shook his head slowly. From the corner of her eye she saw him scuff one boot into the snow, disgruntled. 'I gave you the wrong impression then. I do regret that,

Jodie. I regret a lot of things from back then. I was sorry to hear you got divorced.'

Jodie bristled. She'd been after some kind of explanation as to why he'd changed his mind about her, and Edinburgh, not to hear him admit he'd felt sorry for her circumstances after sending her off, albeit unwittingly, into a marriage she and Ethan had both known would be over before Emmie had even reached her teens.

'It was never going to last for ever,' she admitted quietly. 'Me and Ethan.'

He raised an eyebrow in interest. 'Casper said you got divorced right after you graduated.'

She kept her head high. She didn't want his pity and she certainly didn't owe him any explanations about the quiet untethering she and Ethan had agreed to once they'd both completed their studies successfully and all prying eyes had stopped paying much attention. But it wasn't like Ethan's name wouldn't keep coming up.

'That's right, we did. We decided we were much better as friends.'

She couldn't read him, but she continued matter-of-factly, 'We're a good team, you know? We make everything work for Emmie. They spend a lot of time together with Saxon, her horse. Ethan's as mad about horses as you.'

'Is that right?' Cole's lips curved. She thought he looked smug. They both knew that probably wasn't true.

She realised her heart had quickened under her ribs. 'Emmie doesn't know about us. You and me, I never told her about our history, Cole. I haven't tried to hide anything but at the same time I didn't think she needed to know. She hasn't been herself lately, since Ethan moved in with Saskia. I think she's still processing it.'

Cole held his hands up. 'She won't hear anything from me.'

Jodie let the pent-up air leave her mouth. She probably shouldn't even care, but it *was* her duty to protect Emmie from any information that might make her feel awkward while they were here. She hadn't mentioned the inheritance to her yet, let alone any of the 'rules' Casper had made.

A tall, skinny kid in a flat cap, thick black-rimmed glasses and bright blue welly boots wandered out from the storeroom. He'd been talking to Emmie at the funeral. 'Cole, I'm done with the dog food delivery, it's all stacked up. What else can I do?'

Cole pointed with his flask at Emmie. 'Can you help Emmie over there with the snow blower?'

'Sure thing. Oh, hi, Ms Everleigh, I saw you yesterday in the house. I'm Toby. The kid held out a hand to her and Jodie shook it in mild amusement before he set off purposefully up the path after Emmie.

'Toby lives up at Forster's Nursery,' Cole explained. 'He started showing up every day last summer to help out in the kennels. He walks and feeds the dogs, and we let him ride the horses.'

'Sounds like a fair trade.' It hadn't escaped her attention the way Cole was handling everything here so stoically, knowing he was grieving for Casper. Then again, he'd always been good at keeping his emotions in check—even when he'd broken up with her, he hadn't flinched. Had he ever really loved her?

'He's here most weekends and holidays,' he told her, picking up a thick black hose off the ground and coiling it around his arm. 'Keeps him out of trouble while school's out. He loves his school.'

'Nice for Toby. Emmie stays with her dad most holidays, or with her friend Claire. We go riding with Saxon together sometimes…when I have time.'

'You can bring Saxon here when you come,' Cole offered.

'That might be nice,' she admitted. 'I'm not sure what Ethan would think about that, though. He loves that horse as much as Emmie.'

Cole's jaw was spasming now. She thought for a second he was going to say something else about how her busy schedule might impinge on the requirements of Casper's will because she was already thinking it herself. But he didn't.

'He sounds like a great father.'

'He is.'

Cole looked like he was about to ask her something else but his phone pinged. He looped the heavy hose over its hook on the stable wall as if it weighed nothing. As he talked on the phone she studied the shape of him, the way his shoulders had broadened and his muscles filled out. She found herself remembering a water fight right here that had dissolved into furious lovemaking. Her cheeks reddened. *So many memories.*

'Do you want the good news or the bad news?' Cole asked, sliding his phone back into his jeans pocket and running a hand across his beard.

Jodie pulled a face at him. 'The good news?'

'The Ship Inn's heating system is fixed. Your rooms are ready if you still want them. I can drive you up there later as Barry still needs a part for your car. The way it is, I wouldn't trust it to get you very far.'

'Thanks,' she said, wondering who the heck Barry was. Cole knew so many people. She hadn't even realised he had taken it on himself to get her car fixed already, but she was grateful. 'What's the bad news?'

'The solicitor left a message. Her daughter picked up some bug and she needs to stay home with her a bit longer.'

Jodie frowned.

'We can reschedule,' Cole said, shrugging.

She tried not to look like she was unravelling. 'I have to get Emmie home for school, and I'm due back at West Bow on Monday.'

Emmie emitted another shriek of laughter in the distance, and Toby's own voice travelled indistinguishably up the driveway. Their happiness didn't match her mood. This messed up her whole schedule.

She followed a silent Cole into the stables. 'I guess I could still leave, and we could have the meeting on the phone,' she started, watching him pull two pitchforks from their hooks on the wall. 'But, then, what if we need to sign papers? I don't know, Cole, I think we should both be present for this. I've come all the way here.' She turned for the door. 'I'll go and make some calls…'

'Jodie,' he said calmly, catching her elbow. 'There's nothing we can do about any of this now.' He held out one of the pitchforks. 'Let's just focus on Blaze. He's going to need us.'

CHAPTER SIX

COLE HAD RATHER enjoyed the sight of Jodie wielding the pitchfork in the hay in the stalls, shoving her hair behind her ears every ten seconds and trying to look like she still enjoyed getting this dirty.

She was watching him now from outside the horse trailer, standing on the snow-free gravel, keeping both Toby and Emmie at a safe distance. Cole and Russell, his stablehand, were attempting to move Blaze out of the trailer into the outdoor enclosure, but so far he wasn't budging.

'He's extra fired up after being in here,' he called back to Jodie. 'Stay well back, all of you.'

He slid around to the side of the trailer with his back flat to the wall. He had to move slowly so the horse would know he didn't pose a threat. But Blaze seemed to be going out of his way not to make his job easy and kept shuffling away from his eye contact.

'You've met me before, boy.' He offered a chunk of apple as a peace offering. The horse refused to so much as sniff it.

Cole stood stock still, studying the deep, black flesh wounds around Blaze's left eye socket. He was on meds, but still losing weight after the barn fire. His ribs were almost jutting through the flesh and the horse was a whirlwind of emotions. Cole could almost see the tension rippling through every muscle. 'What you must have been through, buddy…'

He saw it coming half a second before it happened. With a wild sound the horse reared up and almost slammed his own head on the trailer roof.

'Watch out!' Russell leapt from the back doors to the ground to avoid being kicked, leaving Blaze's reins swinging.

'Enough,' Cole ordered, reaching for the reins. Blaze was too fast. The horse startled back, whinnying in fear, and darted from the trailer half a second before Cole could reach him. As he watched, Jodie urged the kids away and moved towards Blaze.

'Jodie, move!' Cole was on the ground now. 'What are you doing?'

Blaze bypassed the gate to the enclosure and reared up again, right in front of Jodie. 'It's OK,' she said, holding out a hand.

'Mum!' Emmie looked panicked, and Jodie made a valiant grab for the reins before Cole skidded across a freshly iced-over patch of grass and yanked her away, shielding her with his own body.

'Don't move,' he told her, one arm wrapped tightly around her heaving chest, beneath her breasts. He held the other up at Blaze, who snorted indignantly. If Cole hadn't stood six feet two, the horse might have attempted to jump over his head; Blaze looked determined as hell.

'I almost had it,' Jodie panted indignantly when he released her. She hurried to Emmie behind the enclosure and Cole cracked his long leather lash on the ground in front of Blaze's forelegs, forcing the horse backwards into the enclosure before he could lunge again. Russell was quick on his feet. He slammed the gate shut behind them.

'Better we just have me in here for now, Russ,' Cole told him, checking Jodie was safe behind the fence. 'Can you go prep the stall, make sure the others are calm when we bring him in?'

'His face,' Emmie said in horror. He had to agree Blaze's injuries looked bad. He was scuffing at the ground with one bandaged hoof then the other. His red-raw ears were pointed high and alert. His blackened nose twitched as he snorted at them both, swishing what was left of his thick brown tail.

Cole knew the horse felt cornered and defensive, and both he and Blaze loathed the lash, but right now it was necessary for everyone's safety.

'The poor thing,' he heard Emmie say. 'He looks so…scared.'

Blaze started snorting in fury, giving him a look like he was going to charge. Cole cracked the lash on the ground at his side, whipping up the snow.

'Mum, what's he doing?'

'It's OK, Emmie, Cole's just showing Blaze who's in control.'

'But he's hurt!'

'He needs to learn some respect. Cole can only help him if they can trust each other.'

Cole got to his knees in the snow, a metre from Blaze, half listening to Jodie. The way she was explaining things to Emmie was just like how Casper used to speak to her back when she'd known nothing about horses.

He sat there in silence, letting Blaze know he wasn't

moving, but wasn't there to harm him either. The horse was starting to understand.

'When Mustang first arrived, Cole sat there for three hours in a face-off. He had to wait till Mustang came to *him*,' Jodie explained quietly.

'He'll look like a snowman soon if neither of them moves,' Emmie replied, though Cole hadn't really noticed the snowflakes settling on his jacket. He was trying to stay still and maintain eye contact with Blaze.

Eventually, after what felt like a long time, Blaze walked tentatively forward and nuzzled his hat. 'There you go,' he said calmly, placing a hand gently on the horse's forelock. 'Are you OK with this?'

The horse met his eyes, and finally Cole was able to stroke around the burns on his face without the animal startling. He murmured in reassurance.

'How did he do that?' Emmie sounded incredulous as they watched Cole mount Blaze and canter around the circumference of the enclosure, the horse kicking up the snow as the driver of the trailer rattled off up the pathway.

'It's just what Cole does, sweetheart,' Jodie replied. 'It's what makes him…'

Cole heard her pause. He knew she'd been about to say something like 'special' but had stopped herself.

'I think Blaze knows no more harm will come to him here,' he said, exchanging a look with Jodie on his walk over to the fence. 'He's OK, but he's still a little apprehensive. We can't blame him.'

'He's just like Mustang used to be, so I know you'll get there,' she told him, putting a reassuring hand on his shoulder before removing it and looking away.

He nodded thoughtfully, his thoughts focused solely

on Blaze again. He had a big job ahead of him with this one. Jodie knew as well as he did that connecting with this horse enough to help him make a full emotional and physical recovery was going to take time.

There was so much to do in Casper's absence. The last thing he needed was for some other buyer to come in and change the way they'd always done things. If Jodie sold her share, changes were imminent. The thought made his breath catch in his chest. He didn't like change. Only the two of *them* knew how Casper had worked, and the faith he'd had in Cole.

'Are we leaving him in here?' Emmie asked, looking between them.

'For now,' he replied, realising his eyes were fixed on the blush of Jodie's cheeks. 'We'll put him inside when he's calmer.'

'Can we give him a reward for backing down?' The kids both looked like they were about to climb on the fence to try and give Blaze more treats he probably wouldn't eat.

Jodie stepped in before he could. 'Give him space,' she warned them. 'Leaving Blaze alone is the greatest reward we can give him for now.'

'Dinner!'

The call from the porch sent the kids running.

'It's *we* now, is it?' Cole remarked, once it was just him and Jodie standing there. He brushed the snow from his hat and drew the double bolt across the gate, fighting back a smile as she pulled a face and shrugged.

This was the Jodie he'd known before. In spite of everything they'd been through in the years apart from each other, Cole felt mild relief to see *some* things hadn't changed.

* * *

'So how long are we staying here now, Mum?' Emmie asked.

'I'm not sure yet,' she said. 'I'm sorry, sweetie. We might have to take you out of school for a few days this week.'

Emmie grinned. 'I don't mind. I mean, about school. I do miss Saxon, but Toby says there's a litter of puppies here due any day. We can help look after them and then we can find them new homes. And Cole says I can go for a ride on Mustang.'

Jodie watched Emmie's face light up in the glow of the fire from the pit. 'Did he now?'

She had expected a different reaction to the news that they had to stay a couple more days, but first Cole and now Toby seemed to be swaying her city-loving daughter in favour of country life.

'I like Cole,' Emmie said suddenly.

Jodie felt adrenaline spike as Ziggy laid his soft head across her boots on the gravel. She was slowly processing the fact that she'd inherited half of everything Cole and Casper had been working on in her absence. But she hadn't been prepared for the way just looking at Cole made her feel every time he walked into a room.

His gravitational pull was just as strong as it ever had been, but he was also a grown-man-sized reminder of the heartache she'd suffered over him. She couldn't think why Casper would make it so she had to spend all this extra time here when he must have known it would open Pandora's box. Was he laughing about this somewhere up in heaven?

The sooner she could discuss her options with the solicitor the better.

'I like the way he's so good with the horses,' Emmie

continued, just as Cole's broad silhouette appeared before the warmly lit cabin and he made his way over. 'And I'm learning a lot more here than I would at school. I just made a fire. I sent a photo to Dad while you were in the house, look!'

Emmie thrust her phone at Jodie, and Jodie got a glimpse of the snap. Emmie and Cole together, holding up chunks of wood, both of them grinning like they'd felled the tree themselves.

'You sent that photo somewhere?' Cole asked in interest over Jodie' shoulder.

'To my dad.'

Cole's eyes flickered towards Jodie as he took his seat at the firepit. The centre of the ring was ablaze after he'd sent Emmie to gather wood from the shed, and taught her how to start the fire carefully and slowly without sending a cloud of black smoke billowing across the estate.

Cole knew she hadn't told Emmie about their romantic history, so of course Emmie wouldn't think twice about sending Ethan a photo of them together. Ethan knew where she was, of course. She'd told him she was going to have a reunion with the guy she'd been trying to get over all those years ago when they'd met at college—he'd even wished her luck.

But she hadn't told him why they were staying a few more days, exactly. She wanted the chance to discuss this inheritance and the terms of the will with him in person. It would involve him, either way, because if she had to be down in Dorset more, he would have to consent to having Emmie more often when he'd only just moved in with Saskia. She couldn't have her missing a lot more school.

Cole placed a bag of marshmallows on the ground and handed her a wooden-handled toasting fork.

'For old times' sake,' he said, and she raised an eyebrow. She had no interest in doing anything for old times' sake with Cole, not that she could stop the barrage of memories flying at her unannounced, like hungry birds. It wasn't particularly difficult to conjure up the sweaty, stormy nights they'd spent locked in each other's arms, but it also wasn't too hard to recall throwing up in the bathroom of the train station after he'd told her it was over. She'd half assumed he'd roll up and apologise, or change his mind, and she'd waited for him so long on the platform she'd let three trains go by before finally getting on one.

Still, she wasn't about to show hostility towards the man with Emmie here.

'Crispy on the outside, runny in the middle,' Jodie heard him say to Emmie, quoting what Casper had always said. 'Stuffed between two biscuits. That's the way to do it.'

'With a gourmet chocolate flourish,' she mumbled without thinking.

She realised Emmie was looking between them quizzically now. 'How long did you say you've known each other?'

'A very long time,' Cole answered as Jodie ran a hand through her hair, feeling frazzled.

'How come I've never heard about you before?'

'Maybe I'm just not that interesting.' With a wink Cole crouched down beside Emmie and pierced a marshmallow hard straight from the packet with his fork. 'Are you ready for the Everleigh delicacy? We call these s'mores. It's an American recipe, if you can call it a recipe, but they taste just as good here. Hold your marshmallow above the fire, not in it…like that…yes.'

Thankfully Emmie seemed to forget her probing questions and soon lost herself in the art of making s'mores with Cole. Jodie wasn't sure what to make of the fact that Emmie seemed to be forming a bond with him already.

Her eyes found the old scar on the back of Cole's neck as he leaned over the fire with his stick. He'd got cut as a kid, crawling under barbed wireas he went after an escaped chicken. She hadn't seen him do it, but she'd seen the way it'd bled through the plasters. She'd had to help him change them, more than once.

'Maybe I can help with the other horses while you're training Blaze,' she heard Emmie say to Cole. 'Mum always says I should stop being so amazing and try being useful, too.'

Cole let out a snort that turned into a laugh.

'Emmie knows she has to work for her rides,' Jodie explained quickly, shifting in discomfort. He was putting her on edge, being nice to her daughter when Emmie had no clue about their history. She couldn't exactly tell her eleven-year-old she'd still been heartbroken over Cole when she'd slept with her father.

'If we need to stay after tomorrow I can organise more nights at The Ship Inn…'

'Fine by me.' Cole shrugged. 'But there's plenty of room here, too.'

'I'll have to see if the locum can cover for me,' she said. 'I'm running a staff of five but there's a surgery on a beagle I'm supposed to be doing with Aileen…' Jodie stopped, realising she was blabbering.

'Everyone there loves you, Mum. You know Aileen will be fine with someone else,' Emmie pleaded. 'It makes sense to stay here at the house too. We already have all our stuff with us.'

Jodie was defeated. She studied Cole surreptitiously in the firelight as she ate her first s'more. She really liked his beard the more she looked at his face. She supposed it was also nice that he was so intent on showing Emmie the exact right way to squish the hot, runny marshmallow over the chocolate.

'Mmm-mmm.' Emmie rolled her eyes back dramatically, chewing her own first heavenly bite. 'Where have these been all my life?'

'You look like your mum did when she had her first s'more,' Cole told her, before taking a bite of a lone marshmallow and chewing slowly, purposefully. He held Jodie's gaze, like he was reminding her how his mouth could move…as if she didn't vividly remember. She groaned internally.

They'd spent so many nights here, that summer they'd first kissed, melting into each other's minds, and mouths. They'd had a competition one night to see how many marshmallows they could toast at once, and they'd almost set themselves on fire.

Jodie had asked to go back to his house with him that night, seeing that she'd never stepped foot beyond the gates of Thistles. She was curious by then about what his home life was like. He'd refused to let her, she remembered now. It was the same night they'd had their first argument.

'What was it you used to say?' Cole was gesturing at her with his fork. 'The s'more you're here, the s'more I love the summers.'

She realised she was frowning over all the puzzle pieces of Cole. 'I love you a little s'more every day,' she followed anyway.

'My love for you is s'more than I can handle.' Cole admired his marshmallow as he said it.

'The s'more I eat, the s'more I want,' Emmie joined in, chomping into a biscuit.

Jodie hoped she didn't look as torn as she felt. She hadn't meant them all to get so cosy like this. She'd had every intention of avoiding Cole as much as possible but with Blaze's arrival and the cancelled meeting…and the broken-down car…and the way Cole did that thing to her heartbeat, like pushing a fast-forward button in spite of his reserve. Cole had kept a lot inside as a kid, that much she'd always known. But she'd always felt special when he'd focused on her and forgotten the mask he'd worn for other people. Maybe that's how Emmie felt now.

What was she supposed to do?

CHAPTER SEVEN

THE SNOW WAS MELTING, the horses seemed calm, even the kennels were quiet as Cole crossed the sodden grass in the dark and let himself into the main house.

It was just after five a.m. His head was busy crafting a to-do list for the day as he grabbed a packet of ground coffee from the pantry.

Hickory Farm for the sick lamb... Check up on Rob's heifer... Blaze's first vital stats check—if I can even get close to Blaze today...

'Cole?'

Jodie was standing in the kitchen doorway, drawing a thick pink dressing gown around her, scraping her hair back from her forehead in embarrassment. She clearly hadn't expected to see him either. He noticed she was holding an old copy of *The Wizard of Oz*. It had always been her favourite. Something about the characters finding their courage had appealed to her. It didn't sit well with him to this day.

He smiled, holding up the coffee. 'I ran out, but there's always spare coffee here.'

'Good to know.'

He couldn't keep his eyes off her figure in the dressing gown, her messed-up hair and sleepy eyes. He hadn't seen her just-out-of-bed look in a long time, but it seemed to be affecting him just the same. He ached to get out of there, but he was glued to the floor now. 'Why are you up?'

'I couldn't get back to sleep. It's too quiet here. Thought I'd make some coffee, catch up on some reading.'

'Too quiet, hmm? Maybe your mind is just noisy, like mine.'

She tightened the belt on the dressing gown, blocking his view of her cleavage. 'Since when? You're the calmest person I've ever known.'

'Not since you showed up, Jodie.'

Jodie blinked. Colour flared visibly in her cheeks as she stared at him with her mouth slightly open, like she didn't know what to say. Suddenly he didn't either. He didn't even know why he'd admitted that—it was too early, he wasn't thinking straight yet.

'Seeing as you're awake, get dressed and meet me at the cabin,' he grunted, before he could change his mind.

It took her less than twenty minutes to knock on his door. She'd dressed in grey jeans and the same boots, which were appropriately muddy now after treading through muck and snow. She was clutching her coffee flask like old times.

'There's a lamb with a swollen face at Hickory Farm, I need to check it out,' he said as she stepped over the threshold. He regretted that he'd just admitted that her presence here was rattling him. He supposed he'd have to get used to it, but the sight of her in that dressing gown…

'Nice place,' she commented, following him through to the kitchen.

'I like it.'

Luckily the cabin was relatively clean and tidy, apart

from Ziggy's toys scattered around the fireplace and couch. And the plates and cutlery in the sink…and the messy home 'office' in the corner where he'd recently dismantled a broken printer.

The sound of her boots on the floorboards made his insides twist with some long-dormant memory. Jodie, aged eighteen, dancing around her room in the main house in nothing but her boots and underwear. Just for him.

'Remember Liam Grainger?' he asked, lifting a jumble of jackets and computer cables on the bench and locating his own coffee flask. The pot was ready on the counter top.

'That big old farmer who always had all the holes in his jumper, and the bright red face?' Jodie had stopped by the kitchen door, and was studying the photos on the wall around the giant chicken-shaped clock. She seemed to pause a second by the one of him and Diyana on their elephant.

'That's the guy. Liam will get a kick out of seeing you at Hickory again. Emmie will be fine here with Evie while we're gone. Pass me your flask.'

She held it out without looking at him. She was still studying the photo. 'Is that Sri Lanka?' she asked, eventually.

Cole poured them fresh, hot coffee. 'Yes, that's Sri Lanka. That was our elephant, Khalua. We rescued her from a temple in the Ancient Cities—she was about to be culled instead of retired.'

'She's beautiful.'

'She has a temperament to match. I'd never seen an elephant cry before I saw Khalua in those chains. The tears started pouring from both her eyes the last time we left her in the temple. We knew we had to go back for her.'

'We?' Jodie was still looking at the photo. 'You mean…you and this woman?'

'Her name's Diyana,' he said, screwing the lids on both flasks, maybe a little too tightly.

'You had an elephant together?'

He shrugged. 'It was too soon for a baby.'

Jodie's lips became a thin line. Cole immediately regretted his words but he had no clue why Jodie had felt the need to get married so young in the first place. Ethan was a staple in her life still, and a great father, that much he knew, but he was burning with more questions he knew he had no right to ask. All this curiosity over the photo was flicking his triggers.

He'd met Diyana during a summer break long after Jodie had walked down the aisle with Ethan. Diyana had been a welcome distraction, like sticking a plaster over a wound. She'd been interesting and new and she'd taken his mind off Jodie for a while.

'I spent a couple of summers in Sri Lanka between studies. Casper said it was important to see other places, see more of the world and its creatures, great and small,' he said. 'I heard about a rescue centre for giant flying squirrels in the hill country. Diyana was one of the volunteers. She introduced me to some of the best vets, technicians, researchers… I helped where I could. I travelled around with them. I learned a lot from the animals there. And the people.'

Jodie was looking out of the window. Dawn was starting to break outside and Russell was pushing a giant green wheelbarrow loaded with tools out of the outhouse. 'Was it serious with Diyana?' she asked quietly.

There it was. The green-eyed monster. Cole was well

acquainted with this beast. He flipped the lid on his flask, took a sip, letting the hot liquid scald his tongue for a second. 'I came back here without her,' he offered quietly. 'And she isn't here now.'

He almost told her exactly why Diyana wasn't here now. He had no doubt she would have come if he'd asked her to. But he couldn't give her the ring and the happy family she wanted, even after all the time they'd spent dating, because the whole time they'd been together he'd never quite managed to push Jodie out of his head, even if she'd had no difficulty forgetting him.

'Why did you come back to Dorset if you had so much going on elsewhere in the world?' she asked him suddenly. 'You could have gone anywhere, Casper would have still supported your decision.'

'This will always be my home, Jodie. I never wanted to be anywhere else. Ziggy, come, let's go.' He signalled to the dog, then swiped up his car keys from the counter before they could start another discussion about their pasts or their romantic lives that he really didn't have the time or inclination to continue.

Jodie put her hand on the door before he could open it. Her gaze sharpened on his face.

'You're worried I'm going to sell my half of your home, aren't you?'

His heart felt like she'd tugged on it.

He studied her a moment. Her eyes were still like oceans, luring him in, threatening to drown him. Of course he was worried about someone else coming in, but he was more concerned that one of the reasons Jodie was planning on selling was just so she could stay away from him.

'Like I said before, this is your home too,' he said coolly, pulling his plaid jacket from its hook.

'I was never invested in this place as much as you were, Cole.'

'You wanted the rescue centre as much as me,' he said, shrugging on the jacket. It was true and she knew it.

She faltered a second. 'Maybe…once. When we were happy here together. But my home is in Edinburgh now. Ethan is there… Emmie's school is there.'

He turned his back to the door, facing her. She was wearing the too-clean jeans again, another reminder of her city-girl life; a life that wasn't here. 'So you're happy up there in Scotland? Logistics aside, are you so happy you'd never even consider being anywhere else, even part time?'

Jodie tilted her chin, meeting his eyes dead on. 'I don't know why you're suddenly so concerned about my happiness, Cole.'

'Look,' he said, keeping his emotions in check and his voice level. 'I know you want to sell because of me, because of our history.'

'Can you blame me?'

He sighed sharply through his nose. 'No. But Casper wanted us to do something together when he put Everleigh in our hands. Maybe the rescue centre was it, we were always on the same page about that.'

Jodie's voice was indignant. 'I thought we were on the same page about a lot of things, Cole. Turned out I was wrong.'

He opened his mouth to counter her, but what could he say? It was sounding more and more like he'd tainted her whole view of Everleigh when he'd broken things off. She'd loved it because she'd loved him, and now… she despised him.

Jodie pulled the door open, sending a flood of light

into the cabin and releasing a pent-up, eager Ziggy, who bolted for the Land Rover. 'It doesn't matter now,' she muttered in annoyance, following his dog. 'Let's just get through this. We should go. The sun's coming up.'

'It's either a blocked saliva gland or she's got some kind of infection,' Cole said. 'I think it's an infection.'

'I trust your instincts by now, Crawford.' Liam Grainger still had the same pot belly and ruddy cheeks Jodie had known before. He was standing with his arms folded behind the wooden fence, observing Cole in action. 'I have to say it sure is nice to see you two together again. How long are you sticking around Everleigh, Jodie?'

'I'm not sure yet,' Jodie told him. 'I have some business to care of at the estate.' She glanced at Cole. '*We* have some business to take care of.'

The bleating of the sheep and other lambs was a symphony all around them. Jodie was still wrestling to keep her mind on the situation at hand, and not on their heated words back at the cabin, or the photo of Cole's beautiful ex-girlfriend riding the elephant with him in Sri Lanka. Maybe that's what had riled her up, more than the terms of Casper's will or Cole's expectations of *her* after all this time.

Every time they talked about anything remotely involving the past, they ended up having some kind of disagreement. Of course he was a big factor in her wanting to leave and sell her share of Everleigh…he wasn't about to guilt her into keeping it just to stop someone else moving in on his precious rescue centre plans.

But seeing that photo framed on the wall had made her feel quite nauseous. And the dig he'd made when she'd let on her surprise at their elephant: *'It was too soon for a baby.'*

That had been unexpected.

If he was jealous in any way of her relationship with Ethan, he only had himself to blame, she thought angrily, watching him now. He looked impossibly handsome with the sun on his face, carrying a cute lamb into an empty pen. Damn him.

'Ziggy, give that bag to Jodie, buddy.' Cole held a gloved hand out, motioning for the bag Ziggy was still holding in his teeth.

To Jodie's surprise, the dog let go of the bag right at her feet. Jodie let herself into the pen with it, losing her boots in the muck and hay almost instantly.

Cole positioned the tiny lamb's head between his steady thighs to hold her in place. The little thing had been bleating and writhing in the hay in fear when they'd first arrived, but he'd managed to calm her significantly.

The syringe didn't look pretty when he pulled it out. 'It's filled with infection,' Jodie observed, crouching down in the hay and straw and locating a set of scalpels from Cole's bag. She already knew he'd have to put a nick in the swelling to release the rest of the fluid.

Liam Grainger watched them intently from the fence, petting Ziggy from time to time. 'So, why did you stay away so long, Jodie? This place was always more interesting when you two were running around together.'

'I run a private veterinary practice in Edinburgh now,' she told him, holding up a gleaming 'Everleigh' engraved scalpel.

'And you have a husband and a daughter,' Liam said, as though he was only just remembering. 'I guess life gets in the way, huh?'

'Actually, Mr Grainger, I'm not married any more,' she replied with a tight smile.

Liam wriggled his eyebrows mischievously. 'Is that so? Did you tell her you're single too, Crawford? How long's it been now? We keep telling him he needs to find himself a good woman. The man can't cook to save his life.'

'I wouldn't be looking to Jodie to cook for me, Liam,' Cole said dryly. 'Scalpel, please.'

Jodie handed it over, noting the curve of a smile on his lips at his joke—not that it was a joke. She was absolutely awful at cooking. But even the familiar holes in the elbows of Liam's jumper and the fabric that was struggling to contain his ample girth wasn't causing her as much amusement as it should have been. She had a feeling Cole knew she'd been bitten by the green-eyed monster too, over seeing that photo of his ex. She couldn't un-see it now.

Diyana was clearly from Sri Lanka herself. She had a stunning veil of wavy jet-black hair the same shade as Cole's. Her bright pink sari and wide, warm, infectious smile hinted at a woman who loved life. Cole had looked magnificent sitting on the elephant behind her, his muscled arms wrapped tightly around her waist in a linen shirt she'd never seen him wear on any English farm. He'd been in a different world with Diyana. Had he *loved* her?

'Jodie, the alcohol, please?' Cole prompted now, looking up from the lamb's swollen cheek. Jodie was already unscrewing the lid from the plastic container. 'You want to do it?' he asked her.

'Of course,' she said, maintaining her professional stance as best she could. She was somewhat surprised at how she was working on autopilot alongside him. Cole seemed to be calming the jittery lamb with his usual skill and inexplicable aplomb as she took the moment of stillness to douse the fresh wound around the incision and prep another syringe from the bag with a painkiller.

Why hadn't Diyana come back to Everleigh with him? Maybe she wouldn't have liked his cabin as much as Cole did, or as much as she herself did, she mused as they worked. Maybe the piles of papers and jackets and computer parts she'd seen about the place would have driven the poor woman mad.

In spite of his calm and cool demeanour Cole had always lived in organised chaos. The mess had always been refreshing to her as she'd been growing up. Her mother had kept a clean and tidy home in Greenwich, and Jodie had never been allowed to leave anything lying around. At Everleigh, as long as the animals were fed and happy, Casper and Cole didn't care how many dishes were in the farmhouse sink or how many jackets were lying around off their hooks.

Back then, when their friendship had morphed into love, she'd never dreamed she'd ever see Cole Crawford with another woman. But, then, she hadn't exactly pictured herself married with a child at nineteen either.

Emmie seemed to like Cole a lot, and Jodie had no doubt her daughter would love coming to Everleigh more often. Frowning into her scarf, she realised she was using her daughter and Ethan as an excuse for keeping away, and for selling up, when she and Cole both knew she was only reluctant to be here because of him. He'd said it himself.

'She'll be fine without the antibiotics, Liam,' Cole said now, standing up tall and allowing the lamb to wriggle free. 'She's much more comfortable now the fluid is all out. See how she's bouncing around? She'll be eating again before you know it, you can't keep creatures like this down.'

Cole opened the gate and let Jodie exit the stall first. As he went about packing the equipment up, Jodie watched the little lamb cross on wobbly legs to the corner of the stall, where a fresh batch of straw was tied to the wooden fencing.

As it began munching on the hay with renewed interest, Jodie shook her head at Liam without Cole seeing. She would always be amazed at the way animals seemed to respond to his quiet handling, and how well he could predict and relate to them. She'd met a lot of great vets in her time but, God, all their personal issues aside, the depths of Cole were as sexy as hell.

She was so lost in her thoughts that she didn't hear Cole's phone buzz, but the next thing she knew he was touching a hand to her shoulder. 'Jodie, someone needs our help. Let's go.'

CHAPTER EIGHT

COLE GLANCED AT Jodie's profile in the sunshine as he took the side road by the old stone chapel. She was scanning the fields from the passenger seat. Her hair was falling in wisps from her ponytail around her face, and her rosy cheeks were flushed from the cold. He'd always liked her best without make-up.

It was strange to have her with him out on call, but thankfully the tension had eased somewhat since they'd locked horns earlier. Someone had called to say they'd seen an injured stray dog wandering along an A-road.

It was almost seven-thirty a.m. The sky was a clear blue for the first time in days.

'There she is,' Jodie cried suddenly, making him hit the brakes. Ziggy started barking instantly from his demoted position in the back seat.

'I see her,' he said, pulling over quickly and making his sunglasses slide across the dashboard. Jodie caught them expertly and jumped from the car. The stray was limping awkwardly, tongue lolling out, seemingly disoriented. 'Stay here, boy,' Cole said to Ziggy before he could follow them. 'And be quiet. We don't want to scare our patient.'

Jodie was beside him on the ground in seconds. 'A

husky mix, I guess,' she said as they drew closer. The creature had started to snarl. 'Look at those eyes.'

'Almost as blue as yours,' he noted out loud.

'So you think you can charm me like your horses,' she chided, though she was fighting a smile. 'She's really scared, poor thing. We need to get closer.'

The sun was streaming down now, blinding on the snow. It cast a bright spotlight on the dog's injuries as it whimpered and shivered. The blood on her left back leg was a sinister sight against the shrill morning song of the little egrets in the trees.

'Looks like she was hit by a car.' Jodie went to creep closer with him, but in seconds the creature seemed possessed, growling and snarling even more, baring its teeth. She stepped back quickly, just as Cole forged ahead. He held both hands to the ground at his sides, stayed still and quiet, asserting his dominance, making it clear he wasn't moving. 'We're not going to hurt you,' he crooned.

It was a stand-off for a good few minutes. Cole felt Jodie's eyes on him the whole time, but eventually the dog got to its belly in the snow and let out a deep sigh before starting to whimper.

'She's letting us approach her,' he said, signalling to Jodie. 'Let's get her to the car.'

Cole scooped the dog up gently in his arms and carried her to the back of the Land Rover. Jodie rushed ahead to pull the boot open, and as he laid the scruffy stray in the back he knew Jodie had noticed the same thing he just had.

'I think she's...'

'Look at her, all swollen under here,' Jodie interjected, before he could finish. 'She has puppies around here somewhere.' She pulled on gloves and rummaged for the stethoscope in his bag, then ran a check, trailing gentle hands along the dog's blood-soaked fur. 'No sounds of trauma or fluid,' she told him, visibly relieved. 'But we'll need to run some X-rays back at West Bow... I mean Everleigh.'

'Lock her in the crate while I check for the pups,' Cole told her, not missing her slip of the tongue. She had Edinburgh on the brain. He didn't suppose that would change anytime soon, but he'd realised earlier that he would have to start making her stay more enjoyable. He didn't want the bad blood between them to deny her this time at Everleigh, or a say in its future, and he didn't want Emmie to miss out either. Emmie loved Everleigh already, he could see it in her eyes—exactly the same dusky blue as Jodie's.

Sweeping snow-covered branches aside, keeping an eye out for wriggling puppies, he heard Jodie back by the vehicle, talking to the dog. She was calmer now, at least. She always was around the animals, like him. He was glad they were working together now. Their love for animals surpassed any of their personal rubbish, and he was thankful for that at least.

'Puppies! Here, pups. Where are you? We're looking for you.' He approached a ditch with a trickle of a stream running through it.

To his relief, the tiny whimper of a puppy caught his ear on the breeze and led him to a drainpipe. Crouching low in the dirt and slush, he pulled out his phone and shone the flashlight inside. Junk food wrappers tussled with the wind but behind them...

'Three puppies,' he confirmed aloud, just as Jodie reached him. Her hand landed absently on his back over his jacket as they peered inside the tiny space together. 'We have to get them out, they're still suckling.'

The flashlight revealed their scruffy bodies, writhing around, trying to escape his light. 'No chance of crawling in there, though.'

'We need to lure them out with food.' Jodie's eyes narrowed, then lit up. 'I saw some biscuits in the car!'

She was back on her feet and sprinting back to the Land Rover before Cole could even feel embarrassed about the open packet of oatmeal cookies he'd left in the door.

She came back with them and he grimaced, jamming his phone back in his pocket. 'What can I say? A man gets hungry on the road.' He crumbled bits of the biscuits at the entrance to the drainpipe, annoyed he'd run out of the dog treats he usually kept in the car, and together they stood back, waiting.

'A man like you needs real food,' Jodie told him, fixing her eyes on the drainpipe entrance.

'Like your curry?' He wrinkled his nose into the middle distance, smirking.

'Hey!' She swiped at him, but again her annoyance was pretend and he dodged her, chuckling. They both knew Jodie had always been a terrible cook. She'd tried to make him a curry once. Instead of adding two teaspoons of curry powder she'd added two tablespoons.

'To be fair, you struggled through that masala most valiantly,' she said.

'I only needed about three litres of water to help.'

Jodie rolled her eyes. She'd wanted to treat him. She'd banned the staff from the kitchen and danced around in cowboy boots and cut-off denim shorts, dropping kisses on his lips between spilling rice and spices and French wine all over the place.

He still had a photo from that night, stashed away

in a box. It was of both of them hunched over the bad curry, pulling faces.

He remembered another photo now. Casper had one framed of the two of them with Mustang. He'd hung it on the wall as a surprise when the cabin was finished, but Cole had taken it down again. He hadn't harboured any emotional attachment to Diyana after breaking things off with her, but the photos of Jodie had always made him miss her unbearably. He'd found a whole stash of them once—he couldn't even remember where he'd put them now.

He shoved his hands in his pockets, resisting the sudden ill-advised urge to put an arm around her. He knew she had her guard up around him, even when it looked like she was letting it down. She was well within her rights to be cautious, he supposed, but he should probably seize the opportunity to talk while she wasn't spitting fire.

'So, it seems like you're still pretty close with Ethan,' he said, testing. He was itching to ask what had gone wrong with the marriage.

Jodie just sighed. 'He's the father of my child. We still care about each other a lot. In fact, I'd say we're pretty good friends.'

He took his hands from his pockets at exactly the same time as she brushed the hem of her jacket and their fingers touched.

A flashback came into his mind. Chesil Beach. They'd been 'friends' then but he'd held her hand for the first time, and she hadn't let go for a good ten minutes. He must have been twelve, maybe thirteen. He'd been in love with her even then, but she'd had no clue. He'd hardly shown it as he'd been too caught up inside his head, figuring out how to keep her and everyone he loved away from his father's angry mouth and fists.

A squeal.

'They're coming out!' Jodie dropped to her haunches. Cole signalled for her to wait behind him while he stepped towards the pipe and scooped the tiny puppies up, one by one.

'They're so little! They don't look hurt.' Jodie stepped close, her boots next to his as she took them in her arms. For a moment their eyes met over the fuzzy bundles and they shared a smile that made him want to close the gap and kiss her, for old times' sake.

She would probably slap him if he did, he thought in vague amusement as she carried the squealing trio to the car. He swiped up a blanket from the back seat while Ziggy tried his best to reclaim the passenger seat.

'Keep them in the front with you,' he said, flinging open the passenger door for Jodie and shooing Ziggy back. 'Their mother knows they're safe with us.'

'You saved their lives,' Jodie told him breathlessly, sliding into the seat, bundling up the pups in the blanket and holding them close to her chest.

Cole leaned across from outside and pulled her seat belt across under the puppies. 'My biscuits saved their lives.'

'I'm serious, Cole. They would have died if we'd left without them. You calmed the mother down enough to let us examine her.'

'That's why I'm here,' he said.

She cocked her head. 'Because dogs need you more than elephants?'

'I guess so.' He paused, clicking the seat belt into place, stopping himself an inch from her lips again. He watched her blue eyes rake over his mouth for just a split second and wondered if she'd been thinking the same—about all the passion they'd once poured into their kisses. All the sparks and sexual tension between them had made for some pretty hot times around Everleigh once he'd finally worked up the courage to kiss her.

Time seemed to stop before he spoke. 'We always did make a pretty good rescue team, you and I.'

Jodie pulled her eyes away. 'That was then, Cole.' Her tone was a warning to him not to dredge up the past any more, not to remind either of them how he'd ruined it. 'Things are different now.'

Three days later, Jodie was watching from the fence as Blaze was cantering the length of the manège, kicking up dust and showering the new yellow daffodils around the periphery with dirt. He bared his yellowed teeth in vain protest every time Cole cracked the training whip to make him change direction.

In the space of just a few days Blaze's wounds had healed exponentially and his temperament around Cole was drastically improved. There was still a long way to go. Whenever anyone besides Cole got too close, the stallion did not respond as well.

She was deep in thought when Aileen called.

'Jodie? How's it all going at Everleigh?'

'It's eventful,' she said, unable to take her eyes off Cole.

'We're still waiting for this meeting to be rescheduled. Hopefully it will happen by the end of the week. Is everything OK there?'

'The usual excitement,' Aileen answered. 'We're all thinking of you.'

Cole cracked the whip loudly behind Blaze. Ziggy

barked in excitement and the stallion let out an anxious whinny. 'Maybe it's not as exciting here as there. What's happening?'

'Cole's in a training session with our…his…rescue,' she said, catching Cole's glance over the fence. He was wearing his stetson today. She knew he was probably wearing it ironically, for her sake. Casper had bought him one like it years ago at a horse show in Missouri and he'd worn it everywhere…even the bedroom. Once she'd worn it in the shower, behind the candles, because Cole had said her cowgirl silhouette in the low light was sexy. It took a week to dry.

She flushed at the memories and the slip of her tongue, calling Blaze *their* rescue. Already she was somewhat a partner in Blaze's recovery and treatments. Together she and Cole had given shots and medicines and soothing words to heal his burns, and she'd also been in with the clients. But then it had always been all hands on deck at Everleigh.

He'd been right when he'd said they'd always been on the same page about the rescue centre, and Everleigh in general. It was a special place, a unique place. Everyone knew it. There was so much room to grow.

But every time she looked at Cole, or he dared so much as hint at a flirtation with her, she felt an overriding need to escape in case he burned her again somehow. He was the only one with the power to do that. Just being around him and all his mysteries felt like walking the rim of an active volcano.

'Cole, huh?' Aileen sounded interested and Jodie realised with a frown that she was still looking at him, dreaming. 'The head vet and animal whisperer?'

'He doesn't like being called a whisperer, he's a behavioural therapist, but yes.'

'So, what's it like to be back there?' Aileen asked now. 'Is Emmie OK? Missing her friends yet?'

Jodie stopped two metres from the kennels. 'I wouldn't say that,' she answered slowly. 'She's made a new friend here. She gets to ride most days. She hasn't had a temper tantrum yet, actually…'

'Sounds like the country air is what you both needed,' Aileen chirped, right as Jodie heard the familiar tinkle of the doorbell in the background. 'Oh, I have to go. See you soon!'

Aileen hung up.

Jodie turned her face up to the greying sky. Why had she been letting herself get so frazzled in Edinburgh lately? Not even taking time out to ride with Emmie as much as she used to.

She hadn't had a real holiday in years. Not that this was a holiday by any stretch of the imagination, but all the tension with Cole aside she couldn't deny that the fresh country air was exactly what she'd been craving, without even realising it. Maybe it was the same for Emmie.

'Mum?' Emmie appeared to have noticed her now. She let herself into the kennel, scooping up a puppy from the clean concrete floor as it tried to escape, and a bespectacled Toby scrambled to his feet with a giant sheet of paper.

'Can we put this sign up?' he asked her. Jodie scanned the sign they'd made most creatively by taping four pieces of A4 paper together.

'Oh, it's…' she started, but she couldn't quite finish.

They'd drawn the words out in giant blue and green letters with marker pens and stick-on gold stars. It was impressive work. But her heart was beating so fast at what they'd written that she thought she might need to sit down.

CHAPTER NINE

'EMMIE AND TOBY'S Canine Rescue Centre, huh?' Cole pulled his stetson into a deep dive against the splattering of rain. So much for the nicer weather. The air had held a soft-edged glimmer of spring, but it was threatening to turn into a downpour again now.

Jodie crossed her arms beside him. They were both observing the sign the kids had strung up with string across the kennel bars before Evie had called them in to lunch.

'Doesn't it remind you of something?' she prompted, putting a hand down to pet Ziggy's soft head.

'It's almost word for word what we wrote on our sign, isn't it?'

'Exactly. They even used the same colours! Don't you think that's strange?'

Cole looked up as a bigger raindrop landed with a plop on the rim of his hat. 'Strange,' he agreed.

It was all very strange around here lately. He never quite knew what mood he'd find Jodie in. One minute she was letting him in, the next she was closed off and cool.

Ordering Ziggy to stay outside, he let himself into the kennel and checked on their husky-cross patient.

The puppies were snuggled close, suckling. 'They're doing fine, just like Mama,' he said to Jodie.

'The kids are obsessed with them. Just like we were obsessed with whatever dogs we kept in here. Remember the Westie, Deefer?'

He laughed under his breath, scooped up a puppy, checked its ears. Deefer had followed them home one summer from outside the Crow and Bell pub. Jodie had called him Dee-fer-Dog.

'Wasn't there a tabby, too? You called him called Cee-fer-Cat. I always did appreciate your unique ability for naming stray animals.'

'Emmie has more of an imagination than me.' She smiled. 'Did she tell you what she named this lot? Starchild, Archibald and Lucy-Fur. I can't even remember which one is which.'

Cole chuckled, which seemed to make Jodie laugh too, albeit behind her hair so he wouldn't see. 'She can make up all the names she wants,' he said in a flush of affection, just as a rumble of thunder pierced the sky and made the dogs' ears prick up. 'We've got more pups coming soon. We'll have a puppy overload this spring at this rate. Let's take these guys into the house before the storm hits.'

Jodie was quiet as they left the kennel with the puppies in their arms. Was she thinking how she and Emmie might not even get to see the new litter arrive, if they left Everleigh before the weekend? She seemed to be keeping her guard up around him just as much as ever but perhaps she was reluctant to discuss anything about the will, or Casper's plans for her here, until she'd spoken to Ethan. He couldn't help feeling annoyed that his name came up so often. But, then, she'd seemed just as irked by that photo of Diyana.

'It's nice, how you've taken Toby under your wing,' Jodie said, as they neared the source of the hot soup and toasted cheese sandwiches they could smell, blowing to them on the wind from the main house kitchen. 'Is that because Casper did the same for you?'

'I never really thought about it that way,' he said, truthfully. 'Toby's dad doesn't seem to want much to do with him.'

'You didn't spend much time with your father either, did you? Before he was locked up, I mean? You were always at Everleigh. At least you were whenever I was here.'

'Maybe I just liked it more here,' he said quickly, but Jodie was studying him quizzically again.

'I was thinking before about how you never asked me to come back to your home.'

The depth of her stare made him uncomfortable.

His face must have darkened, thinking about the fists that had beaten him blue and thrown him across the living room, every time he'd gone home dirty, or late, or with an expression his father thought was rude or accusing. He'd taken it on the chin, literally, but he'd had to, or else his father would have hurt someone else instead. Like his mother, or Jodie. He couldn't imagine now, as an adult, that he would have carried out his threats, but as a child he'd had such a hold on Cole he'd been forced to take him seriously.

'And now here you are. You never left Dorset,' Jodie said, taking the wooden steps up to the main house porch. 'Apart from when you went out to Sri Lanka.'

'And college. I wouldn't have stuck it out if it hadn't been for Casper landing me the scholarship. I won't lie, that was tough, being stuck in all those soulless rooms.'

'I bet,' she said. 'Especially for someone like you.'

He nodded, grateful for the change of subject. He wasn't going to say it because who knew, it might have been the same if he'd gone to Edinburgh but he'd struggled in London, away from the horses, and Dorset. In classes all they'd seemed to do was link the minutiae of anatomy and physiology to how they might one day use it in practice. He'd found it hard to see why most of it was important at the time, all the biochemical pathways, the laws and legislations of the vet world. Casper had known better. The qualifications had taken him around the world. Cole's *other* skills had made him his fortune.

Cole nudged the farmhouse door open and put down the two puppies he was holding. Emmie ran over and picked them up instantly as Ziggy slipped inside and shook his wet coat, making her squeal.

Toby took the other pup from Jodie. 'Don't feed them anything bad,' Cole told him. 'We'll be back in a second. Gotta get these muddy boots off or we'll be in trouble.' He winked at them and closed the door again.

'Casper would have done anything for you, Cole,' Jodie continued thoughtfully. 'He knew you were an investment, too, in Everleigh's future.'

Cole murmured noncommittally and dropped to the bench outside the door. He hadn't told her his own net worth—he loathed discussing anything to do with finances. Growing up at home after the strawberry crops had failed, the topic had caused nothing but arguments between his parents. It was the reason his dad had turned to whisky. Then violence.

He was sure it would come up in the meeting with the solicitor anyway—the comfortable sums that had amounted in his bank account since people had started seeking out his skills. He'd ploughed a lot of it into wildlife rehabilitation projects and funding research projects globally, and he had still more to invest in the rescue centre when the time came, but whatever happened with the estate it was safe to say his own future was more than secure. He'd made sure of that.

'This isn't just about the money, Jodie,' he said firmly, shaking off a boot, realising she was looking at him for a reply of some kind. 'I would never sell my share of this place, you know that.'

She looked up from where she was untying her laces. 'And you still think I have no reason to either?'

'That's not what I said.'

He saw the start of an argument in her eyes, but she turned to the floor, as if thinking better of it. He took off the stetson. It was dotted with water…like the day Jodie had stepped out of the shower with it on and it had taken a week for the leather bits to dry. She probably didn't even remember that…or maybe she did. He'd seen the way she'd looked at him earlier outside with Blaze.

Jodie was quiet for a moment. 'Can I ask you a personal question?'

'I feel like you're going to anyway.'

'Why didn't Diyana come back here with you from Sri Lanka?'

'She didn't come back here with me because I didn't ask her to.' He scraped the mud roughly from his boots across the wiry mats beneath the bench. Jodie said nothing, but he could feel the way she'd tensed up beside him.

'You're jealous,' he asserted.

'Don't be absurd. I'm not jealous, Cole.' Her voice was hoity-toity and he arched an eyebrow at her in amusement. She huffed and dropped to the seat beside him. 'OK, you win. Maybe I felt a little spark of jealousy just then…'

'Just a little one?'

'Considering our history, and the way you left things, I thought you'd be happy here with your horses, but you look so happy in that photo with her.' She paused, looked into the rain. 'The one in your kitchen with your elephant.'

'You looked pretty happy in your wedding photos, too,' he countered. 'And we'd only just broken up.'

Jodie closed her eyes. 'You didn't want me, Cole. You made that very clear.'

He couldn't stop himself now. 'You got pregnant, Jodie, *six months* after we ended things.'

'After *you* ended things, you mean.' Her voice was level, measured, but he could sense her simmering. Something made him push her.

'You slept with another guy. And then you married him.'

She stood and faced him. 'Was I supposed to call you up and ask for permission? What is this about, Cole? You told me you didn't love me, so why did you care?'

'No, I didn't. I never said I didn't love you.'

'Not in so many words but…' She paused, like she was only just considering she might have heard things he hadn't said as well as things he had. 'Anyway,' she huffed, 'both Ethan and I were totally drunk the night the accident happened…'

'Accident?' Cole gripped the bench hard beneath him as he processed this new information. 'Your pregnancy was an accident?'

'Of course it was, Cole,' she snapped. 'I was nine-teen.'

She sat back down again heavily with a sigh. Thunder rumbled in the distance. 'Ethan was my good friend, my flatmate. He took the place in the flat share that *you* were supposed to take, actually. My parents wanted me to abort the baby, obviously, you know what they're like. But I couldn't do it.'

'So you *married* him?'

'Yes, but…it was more complicated than that.'

'What do you mean?'

She huffed. 'I don't want to talk about this with you.'

Cole sucked in a breath and let it out into the mounting storm. He felt his shoulders tense as her fingers started drumming on the bench beside him. So she *hadn't* loved the guy? She'd married a man she hadn't loved? Why?

He turned on the bench, took her face in his hands and brought his forehead to hers. Heat surged through him and made him hold her tighter. 'Jodie. It's *me* asking you this. Why did you marry Ethan if he was only a friend…if you'd just made a mistake? You were nineteen years old, you had everything ahead of you.'

'I told you before, we made it work.'

Her eyes had clouded over. She raised her hands over his, then back to his open jacket. Maybe they had made it work somehow. She had graduated after all, but if Cole had gone to her sooner, instead of appeasing his useless, abusive father or listening to Casper advocating caution once his father had died, she might not have married Ethan. She might have married *him*…

The smell of cheese toasties was so damn good but suddenly he'd lost his appetite. She was breathing hot and sharp against him, her fingers fisting and unfisting on his jacket. 'Jodie?'

She seemed to wrestle with her emotions and he could almost feel her walls crumbling down before she pulled away from him and composed herself. Emmie was still giggling at something in the kitchen.

'I'm not going to do this with you, Cole,' she hissed in a whisper, breaking free and making for the farm-house door. 'How can you ask me to explain my life's decisions after you broke us and then did *nothing* to fix it? This is getting us nowhere.'

'So I set up the new account. Dacey had to approve it because technically we're too young to have social media…but you're on—see?' Emmie passed the iPad to Cole over the kitchen island and Jodie watched his eyes widen over his bowl of tomato soup.

'I've posted four photos so far,' Emmie said. 'One of the kennel with our new sign, and one of each puppy. Lucy-Fur has the most likes, so we'll use the same hashtags again for the next post. It's really trial and error, you know? We have to figure out which hashtags are more popular with people looking for rescue animals.'

'Either way,' Toby added, 'we think we'll have homes for them all by the end of next week.'

'All three puppies? Without anyone coming to see them?' Cole looked impressed, and maybe a little awed; it wasn't a look Jodie was used to seeing on Cole Crawford's face. She realised his toastie was untouched. She could tell his mind was elsewhere, churning over the information she'd just shared about Ethan, no doubt, but he was doing his best to seem normal.

'People can still come and see them.' Toby put one of the puppies down on the counter top and let it sniff around their plates. 'This just helps us weed out the most suitable owners, so we can send them a personal invite.'

'I see.' Cole took a tiny spoonful of soup and moved his bowl away from the puppy's snuffling nose.

Jodie was grateful for the kids easing the tension after what had happened outside. She wanted to blame it on the storm but she knew better—there was so much about their past together that neither of them had been expecting to still rattle them, and the explosions were getting to be a regular thing.

If he hadn't teased her about her jealousy over Diyana, she might not have been as flustered as to admit that she and Ethan had conceived Emmie by accident. She already regretted letting that slip.

OK, so she hadn't told him anything about how she and Ethan had basically been *forced* to marry or risk having to drop out of their degrees. And there was no way in hell she was admitting she'd been so weak at the time, so lost without Cole that she'd waded through most of that year not caring at all what went on around her, but, still, Cole had no business pushing her for details when he'd been the one to break things off in the first place. And he was still keeping secrets from her. She knew it.

I never said I didn't love you. She couldn't forget the way he'd just said that.

Emmie squealed with laughter as the puppy wagged its tail against her glass of juice and sent it sliding along the counter so fast that Cole had to grab it before it toppled over the edge. Jodie went for it at the same time and her fingers landed over his.

'Be careful,' they said at the same time, catching eyes, just as a lightning bolt lit the room from outside.

Toby clapped his hands. 'I love storms.'

'You can feel the energy in the air,' Emmie said, looking between her and Cole. Jodie pulled her hand away as though she'd been stung.

Cole scooped up the puppy in one swoop and deposited it back on the floor before Evie could see and reprimand them. The bustling housekeeper was busy adding more coals to the hearth in the corner, which was already blazing with a fire.

'So, have you guys been studying marketing up in your rooms when most kids are watching cartoons?' Cole teased, stepping over the skittish puppy and crossing with his bowl to the wide copper sink.

'I never watch cartoons,' Emmie said. She was twirling her ponytail around her fingers at the back of her baseball hat. 'And it's not really marketing, Cole, it's just using common sense.'

'It's all about common sense,' Toby reiterated.

Jodie couldn't help smirking a little at the way they were putting him in his place when it came to modern technology. Emmie was pretty good at reaching her father on social media already. She'd been given a phone on her eleventh birthday for that purpose alone, but she'd never seen her daughter try to put her skills to use in this way before.

Cole was watching her now from over by the sink, drying his bowl diligently with a dishcloth. His leather jacket was undone, his jeans were smudged up one side with mud from the manège. His stetson was almost skimming a copper cooking pan that hung from the beams. She realised she'd barely touched her lunch either.

'Don't you want that soup, Mum?' Emmie asked.

'I might have some later instead,' she said, flustered. Cole was still staring at her.

'So, Cole, it looks like you've found yourself some new social media managers,' Evie said now. Had she picked up on the stormy atmosphere between them?

'Did Casper not have any social media set up for this place at all?'

'None,' Emmie answered for him, pattering over to the sink in thick pink woollen socks, with both of their bowls. 'But don't worry, Cole, Toby and I can handle it for you guys. I'm sure you and Mum have better things to do together.'

Emmie ran the hot tap, then started pulling on a pair of rubber gloves. Jodie watched in amazement. Emmie never volunteered to do her own washing-up at home, gloves or no gloves. She never even unloaded the dishwasher unless she was asked to.

She was so taken aback that it took a moment for Emmie's words and tone to sink in. Had she really just said, *I'm sure you have better things to do together?*

'We'll find the next litter of puppies homes, too. Then we can move on to any horses you bring in. There will be more after Blaze, right? Can we ride him soon? Oh, can we go to Green Vale with Dacey and Vinny tomorrow for the animal show?'

Emmie was looking expectantly at Cole now.

Cole hung the dishcloth on its hook on the wall and flicked the rim of her hat affectionately with a thumb. 'So many questions,' he said. 'You're just like your mother.'

'I tend to stop, when I don't get any answers,' Jodie shot back. She regretted it when Emmie raised an eyebrow at her, then Evie. 'What's Green Vale?'

'It's my school,' Toby replied.

'I guess you could call it alternative.' Cole shrugged. 'They have some pretty interesting activities during half-term too. I'm a big fan of the woodland yoga classes.'

Jodie scoffed. She knew he was joking. At least, she *thought* he was.

'Uncle Cole helped me get a place at the new school, Ms Everleigh,' Toby explained. 'This one's way better, we have maths and geography lessons in 3D! There's no headteacher and no hierarchy, the school is jointly managed by students and staff. And we have pigs and donkeys, and we make organic lunches. Before half-term we had to learn to build a fence to keep the pigs off the vegetable patch.'

'They have a yoga studio *and* a photography lab,' Emmie added. She had clearly been told all about it already.

'And they teach them useful stuff, like debating and cooking,' Cole said. 'Not that you couldn't have learned all that at Everleigh too, right, Toby?'

Toby pulled a face. 'Maybe not cooking, not from you, Cole.'

Cole nodded sagely. 'That's fair.' Jodie stifled a snigger.

The wooden door to the practice creaked open and Dacey, one of the vets, walked in, followed by a tiny, wobbly white lamb.

Emmie and Toby both sprang from the sink and started fussing over it. 'Want to help with feeding?' Dacey said, holding up a baby bottle filled with milk. 'She was brought in this morning for a check-up after her mother died, poor sweet thing. What should we call her?'

'We'll call her Annie,' Emmie announced, before anyone else could make a suggestion. 'Like the orphan. Toby, get the iPad, can you, and take a photo of me and Annie for the new social media account. Should I wear these rubber gloves in it?'

'Yeah, that would be funny!'

All of a sudden there was a ruckus of paws and giggles and soap suds and hooves across the floor tiles, a spilled bottle of milk, the clicking iPad camera, the lamb bleating, dogs barking and rain lashing at the windows.

There was never a quiet or dull moment in the Everleigh kitchen, Jodie mused nostalgically. There had always been so many people, so many opinions flying around, so much to do. She was deeply touched that Cole cared enough about Toby to help get him into a new school, too.

They needed to talk more, clear the air. It was ridiculous, carrying all this ancient resentment and tension around—she was here for Everleigh, not Cole. They had to put all that behind them and move forward, for Emmie's sake more than hers. Emmie would only get caught in the middle if this bitterness continued.

Then…the door to the porch swung open again. The stablehand Russell stumbled in, along with a gust of wind and rain. 'C-Cole,' he stuttered, clutching his leg and wincing in pain. 'Cole, man, we have a problem.'

Evie sprang for the old-fashioned telephone on the wall. 'I'll call an ambulance.'

Dacey and Emmie both grappled to stop the lamb from fleeing out the door as Cole hurried to Russell's side. The bottom of the poor guy's jeans was soaked in mud, rain and blood.

'Blaze is gone,' Russell said, grimacing at the sight of his own leg. 'He freaked out at the lightning. I couldn't stop him.'

CHAPTER TEN

'WHY CAN'T YOU take the Land Rover? It's pouring with rain!' Jodie's blue eyes were imploring as Cole heaved the saddle over the back of one of their thoroughbred hotblood mares, Aphrodite.

'Ziggy needs to follow Blaze's scent,' he explained, yanking the straps tight on the left stirrup.

'Blaze won't have gone far *because* of the rain,' he told her. 'But he doesn't know the area so he could be anywhere.'

'I'll come with you.' Jodie was hot on their heels. She was already wearing a riding helmet she'd plucked from the wall and wielding a bridle, awaiting instructions. 'Which horse can I take?'

'You're not coming with me, Jodie,' he told her, hurrying down the aisle with Aphrodite. 'It's too dangerous. I need you alive.'

'Don't be ridiculous.'

He knew she was concerned for his safety, but he was more concerned for hers. Cole was kicking himself for not checking in when the storm started. He'd been distracted by Jodie, and the cozy mayhem in the kitchen. What had happened to Russell was *his* fault.

At the door he prepared to mount, but Jodie's willowy frame blocked him.

'Tell me which horse or I'll take Mustang.'

'Mustang couldn't keep up.'

'Then give me another one. Stop trying to protect me, you're acting like I've never ridden before when you know damn well I'm as capable as you are. What if you need my help when you find him?'

'Fine.' She wouldn't back down, he knew it. Admittedly he was treating her unfairly. 'If you insist. Grab the saddle.' He took the bridle from her and clasped his hands around her waist. He heard her gasp as he put a hand to her pert backside and hoisted her onto Aphrodite's back with one swift movement.

'Do your helmet up,' he ordered as she landed astride the horse. He threw her up the reins. 'I'll saddle up Pirate.'

They took to the road and Ziggy set off ahead, nose to the ground around the rain-crushed daffodils.

Blaze had kicked Russell in the shins, charged past him on the way out of the manège and leapt over the gate to the property like it was nothing but an oxer in a lower showjumping division. A wounded, frightened stallion like him on the loose yet again was a serious liability.

'Has Ziggy done this before?' Jodie called out from behind him.

'He can find anything,' he shouted back against the wind.

They'd only been out on short, fun rides with Emmie and Toby so far, but this was something different. Secretly he thrived on the adrenaline, especially with Jodie at his side…but she was a mother now. Things were not the same as they had been before, so he had even *more* reasons to be careful with her.

Near The Ship Inn, Ziggy suddenly let out three sharp barks at the crossroads by the old red phone box.

'He's got something!' Jodie yelled.

'Get closer to me,' he called to her. He trusted the mare in all weather conditions, but he needed to be able to grab Jodie's reins if anything *did* go wrong.

The mud and dirt splattered Aphrodite's pristine grey legs as they broke into a gallop. Ziggy led them down side roads, across a field of cows. Jodie's helmet did nothing to stop the rain drenching the ends of her hair.

Cole ran over their previous conversation as his horse pounded a new gravel track beneath him and the cold wind whipped his face. He was surprised he'd managed to hold a conversation with the kids at lunch, knowing that Jodie had probably only got married to save face after getting pregnant. She hadn't admitted it, she was likely too embarrassed, but why else would she have married a friend?

Shifting his weight to his outside hip, he nudged his heel into Pirate's right side, and Pirate picked up the pace in perfect rhythm. He could almost see Casper on the horizon, as he always had been before, riding up ahead of him.

This had been their place, where they'd made all their troubles disappear. Just listening to the steady pounding of hooves, the tail-swishes, it had always put his mind at ease, but so had their conversations. Except one, he thought now, back when Casper had told him Jodie was pregnant and getting married. He thought back to writing the letter that same night. He hadn't thought about it in a long time. He had told Jodie everything in that letter. Would it have made a difference for *them* if he'd sent it?

He considered giving it to her now.

No, he couldn't. If she found out this late how he'd broken it off to try and save her like some storybook hero... God, she would never forgive him. She might not regret having the amazing Emmie, but he'd sent her off into some other guy's arms, who'd got her pregnant by *mistake*. All that, just because he'd never had the guts to face up to his father and call his bluff.

'Do you see anything yet?' Jodie was breathless and flushed and her jeans were drenched as she came up alongside him on her horse.

'Nothing, but I trust that dog.'

Some way up the path, Ziggy upped his barking, urging them down an even narrower path at the side of some old storage barns. 'The river's down there,' he yelled to Jodie. 'It runs through the woods. Follow me, it could be dangerous in this wind.'

Cole had been bucked off, bitten, kicked and bowled over himself over the years...but he'd also never, ever blamed a horse for its hostility. Horses were aggressive for two reasons only: if they felt threatened, or if they'd been taught to dominate humans. There was every chance Blaze would feel threatened if they cornered him in the woodland. He'd have to take the chance.

'Go slowly, please,' Jodie urged him, close behind him on the narrow trail. 'You don't know what he's capable of.'

'I won't let anything happen to you,' he told her. He would protect her at all costs. Maybe it was in his biological make-up, or maybe it came from sheltering her for all those years. Maybe it would always be in his wiring, he didn't know, but he felt it like a duty. To this day, he would put Jodie's safety and well-being over his own, in any situation.

The storm seemed to be subsiding, and the rain was finally easing off. Jodie remembered the gushing river to her left. Casper had warned them about the fierce undercurrents when they were kids, especially after heavy rain. It was bulging now, after all the snowmelt they'd had.

Casper's words came to Jodie's mind as Cole crouched down in the sodden moss and leaves, two metres from an anxious-looking Blaze. *The most dangerous part of a horse is its feet, Jodie.*

In a heartbeat, Blaze bucked beneath a giant oak, sending the birds scattering. With a gut-wrenching whinny he charged at Cole, kicking up the leaves in a power play.

'Jodie, don't move an inch,' Cole warned. He didn't even make a move himself, but the horse swerved at the last second and made for the rushing river.

'There's nowhere to go, bud,' she heard him say calmly. He inched towards him again, swiping at low-hanging branches.

Blaze trotted manically up and down what exposed bit of riverbank he could get a footing on. The stallion's neck was lathered in a thick sweat, more from his nerves than from the warmth of the sun, she could tell. His wounds and scars, lit up in a shaft of sudden sunlight, were almost unbearable to see.

The meds had brought him a long way, and his ribs weren't as prominent. But she knew the scars on the inside must be painful for him to act like this, especially when Cole had already worked so hard on gaining his trust.

'Cole, please be careful,' she heard herself say. He wasn't even wearing a hard hat. She almost threw him hers but he put a hand up to stop her, to keep her still.

She was sweating now as she stood there, clutching their horses' reins. One kick from Blaze to Cole's head, and his face would look worse than Russell's shin, if he even survived at all, but she trusted he knew what he was doing.

Blaze was eyeing Cole suspiciously, creating showers of wet chestnut leaves, mud and torn-up daffodils. His scorched nose snorted air. His ears were pinned back and his head jerked this way and that as Cole crept ever closer to the riverbank.

Jodie felt like she'd gone at least ten minutes without taking a breath. But thankfully it wasn't long before Blaze's ears returned to normal, and she watched in wonder as the horse lowered his head in apparent surrender.

'Good man, you know you can trust us.' Cole got close enough to fix the bridle over Blaze's head. Jodie drew a sigh of relief when she saw the reins in his hands. Finally, he was back in control.

She turned to mount Aphrodite…but a sudden commotion behind her made her spin back.

Cole yelled something to her about a rabbit, right before Blaze reared up in fright. The next part seemed to happen in slow motion. Before she could get a mental grip on the situation, Cole was forced backwards into the river.

'Cole!' Jodie raced to the edge and made a futile grab for his billowing shirt. The river was freezing. To her horror, in a nanosecond she couldn't see him at all.

She tore off her jacket, ready to jump in and swim after him…where to, she had no idea. Ziggy was barking hysterically. She saw the dog crouch before she could stop him. 'Ziggy, no!'

With a giant leap Ziggy dived in and started paddling furiously. She flailed for his tail but he drifted out of reach. The world went white and then back to colour.

She couldn't see Cole, still. Maybe he'd hit his head. The thought filled her with sheer terror. A thousand possible scenarios made her feel sick to her stomach as she scanned the river surface up ahead. *Where was Cole?*

A thud in her side almost knocked her fully into the water. Blaze's reins. Grabbing them in one fist, she held on so tight that her hands blistered instantly beneath the leather. With her other hand, she fisted tufts of grass to steady herself, and realised what the horse was doing.

Blaze was trotting in a strange dance, backwards from the riverbank, stomping over shrubs and flowers, biting and yanking on the reins, which were attached to...

Cole. Cole still had hold of the reins.

'Jodie! Don't move. It's OK.' She heard his voice before she saw him. Thank God, he was conscious.

He was getting closer to her now, bobbing back towards her on the white lip of the current. He almost collided with Ziggy but somehow he scooped the struggling dog up in one arm and held him protectively.

Blaze was pulling him back in. Jodie couldn't believe what she was seeing. Foam was still frothing at the corners of the horse's mouth from the sheer effort, but the whole thing had happened in seconds, maybe thirty at the most.

Blaze had purposely lengthened the line between them and was using his strength to pull Cole back in from the water. He was saving Cole's life.

CHAPTER ELEVEN

'PARACETAMOL… ASPIRIN… I need something.' Her nerves were shot. 'Cole, where do you keep your medicine?' She knew he couldn't hear her as he was in the shower.

She pulled open the middle drawer, the top drawer, the bottom drawer… Nothing but cutlery, pens, cables, dog treats. He hadn't told her where it was. He'd insisted he was fine, but she knew he'd be in pain soon enough, if he wasn't already.

They'd ridden the horses back slowly, with Blaze beside them. Cole was bleeding under his jacket, she'd seen it when she'd peeled it off him as soon as they'd reached the cabin, but he'd brushed off his injury. 'Go shower, get warm,' he 'd told her.

So she had, and now she was back. How could she leave him? Russell was in the hospital, and she could tell Cole blamed himself for not checking on Blaze sooner. She knew the way his brain was wired. He would never blame a horse.

You could have lost him. He could have drowned.

The thought was like a knife wound to her heaving chest as tears threatened to consume her.

'Where would you keep your medicine?' she said to his kitchen walls, moving mugs and coffee flasks, and an empty bread bin. Cole would keep the medicine somewhere odd, she thought, like under the sofa.

Her eyes caught on something under the bench by the door, covered in jackets.

Dropping to her knees in her track pants, she pulled out the bright red medicine kit and flipped the latch under the huge white cross. Paracetamol. That would have to do.

She slid the box back, but it was stuck now, jammed halfway out. Reaching behind, it her hands landed on something smooth, made of glass. She pulled out a photo frame covered in dust and swept a hand across it.

Cole and her, sitting on Mustang, bareback.

She fell on her bottom, holding it.

There was another box, she noticed now—the box his stetson had arrived in. She slid it out from under the bench and sifted through photos from their summers together. *He'd kept all these?*

One fell out.

There was Cole, looking up at her from the floor, leaning with his arms crossed and his leg kicked back against a red tractor. She was behind him in the photo, grinning from the driver's seat. It must have been taken the first summer they'd met.

There was Casper in another one, just as she remembered him in his trademark waxed cotton cap and quilted moleskin jacket, with one arm around her shoulders and the other holding a chicken.

Another photo. Her and Cole at twelve or thirteen. She recognised Chesil Beach—this must have been the day they'd gone on a fossil hunt. She held it closer, studying his tanned hand wrapped tightly around hers on their bucket of treasures. That had been around the time that parts of her had started tingling in anticipation of his touch. Just his hand, hauling her up to a rock for a photo, had felt like another moment in heaven.

Another photo. Her and Cole at fourteen. Cole was even more tanned in this one, holding a pitchfork like a guitar out in the stables. He'd been skinny before but now he was filling out. He had muscles from labouring with hay bales and farming equipment, and a wild mop of curls. This was right before he'd taught her to ride bareback, solo, she remembered with a smile.

This was the summer she'd thought Cole was finally going to kiss her…but he didn't. The kiss had come at fifteen. There was no photo from that year, but she could see it as clear as day. They'd been swimming in the river, looking for kingfishers. Cole had swum right up to her beneath the wrought-iron bridge.

She'd thought he'd been about to dunk her; she'd been laughing and splashing him in his new blue board shorts. She'd been self-conscious of her new womanly body, and awed by his new broad chest and the thick, dark hair in places he hadn't had hair before. But his hands had found her waist under the water. Without a word, he had pulled her into the shadows under the bridge and kissed her. Her first kiss. Cole had been her first everything.

Jodie pressed her bare feet to the cold tile floor, clutching the photos to her heart as the mental image of Cole slipping away in the river tore a new hole in her chest. They'd had their disagreements and spent the last twelve years apart but if anything happened to him she knew she would die herself, even after all this time.

The tears wouldn't stop now. She didn't know how long she sat there, falling apart, on the floor, but Ziggy laid a sympathetic head on her lap and she was very grateful for the comfort.

A sound from the bathroom made Jodie shove the photos and medicine kit back, but a letter slipped out from the pile. At least it looked like a letter, sealed in a cream-coloured envelope. There was nothing on the front, but she recognised the old-fashioned wax stamp Casper had always used, sealing the back closed.

Hearing Cole moving about, she put it back with the photos and laid the framed photo back on top, wiping her dusty hand on her tracksuit bottoms.

By the time Cole stepped from the bathroom, running a towel over his hair, in nothing but clean jeans, she was stoking the fire, trying to dry her eyes, as well as her wet hair and damp tank top.

'How are you feeling?' he asked her, dropping to the leather couch then wincing at the pain to his shoulder.

'Better than you, I think,' she said, still fighting to gain control of her shaky voice and limbs. He was here, he was OK, and she had to pull herself together.

The buckle of his jeans blazed red from the fire behind her. Her eyes fell to the lines on his body from his belt to the trail of dark fuzz up to his belly button. Shuffling between his knees on the rug, she popped the paracetamol from their foil case.

It had been a long time since she'd seen Cole without his shirt on. He looked even better now than he had then, only he was still bleeding.

'You're really hurt, Cole.'

'I told you, I'm fine.'

'That's what you always say, Cole, even when you're not.'

He tipped up her chin with a finger, looking her deep in the eyes. 'Hey, I'm sorry I scared you.'

'What if you'd died, the same way your dad did?'

Cole's face darkened. 'I'd have hoped more people would miss me.'

The shadows on his abs caused a flicker of a memory. One hot second of them making love. Then another memory, years before they'd been an item, of Cole telling her he'd broken his finger. It had been over Christmas, when she'd been back in Greenwich, so they'd talked about it on the phone.

When she'd offered to fly down on Christmas Day to be with him, he'd told her not to be so dramatic. *'I told you Jodie, I'm fine. It was an accident, he didn't mean to...'*

'Who didn't mean to?'

'The dog, when it jumped up at the door and slammed it shut on me! Tell me what's going on with you?'

She took his strong, gentle hand on his lap, opened his palm and put the pills in it. Why was she remembering that now? Because he was in pain and embarrassed that someone might want to help him?

'Swallow,' she said, reaching a tentative finger to his wound. His right upper arm was bruised from a collision with a rock.

'You got lucky, you won't need stitches,' she told him, but his skin was already a wicked shade of purple around the cuts. His biceps stretched out another deep red scratch as he chased the pills with water from a mug.

'Cole, that horse saved your life today.'

His gaze fell to her lips, right before he leaned across her to put the mug down, sending the scent of familiar musky soap to her nose, deep to her core. 'Not many people would believe that.' Her stomach flipped as he caught her fingers and pressed a hard kiss to her knuckles.

'I saw what he did. I saw Ziggy dive in after you, too,' she managed, though her heart was thrumming.

He cradled her face in his hand, and his thumb caressed her cheek. She leaned into him, closing her eyes. Every nerve ending flared at his touch.

'I need to tell you something,' he said.

She held her breath. Her gut told her she wasn't going to like this.

'Casper left a photo of you out on his desk, not long after he got back from your wedding in Edinburgh.' Cole ran a finger softly across her lower lip, sending a flock of butterflies straight between her legs. 'Seeing you in that white dress, married to someone else, knowing you were carrying his baby... Do you want to know what I did?'

'What?'

'I rode Mustang out to West Bay cliffs. I yelled at the sea until my throat was on fire, and you know I never yell. A guy with a dog ran over and asked if I was OK.'

'Jealousy almost drove you off a cliff, huh?' Jodie joked weakly, swiping her hair behind her ear. 'And yet you never once tried to come and get me back.'

The rug was hot under her knees as she knelt between his legs. He lowered his head, urging her lips ever closer. Her fingers inched around the waist of his jeans, tracing across his hip bone before curling about his belt, urging him down from the couch to the floor without any words. He let out an anguished groan as he slid to the rug, still lacing his fingers through her hair, keeping her head close enough to kiss.

'Why didn't you try to get me back, Cole?'

'All this time, I thought you'd fallen in love with someone else.'

They seemed to hover there in silent longing, until she'd had enough. She crushed her lips to his. She wanted...no, needed him. All of him. Cole's body loos-

ened. His arms encircled her like a cage, more posses-
sive by the moment.

'You have no idea how much I missed you,' he
growled against her lips, as his fingers found her bra
straps and slid them down her shoulders.

She realised he probably meant he'd missed their
amazing sex but she wasn't about to ruin the moment
with more questions.

In seconds he was worshipping her bare breasts with
his lips and kisses in the firelight, and her breathing was
ragged and raspy in his hair. He urged her down onto
the sheepskin rug, hovering over her, taking her in. She
was older now than when they'd last been together like
this, and she wasn't used to a man's gaze on her body,
not the way Cole was looking at her.

His eyes showed nothing but admiration and lust
as she traced her fingers along the lines of his abs. He
knelt between her legs, reached up and pulled his shirt
over his head, tossing it to the couch. He was all man;
broader, bigger, muscled from a life outdoors intensi-
fied by lifting saddles and straw bales and labouring
over the gardens at Everleigh.

Every muscle on his torso rippled in the firelight.
Their bickering and unresolved issues seemed to melt
away. She blocked it all out, or rather her tendons, muscles and limbs ignored her head and its burning questions. The thrill of his touch was too intense to deny.

Heat was all she felt. Heat from the fire, heat from
Cole, heat from the sparks between them as he came
back over her, his good arm getting lost in the sheepskin rug as he trailed a finger from his other hand over
her breasts, slowly down to her belly, tracing more delicious kisses in its wake. His close-trimmed beard left
trails of delicious tingles on her skin.

She'd used to love it when he'd worshipped her like this, sometimes more than the act of making love itself. The gentle, teasing touch, as soft as a moth on her skin, created tingles of anticipation all over her.

Lying on her back, Jodie shivered at his touch, arching from the rug to allow him to lower her sweatpants, then allowing a pent-up moan to escape her throat as his fingers found the once-familiar path to the parts of her that only *he* had ever known how to truly make tremble.

'I'll stop if you want me to.'

Somewhere in a distant galaxy another version of herself screamed *Yes, stop*, but in his hands she was mute, relishing in the chemistry bubbling and fizzing between them. It was theirs and theirs alone.

His fingers wove through hers on the rug above her head, and every few kisses he squeezed them tight, as if he needed to check if she was really there with him, doing this, after all this time. She was here, she realised, heart and soul, inching out of her underwear with her lips still glued to his.

'Jodie…' He stopped, as if to question their actions again, or tell her something he'd been keeping to himself. She couldn't tell, but she didn't care now. She was already gone, into him, consumed by him. Her naked body seemed to remember his, like a song that had been on the tip of her tongue but which she'd somehow forgotten the words to till now. They didn't need words, she remembered that now. Making love had always been their principal means of communication.

'How is your daughter doing?' Jodie asked the solicitor, crossing her legs under the desk in fitted green military-style trousers that she knew Cole hadn't seen before.

She'd felt his eyes on her bottom walking in here, but she hadn't known quite how to look him in the eyes yet.

Ms Tanner looked up from the papers on the desk between them. 'It was nothing serious but she's much better now. Thank you for asking. Again, I'm sorry this meeting had to be rescheduled. My husband was away on business so there was no one else to watch her.'

'It's not a problem. It gave us time to...' Cole trailed off, catching Jodie's eye as Ziggy stretched out across his feet under the desk. Her insides jolted. She could still feel the slight burn of his kisses on her lips and an echo of euphoria that was now disguising itself as mild discomfort between her legs—the kind of physical afterglow you only ever experienced after making love more times than you can remember in one night.

It didn't take much to send her mind back to how she'd melted into him, but in the cold light of day she was starting to regret her raging libido already. *Time to what?* She wondered what he'd been about to say. Time to fall back into bed together? Of course he wouldn't say that in front of the solicitor, but what if he was thinking it?

She'd given herself to him willingly, and she wasn't particularly proud of that. Whatever force of gravity that had seemed to bring her body back to his had left her reeling and fumbling through the morning, wondering what the hell had happened to her brain.

They'd both returned to earth to find missed calls from Ms Tanner about the meeting. Jodie had almost forgotten they still had to talk with her.

'You were lucky. Casper had this all planned out,' the round-faced, flame-haired Irishwoman told them from the leather-backed chair.

'For how long?'

Ms Tanner leafed through the pages in front of her with neatly manicured fingers. 'For almost five years.'

'Five years?' Jodie was stunned. Cole dragged a hand through his hair. She knew he was probably still in pain from yesterday. He hadn't exactly been careful with his arm, rolling around in the living room with her all night, but he was doing his best to hide any discomfort.

'We find it's better to initiate conversations about estates by focusing on the owner's wishes and concerns, rather than on who gets what,' Ms Tanner explained, pushing her glasses up her nose. 'So that's what we focused on when Casper came to us. The potential long-term care needs he had in mind for Everleigh came back to you, Mr Crawford, and you, Ms Everleigh.'

'Ms Tanner, can I see that plan?'

'Of course.' She slid the papers over the desk to Jodie. 'You're free to look over all this again in your own time. You can come to an agreement between yourselves. If selling is on your mind at the end of the stipulated time spent here, Ms Everleigh, you should know there are legal arrangements already in place regarding which assets are held for designated beneficiaries without the need for a court process...'

Jodie scanned the documents, listening dutifully, swigging from her coffee cup as Ziggy warmed her cold feet as well as Cole's, like the dog had accepted her into his pack already.

She hadn't even contemplated probate, or the prospect of divvying up what would be hers and what would be Cole's. That would feel more like a separation than the day he'd broken up with her; not that splitting away from Cole in any way, shape or form should bother her now, she thought defiantly.

And yet here we are now...

They'd just made incredible love and her heart was rioting in her chest.

'Do you have any thoughts about selling, Mr Crawford?' Ms Tanner asked him.

Cole sat up straighter on his chair. Again Jodie noticed him trying not to wince at his shoulder pain—stubborn fool. 'This is my home,' he stated bluntly. 'I'm not going anywhere, and I wouldn't particularly want anyone else coming in as a partner either. Jodie knows what Casper wanted for this place better than anyone.'

She caught his eyes again and he held them this time, searching hers like he was waiting for her to either agree, or thank him, or maybe even confirm here and now that she wouldn't be selling anything either, once she'd done what Casper had asked of her.

Shame, guilt and irritation flared up out of nowhere. She'd put herself in an awkward situation last night. She'd been so caught up in Cole and the moment that she'd completely forgotten she was supposed to be staying away from the man who'd, oh, so casually ripped the rug out from under her once. She might know Everleigh better than anyone else who might walk in off the street, wanting a piece of it, but she owed Cole nothing. He was the one who'd kept her away from here for so long in the first place by ending their relationship.

And yet you still slept with him!

She tried to squish the delicious flashback of their bodies moving as one, the absence of space and time, or past and future that she'd felt in his arms. She owed him nothing. She'd just been weakened in the moment, seeing all those photos, remembering how she'd loved him once.

But it had felt so incredible. Like nothing else mattered.

Cole was still looking at her, and Ms Tanner cleared

her throat, as though sensing the tension. 'Well, from your personal financial statements I see you're quite comfortable here, in more ways than one, Mr Crawford. And as for you, Ms Everleigh, I see you fare the same in Scotland. You are of course entitled to review the situation once the conditions stated in the will have been met in a year's time.'

'I'm aware of that, thank you,' Jodie said. 'As you can imagine, it's quite a lot of information to take in. I owe it to my ex-husband, Ethan, to discuss this with him. Neither of us would want our daughter or her education to be disrupted. I also have my own practice and staff to consider in Edinburgh, so I can imagine selling my share of Everleigh at the end of the year is probably still quite likely.'

'I quite understand. Maybe you'll feel differently in a year.'

Jodie chewed her cheek. Beside her, Cole's jaw had started to spasm. Ziggy seemed to sense the general air of discomfort and whimpered softly as Jodie shook her head. What was she supposed to do?

Reality was probably taking a fist to Cole's ego right now and her suspicions were getting the better of her. If he thought one night of sex…even if it was the best sex they'd ever indulged in, as far as she could remember…would somehow secure her decision to keep her half of the estate, he was wrong.

Emmie was her priority now. Even if Jodie had very much enjoyed last night, *everything* she'd known for the last twelve years was in Edinburgh.

'Who's to say someone else wouldn't do a better job than me?' she added now, trying to make herself believe it at the same time. 'Someone with more time and fewer…commitments.'

'Sounds like you need this time to figure things out between yourselves,' Ms Tanner said, looking from one to the other.

'Or to find another suitable partner for Cole,' Jodie added.

Cole had a face like thunder now but he remained silent and stony. Ms Tanner raised an eyebrow. Jodie swore she saw her smirk.

When the solicitor had wished them both goodbye and good luck, Jodie realised she was quite wound up. They were business partners with a sizeable fortune and even more sizeable responsibilities. Everything about the meeting had hammered that home.

What had she done, giving in to him like that last night? Worse than that, hadn't she initiated it?

She braced herself to take Cole aside and ensure he knew that last night had been a mistake, and that they should leave things on a platonic note and remember their priority was Everleigh going forward.

He didn't give her a chance. 'I have an appointment,' he told her curtly and strode in the direction of the stables without looking back. She watched him go, stunned.

CHAPTER TWELVE

Toby looked genuinely sad as he helped to put Emmie's bags in the back of their car. Emmie looked torn as she hugged one of the puppies to her for the last time. 'I can't believe you're leaving before the next puppies arrive. And we've got that girl coming to see Lucy-Fur later.'

'I have to get back to school, and Saxon.'

'But you'll be back soon, right?'

Emmie shrugged. Jodie offered a weak nod in their direction and pulled her sunglasses down over her eyes. She felt nauseous from drinking too much coffee on an empty stomach and totally drained of energy. She'd watched them bond and now she was pulling them apart, like her father had done to her and Cole.

She pulled out her phone, distracted. *Where was Cole now?*

He hadn't returned from his appointment yet and she had no idea where he'd gone. One of the staff said he'd saddled up Pirate and gone out, even though he shouldn't have been riding after injuring his shoulder.

A laugh from the manège pulled her eyes away. Emmie and Toby were heading for the paddock, where Blaze was grazing on a fresh load of hay. Her heart lurched. 'Emmie, don't get too close,' she called.

She hadn't told her what had happened by the river. Yes, Blaze had shown a gentler side of himself to Cole, but he was still unpredictable. She crossed the grass towards them quickly, but Emmie was already standing on the fence, reaching a hand out.

'Emmie, be careful!' she warned, but she soon stopped in her tracks. Blaze had ambled over and gently rested his muzzle in her daughter's outstretched palm.

Emmie giggled. Jodie half expected to see Cole coming out of the stables. Maybe he was close by, making Blaze feel safe. But he was nowhere around. Her annoyance at him simmered.

He'd said in the meeting that he didn't want anyone but her taking over at Everleigh, but when she'd refused to commit beyond the year he'd gone AWOL. She didn't want to think he'd slept with her out of any ulterior motive, but he was acting like it now.

'Jodie!' Evie was crossing the garden towards her in her apron, holding two brown sandwich bags. 'For your supper.' The housekeeper beamed, plopping kisses to both cheeks and squeezing her shoulders warmly. 'I really hope you'll be back with us soon. It's been lovely having you and Emmie here.'

'Thank you so much, Evie.' Jodie hugged her warm, stocky frame, surprised to find tears in her eyes again behind her sunglasses. She wasn't prepared for this muddle of emotions.

'Where's Cole?'

'I don't know.'

Evie frowned, peering into the car as though she might find him hiding in the back seat. Jodie knew her face must have given her away as she sighed and placed the sandwich bags on the passenger seat.

'You know what he's like,' Evie said, lowering her

voice as Emmie came running over to the car. 'He's always been better with animals than people. Keeps a lot inside, that one. But I *know* he thinks the world of you.'

The wind whipped Pirate's mane into the air like flames as the animal's muscles rippled under powerful legs, propelling Cole back towards the village from the cliffs.

He'd been trying to gallop away from the sense of self-loathing that had consumed him in the meeting and sent him into his usual fight or flight mode. Every time Jodie mentioned Ethan, he was reminded of how, divorced or not, their unconventional little family unit was her life. Everleigh wasn't. *He* wasn't.

He didn't deserve her as anything more than a business partner. He had no right expecting anything else to develop between them. But, then, he hadn't exactly been expecting to spend the whole night having sex with her on his living-room floor, making up for lost time. He sucked in the sky as he flew through the air, recalling her moans of pleasure as she'd put herself heart and soul into his hands. It had been impossible to deny himself, even though he'd known there would be consequences afterwards. She'd wanted it to happen…she'd started it, even…but he should have been stronger.

'Faster, Pirate, boy!' he yelled.

The feel of her after all this time…he couldn't stop reliving it. No one else had ever come close to fitting him like that. But Emmie was her life now. Edinburgh was her life.

It was clear that Jodie was intent on selling after the year was up, no matter what she felt, or didn't feel, for him. He'd hurt her too much in the past, pushed her too far away. To him, last night had felt like a reconnection, but maybe she'd seen it as closure.

For Emmie's sake, he had to make sure they both knew they could come back here any time without any underlying awkwardness.

'Mum!' Emmie's voice in the back seat brought her out of her gloomy thoughts.

'What's wrong?'

'Mum, is that Cole?'

Jodie slowed the car. They were right outside The Ship Inn. His horse appeared in her rear-view mirror, sending the gravel flying as her heart kicked into overdrive. Cole was galloping towards them under the clear sky, startling the cows with his speed.

Jodie held her breath. She flung the car door open, right as Cole dismounted in one jump.

'I'm sorry I got held up,' he said as his boots hit the ground. He clasped the reins in one hand and raked a hand through his windswept hair with the other.

'Were you trying to avoid me?' she asked bluntly, folding her arms. The breeze sent her hair flying out, tickling her face, and it reminded her of when they'd stood here on the day of the funeral, facing each other. A lot had happened since then. *What might happen in a year?*

He grunted and tipped his hat. 'I'm not great at goodbyes.'

'I already know that, Cole.'

Cole's very presence was making her heart race but she hoped her face didn't show it. She wanted to tell him last night had been a mistake, because it had been… they had to work together from now on. She couldn't put Emmie through any more drama, and she refused to put herself through any more emotional stress at the hands of this man.

His hands. She looked at them now, remembering the feel of his fingers in places they hadn't been for a long time.

She studied the mouth that had spent all night exploring her and felt the shakiness return to her knees. The remnants of last night's actions lingered between them, bringing Cole to a stop almost at the tip of her now-scuffed boots, making him shove his hands into his pockets.

'Did you chase us all this way so you could tell me something?' she managed.

Pirate snorted softly through pink nostrils. Cole lowered his voice, and threw her into his shadow as he stood over her. She swallowed.

'I wanted to tell you I'm sorry about last night,' he said, glancing at the car to make sure Emmie couldn't hear. 'It went too far, Jodie. I know you have a lot on your mind, a lot going on, and this has all been a shock for both of us. We got…carried away.'

Jodie felt the impact to her heart like a horse had rushed up and kicked her. She hadn't been expecting that. He continued. 'If you're going to be spending more time here, as equal partners, we should probably keep things professional. Don't you think? I know Emmie has been through a lot with your divorce already…'

She bit her lip, but he was only saying what she'd planned to say herself. She took a deep breath. 'I one hundred percent agree with you.'

Cole looked taken aback. 'You do?'

She swallowed, maintained her cool. 'We were just two people giving in to their…biological urges. You're not to blame, I'm not to blame. We're two very different people now, Cole, with very different lives. From this point on we are colleagues, equal partners in creating a sustainable future for Everleigh over the next year, that's all.'

He nodded, adjusted his hat awkwardly. 'And we don't know what will happen after that.'

'We'll find a new partner for you,' she replied, 'I'll help you do that.'

He was quiet for a moment, nodding slowly and thoughtfully the way he did when his brain was working overtime and he didn't know how to express himself. Or didn't want to. *Infuriating.*

'I guess I'll see you soon, then,' he said, lingering on the spot.

She kept her arms crossed tightly, resisting the urge to reach for him, or yell at him. She wanted to do both. What was happening to her? 'I guess you will.'

Cole stepped to the car window and tapped on the glass. Emmie rolled down the window in response.

'Emmie, look after your mother, she needs you,' she heard him say.

'I'm perfectly capable of looking after myself, thank you,' Jodie snapped, brushing past him and re-inserting herself into the driver's seat.

'We should get going, it's a long drive.'

Three weeks later

'It looks a lot like your dog has eaten something that she can't digest,' Jodie said to the harried-looking woman. Aileen shifted the unhappy Doodle on the table between them. 'We can see a foreign body on the X-ray here, but at the moment we can't tell what it is.'

'You can't tell what it is?' The woman looked annoyed.

Jodie frowned at the X-ray again. 'No idea. But we'll have to remove it for Ringo's safety.'

The woman sighed. 'Please, do whatever you have to do for Ringo. I have to run. Will you let me know once you find out what it is? I can't think what he could have eaten. We don't leave things lying around the house… Mind you, I've been away a lot lately, and I don't know if my boyfriend's been spoiling him.' She looked thoughtful for a moment, petting the dog's head.

'He'll be fine with us,' Jodie said, though she knew Aileen and Maxeen would be performing the op. She had to run out to pick up Emmie's iPad and take it to Ethan's new place. Apparently she had a video call with Toby at Everleigh and she'd left the essential item at home by mistake. It was imperative she log in on time.

Jodie thought it was sweet how much they'd enjoyed each other's company on the estate. Emmie talked about it non-stop. On the other hand, she was annoyed that Cole hadn't so much as picked up a phone, let alone tried to initiate a video call. She supposed it was up to her to let him know when she'd be back, as per their agreement, but his stony silence wasn't making the prospect any more appealing.

When Jodie returned to West Bow, the operation was still under way. With less than twenty minutes till the next appointment she poured herself a cup of coffee in the little kitchen and resisted the temptation to call Cole.

She was back now. Back at West Bow, where she belonged. She was living her normal life, in her normal routine. She'd needed normality to come to her final decision without Cole clouding up her thoughts. She was going to sell her share of Everleigh, just like she'd told him and the solicitor.

Or was she?

She frowned. She couldn't quite stick to a decision. Emmie was talking about it like it was some sort of utopia, all the horses, the puppies, the lambs and the marsh-mallow nights round the firepit…and Toby. Maybe they just needed more 'normal', she thought. Just a couple more weeks to forget the way her heart had fogged up her head around Cole, and for Emmie to remember she was a city kid who hadn't even wanted to go to Dorset in the first place.

Normal is good, she reminded herself yet again, glancing at the 'normal' moody dark sky and cobble-stones on the narrow, cramped street outside. A far cry from the changeable skies over Dorset and the mud-splattered pathways they'd walked and ridden down, she thought with a slight pang.

A far cry from the feeling of home she didn't want to feel in Cole's arms but still did.

'Everything went to plan,' Aileen said, bustling into the kitchen. She deposited her gloves in the bin on the way past. 'But I think Ringo's humans have another problem on their hands now.'

'What's happened? What did the dog eat?'

'A pair of lacy red knickers.'

'You're kidding?'

'Nope. I showed them to the client and she said they weren't hers. Then she stormed out, yelling into her phone. It's not a great way to find out your boyfriend's cheating, is it?'

Jodie grimaced. 'The poor woman.'

'Well…you know what they say about love,' Aileen sighed.

'What do they say about love?'

Aileen frowned. 'You tell me! You've been in a different world since you got back from Everleigh. Something to do with your horse whisperer, and inheriting your uncle's estate?'

Jodie winced. 'Is it that obvious?'

'Very.'

'I'm sorry.'

Aileen put a hand lightly on her friend's arm. 'Why are you apologising? A lot has happened to you lately.'

Jodie let out a long sigh. 'I don't even know. The inheritance is one thing. I mean, I'll have to spend a lot more time away from this place.'

'That's why you have all of us,' Aileen said.

Jodie nodded, grateful for her team yet again. She knew that was only half the issue, of course. 'I feel guilty, I suppose,' she admitted. 'And a little bit silly. I didn't tell you…but I went back to him.'

Aileen grinned. 'Now we're getting to it! Like, *back* to him back to him?'

'Several times,' she groaned, putting her head in her hands. 'In one night.'

'Wow.'

'Yes, wow. But then we both agreed it was a mistake.'

'And why was it a mistake? You're both single.'

'Emmie asked me questions in the car…things about me and Cole,' she said, running her hands anxiously along a stethoscope on the desk. 'I didn't really tell her much about our history, Aileen. She doesn't know I was with Cole before I met her dad.'

'I don't see why any of that matters. You were faithful to Ethan when you were married, raising Emmie.'

'Yes…physically. But not mentally.'

'Jodie, you're only human.' Aileen looked exasperated. 'Don't beat yourself up, you're a great mum. Tell me about this man, please. What kind of romance did you *have* with this Cole guy? He seems to have quite the hold on you.'

'A big one.' Jodie looked defeated. Aileen was always

blunt and she was glad of it. It was what she needed. 'But then he broke me to pieces.'

'There's always one that does that.'

'I know, and you swear you'll never let them anywhere near you again…'

'And then your raging hormones take over,' Aileen said knowingly. 'The insufferable consequences of human imperfections, huh? Animals don't suffer this problem.'

'I don't even know why I did it.' Jodie grimaced. 'I don't know what happens to me when I'm with him. It's not normal. I went there for Everleigh, but he *is* Everleigh.'

In a flash she was back on the riverbank, watching Cole go under. Then back in the cabin, seeing all the photos of them he'd kept for some reason. Maybe he hadn't been over her when he'd said he was. And if not, why had he called things off?

It was too confusing, but she could have lost him in that river and the notion still killed her. It was all too much to think about.

Aileen took her stethoscope and shooed her towards the door. 'Go.'

'Go where?' Jodie almost stumbled in her non-slip shoes.

'Go back to him again. Or at least clear your schedule and talk to Emmie first. She can handle the truth. You owe it to yourself to be happy, Jodie, and I've never seen you like this before. Everything's under control here.'

As she said it, a dog barked and a cat yowled loudly in the kennels, making Aileen jump and curse, and Jodie burst out laughing for the first time in days.

'Normal is boring, by the way!' Aileen called after her down the corridor.

CHAPTER THIRTEEN

'WILL YOU BE OK, staying with your dad?'

Emmie looked up over her bowl of soup. 'Why? How long will you be gone?'

'I don't know yet,' she replied honestly. 'I've booked time off from West Bow for the next week, so...'

'This is about you and Cole, isn't it?' Emmie asked. 'There's something going on with you two. I'm not blind, Mum. Why don't you want to tell me?'

Jodie's heart sped up. She'd been anticipating this, and had wanted to sit down with Ethan, but when she'd filled him in, Ethan had suggested it might be best just coming from her. She took the butter out of the fridge and then sat next to Emmie.

'Truth time,' Emmie said, dropping her spoon.

Jodie picked up a bread roll and started buttering it absently, feeling the heat prickle right up her arms. 'Uncle Casper left me and Cole equal shares in Everleigh in his will. The meeting we had to stay for, that was so we could talk about it and all the legal implications.'

Emmie just blinked at her for a moment. 'You own half of the estate?'

'Yes.'

She scraped her chair back on the kitchen floor.

'Isn't that worth…like millions? Can I tell people we're rich now?'

Jodie rolled her eyes. 'I didn't raise you to talk like that. But it's worth a lot, yes.' She shot her daughter a sideways smile. 'A *lot*.'

Her daughter's eyes grew as round as saucers. 'Mum! What the—'

'Listen.' Jodie discarded the knife, putting a hand out over Emmie's. 'The will states I have to go back there over the course of a year as often as I can before I can sell my half. I have to work things out with Cole, help him find someone else who can—'

'Why would you *sell*?' Emmie was looking at her like she'd gone insane. Jodie sat back in her chair as Emmie gazed at her imploringly. 'Mum, seriously, why you would sell your half of Everleigh? I thought you loved it there. It's amazing. I mean, I know I didn't want to go there at first, but that was before…'

'Before you met Toby?' Jodie raised an eyebrow. Emmie scrunched up her nose.

'What? No, Toby's cool, but the horses… Mum, the animals, the veterinary practice, all the stuff Evie showed me how to cook. I didn't watch TV the whole time I was there.'

'I noticed.'

'Can I come back with you?'

'No, not this time, you have school.' Jodie pushed her own plate aside, preparing herself. 'Emmie, there's something else.'

'Is this the part where you tell me something's going on with Cole?' Emmie grinned impishly. 'I knew it!'

Jodie felt her face flush. She'd deflected the questions up till now but she knew Emmie deserved the truth. 'Cole and I were together for a few years. We just…fell in love as kids, then it suddenly got serious when we were older.'

'OK.' Emmie put her chin in her palms, listening intently.

'But he broke things off when we were nineteen, before I moved to Edinburgh, and that's when I met your dad. There wasn't much of a gap between those relationships.'

Emmie's eyebrows shot up. 'Are you trying to tell me Cole Crawford is my real dad?'

Jodie laughed. 'Don't be ridiculous. Emmie, listen, all you need to know is I love you, and so does your dad. And I loved Cole for a long time before that. He just wasn't too hot at communicating with humans when we were together.' *He still isn't*, she thought, but she didn't say it. 'He's always been better with animals.'

'You mean you *love* him,' Emmie corrected her. 'I don't know what went wrong with you two, and I thank him for breaking up with you because it meant I was born. I am totally awesome…'

'Yes, you are.'

'But you still love each other. I've seen the way you look at each other when you both think the other isn't looking. And Toby said you spent the night with him before we left.'

Stunned, Jodie shifted in her chair, looking for signs of disgust or disdain in her daughter's blue eyes, but there were none.

Emmie was growing up so fast, she realised helplessly. She was losing the softness to her cheeks but getting tougher. She admired her daughter for the millionth time, even as embarrassment flared through her. 'I don't know what to say.'

Emmie smirked, rocking back on two chair legs. 'It's OK, Mum, we've had the sex talk at school.'

Jodie shook her head, biting back a smile. 'You're the best thing that ever happened to me, do you know that?'

'Mum.' Emmie's eyes filled with love suddenly, a love so pure it shocked Jodie.

'We're not together now,' she explained quickly, wondering when her daughter had got quite so mature. 'I just wanted to let you know the situation with the inheritance, and everything that comes with it. There might be times when you have to stay with your dad and Saskia a bit longer.'

Emmie frowned. *Now* she looked disturbed, but thankfully not at the concept of staying with her dad more. 'You're not with Cole now? After you…? But you guys were so angsty.'

Angsty? 'Emmie, it's complicated.'

'Adults are always so complicated.'

'Well, you're going to be one soon enough.' She smiled.

Emmie rolled her eyes. 'So when are you leaving again?'

'Tomorrow,' Jodie said, opening her arms. 'Can I get a hug?'

'Can I get a promise that you'll keep your share of Everleigh, so I can tell my friends my mum has an estate in Dorset with horses?'

'Not just yet.' Jodie's insides twisted, remembering how she'd left things with Cole. To her surprise and relief, Emmie hugged her anyway.

Jodie had hoped she would be able to get through some of West Bow's paperwork on the train journey to Dorset, but her mind was a whirlwind as she stared out the window. She felt a pang of sadness over leaving Emmie. They'd been getting on surprisingly better since coming back from Everleigh the first time, but she couldn't pull her out of school. And as much as Ethan supported her, he adored spending time with Emmie. She didn't want to deny him that.

She'd told Cole that what had happened had been a mistake. He'd said the same thing. Rejection had seen her building her defences back up again, and he had done that too, perhaps. Neither of them had been particularly nice to the other when they'd said that awkward goodbye.

She knew it was for the best if they focused on the rescue centre from now on, and the plans for the estate going forward.

Yet here she was, watching the three hundred and forty miles speed past in varying shades of green, feeling nauseous at the thought of seeing him again. She was heading back to the man she'd sworn just weeks ago that she had no feelings for whatsoever. But it wasn't exactly indifference causing her butterflies.

She pondered Aileen's final perspective on the inheritance clause:

'Maybe that's why Casper left you both the property? Maybe he knew it wasn't too late to fix things between you and Cole?'

Jodie looked up at the drizzly sky. If that was it, he wouldn't be getting his wish. Emmie might love Everleigh more than Jodie had ever expected her to but it didn't change the fact that Cole was still a locked-up tower of secrets that infuriated her.

There was no way she could keep her share of Everleigh and work with him beyond the allocated time unless he started to communicate with her in the same open, trusting, honest way he seemed to communicate with his horses.

Twilight was settling on the paddocks by the time her cab rumbled down the gravel pathway. The lights were on in Cole's cabin and she could make out two cars outside. The Land Rover and a sedan she didn't recognise.

'Ms Everleigh?'

Toby's voice took her by surprise as she stepped out from the cab and paid the driver. He was hurrying towards her from the kennels with a puppy under his arm. She didn't recognise it from the litter they'd rescued, but he had probably found homes for Lucy-Fur and co., thanks to his and Emmie's social media efforts.

'Where's Emmie?' he asked her. His eyes were wide and hopeful behind his glasses.

'Sorry, Toby, it's just me this time.'

His mouth twisted in disappointment. 'She told me it would just be you. I was hoping she was planning to surprise me. This is one of the new puppies!'

'Cute,' she said, pulling her bag from the back seat.

'I guess you're looking for Cole. He has a client, but I can take you over there.'

'Oh, no, let's not disturb him,' she said as the cab crunched back up the driveway.

'He won't care. I have to feed Ziggy anyway. I always feed him when Cole has clients.'

Toby was persistent. He even carried her bag to the cabin porch. She followed him inside and the familiar scent of Cole, cleaning products and coffee filled her nose and made her empty stomach shift uneasily.

'Cole!' Toby called out as Ziggy made a beeline

straight for her from the sheepskin rug by the fire, and started sniffing her ankles.

She heard Cole's voice behind the door to his consultation room, the extension he'd built onto the cabin where he saw his clients and their animals.

'One second, please, I'll be right back.'

The door was flung open and his deep voice pierced the air. 'Toby, hey, there's a new bag of kibble by the bench, thank you, buddy. Can you walk Ziggy too?' He stopped in surprise when he saw her. 'Jodie.'

She raised a hand awkwardly as Toby dropped her belongings on the floor by Cole's old weathered leather boots and went about fetching the giant sack of dog food. Ziggy padded after him expectantly.

'I left you a message to say which train I was getting. But I know you're busy. I can wait,' she said.

He'd shaved his beard off, she noted. He looked younger, like he had when he'd been nineteen, only there was muscle on him now, and biceps stretching out the fabric of a smart blue shirt. He looked good. Tired, but good.

She knew she didn't look great herself after a day of sitting on trains, but then again so what? He'd seen her look far worse. And she shouldn't even care what she looked like, it wasn't like she'd come back to romance him. She was here because Casper had given her no choice, and because she wouldn't have heard the end of it from Aileen if she didn't at least attempt to talk to him about some of the more personal stuff still left unaddressed.

'You're still going to sell,' he stated, stepping towards her.

She frowned. Trust him to get straight to business now that she'd hurt his pride. 'I don't see why anything should have changed,' she told him, adjusting her hand-bag on her shoulder. 'Evie's fixed me a room in the house while I get to know the property a little better. I can shadow others here if you don't want me with you.'

He ran a hand across his chin then dashed it through his hair like he was trying to figure out what to do with her now she was standing here. He hadn't responded to the message she'd sent on the way here, but she could see his phone now, abandoned on the arm of the couch.

She heard the kibble hitting the metal bowl in the kitchen, right before Toby slid past them, flashed them a cheeky, knowing grin and slipped back out the door with Ziggy.

They were alone.

Her breathing constricted as Cole stepped closer, his brown eyes boring into hers. Without warning, he closed the space between them, brought a big warm, gentle palm to her cheek then ran a thumb across her lower lip.

'I definitely don't want you with me after what happened before,' he stated. His gravelly voice was almost a growl.

A maddening half-smile quirked his mouth before he lowered his lips to hers and pressed a kiss down possessively, like a stamp.

Jodie sank into him instantly, heating up at the thrill of his hands following the curves of her body and the hard spines of his prized books against her back. She couldn't recall how she came to be backed against the bookshelf. The passion overwhelmed her like it always did. She almost forgot where she was as she brought her arms around his muscled shoulders and her legs around his middle, losing herself in their kiss. She was losing her mind.

What was she doing? 'Cole!'

Quickly she broke free, scrambling breathlessly to pull her skirt back into place. She stepped back from him, hands to his chest as a barrier. 'I thought we said—'

'You're right, we did,' he interjected. He looked amused now, scanning her eyes. 'Old habits die hard. I guess you woke something up the last time you were here…so to speak. It won't happen again.'

She wanted to slap him but she'd kissed him too, hungrily, the way she'd been thinking about doing during the whole train ride, in spite of trying not to. 'Well, please make sure it doesn't,' she said, flustered, 'I'm serious, you know that's not why I'm here. Don't try that again.'

'As you wish.'

Cole stepped away like nothing had happened, leaving her colder. 'Meet me in the main house. I'll bring Miss Edgerton over to the surgery,' he said.

She blinked at him, bringing a hand up to her messy hair and smoothing down her skirt again. *What was happening?* 'Who?'

Without answering, he made for the consultation room and disappeared inside again, leaving her reeling. It was only then that she remembered he still had a client waiting.

CHAPTER FOURTEEN

ONE LOOK AT the bulldog bitch's quivering frame and bulging abdomen, and Cole knew the C-section couldn't wait. Blue was in the early stages of labour already and not happy about it at all.

'You got here just in time,' he told Jodie in the surgery, handing her a fresh white coat. It was dark outside now and he was on emergency call tonight, much to his chagrin. Or maybe it was a good thing, he mused. It would stop him making his way to Jodie knowing any more intimacy was off limits. 'Dacey finished her shift an hour ago, but this will take more than one pair of hands...'

'Usually one for each puppy, I know.'

'We'll do what we can. I hope you don't mind.'

'Straight in at the deep end, huh?' She smiled.

Jodie buttoned up the coat he handed her and he lowered his voice, glancing behind her at the woman who'd brought Blue in. 'About what happened back there, I really am sorry,' he said. 'I know we said that spending the night together was a mistake. I respect that you're here for Everleigh, I hope you know that.'

He was telling her the truth, but the sight of her in the cabin again had just rebooted his desires. He'd been thinking about her ever since she'd left, but he hadn't once pestered her for details about her return. He'd known he had to wait for her to come to him and she was bound to still have her guard up.

Jodie let out a sigh and he swore he saw desire in her eyes, along with frustration. 'I kissed you back. Let's just get to work, shall we?'

'Blue's owner didn't know most French bulldogs can only give birth by C-section,' Cole told Jodie, barely murmuring. 'She brought Blue in to me because the labour was going on too long, and she thought there might be something else wrong with her. The dog was trying to bite her before I stepped in, too.'

He watched Jodie fix her hair up in a quick bun. 'I've met plenty of people who don't know enough about the pets they choose to keep,' she said quietly.

He was glad she'd shown up when she had. He could handle things like this himself, he always had, but Jodie's presence and opinions were invaluable. She looked damn sexy too, all dishevelled after her train ride. Not that he should be thinking things like that. This was business now. Strictly business.

'So why can't she do this on her own?' the dog owner asked the second Cole and Jodie reached the operating table.

'Their hips are too small for them to do it naturally, Miss Edgerton,' Jodie said, pulling on a pair of latex gloves from the box he passed to her. The dog jerked her head suddenly, as if it was aiming for a bite at Jodie. It caught the end of the glove but no flesh, thankfully. Jodie pulled her hand away fast. 'Whoa, little one, we won't hurt you.'

Cole could tell the animal was fearful and wary, but judging by the animal's behaviour in this woman's presence it had more to do with the owners, unfortunately, than the pending C-section. Not that he was going to say that now.

He took a step back, one hand on the table, the other stroking the dog's velvety ears. Jodie's expression softened when the dog calmed in his hands and laid her head on his palm.

'I haven't seen her trust a stranger like that in a while. So it's true what they say about you.' The other woman was looking at Cole in mild suspicion.

'And what do they say about me?' he asked, signalling Jodie to administer the anaesthetic.

'They say you're a pet psychic.'

Cole felt his mouth twitch. People called him all kinds of things when 'vet' seemed too pedestrian for what they witnessed him do. He'd been called a counsellor, a therapist, a psychic, a healer, an animal whisperer and countless other things based on vague pseudo-scientific theories. He didn't care for any title really; but it seemed to make people happy to give him one.

'What do you consider yourself, then?' Jodie asked him.

He thought about it, looking at her like the answer might be in the shape of her mouth in the surgical lights, the flecks of amber in the blues of her irises. 'I'm just a man. I don't do anything we can't all do if we choose to listen.'

Jodie smiled behind her hand as the woman frowned in contemplation. Cole wondered if Jodie had told anyone what had happened with Blaze on the riverbank. He'd been making great progress with the horse but he hadn't expected that. Ziggy had surprised him too, leaping into the water after him.

Neither had surprised him as much as Jodie, however. Surrendering herself to him with such longing and passion, no wonder he hadn't stopped thinking about getting her back here. He had to smash her guard down more often, but he knew there were things he'd have to tell her about the past for that to happen. And those things from the past might end up turning her against him even more in the future.

'Sometimes it's better to get them spayed so they don't have to go through this,' Jodie was saying now, turning the woman's attention back to Blue as they laid the dog on her side. 'I'm surprised she's pregnant at all. A lot of Frenchies need artificial insemination.'

'My boyfriend brought the stud over,' the woman explained. 'He said we could make good money from the puppies. He lost his job at Christmas.'

Cole knew exactly what Jodie would say before she even said it. Sure enough, she crossed her arms and looked disparagingly at Miss Edgerton across the table.

'Putting a dog through this just to make some quick cash…'

'I know, it's not fair. I didn't know it would be so hard on her. We do love her.'

She produced a photo from her purse. They scanned it together quickly side by side. In it, the woman had her arm around a guy in his mid-thirties wearing bright blue trainers. The dog had her tongue lolling out between them.

'It's OK,' Cole said quickly. 'We're here now, and we're going to help her. It might be best if you waited outside, Miss Edgerton.'

Jodie gave him a look as if to apologise for speaking out of turn, but he wasn't about to make her think she should be sorry. She could say what she liked, she was entitled to speak her mind. People who loved animals weren't always the best owners.

* * *

'I can tell you something else about Blue,' he said some time later.

'What's that?' Jodie was inserting the last of the stitches to the Frenchie's belly. He watched her eyes with their blue laser focus.

He didn't usually say things like this to Dacey or Vin as he didn't want to compromise their own judgements or skills in training. But Jodie's bluntness with the owner was proof that she still trusted his instincts. 'I think the dog's been mirroring what's been going on at home.'

Jodie narrowed her eyes over her mask, intrigued. 'You think she's aggressive because someone else around her is aggressive.'

'Unfortunately yes. I've seen it a lot. I saw it in my own pets as a kid.'

'What do you mean?' Jodie looked confused and he cursed himself. But he'd started now. 'Well, you saw my dad drunk that time,' he said carefully. 'But that wasn't the first time. Animals pick up on unsettling behaviour. Sometimes even the chickens would act up if he went out there in the coop with too many beers in him. I had to learn pretty fast how to calm them down.'

He realised as he said it that his dad had driven him to discovering his special talents with the animals. In some strange way he was indebted to him for that as much as he was to Casper for nurturing them.

To his surprise, Jodie put a hand on his arm and squeezed it. 'I had a feeling something else was going on at Thistles,' she said, with more compassion than he probably deserved. 'You never told me your father was an alcoholic. Is that why you never took me back to your house?'

He held her gaze as the shame roared through him again. It had been worse than his father being drunk most of the time, but of course he'd never got the chance to tell her that in person. It was all in the letter.

'Of course, I forgot, we don't talk about you, do we,' she said coolly, obviously disappointed by his silence. 'But I trust you to do the right thing for Blue. Do you want to talk to her owner together?'

He nodded, appreciating her all over again, not just her body, which he could rediscover every day for hours, but her inestimable capacity for her faith in him, in spite of the tension bubbling up between them again. He didn't want sympathy over his father, he never had, not from anyone. He simply saw it as his duty to help prevent another human or animal from having to endure what he had.

He knew she deserved some answers, though. Maybe he should just give her the letter. Either way, they needed to talk. He was just as perceptive around Jodie as ever. There were things she wasn't telling him too. About Ethan.

When Blue was in recovery, Cole told the woman they would prefer to keep the dogs at Everleigh, where they'd be registered and licensed before being up for adoption.

'Will we still get to sell them?' She looked hopefully between them.

'We can't stop you claiming money for them, Miss Edgerton, as a hobby breeder,' Jodie said tactfully. 'But they'll get the proper treatment here while they're waiting for their new homes, and so will Blue while she's nursing.'

'Toby will find them homes in no time,' he added from across the room. He'd just checked his phone for new emergencies. None. *For now.* 'He's my self-appointed social media assistant. He and Jodie's daughter here have been finding good homes for all our animals through a social media account.'

The woman looked appeased, but Jodie was quiet as they cleaned up together afterwards.

'Did you know Toby and Emmie have been in touch pretty much every day since we left?' she asked him.

'I had some idea about that, yes.' He watched her shake out her hair and unbutton her surgical coat, looking pensive for a moment. He admired how protective she was over Emmie. 'It's not a romance, though. They're much too young for that.' He slid up to the polished counter beside her. 'We'd know if it was.'

'I guess we would,' she replied tentatively, shooting him a sidelong glance.

He kept his hands to himself, though they itched to touch her again. He almost said their lovemaking a few weeks ago had been the best they'd ever had, and he knew she hadn't forgotten their encounter in the cabin earlier either. Desire was written all over her face even now. But he wouldn't make a move; he'd promised he wouldn't.

He put his hands to the bench on either side of her. 'I missed you,' he admitted. 'The last three weeks…the last twelve years. You weren't happy, were you, getting married? You looked like you were in the photos, but you didn't love Ethan.'

'Cole…' She met his eyes. 'Why do you care so much about Ethan?'

'I guess I care that there were things we both could have done differently back then,' he said.

She looked affronted suddenly. 'We? I don't regret having Emmie.'

He bit his cheeks for a second. 'That's not what I meant.'

'I'm tired of trying to read between the lines with you, Cole.' She tossed her coat into the laundry basket. 'It's been a long day. Can we pick this up tomorrow? We need to discuss things when we're in a better frame of mind—like who you'd like to approach as a potential partner for this place when I sell.'

He raised an eyebrow but didn't move from the counter. He wouldn't make a move, and he wouldn't react to provocation like this either. He had no intention of doing anything that might make her turn around and leave again. While she was here, he had to remind Jodie why this could be *her* home again, and Emmie's too.

'I'll see you in the morning, then,' he said. 'Bright and early. I'll make the coffee.' An idea was already forming in his head.

CHAPTER FIFTEEN

BLAZE'S WOUNDS HAD almost healed completely. The cuts and scrapes she'd seen before were nearly back to normal, giving the horse a new majestic prowess. 'He looks like a different animal,' Jodie said, sending out her silent gratitude for what Blaze had done to save Cole.

'He's coming around slowly.' Cole ran his hand over Blaze's forehead and muzzle. 'Russell can get closer now, without any trouble.'

'Not as close as you, I bet. How's his leg?'

'He's fine,' Cole said. 'He's strong. I wouldn't have hired him otherwise. Blaze won't be the only temperamental creature we have in here if the rescue plans work out.'

Cole hadn't mentioned the rescue centre in a while, but the thought of bringing it to life made her feel fuzzy and content, like a daydream she was nurturing, until she remembered everything she would have to uproot and change if she were to become a permanent fixture here.

Selling still seemed like a viable option, for many reasons, but Emmie kept messaging her, asking if she'd decided to keep it yet. Ethan had also asked again. She had a feeling he was getting more concerned than he was letting on, hearing Emmie rave about the place.

She'd told him she was planning to sell, just as she'd told Cole. But every time she said it now it didn't seem to feel right. Especially on beautiful mornings like this.

The stable was warm and made her nose tickle with dry grass and anticipation. It was barely sunrise. They were loaded with coffee and a bag of pastries and she still didn't really know why they were going to Portland Bill. Cole had just said he had something to show her.

'You're not going to ride him, are you?' she asked suddenly. Cole was holding the reins up to Blaze, like he was measuring them to his face.

'He's not quite ready for that yet,' he told her. The bulk of him was reassuring beside her; he knew what he was doing, and she knew he'd never put her in danger. It didn't stop her worrying about him, though.

He might have broken her heart once but it pained her to know he'd had to deal with a drunken father as a kid, before he'd met her. Maybe even after that too... She frowned to herself. Come to think of it, she and Cole had only got together after his father had been locked away. And as soon as he'd got out, Cole had broken up with her. Something about it didn't add up.

'Evie told me she saw Emmie with Blaze, before you left the first time. Emmie could get close to him,' he said now, bringing her back to the moment. He was patting Blaze's long, sleek neck with a firm hand. 'Sounds like progress.'

Jodie watched the dust fly from Blaze's coat, remembering what she'd seen. 'He put his nose in her hand,' she confirmed, studying Cole's profile as he did the same, letting Blaze nuzzle his hand.

Cole looked impressed. 'He won't let anyone else do that yet, except me.'

Blaze wasn't wary of Cole at all any more, but as

for her, she couldn't be sure. They had a couple of hours on horseback ahead to reach Portland Bill. Even though Blaze had displayed a couple of heart-warming changes in character since his chaotic, hostile arrival, Jodie didn't much care for the idea of taking such a temperamental stallion out on a long ride.

She watched as Cole seemed to pause time and space while he stood at the stall's gate, neither touching nor talking to Blaze.

After a moment Blaze lowered his head in what she took as submission and started munching on hay in front of her.

'I guess he's still a little self-conscious,' Cole said, turning to her with a smile. 'Maybe he considered himself a perfect specimen before the fire. Now not so much.'

She shook her head. 'He's still beautiful,' she said, without taking her eyes from Cole.

Jodie watched Cole during the whole ride towards Portland Bill, as the wind whipped their hair under the moody sky. She was back on Aphrodite. Cole was riding Jasper ahead of her like he owned the entire coast. It was clear that he belonged here.

Emmie would love being out on this ride right now, she thought, missing her already.

The rolling fields were like verdant green blankets, knitting into one as they galloped along the flower-strewn coast. When they finally dismounted, the rocky, windswept area around the lighthouse brought memories in with the waves. She was racking her brains now, trying to remember anything else Cole might have said about his dad. She drew a blank every time—he'd hardly ever mentioned him at all.

After his dad had got locked up, she'd thought maybe Cole had known what he had been doing all along. When she'd asked him that outright, he'd told her she was crazy and he'd seemed so affronted that she'd never mentioned his father again. He seemed to want it that way and she'd been so in love, so under Cole's spell she'd forgotten he'd had a father in jail at all.

Why was all this bugging her now?

At Portland Bill, Jodie tilted her head and tried to breathe in the sky as Cole walked the horses to a private paddock and tied the ropes around a giant post. It was covered in moss. The paddock hadn't been here before, she thought, taking in the fenced-off property around it. Apart from that it looked exactly the same. Casper had brought them here lots of times.

She trailed her gaze up to the red and white striped tower. They'd taken the one hundred and fifty-three steps up to the top countless times as kids to look down in awe at the Jurassic Coast from the lantern room.

'Are you ready?' Cole came up behind her and looped his arms around her waist. For just a second she was thrust back in time, to when he'd done that every single day. The steadiness of him against her back in the wind took her breath away, then flooded her with fresh intrigue as he pulled a key from his pocket and dangled it in front of her.

On the tiny but shiny, expensive-looking motorboat, Cole steered them over the waves expertly. The wind tussled with her hair and the engine powered them over every wave bump, and Jodie appreciated Cole in silence, not least when he pulled her against his shoulder to shelter her from the wind. She didn't want to like the way that physically he made her feel so safe and protected, but she did.

'Remember when you told me which dinosaurs used to live around here?' she said into his shoulder, flashing back to them looking out together from the top of the lighthouse. 'I always pictured you taming a T-Rex, living amongst them all quite happily.'

Amusement played on his lips. 'I would have given it a go.'

He slowed the boat till they were bobbing gently on the blue. She took the seat opposite him and studied his muscles in the sunlight as he poured them thick hot coffees from a red flask. He was wearing a cream fisherman's knit sweater with the sleeves rolled up and clean jeans with the same brown boots. He might have even polished them, and Jodie found herself admiring the boat they were in. It was gleaming too, like whoever owned it saw it as their pride and joy. 'How long have you had access to that paddock and this boat?' she asked.

Cole sat back with his drink, stretching his long legs out between hers. 'I bought the boat about five years ago.'

Jodie raised her eyebrows. 'You own it?'

He slapped its side, like it was a stallion he'd broken in. 'Every last inch of fibreglass. I bought the land too, where I built the boathouse and the paddock. The plan is to put a guesthouse up eventually. I'll give people access to the boat and fishing rods, and we'll do rides along the coast… It's only a rough plan. But I have time. I'm not going anywhere.'

His eyes seemed to burn that last statement into her brain as he put the flask down at his side. 'Stop trying to make me not want to go anywhere either,' she muttered, so quietly she wasn't sure if he caught it.

He smirked, holding her gaze. 'Why would I do that?'

'You only want me to keep my half of Everleigh so some stranger won't come in and change things,' she challenged him.

He shoved his sunglasses up to his hair. She sensed the smugness fading, and a silent urge to prove something take its place before he reached across the gap for her hands. 'Come on, Jodie, you know that's not the only reason. Who are we kidding here? I was trying to do the right thing by you and Emmie, making this all less awkward. If you want to keep this strictly business we will, but I don't think you really want to.'

The wind caught his hair. The lighthouse loomed behind him. Before she knew it he was on his knees in front of her, making the boat rock. 'We have the chance to make something of this place together, like we always said we would.'

'I can't bring Emmie into this,' she told him as her heart skidded.

'Into what?'

'This!' She dropped his hands and indicated the salty air between them. 'I know you're still dealing with some stuff from the past, Cole, and you don't have to tell me what it is, but if you don't, it's always going to be there, between us. Was it something to do with your dad?'

Cole looked lost for a second. He sat back on the seat, drew his sunglasses down over his eyes and turned to the lighthouse, closing himself off again the way he always did. She wrapped her arms around herself, waiting.

He'd done so much without her. He'd made a name for himself and bought his own piece of Dorset. She had almost forgotten what it was like to feel this fire burn through her entire body and soul. She'd felt snatches of it over the years, enough to squish the silent longing for something more perhaps, but Cole was something else. Even his secrets kept her hooked. But it wasn't enough. She had to put Emmie first, above her urge to fall into him regardless of the issues that had kept them apart.

'You still won't talk to me?'

She could tell by the look on his face that she'd hit a nerve, or touched on something she wasn't supposed to know about. She continued, softer this time. Whatever it was that he didn't want to talk about had clearly affected him deeply and her heart went out to him suddenly.

'Look, I wouldn't have had Emmie if you hadn't broken things off with me, so how I can regret that, really? But you need to tell me what happened.'

'Dad refused to pay—or let Mum pay—for me to study in Edinburgh when he got out of prison, Jodie,' he said. 'And I didn't want you to waste your life waiting around for me in case I never made it.'

Her hand came up over her mouth before she had to grip the side of the boat again. 'Why didn't you tell me?'

'I didn't want anyone's help either, you know what I was like. I thought I could figure things out, but then you got pregnant and Casper told me not to go to you.'

The boat started rocking harder in the wind. Jodie's hair lashed her face but she swiped at it, zoning in on Cole. 'Wait… *Casper* told you that?'

Her knuckles were white. Her throat turned as dry as parchment. She felt sick, and not because of the sea, although it didn't help. 'Why couldn't you have come sooner?'

Cole looked anguished. 'I wish I could explain. It was a difficult time, Jodie. I thought you'd be better off without me.'

'Well, I wasn't.' Jodie couldn't stand it. 'Ethan and I had an agreement, Cole. His dad was on the verge of winning his constituency seat again, and he didn't need a teenage pregnancy right in the middle of his campaign. Ethan's and my parents offered us support to finish our degrees, but only if we married, so we made it legal and carried on with our studies too, but we always knew we'd get divorced once we graduated.'

Cole's fists were clenched. 'So you got married for some rich, upper-class guy's political gain.'

'No one forced me into anything, Cole. I was just so in love with you I didn't care what happened to me!'

Cole crossed the boat on his knees towards her, at the same time she went him, and the boat rocked so hard she let out a shriek that dissolved in his mouth as they met in a kiss. He fisted her hair in bunches and her hands fumbled at the buttons on his jeans.

Then…

Over his shoulder, gulls were squawking, circling something under the surface. Jodie sprang away and sat up straighter. 'Cole, look!'

Dolphins' fins were skimming the water, one followed by another, then another, making a glistening whirlpool in the sunlight. She gripped the boat side in awe. '*This* was what you brought me here to see?'

Cole's eyes were fixed on the horizon behind his sunglasses, surveying the dolphins' frenzied swimming. They were starting to create a frothy white foam on the water. 'There's usually ten or eleven around this time of day,' he told her. 'They know this boat by now. I come out here to read. Normally they swim right over.'

Yanking his sweater straight again, he crossed the benches with two strides and crouched in the bow. Adrenaline flooded her as he took a moment to observe the situation. Then he gestured to the driver's seat, urging her to steer. 'Jodie, get us over there.'

* * *

The fishing net was tangled around the dolphin calf's nose and dorsal fin. There was no boat in sight but the net could have come in on the tide and cost this creature its life.

'Cole, we have to do something.' Jodie echoed his thoughts beside him. She was hauling the net in with him over the side, splashing ice-cold seawater all over herself as they tried and failed to raise the tangled dolphin higher.

Cole was fuming inside. This was something he'd never seen before. He would never have expected this around the lighthouse, these waters were supposed to be protected.

'Grab that box under the driver's seat,' he said to her when they couldn't raise the net any higher. 'The net's stuck on something, I need the knife.'

He figured the dolphin pod had been sending his boat a plea for help by not coming over to him, like they normally did. One or two were calves, including the one in the net, and the rest were eleven-foot adults. He knew them all by sight but he'd never seen them behave like this.

An adult female prodded the air with her nose, coming up alongside him and squeaking in earnest as he worked the oar to bring the net up to the surface. Her body language told him she was distraught; this must be the mother.

Standing up, he started taking off his shirt.

'What are you doing?' Jodie slid him the medical kit. 'It's too cold…'

'We'll have to cut the calf out of the net and we can't do it from here.'

'Then I'll do it,' she said, undoing her jeans quickly.

He put a hand on her wrist quickly, seeing the goose-bumps on her arms. 'Jodie, you're not getting in the water.'

She pulled back in defiance, unbuttoning her shirt. The gulls above them were deafening. 'You need to be up here to help pull me up and steer,' she said. 'I'm smaller, I'll also dry quicker, but you'll have to keep me warm.'

'OK, *some* of that is logical,' he said, but in a flash she was naked apart from matching black underwear and kicking her jeans aside. She took the knife he was holding and stepped onto the seat. He was too distracted by what he was seeing to stop her jumping in. 'Jodie, you'll get tangled in the net...'

'It's OK,' she said, gasping for a second at the shock of the icy water. 'It's not that bad,' she lied.

The dolphins surrounded her. For a second he worried they might do something out of fear, but he knew they trusted him as he'd been coming here for a year or so, observing their behaviour while they were observing his. It was why he'd bought the boat. But he wouldn't let her do this alone, even though she thought she could.

He dropped the anchor quickly, made sure the tiny ladder was down in the water. In seconds, Cole was stripped bare and in the water beside her.

'Help me hold it, like this,' he said, coming up alongside her. The milky white of her flesh in the water could probably be seen for miles but she wasn't complaining if she was cold.

They had the net under control in seconds, but the poor calf was still struggling below them. They had to take it in turns to dive under with the knife and carve away at the nets for as long as their breath would last.

To his surprise, the dolphins started breaching and

pirouetting around them and the boat. He forgot how cold he was as he took his eighth or ninth dive with the knife.

By the time the last tangle of rope was cut away, Jodie's lips were blue, but her eyes were enchanted when the calf wriggled free and swam around them. Cole tossed the knife back into the boat. He knew they were running on adrenaline, and he had to get them out of the water, quickly.

'Do you think she'll be OK?' Jodie asked, from the ladder. Her knuckles were white, her thighs and arms prickled with cold, but she still wasn't grumbling at all. He had never seen her look more beautiful than she was at this moment.

'She wasn't cut up...she was lucky,' he said, hitting the deck after her. 'And they'll stay away from fishing nets from now on.' He yanked at a pile of blankets and towels at his feet and cocooned her in them.

His brain was still swimming as he hauled the rest of the net up into the boat. It was heavy and his arms were tired. The ropes lashed his skin as he tossed them roughly under the bow. He'd dispose of them where they couldn't cause any more harm. And he'd find out where those nets came from if it meant he had to call everyone he knew.

As he steered the boat, a squeal pulled his eyes from the horizon. The mother dolphin was following. She raced ahead and breached at the bow, sending a shower up over them and forcing Jodie to hide in her blankets.

'She's saying thank you,' he told her as she erupted into laughter. 'She knows you now. She knows you helped her baby.'

'We both did.' Jodie had stood up and was shaking against him with the cold as well as with laughter, and his arm looped around her, shielding her from the sea spray. The coast guard was coming up now. The car he'd called for was waiting up ahead already. He'd come back for the horses when Jodie was safe and dry.

Thanks to Jodie's quick actions and the dolphin's trust in him, they had both changed the fate of that calf—he knew the pod wouldn't have trusted the coast guard like they did him, and they'd cut the net faster together anyway.

'The dolphins will never forget what just happened,' he told her, daring to hold her tighter and drop a kiss on the top of her head.

'Neither will I,' she said, and he almost told her he loved her, but he didn't. He'd already broken his promise not to make a move—not that she hadn't reciprocated.

They cruised towards the coast, which felt like coming out of a storm somehow, but Cole's adrenaline was still spiked hours later, after learning why she'd married Ethan.

The next few days of duties seemed to drag as Jodie went off with various media and staff members at Everleigh, and he continued with his appointments. He found himself looking forward to the next time the sound of her boots would echo out in the hallways, or her laughter would spill from the kitchen.

On the boat he'd told Jodie what she needed to know about his dad holding him back from going to Edinburgh, but somehow he hadn't been able to discuss the part about him being a lousy, abusive, violent man who'd threatened him with such terrible things. A cloud of shame for his former cowardly self seemed to follow him around permanently. He had never told anyone. What would Jodie think of him if he told her now?

All she had ever done had been to love him, but instead of protecting her from being hurt, like he'd tried to, he'd sent her straight to Ethan to be turned into some political pawn, manipulated by two sets of parents who should have known better.

CHAPTER SIXTEEN

THEIR DOLPHIN RESCUE off the coast made the news as soon as word from the coast guard got out, but Jodie hadn't told anyone why she'd jumped into the water first.

The truth was she'd panicked at the thought of Cole not coming up again, for whatever reason. She'd actively put herself first this time. The water had been freezing but she hadn't cared.

She'd almost told him she loved him as they'd sped back to land on the boat. Maybe she had still been high on adrenaline. The words had entered her brain and floated around, and made her heart ache to be heard, but they hadn't made it out of her mouth. She'd done enough to complicate things already.

She didn't want to press Cole for more answers about the past, but it was clear his pride had taken a hit over his family's dire financial status back then, and their wires had got crossed. And she hadn't exactly been honest with him before now about why she'd married Ethan. But she couldn't shake the nagging feeling that he was still hiding something else, that she might have only touched the tip of the iceberg.

Thoughts of what to do next with Emmie were still

heavy on her mind. Jodie had to ask herself whether Everleigh really was the right place for Emmie if she decided not to sell.

One morning she paid a visit to Green Vale, Toby's school. He was giving a presentation to his class about the Everleigh animals.

'You're the woman who was with Cole Crawford and the dolphins! What brings you here today?' asked a woman in a yellow shirt bearing a nametag that said Hetty.

The main hall at Green Vale was a bustling dome, with seats made of straw bales. The kids all had fifteen minutes each for their presentations.

'I suppose I'm interested in seeing whether my daughter might…be a good fit here,' Jodie admitted to Hetty, watching the scene. She had been thinking about this progressive school more and more since Cole and Toby both spoke of the place so highly.

'My daughter is friends with Toby over there,' she told Hetty. Toby was getting ready to make his speech on the makeshift stage. She liked the vibe in the place already, people seemed happy. It wasn't like she'd had a chance to speak to Emmie about any potential long-term move to Dorset, she was merely looking around, garnering information to take back with her.

'Toby's a great student, love his energy. Did you see this, by the way?'

Hetty held out her phone to her. Jodie's throat dried up instantly. It was a photo, just posted on a local news site, of Cole's boat…way out in the distance, thank goodness. Jodie's face flushed. She could just make out the blurry shape of a man and a woman on board.

'Am I right thinking that's Cole Crawford's boat?' Hetty eyed her sideways. 'And I'm not being funny, because what you did for the dolphin was brave…but were you both naked?'

'Not quite—but it was the only way to help,' Jodie told her, as poised as she could manage it. 'Was that posted anonymously?' she asked.

'Looks like it. So you're a couple?' Hetty asked curiously.

'We're working together at Everleigh Estate,' she replied tactfully. 'I'm a vet.'

'Another vet! The perfect pair. He's a mysterious one, always keeps himself to himself. Everyone here's been wondering what kind of a woman would win his heart.'

Jodie didn't quite know what else to say, the woman was practically gushing over Cole. It annoyed her as much as it amused her.

The boat was too far away from the camera to tell for sure if they were clothed or not in the photo. She'd already spoken to a reporter herself, but it made her slightly uncomfortable knowing someone else had taken a photo like that and published it.

You couldn't make out any details, she reassured herself as she excused herself and took her seat.

She tried to focus on Toby and his puppy plan. They had a lot of puppy photos on the social feed suddenly, and Cole had taken a call last night about another rescue horse. Things seemed to be picking up again after Casper's death.

Over the course of the next year she and Cole would work together with the contractors and local land management to build more shelters and stables, hire more staff—technicians, vets, another receptionist and an office manager just for the rescues. Jodie knew Cole would happily start as soon as possible—he'd even brought it up as they were both so encouraged by their progress with Blaze.

But while she had given her go-ahead to the plans, she couldn't commit to being on the ground herself yet, not until she'd spoken to Emmie and Ethan. And as for her and Cole...

What *were* she and Cole now, apart from partners in Everleigh? The rumour mill was spinning but they seemed to be playing a dangerous game, tumbling into each other then taking a step back to process. He was giving her space, no pressure, but the more he did that, the more she wanted to pounce on him again.

'This is how Cole Crawford gets a horse to stop bucking.' Toby's voice jolted her out of her thoughts. A video of Cole was up on the screen, larger than life, as though she'd just summoned him.

From the looks on the parents' faces, Jodie had a feeling most people in the area already knew about Cole's unique gifts. She felt another flutter of pride in her belly and couldn't help but smile. The kids were engrossed— they clearly all loved animals here, just like Emmie did.

When the presentations were over, she headed for Toby. 'Cole would be proud of you,' she said, taking the wriggling six-week-old beagle-cross puppy from his hands.

'I *am*...very proud.' Cole's voice behind her made her spin around.

'Have you been here the whole time?' she asked him in surprise, noting Ziggy at his feet. People around them were already recognising him, milling around like he was some sort of handsome celebrity. Hetty was staring from the lemonade stand, trying to make it look like she wasn't.

Cole cleared his throat. 'Came in a few minutes late. Sorry, had an issue with a lamb out by Abbotsbury.'

He gave Toby a high five then slung his arm around Jodie's shoulders, making her freeze in shock. 'I loved watching your face, when you saw the video of me,' he whispered in her ear, so discreetly that only she could hear.

In spite of her fluttering heart she held the puppy close and joined in with Cole making polite conversation with the people all around them. He hadn't touched her in public before now, not even in the farmhouse kitchen. If he was trying to make a point in front of everyone or create some more public buzz around them to stop her selling up and leaving a spinning rumour mill in her wake…she should have cared, deeply. She should have been offended. She was only here for Emmie—wasn't that obvious?

But to her surprise it *was* starting to feel good, his steady presence, the way he was opening up to her. Not enough perhaps, but little by little. There were things only she knew about Cole Crawford. And things only he knew about her.

She reminded herself she shouldn't care if they'd been seen out there at Portland Bill together, or anywhere else. It was no one's business but hers…but she still couldn't help wondering who'd taken the photo.

CHAPTER SEVENTEEN

IT WAS THREE-TEN a.m. when Jodie woke with a start. She was in Cole's bed and for a second she allowed herself to feel good, not guilty, about how a cosy fireside dinner in the farmhouse had somehow ended with them tearing each other's clothes off again in the cabin. Then she saw his side of the bed was empty. Cole was gone.

The candle on the hearth had burnt out. Lambing season meant all kinds of call-outs at odd hours, so she wasn't alarmed at first…but then she saw the flashlight outside through the window. The beam across her face had woken her up.

Jodie's heart surged as another light flashed fast across the flowers in the window. It seemed to be moving towards the kennels.

Grabbing up her phone, she sprang from the rug Cole had draped over her and pulled on his oversized shirt and her jeans, which they'd left on the couch. Her boots felt rough without her socks as she slid her bare feet into them. Outside, the dogs were strangely silent, which didn't feel right. Some of them always barked, unless it was someone they knew.

'Russell?' she called, expecting the stablehand to answer. Nothing.

She shone her phone light into the night. 'Toby?'

She swallowed her nerves. It couldn't be Toby: he'd be in bed. Cole's Land Rover was gone from the driveway, so it definitely wasn't him either. It was just her, facing a row of quiet kennels.

She called Cole's phone, left a message. 'Cole, everything is probably OK, but I thought I saw a flashlight near the kennels. I came outside to check it out but… there's no one there. It's a bit weird.'

Embarrassed, she hung up. She didn't need to bother him over nothing and he was probably busy. She couldn't see anything out of the ordinary now, but she crossed the yard to the stables, just to check. The grass crunched under her feet. Inside, the horses were quiet. Some were sleeping, some were munching and she lingered a moment by Blaze.

'How are you, beautiful boy?' she whispered, breathing in the heady scent that always soothed her. The horse snorted softly but didn't move or show any agitation. She reached out a palm to an inch from his forehead. 'You can trust me,' she said.

To her surprise, Blaze lowered his head, if only slightly, permitting her to lay her hand flat against him. It was the softest touch, the first time she had ever touched him. Her heart thrummed this time with excitement as she stroked his face, around where his scars were healing well. She couldn't wait to tell Cole.

A noise made Blaze's ears prick up. Jodie raced back outside. It sounded like something heavy had fallen and now the dogs were barking up a storm. Back at the kennels she hovered in the shadows. 'Who's there?'

A black figure slipped behind the last cage in a row of kennels, where they kept Blue and her puppies.

'I'm calling the police!' she announced, as her heart leapt to her throat.

A light flickered on in the main house behind her, just as the figure in black appeared right in front of her. Heavy hands slammed her against the bars of the last cage. Her phone shattered on the concrete. The impact across her back felt like someone had struck her with ten baseball bats and was so painful she lost her voice.

Gasping for her breath, Jodie kicked at the man pinning her by the shoulders, but he was strong for someone so slight. He was in his mid-thirties, wearing a black tracksuit and blue trainers. *She recognised those trainers...* 'What do you want?'

His clammy fists gripped her wrists. Jodie's brain was in overdrive. She thought she'd seen him somewhere before, but she couldn't place him. 'Let go of me!'

'Not unless you promise to be quiet.' His growl was pure alcohol. 'I'll be out of here in seconds, then you can just forget about me. Understood?'

Headlights suddenly roared towards them on the driveway. Her attacker faltered and Jodie watched the satchel he was holding slip from his shoulder. A car door slammed, a puppy yelped from inside the bag before a little head poked out—one of the French bulldog pups. 'Don't say a word,' her attacker warned her.

'Don't threaten me. You were trying to steal the dogs!' Struggling again to free her wrists, she almost kneed him where it would have hurt most. She got so close she could see the anticipation of impact in his eyes...but in a second he was gone, ripped from her at gunshot speed.

'Get away from her!'

Cole was here. A rush of air felt like a whiplash as he slammed the guy up to the bars with one arm and held the other across her like a barrier. 'What did you *do* to her?' he roared.

Jodie gasped and struggled for composure as Ziggy leapt around their feet. She tried to take hold of Cole's arm but he wasn't letting the man go. 'Cole, he didn't do anything. I'm OK.'

She watched his jaw tense as fury ravaged his features. His knuckles were white. A siren wailed briefly in the distance. 'Were you trying to take those dogs?' Cole's fury was pouring over the intruder like magma as she scooped two puppies up from around her smashed-up phone. Her legs were shaking in her boots.

'I was just taking what's mine!'

'What do you mean, what's yours?' Jodie managed, but she remembered now where she'd seen those trainers. 'Cole, he's the guy from Miss Edgerton's photo...'

'I told my girlfriend she shouldn't have left them here with you!' The guy was fuming but Cole ignored him.

'Are you OK?' His eyes were slits of black, shimmering in fury and contempt. It shocked her.

'I'm fine.' Her back throbbed as she pickeded up the last pup. Cole saw her struggling a little on her feet, and the sight made his mouth contort before he hauled the guy into an empty kennel.

He swiped the bars across, bolting the iron gate shut. 'Stay quiet, you're on camera,' he snarled, jabbing one finger to the hidden security cam inside one of Ziggy's old dog toys.

He turned to Jodie and held her at arm's length. 'You're hurt.'

'Maybe a little bruised, but I'm fine. I'll be all right.'

Cole scanned her face like she was a precious jewel about to crack. Jodie's back was still throbbing but she knew it was nothing serious. She was just glad the man hadn't got away with his crime.

'I would have kneed him in the privates if you hadn't

got to him first,' she told him. 'You came when you got my message?'

Cole's nostrils flared, and for a second he looked like he wasn't even there behind his own eyes. He was someone she didn't recognise at all.

'Cole?'

The police car was pulling up next to the Land Rover and double headlights shone accusingly on their locked-up perpetrator. Russell ran towards them, a police-woman close behind.

Cole seemed to retreat into himself as he strode down the line of kennels, somehow silencing the barking dogs in seconds. She noticed a shower of dog treats on the floor around the kennels. The perpetrator had stopped them barking by giving them food—the preparation was impressive for a drunk.

It transpired the man—John Kowara—had been following Cole, working out his schedule, planning on when to take the puppies back so he could sell them himself on the black market for a disproportionate price.

'It could have been him who was watching us from the lighthouse with a camera,' Jodie told the police-woman, hugging her arms around herself.

'We'll check his phone when we get to the station,' the policewoman told her. 'Meanwhile you should think about pressing charges for assault.'

'Yes, you definitely should,' Cole said through grit-ted teeth. His arm tensed around her shoulders as Kowara was carted away to the police car.

Later, in bed, she listened to the sound of Cole's steady breathing like a lullaby she'd missed for longer than she could remember, but Jodie still couldn't sleep. The scene kept playing on a loop inside her head—the attack, the residual shock of it, the poor pups, who must have been terrified, and Cole… Cole had gone crazy seeing her being threatened by that guy. He'd looked haunted more than anything and it was haunting her now. She had never seen anyone look like that in her life.

Cole passed the kennels, raising his hand in greeting at Toby, who was sweeping the cages eagerly like he did every Sunday morning. They had three more people coming to look at adopting dogs later and another crazy day ahead, enough to keep him and an army busy, but he couldn't stop his brain rehashing the break-in.

He'd just watched the security footage. Twice. It made his blood run cold, seeing Kowara making a lunge for Jodie.

Jodie and Dacey both looked up when he walked into the kitchen, and a little lamb wobbled out from around the fridge, knocking a magnet off the front as it passed.

'Did you watch it? Can you see him taking the puppies?' Jodie's eyes were brimming with concern as Dacey left the room to greet a client in the surgery.

He dodged the lamb and retrieved the magnet. 'It's all on film,' he said, sticking the photo of Evie's grandkids back on the fridge. 'It's with the police report.'

'OK…good. Well, if they need me, I can talk to them from the road.'

The sudden tightness in his chest made him put his coffee cup down without pouring anything. Jodie had to be at the airport in a matter of hours. She had been here just over a week already. He still didn't really know when she'd be back at Everleigh. It depended on Emmie's school and her ex's schedule, he supposed. He didn't want to pressure her by asking, especially after last night.

She probably *wanted* to go back. She'd been in danger here. He had put her in danger. He'd gone out on a call with Ziggy and he hadn't locked the door of the cabin behind him. Something far, far worse could have happened to Jodie after Kowara had scaled the fence at the entrance and sneaked in while she'd been sleeping to get the keys to the kennels.

Jodie crossed to him. 'Cole, are you OK?'

He glanced at her hand on his arm as his guts twisted up into a knot. 'It will be easier to press charges if they find evidence he was watching us before he broke in,' he said, picking up a chunk of ham from Evie's chopping board and tossing it to Ziggy.

'I probably won't press charges myself,' she announced suddenly, folding her arms.

She couldn't be serious. 'He attacked you, Jodie. You have to press charges.'

'He's already being prosecuted for theft and you got to him before he could do anything worse. Not that he would have done, he was just trying to scare me into letting him take the dogs. I told you, I was about to knee him where it hurts.'

Cole just stared at her, raking a hand across his chin, then shoved his hands in his pockets so she wouldn't see his fists clench. He'd been picturing his father the whole time he'd been staring at the footage. Kowara could have been him, laying his filthy hands on Jodie. It had brought everything back, the way he'd had to fight his father off, time after time.

'You don't know what he would have done to you, Jodie,' he growled. 'He was totally wasted.'

She poured herself a glass of water from the sink, sighed. 'I don't want to think about it, Cole. I have to get back to Emmie. I'm too busy—'

'Too busy?'

'Yes, and if we start that process we'll have to keep on thinking about it! Everything is OK now, isn't it? The police won't let it happen again and neither will you.'

His jaw clenched. The security footage still wouldn't leave his head. There was Jodie, wearing his shirt out in the yard. One second she'd been shining her phone around the kennels and the next she'd been pinned against the bars. It had made him see red. It had been his childhood all over again. He'd been the victim so many times, too damn scared to bring the man to justice; thinking he'd be hurt even more just for speaking out.

'I can't let you go without facing this, Jodie, and I'll be with you.' He wanted to rewind real time like he'd rewound the security footage, but he couldn't go back and stop Jodie being attacked on the property. *Their* property. She'd been adamant on selling her half before…she'd be even more determined to do so now. At least, he wouldn't blame her if she was.

He couldn't believe she just wanted to forget about it. Maybe she was frightened of the consequences of pressing charges, like he'd been all those years ago, fending off the fists that had always come at him.

'I told you, I'm OK. Please, just let it go,' she said gently, as if she was reading his mind, God forbid.

'I can't do that.'

Vinny came into the room with a bottle and took the lamb over by the fire for a feed. 'We have two kids and pigeon in there,' he said to Cole, nodding towards the surgery, oblivious to their conversation.

'I'll go and help. You rest,' Jodie said quickly, like she was trying to escape him. Cole followed her to the door.

'It's your last day and I'm not letting you out of my sight,' he said, keeping his voice low. Already it felt like she was slipping through his fingers.

She turned, eyes narrowed. 'Cole, you do know that what happened last night wasn't your fault? If anyone is to blame for him getting in, it's *both* of us. We were both distracted, doing things last night that we'd said we wouldn't do...'

'That's no excuse for what he did to you, Jodie.'

'You don't have to worry about me.'

But I do, he thought to himself, holding the door open, resisting the urge to reach for her. *I always worry about you, I always did everything I could and I still couldn't protect you.*

Jodie was downplaying her injuries and the shock of what had just happened to her to save *his* feelings, but he knew when she was hurt, inside and out. He spotted her stretching out her back a couple of times as she pulled her white coat on. She caught him looking, pretended she was fine. Just like he always used to do in front of her.

It was too late for pretence. He'd seen the bruises on her flesh in his bed this morning, angry black and blue marks along her spine. She was leaving Everleigh for Edinburgh hurt today, and that was everything he'd always done his best to prevent.

CHAPTER EIGHTEEN

THE TWO YOUNG boys studying the pigeon with Cole were a little older than Emmie and Toby, but it turned out they went to the same school. 'What happened here, guys?'

'We were playing in the field when we saw it. We think its wing is broken,' one of them said despondently.

The pigeon was silent in Cole's steady hands on the table. He held it up, showing them the tag on its bony pink leg. 'It's a racing pigeon. We can find out who set him off on his flight if we type this tag number into a special website.'

'Really?' The kids looked fascinated. Cole offered them seats so they could watch them at work, and their presence in the room eased Jodie's thrumming heart.

She was worried about Cole after last night. He blamed himself for leaving the door to the cabin unlocked so Kowara could help his sticky fingers to the kennel keys. It creeped her out, thinking how that guy must have seen her lying in bed, sleeping. Cole was driving himself crazy over it, but she didn't blame *him* for it.

'You were right about the broken wing,' Cole said to the kids as she set about cutting a twelve-inch strip of bandaging tape.

He folded the bird's wing against the side of its body in its natural position. The poor little thing kept turning its head and clucking as if it was searching for Cole's eyes, seeking comfort.

'Now we wrap the tape around the bird's body, which will hold the wing in place,' Cole explained to the boys, looking towards her for the tape.

She picked up the iPad to check the tracking number on the tag. 'Turns out it's from Cambridge. I'll give them a call and see what they want to do,' she said.

Sitting on hold with the Royal Pigeon Racing Association, her back felt uncomfortable again, but she wasn't about to let on and worry Cole. It was just bruised. He gave instructions to the kids if they wanted to look after the pigeon a while but, still, she could feel him watching her like a hawk, as if he was scared to let her out of his sight for more than a second.

Jodie glanced around at the oak-panelled walls and Casper's certificates, and the paddocks through the windows, where Blaze was trotting around. The sun was shining and spring was taking a firm hold—it seemed like for ever ago that they'd arrived in the snow.

Everleigh had always meant surrounding themselves with excitement, one way or another, good and bad, she thought. Things were no different now but her ties in Edinburgh were too tight for her to be on the ground here at Everleigh any longer.

Right now, it wouldn't be fair to anyone to commit to coming back in person, least of all Emmie. But already the thought of leaving Cole for any undetermined length of time was making her heart flap in her chest like another pigeon was stuck inside.

She wouldn't tell him but the image of Kowara's face bearing down on her against the bars of that kennel was getting harder to block out. She didn't want to sleep alone tonight back in her bed in Edinburgh, but she had no choice.

Cole stepped into the pen, flipping the latch back behind him. Jodie was stroking Blaze along his mane and he couldn't believe his eyes. She turned to him and shrugged, seeing his look of surprise.

'Didn't I tell you Blaze let me touch him last night, when I came in here?'

He frowned. 'When?'

'When I came into the stables to check these guys were all OK. I heard Kowara from here—' Jodie stopped what she was saying abruptly, like she was afraid to bring it up again.

'Maybe he'll be ready to ride sooner than you thought,' she said. He could tell she was desperate to change the subject.

'Only for someone he trusts,' he told her, taking her hands and drawing her close by the waist in her city-girl dress and sweater. She was dressed for somewhere else already; her boots in the hay were even shiny again. The thought of her suffering at all back in Edinburgh because of him made him feel sick to his stomach, even as he fought to transmit composure.

'I know last night affected you more than you're telling me,' he said, eyeing the saddle on the fence. They'd agreed to try and saddle Blaze before she left but he had other things on his mind now.

'I told you, I'm fine.'

'You're so stubborn.'

'Pot, kettle, black.'

They were waiting for her car. Her bags were all packed up outside, and he had no idea when he'd see her next. All he knew was that she'd be out there thinking about John Kowara and what he'd done…and how *he* hadn't been there to protect her. It would hit her eventually, when she got home.

'I want you to press charges,' he said firmly.

'This again?'

'You don't want to because it's not very nice to think about, but people like that need to get what's coming to them, Jodie. What if he hurts someone else?'

She pulled her hands away. 'What's wrong with you, Cole? Is this to cover Everleigh's reputation, because you think I'm still going to sell my half?'

'I don't care about that, I care about you!' Infuriated, he pulled the envelope from his jeans pocket. 'There's something I haven't told you.'

Blaze grunted behind them, sending dust clouds into the rafters. Cole knew he was picking up on his mood. He urged Jodie out of the pen by her hand, and shoved the letter into her other palm, ignoring the pounding in his chest, the foreboding feeling creeping like a freezing river around his body.

'I saw this before, with the photos, by your medicine box.' Jodie turned the envelope around in her hands, studying the red wax seal.

'Read it,' he ordered her. 'Maybe then you'll see why you need to press charges.'

Jodie's heart was like a leaden weight in her chest. She could barely finish the letter through the tears in her eyes. It was true, Cole had been coming to get her, and Casper had stopped him, but that wasn't it.

I told myself when I broke up with you that I
was doing the right thing. I thought I was saving

*you from worrying about me, or getting yourself
involved in any of my family's mess...*

'Oh, my God!' she cried, looking up at him. The
sun was streaming onto his hair and the wisps of grass
and hay stuck to his jacket but it was like looking at a
stranger now. Her fingers were trembling around the
piece of paper.

'All those years I thought we'd told each other everything, I thought you'd let me in. But all the time you
were keeping secrets, lying to me about how you got all
those injuries. You were suffering all that alone, Cole?
You didn't even trust me to try and help you?'

Cole's eyes widened then narrowed. He stepped towards her but she held up her hands to stop him.

'Jodie, I didn't let anyone try and help me. I thought
I was protecting you.'

'You were the one who needed protection, Cole! He
ruined us...and you just let him!'

She was so incensed she almost fell over her bag at
her feet. The cab was coming to take her to the airport,
and it couldn't arrive fast enough. The thought of how
things could have been so different if he'd just opened
up to her was suddenly all too much. 'You should have
let me make up my own mind whether I needed you to
protect me.'

'I knew you'd have gone to him, tried to defend me!'

'Damn right I would. I'd have done *something*, because I loved you so much.'

She could hardly think about what she'd read, or
the fact that she was only just learning this now. Cole
looked like a restless rescue horse with nowhere left
to run.

'I understand you didn't want to see me hurt but

you hurt me, Cole, more than your father or Kowara ever could. Do you have any idea how long it took me to get over us? You let me think you didn't love me! You would've rather lost me…us…your education… your whole life, Cole, than confide in me so I could help you make a call to put your father back in prison where he belonged.'

The cab was pulling up. It was just like twelve years ago, she realised, when she'd driven off after a monumental row. But surely that day could have been prevented if he'd just told her the truth back then. 'I need to process this,' she said, and this time her voice came out as a croak. Part of her knew she was being unfair, but she couldn't help how she felt: sick with the knowledge of what he'd suffered at his father's hands but devastated that he'd kept such corrosive secrets from her for so long. Secrets that had ruined their relationship.

Cole's cheeks were pinched. He looked pale and angry. 'I know it's a lot to take in, but you must see now why you have to press charges, Jodie.'

'Yes, I do. Because *you* didn't, back when it mattered. Your father died before he could face any justice for what he did to you, and us! But what I do now won't change that, Cole.'

'Maybe not, but you can do it for Emmie.'

She flinched. 'Emmie? Emmie will never come back here now and neither will I.'

She pressed a hand against her mouth to stem the sobs the second his face broke into a dark scowl. He wasn't seeing anything from her perspective, even now. She could tell. He was still stewing over his own cage of secrets. Would he even have told her if she hadn't been attacked by Kowara? Love couldn't flourish where there was no trust.

'You're impossible, Cole.' She grabbed her bags, threw them into the back seat of the car.

'Airport,' she told the driver. And this time she didn't look back.

CHAPTER NINETEEN

One week later

'PENNY FOR YOUR THOUGHTS,' Ethan offered, sliding onto the leather chair opposite the sofa and putting his feet up on the coffee table.

'Does Saskia let you do that?' Jodie quipped from the posh leather couch and Ethan pulled a face then removed his trainers. Jodie laughed. She was at Ethan's new place, waiting for Saskia to bring Emmie back from a shopping trip. Jodie had made restaurant reservations for herself and Emmie close by, but she wasn't really in the mood.

'I don't know if my thoughts are worth a penny right now,' she said miserably.

Ethan pulled a mock frown. 'Are we still feeling mortified for flying off the handle at Cole?'

She groaned. 'OK, yes, I know I was way too hard on him, considering what he went through.'

She'd done a lot of reading on domestic violence in the last few days, and had discovered the hold abusers often had on their victims. He'd kept all that inside whilst caring for others, pouring out his compassion without measure yet never knowing how to ask for it himself, not even from her—not until he'd asked her to press charges against Kowara. Cole must have felt he'd had no choice but to let her go back then, and she'd just screamed at him selfishly for ruining *their* plans.

'Have you pressed charges against that guy yet?' Ethan eyed her sideways, just as Jodie's heart went haywire. He'd struck at the heart of the matter, as usual.

'I know I should,' she replied with a sigh, rummaging in her bag to find her ringing phone. It wasn't Cole. But, then, it never was. The two of them seemed to have reached a stalemate of sorts since she'd left Everleigh.

'It's getting to you, Jodie. Or maybe it's Cole, hmm? You told him you wouldn't ever go back there but you know you want to. You obviously still care about him.'

She stared at her manicure, wishing Ethan didn't know her so well. She'd told him everything. The two of *them* had never had any secrets. Sometimes she wished they were in love, instead of just being co-parents and best friends. She told him so and he smirked.

'You know, Emmie doesn't stop talking about that place.' He reached for her hand. 'I can't imagine why, but sometimes I think she'd rather be there than here, even with my giant plasma screen TV! Did you see my organised T-shirt drawer, by the way?'

She laughed again. He was being sarcastic, but Saskia's living room was catalogue perfect, and Jodie couldn't help imagining what she'd do if a lamb or chicken waddled across it like it might at Everleigh. She'd got used to the buzz and muck and mayhem of Dorset life yet again, and everywhere else felt too quiet now.

'I wouldn't want to take Emmie away from you, Ethan,' she told him. 'We raised her together, we went through all that nonsense our parents dished out together. We promised to always live close by, put her through school, college together...'

Ethan tutted. 'You wouldn't be moving her to Mars, Jodie. Besides, I quite like the thought of a little riding holiday in Dorset myself every now and then. Do you think Saskia will let me go?'

'If you keep putting your nasty feet on her coffee table I should think she'll pack your bags for you.' Jodie smiled. Ethan squeezed her fingers in solidarity. She should have known he would be fine with whatever decision she made about Everleigh: he was a good man.

It had been Cole as much as Ethan and Emmie's tight bond here that had been holding her back in her head. She'd created enough barriers herself to protect her own heart, and the more days that passed without him now, the more she regretted overreacting to his letter.

The security footage *had* been pretty shocking, she'd seen when she'd summoned the courage to watch it. It felt like she'd been watching someone else, not herself. Cole's fury at Kowara and then at her for not pressing charges had been a direct result of the pain he still harboured inside from his father doing the same thing to him. She couldn't bear the thought of him being hurt... all those cuts and bruises he'd tried to cover up.

The thought of how she'd left him flooded her with guilt all over again. She knew she should press charges for Cole as much as for herself and Emmie—and for the Cole she'd *used* to know, who'd lived in anticipation of his father's despicable, violent whims...

She should do it for Cole and for everyone else who'd ever been attacked or abused or violated like that. He had lied to her for so long only because he'd been afraid.

'When will you see Cole next?' Ethan asked in interest, but his phone was ringing now. Ethan answered, and the look on his face made her gasp.

'He's sick? How sick?'

'Who?' she mouthed, but Ethan was already grabbing both their jackets on the way to the door.

Cole hadn't been planning to go to The Ship Inn for the three-hundred-year anniversary party, but he thought it would be a good way to answer some of the questions the locals had been choosing to call him.

The recent media interest about the dolphin had got people talking, but at the party all people seemed to be interested in was him and Jodie.

It still made his fists curl to picture that guy's hands on her. The thought of her experiencing even the slightest bit of what he'd felt when his father had been loaded on the drink still made his blood run cold, but he could hardly blame her for reacting to his letter the way she had. He'd lied to her repeatedly, he'd shut her out and he hadn't given her the opportunity to try and help him. She was right, he'd been the one to ruin them in the end, not his father.

It was almost midnight when he got home. He pulled off his jacket and greeted Ziggy at the door, and spotted the photo of them in its frame, sticking out from under the bench. He should have put it up before. He'd built the cabin for her after all. He'd built everything around Jodie since he was eleven years old.

Dropping to the bench, he dusted the frame off, studying her expression in the picture, the youthful Mustang who'd been so much like Blaze. They both looked so young. He had no excuses for not hanging this picture up now, he thought…unless she really wasn't coming back.

It killed him how his own secrets from the past had messed up the future. And the sex…that was where they'd always talked without words. Damn, he missed that. Damn, that whisky was making him feel sad. He picked up his phone where he'd left it on the couch.

Three missed calls from Emmie?

Shaking off the alcohol that Liam Grainger had forced on him, he dialled into the voicemail.

'Cole, Cole, it's me, Emmie. I'm sorry for calling you but I didn't think my mum would want to. It's Saxon, my horse, he's sick. We're at the farm with him…we don't know if he's going to make it. Can you help me, please? You're the only one I can think of who might save him.'

He crossed to the messy desk. Swiping the papers and cables aside, he located the laptop and searched for a flight.

'Dammit,' he cursed aloud at the screen. Just when he really *needed* to go to Edinburgh, there were no flights he could take before two p.m. the next day.

According to the rest of the message, Saxon had been refusing food and walking unsteadily, and now had diarrhoea at sporadic intervals, as well as excessive urination and chronic fatigue. It sounded like some kind of poison but the vet on the premises couldn't identify it.

He only hoped *he* could, but he would have to get there fast. The overall prognosis for ionophore toxicity in horses was poor to grave… Jodie would know that as well as he did.

With Ziggy on his heels, he pulled down a bag from the closet, catching sight of his face in the bedroom mirror by the dresser.

Shaking his head at himself, he dragged a hand

across his chin and witnessed himself coming full circle. It was twelve years overdue, but it was about time he got on that train to Edinburgh.

CHAPTER TWENTY

'COLE!' JODIE'S HANDS came up over her mouth as she met him halfway across the forecourt. 'What are you doing here?'

'I hope I'm not too late.'

Cole dropped the backpack at his feet and crossed the last foot between them. He was wearing his plaid jacket and the jeans he always wore in spite of having twenty pairs. The sight of him so out of context was surreal, but suddenly it hit her... Emmie must have called him.

'She didn't tell you I was coming, huh?'

His broad shoulders seemed to hold the weight of the world until he put his arms around her and sighed deeply into her hair. She felt it too, as if something lifted inside her as he held her face in her hands. 'I missed your eyes,' he said gruffly.

'I missed yours too. Cole, I am so, so sorry. I totally overreacted to your letter.'

'I deserved it. I know I should have told you everything way sooner. I was being selfish, not wanting to lose you again.'

'Well, I was being selfish too, only thinking about how I felt. You had to do what you had to do to protect me and your mum, and so did I when I married Ethan. We always wanted Emmie, Cole, and I don't regret making that decision. As for you and me…can we please start over?'

He still loved her very deeply, she could see it in his gaze. If it had been anyone else, the intensity would have made her look away, but he held her eyes like magnets, then drew her close to his chest and kissed her. For a moment as she sank into him she almost forgot why he'd come.

'Emmie,' she cried, breaking away from the kiss at the same time he released her. He slung his backpack quickly onto one shoulder over his jacket and took her hand.

'Let's go.'

In the stables Jodie watched with wet eyes as her daughter clung to Cole's middle, in tears. 'Thank you, Cole. Thank you for coming here. Can you help him?'

'Let's see, shall we?' he said, putting a steady hand to the top of her head and throwing Jodie a look of mild surprise.

It crossed Jodie's mind that maybe Cole didn't know what an impression he had left on Emmie during the brief time she'd spent at Everleigh. Her daughter was overcome with gratitude that he'd come all the way here.

The gelding was looking very poorly indeed and secretly Jodie feared the worst. They'd all been up all night, watching him deteriorate.

'The vet just left to get breakfast with Ethan, while he's resting,' she told Cole, watching him crouch at Saxon's side. She hoped and prayed Cole would be able to reach Saxon in a different way. She'd seen him do it a hundred times with other horses, but this was different. This was Emmie's horse. If anything happened to Saxon, her little girl would be devastated.

* * *

Outside in the sunlight he accepted two coffees from a kindly woman in overalls and took one to Jodie, who was by the stables, tapping something on her phone. Saxon was now on his feet. Cole had managed to get him to stand, albeit weakly, and Emmie was over the moon.

'Ethan sends his thanks to you for you coming,' Jodie said, pushing her phone back into her pocket and dashing her hand through unkempt hair—just the way he liked it. 'You might have saved Saxon's life.'

'Tell him he's most welcome,' Cole replied. 'I'm just glad I could help.'

It transpired that poor Saxon had eaten something from the yard that had been left for the chickens. Cole had been able to tell from his stance, the way he had been pressing his belly to the ground. He'd calmed him enough to allow them to give him a second full flush and on close inspection they'd located a chicken feed container spilling into an open paddock. Luckily no other horses had tucked in.

'I don't think she'll be able to ride him any time soon. I'm sorry,' he said to Jodie in private, sipping the coffee.

'He'll need electrocardiograms and ultrasounds to monitor his heart. It's pricy stuff, and it could take time for Saxon to heal properly.'

Jodie looked determined to bring Saxon back to full health through sheer force of will. He tossed both their cups into a bin and tilted her chin up. 'Everleigh's insurance will cover it, it's tied into the inheritance. I can arrange for Saxon to come back with me, where I can keep a proper eye on him. We can watch him round the clock until he's out of danger. You can come down whenever you're ready.'

'Are you sure?' she said, swiping at her eyes. The Scottish sun was high in the sky now, and behind her the craggy mountains looked like a movie set.

'You can both come,' he told her, hoping she'd agree. 'It's almost Easter holidays. Emmie will be close to Saxon. Meanwhile, she can ride Blaze.'

Jodie's eyes lit up. 'He's ready to ride?'

'For someone he trusts, like Emmie. Look, if you're worried about security after what happened, don't be. I had the place rigged up—'

'I'm not. But I was going to tell you before this happened, I'll press charges,' she told him, clasping the front of his jacket and pulling him closer. 'You were right, people like that need to be locked away.'

Her back was against the stable wall. She was looking at him with fierce determination and suddenly all he wanted was her, for ever. 'Do you know how much I love you? My protector?'

He pressed his smile to her forehead and she laughed softly. 'And I love you. We'll look after each other, Cole, and Everleigh. That's what Casper wanted.'

'I think you're probably right about that.'

'And by the way, I spoke to Ethan about moving Emmie down to Dorset on a more permanent basis.'

'Oh, yes?'

'He likes the idea. But only if he can come riding sometimes.' She grinned at the look on his face. 'I think he was joking.'

'Whatever makes you happy,' he said, going in for another kiss. She put her hands up to his handsome face and realised that she'd never loved him quite as much as she did now, knowing he had finally made it to Edinburgh, not just for her but for Emmie.

'*You* make me happy, Cole Crawford.'

Eighteen months later

The lighthouse loomed behind them as Cole steered the boat, and Jodie gripped the sides in anticipation. 'Do you think they're here today?'

'They'll show us if they are,' Cole said, and she watched his profile in the loose blue shirt and blue baseball hat as he stopped the motor to reach for his camera.

They weren't here for the dolphins specifically on this sunny, warm, late September day. Toby had taken some great shots of the new Portland Bill Everleigh Suites from the land, but Cole was determined to take his own promo shots from the water.

They had more staff than ever but he still liked to do as much as possible himself when it came to Everleigh, just like Casper had always done. As if he didn't have enough on his plate, she thought in admiration.

Jodie felt the little red boat bob beneath them as Cole positioned the camera on his lap. She pulled her cardigan tighter around her, and the shimmer of her wedding ring in the sun cast a rainbow reflection on the seat.

She loved the way the different seasons brought such different opportunities for them in Dorset, from organic farming and nursing newborn lambs in spring, to inviting their guests to marshmallow singalongs round the fire pit in winter. Her veterinary duties had expanded in every way she could imagine now that Aileen had taken over at West Bow. Everleigh had never been so busy or exciting. She had a feeling it was about to get even better...once their baby arrived.

'Did Emmie tell you, she and Toby are doing their next presentation together at school?' she said to Cole, putting a hand to her swollen belly. 'They're sharing how they've been making all their own dog food from organic ingredients. It's a pretty entrepreneurial business venture, don't you think? Everleigh K9 Complete.'

'I suppose they learned from the best,' Cole said, with faux smugness. 'I know Ziggy appreciated trying out all their samples.'

Ziggy cocked his head up from the bottom of the boat at the sound of his name, and Jodie reached down to stroke his soft, warm fur. He'd been extra-protective of her since he'd sensed the baby growing inside her. 'At least they'll pay for their own college educations at this rate,' she said.

'As long as they don't stick my face on the dog-food labels, I'm OK with it.'

Cole saw her wrestling with her cardigan in the breeze and quickly reached for a blanket under the seat. 'Are you cold?'

She shook her head as he draped it across her shoulders and laid a hand on the small bump. He was even more protective of her than Ziggy was, and every now and then she'd catch him looking at her in wonder, like he couldn't believe she was carrying life inside her—his own son. He was going to be the best father, she knew it would come naturally to him.

Five months in and she was showing through her clothes—the mums at the school were already planning her baby shower. Cole dropped a light kiss on the bump over her stretched cotton T-shirt, and she ran her fingers contentedly through his hair as he went back to looking through his camera lens.

The new Everleigh Suites looked like somewhere

you wanted to be, she thought proudly. They'd had each block painted a different colour, casting a red, blue and yellow splash across the shore behind the boathouse and the paddocks.

They were already all booked out for the rest of the year—most were guests with disabled or autistic children who were engaged in animal therapy with Cole. It hadn't been Cole's plan for the space initially, but after she'd fallen pregnant, the idea had struck her, and it had stuck for both of them.

The first paying guests were due to arrive any day. They even had customised snorkels and wetsuits in the boat, and Jodie and Evie had personally arranged wine glasses and bedspreads featuring real prints of their rescue horses for the guesthouse bedrooms. The Blaze Boudoir was their best suite. He was the star horse of Everleigh after all, who only Emmie got to ride.

Jodie was lost in a dream about teaching their son to ride when a movement in the corner of her eye made them both look up. She recognised the fin instantly.

The mother of the dolphin calf they'd rescued was here.

'She's coming over,' Cole said, putting a steady hand on her knee. Jodie was mesmerised. The baby dolphin was fully grown now, at least eight feet long. She watched in awe as the pair of them swam eagerly to the boat, then leapt right in front of the bow, making her gasp. 'They haven't come that close in a long time,' she said, although she and Cole were always greeted like friends.

She leaned over the edge, feeling Cole's arm snake around her protectively. The baby dolphin was hovering at the side of the boat, its head above water, eyeing her with what she was sure was a smile. 'You can tell she knows,' Cole said, wrapping his arms around her more tightly.

'Knows what?' Jodie asked, as the creature beamed with intelligence and curiosity in the water below her.

'That you're pregnant,' Cole said. 'Did you know that dolphins can sense when women are pregnant? She's excited by the heartbeats inside you.'

Jodie turned to him in surprise as the dolphin let out a squeak and bobbed her head. Dolphins did that all the time but it looked like she was laughing. 'Is that right?' she said.

Cole took the camera up again and positioned her with the dolphin just behind her. 'Put your hands on your bump,' he said, as he started clicking the shutter in her direction.

Jodie laughed, self-conscious all of a sudden. 'What are you doing?' she said, just as the mother dolphin leapt into the air with the lighthouse behind her.

'I think we need new photos for the wall,' Cole said. 'And this moment, right now, is absolutely perfect.'

* * * * *

RESCUING THE PARAMEDIC'S HEART

EMILY FORBES

MILLS & BOON

For James,
Twenty-four years as husband and wife and I'm having
as much fun now as I did when we were first married!
I couldn't do this without you.
With love, now and always,
Emily
16 March 2021

CHAPTER ONE

'EASY? KEEP AN eye on Backpackers' Express, I reckon we might have trouble.'

Jet Carlson's voice came through the radio, catching Ryder's attention as he stood beside the lifeguard buggy. Jet was up in the circular lifeguard tower that overlooked Bondi Beach, keeping watch over the one-kilometre curve of white sand, issuing updates to the lifeguards on patrol. Ryder reached into the buggy and picked up his binoculars and scanned the beach, looking towards the troublesome rip to the south. He picked out a dark-haired man swimming alone where the first waves were breaking as the Pacific Ocean rolled into the shore.

He picked up the walkie-talkie, certain he was looking at the same man Jet had spotted. 'Copy that, Central, I see him,' he responded.

He stood by the buggy as he kept his eyes on the swimmer. The water to the man's left was deceptively calm between two sets of rolling waves. Ryder knew the tide was turning and the calm water indicated a passage of water flowing out to sea. If the man got any closer, he'd be pulled out to sea with the tide.

It was the danger period, after lunch on a hot Sunday. It wasn't peak season yet; it was only the middle of spring and school hadn't finished for the year but the beach was still busy. Holidaymakers, shift workers and backpackers all flocked to Bondi at any time of the year. The tide was going out and the notorious rip was going to cause grief. Most likely to an unsuspecting tourist.

No matter how hard the lifeguards tried, it was impossible to get all the beachgoers to swim between the flags. Ryder knew it was sometimes because they didn't understand English or the dangers or where to swim, at other times they just chose to ignore the lifeguards and the risks, thinking their swimming ability was better than it was or that the warnings were some kind of joke or scaremongering tactics and the treacherous conditions wouldn't affect them. It didn't help matters that the main access point to the beach was closest to the dangerous southern end.

But no matter what the reason was for swimmers ending up in the wrong place, the lifeguards' job was to look after them all. The drunk, the stubborn, the unlucky.

Life was precious and Ryder felt a strong sense of responsibility and, at the end of the day, a strong sense of satisfaction in a job well done, whether that had been saving a life or just preventing a disaster. Not every day brought an emergency, although there was always some excitement, but a quiet day on the beach was preferable to one filled with drama.

Either way he enjoyed the work. It was interesting and varied and he met people from all over the world and from all walks of life and he reckoned that would hold him in good stead for his future career as a psychologist. If he could cope with the Bondi beachgoers, he could cope with anything.

He hadn't worked at Bondi long. It had only been a

couple of months since he'd been offered a position and had become one of several lifeguards employed by the local council to patrol the popular beach three hundred and sixty-five days of the year. It was a highly coveted job and usually went to qualified Sydneysiders who had grown up surfing the waves at the local beaches and had years of experience of the conditions.

He'd had years of experience as a surfer and as a lifeguard at Cottesloe Beach in Western Australia but that was on the opposite side of the country, on the shores of the Indian Ocean. But the Pacific Ocean was familiar to him—he'd spent his childhood surfing the breaks at Byron Bay, on the coast north of Bondi. The ocean on Australia's east coast had been home to him until one fateful day, just before his eighteenth birthday, when he'd been uprooted from everything that was special to him and moved thousands of kilometres away to the other side of the continent.

Eventually he'd settled in his new home and when he'd arrived in Bondi, part way through his transcontinental road trip, he hadn't planned on staying but he'd been offered a temporary position and it had been too good to refuse.

He'd landed in Bondi at just the right time. Two lifeguards had sustained serious injuries that would keep them off the beach for several months over the busy summer period and the council had been desperate to employ qualified replacements. Ryder had fitted the bill and, fortunately for him, he also had a personal reference from his childhood friend, Jet Carlson, the lifeguard who was currently manning the tower and giving Ryder his instructions.

He was happy with temporary. He knew he couldn't stay for ever as he was needed back west, but for the moment this was good. Casual work would allow him to extend his break and make sure he was refreshed and energised when he went home.

It was a perfect situation, he thought as he had a quick glance along the beach, trying to figure out if there was anyone else keeping an eye on the man he had under watch. Was anyone else aware of his position? In situations like this it could be helpful to speak to someone who knew the swimmer. It could help determine how competent they were in the water.

But he didn't really need confirmation, he'd bet his next pay cheque on the fact that this guy wasn't a strong swimmer. He could see him pushing off the bottom, not wanting to get out of his depth, but the outgoing tide was already taking him further from the beach and the minute he got washed off the sandbar he'd be in deep water.

As Ryder watched, a wave broke over the man's head, submerging him. That second or two when he went under was long enough to make him lose his footing. As he surfaced, he was swept into the channel and away from the beach.

He was in trouble.

'Easy?' Jet's voice came through the radio, using Ryder's nickname.

'I'm on it.' Ryder leapt out of the buggy, whipped off his distinctive blue lifeguard shirt, grabbed the rescue board from the rack on the side of the all-terrain vehicle and sprinted into the surf. He threw his board in front of him and dived onto it. He paddled strongly out past the small waves that were crashing onto the shore, past the swimmers who were oblivious to the drama unfolding a few metres off the beach, past the break.

He scanned the sea as pulled his board through the

water and caught a brief glimpse of the man's head as it appeared behind a wave before he lost sight of him again. He dug deep, paddling harder, knowing time was of the essence. His shoulder muscles bunched and already he could feel the burn but he was used to that. He was breathing deeply, his lungs straining, and he could feel his heart racing but he wouldn't stop. He was getting close now.

He crested a small wave just in time to see the man go under again.

Two more strokes.

He reached over the side of the board, plunging his arm into the water up to his elbow. He scooped his arm through the water but came up empty. He could see the man's dark hair. He leaned over further, plunging his whole arm into the ocean, the sea reaching to his armpit, and this time his fingers grabbed hold of the man's head. He pulled him to the surface by a fistful of hair. He knew it would hurt but having your hair pulled was a small price to pay in exchange for your life.

He dragged the man from the water, holding him by one arm. He wasn't breathing. Ryder needed to get him securely onto the rescue board and back to shore. The man was of slight build and probably weighed no more than seventy kilograms. Ryder was six feet three inches tall, fit and strong, a muscular ninety kilograms with no excess weight, but even so he strained with the effort of pulling a dead weight out of the water.

He grabbed his patient under his armpits and hauled him up, draping him across the board. He pulled his legs out of the ocean and waited to see if he would start breathing on his own.

The man coughed twice, expelling sea water, and

began breathing. Now Ryder just had to get him back to the beach.

He got the man balanced, getting him to lie on his stomach in front of him. It was a long paddle back to shore and he didn't want the board tipping. He didn't want to lose his patient and have to go through the process of getting him out of the water a second time.

As Ryder brought his board onto the beach two dark-haired women hurried down to the water's edge. His patient fell off the board into the shallow water as the rescue board hit the sand. Ryder grabbed his board with one hand and hooked his other hand under the man's armpit, helping him to his feet. His legs were shaky, the small waves almost knocking him off balance, and Ryder kept hold of him, helping to keep him upright.

'Thank you. Thank you.' The man had recovered enough to speak but his English was heavily accented.

'No worries,' Ryder replied, even though it *was* a worry. Beachgoers needed to be aware of the dangers. He didn't want to be rescuing the same man again today, something that had happened many times before.

'Do you see those flags?' he said as he pointed north along the beach. 'Red and yellow? You must swim between the flags.' He gave the warning, even though he doubted he would be understood, but he had a duty to explain the risks and to attempt to get them to follow the rules.

'Yes, yes.' The man and his friends all nodded but Ryder suspected none of them fully comprehended his caution.

'Here—very dangerous,' he emphasised as he waved his hand out to sea in the direction of the rip and tried one last time to stress the need to avoid this area, but he didn't have time to repeat himself, or to give any other advice, before he heard Jet's voice again from the radio in the buggy.

'Easy? There's another one in Backpackers'. I'm sending the jet-ski out but you'll be faster.'

Backpackers' Rip hadn't finished creating chaos yet and the day was going downhill fast.

'No worries,' he replied. 'I've got it.'

The Asian tourists were still thanking him as he picked up his board, turned and sprinted back into the water.

'Hello! I'm here. Anyone home?'

Lily jumped as she heard the front door slam and her sister's voice calling for her.

Poppy had arrived and the energy in the house kicked up a notch, swirling around Lily as the serenity of the day evaporated. From the time she could walk Poppy's life had moved at a million miles an hour. She was loud and fast and hectic. By comparison, Lily and Daisy, the eldest and youngest Carlson sisters, were quiet. Only their brother, Jet, could give Poppy a run for her money in the volume stakes and that was only at certain times. Jet had two settings—quietly monosyllabic or loud and boisterous. Poppy constantly operated at full volume and top speed, as if there were too many things to get done, no time to stop.

Poppy was standing just inside the front hall. She had two bags slung over her shoulders but she dumped them on the floor to hug her sister.

Lily hugged her tightly before stepping back to look at her younger sibling.

Poppy was a mixture of her older and younger sisters physically but there wasn't much of either of them in

Poppy's personality. Lily wondered momentarily how disruptive Poppy's arrival was going to be. But when Poppy had called and said she needed a place to stay, Lily hadn't hesitated. They might be like chalk and cheese in many ways but they were family and, as the eldest of the Carlson tribe, Lily had always made her siblings her priority. Poppy could be exhausting but Lily would deal with the logistics of her arrival just like she dealt with everything else—almost everything else, she amended silently, knowing there was one issue she was continuing to ignore. Having Poppy stay might turn out to be a bonus—someone else's drama might be a good distraction from the mess of her own personal life.

'Why don't you put your things in here?' Lily pointed to the bedroom off the hall on their right. 'And I'll put the kettle on.'

Poppy threw her bags onto the bed. This room was at the front of the house that Lily used to share with her husband. Poppy wondered if Lily had spoken to Otto recently or if she was still struggling with what had happened between them. She'd had a difficult time and she had Poppy's sympathy.

Thinking about Lily's love life reminded her to try calling Craig. Again. She took her phone out of her bag and brought up his number but, for the second time in as many hours, her call went to voice mail. This time she left a message, letting him know she'd arrived safely and asking him to call her back. She ended the call, annoyed that he hadn't phoned her after the last message. He would have checked his phone. Surely, he'd want to know she'd reached Sydney safely?

She sighed, knowing there was nothing she could

do about it. She kicked off her shoes and headed for the kitchen.

Lily's house was tall and narrow, it spanned four levels but was only one room wide, and it was in a magnificent position, perched on the hill at the southern end of Bondi with an incredible view looking east over the ocean and north over the famous beach. The kitchen opened onto a deck and Poppy stepped out and tipped her face to the sky, letting the sun warm her skin. She inhaled and let the scent of the sea wash over her. She'd missed the beach.

She had spent most of the past nine years living in Brisbane, which, despite it being the capital of Queensland, was severely lacking in beaches. Having grown up in Byron Bay on the New South Wales north coast, the ocean was in her blood and it was good to be able to step outside and see the waves and smell the salt air.

'Where's Daisy?' Poppy asked as Lily handed her a mug of tea and sat beside her on a high stool that afforded them a view over the sea. The kitchen was on the entrance level but the ground sloped away below the deck and Poppy could look down into the garden or out over the ocean.

'She's at work, she's on an early and I have to go in shortly as there are a couple of patients I need to check.' Both Lily and Daisy worked at Bondi General Hospital. Lily was a first-year resident and Daisy was a paediatric nurse. 'I thought we could have a family dinner tonight, though, I've asked Jet, too. He's on duty today but finishes at seven.'

Their brother, Jet, who was sandwiched between Lily and Poppy in the family order, worked as a lifeguard, employed by the local council to patrol Bondi Beach and neighbouring Tamarama and Bronte beaches. It was a full-time job and one that Poppy knew he loved. Jet's personality was perfectly suited to the role—every day was different, the job kept him fit, he was surrounded by blokes but had plenty of female attention. Some of the aspects appealed to Poppy—namely the excitement and variety—but it wasn't a career she wanted. The financial reward wasn't generous enough for her and job security was another factor. Jet had to prove his physical fitness every year—that wasn't a problem for him, he was a professional athlete as well and trained hard, but while Poppy maintained her fitness for her career as a paramedic she felt that having to pass a test every year to keep her job would be stressful.

'So, how was the drive?'

'Fine.' Poppy had split the long drive south from Queensland to New South Wales over two days to make it manageable. 'I didn't have any dramas but it was a little lonely. It would have been nice to share it with Craig.' Craig's employer was transferring him to Sydney and Poppy had applied to join the New South Wales Ambulance service in order to move with him. But Craig was currently busy on a large project that had delayed his move and Poppy had found herself relocating to Sydney ahead of him.

'Has he booked a flight to come down for a weekend?' Lily asked.

Poppy shook her head. 'Not yet. He said he'll come down in a fortnight's time. I'm hoping that will give me time to line up a few rentals to look at when he's here.'

'What does his time frame look like now? Is he still thinking his move will be a few months away?'

Poppy nodded. 'He doesn't think he'll get here for another three months. He reckons he'll need to work through Christmas and won't be able to move until the end of January. One or the other of us will travel up or down every two or three weeks.' Poppy shrugged and added, 'Lots of couples have long-distance relationships, it'll be fine.' It wasn't until she saw Lily's stricken expression that she realised what she'd said. 'Sorry, Lil, I wasn't thinking.'

Poppy waited for Lily's response to her apology but Lily was silent, her face blank. Lily and her husband had been living separately for almost two years. Otto was in London, doing his medical speciality training, and Lily should have been there with him, but their plans had gone awry and Lily had come home.

'How is Otto?' Poppy asked, filling the silence.

'Can we not talk about this now?' Lily said as she stood and picked up their empty mugs. Poppy knew she was using the activity as a means of avoiding eye contact. 'I need to get to work.'

'Of course.' Poppy didn't want to upset her further. She'd hoped Lily and Otto would have made some progress in healing their relationship or, if that wasn't possible, at least made some progress in deciding how they were going to move forward. She knew their separation was about more than just physical distance but she also suspected the distance was making things more difficult. She hoped they would eventually be able to resolve their differences and while she wasn't about to insist that Lily talk to her right now she did make a mental note to broach the topic again. She needed to check on Lily's well-being.

Poppy changed into her bikini, shorts and a T-shirt as Lily left for work. She'd go to the beach for a quick swim, she decided, say hi to her brother and then come back and make a start on dinner.

She checked her phone for what felt like the hundredth time as she slid her feet into her flip-flops. Still nothing. She tossed it back on the bed. She wouldn't take it to the beach as she wasn't planning to be gone for long. If Craig called while she was out, she'd call him back later.

She left her car parked on the road in front of the house and walked down Edward Street towards the beach. After consecutive six-hour days in the car, driving from Brisbane to Sydney, she needed to stretch her legs and the fifteen-minute walk to Campbell Parade would help to clear the cobwebs.

She turned onto the pedestrian path and walked along the promenade past the skate park and the mural wall towards the lifeguard tower.

She stopped before she reached the tower and leaned on the railing and looked out over the beach. The sun was behind her and the sea shone in the afternoon light. The sand was crisp and white and, despite the fact that it was not yet the summer holidays, the beach was busy. She took a deep breath, filling her lungs with the sea air, and stood for a moment, enjoying the feeling of warm sun on her skin as she watched the water.

The waves were small but she could spot the rips, the deceptively smooth water between breaking waves. She had years of experience as a surfer—growing up in Byron Bay, she and her siblings had learned to surf almost before they could walk—but she could see why the tourists and the locals who weren't familiar with the ocean could be fooled into thinking the rips were safe spots to swim.

She turned to the south to see if she could pick out

Lily's house perched on the cliff before she spun on her heel and headed for the circular lifeguard tower. She knocked on the blue door and waited, if Jet wasn't in there someone would be able to tell her where he was.

'Poppy! You're here.' Jet grinned as he swung the door open. His welcoming smile was wide, his perfect teeth white and even in his tanned face. His blond hair was pulled back into a messy man bun but that was all Poppy had time to absorb before he stepped out of the tower and wrapped her in a tight hug. He stood well over six feet tall, and even with his slim but muscular athlete's build he managed to make her feel small. She was five feet seven inches, not short for a girl, but Jet made her feel petite.

He released her and dragged her into the tower where he introduced her to the other lifeguards.

'Guys, this is my little sister, Poppy. Poppy, meet the guys—Gibbo, Bluey and Dutchy.'

Poppy smiled at Jet's use of the guys' nicknames.

'Are you going to hang around here for a while?' he asked as Poppy finished saying hello.

'No, I just wanted to say hi. I'm going to have a swim and then head home. I hear you're coming for dinner.'

Jet nodded and looked as if he was about to say something else when the radio on the desk crackled into life.

'Central, this is Easy. We've got a problem down here, south of the flags.'

He held up one hand in Poppy's direction, asking her to wait as he grabbed the radio. 'Go ahead, Ryder.'

'The tourist I pulled from Backpackers', he's not looking great. I'm bringing him back to the tower for an assessment.'

Poppy's ears pricked up as she listened to the exchange. Ryder was an unusual name. She'd only ever known one and he had been Jet's best friend when they were at high school. He'd also been her first crush. But the Ryder she'd known had moved away when he was seventeen, breaking her young, impressionable heart in the process—although she'd kept that to herself—and she hadn't seen him since.

It couldn't be him, though, could it? Surely Jet would have said something.

'Ryder?' she said as Jet put the radio down.

'Yeah, Ryder Evans, you remember him?'

Of course she remembered him.

She could feel herself colouring as she thought about the last time she'd seen him. She hoped Jet didn't notice the blush she could feel creeping up her neck.

She nodded. 'You never told me he was in Sydney.'

'Didn't I?' Jet shrugged. 'Probably figured you wouldn't care, you haven't seen him for the best part of twelve years,' he said over his shoulder as he went to open the door to the tower.

He had a point. He wouldn't think it was important. It *wasn't* important really, although that didn't stop a frisson of nervousness from shooting through her at the thought of seeing him again. She hadn't thought about him for years, had finally let the idea of him go, yet at the mere mention of his name all the old feelings rose to the surface along with all the memories of how much he'd meant to her teenage self. She could instantly re-call all her teenage fantasies and the memories made her blush.

The lifeguard buggy pulled to a stop at the bottom of the metal stairs that led from the sand to the tower en-trance and Poppy's jaw dropped as a lifeguard jumped out. Tall and muscular, tanned and fit.

Was that Ryder?

She managed to close her mouth as she watched him help his patient out of the buggy and up the stairs.

She hung back, out of the way, as Ryder got the man into the tower and onto the treatment plinth. Jet went to assist, instructing Bluey to keep an eye on the beach. Poppy stayed near the desk by the windows. The lifeguards had a job to do and she didn't want to be a nuisance but staying out of the way also gave her a chance to check Ryder out unobserved. She knew he hadn't noticed her, he was too focussed on his patient.

The last time she'd seen him there had been a hint of the man he would become, of the man waiting to emerge, but he'd still been a gangly teenager. He'd been tall but he'd yet to have a fast growth spurt or develop the muscle definition that would come with adulthood. But all traces of adolescence had disappeared now. Now there was no hiding the man. And no ignoring the feeling of warmth that was spreading through her belly and into her groin. Poppy leaned on the desk, taking the weight off her suddenly shaky legs.

Fortunately Ryder had his back to her and wouldn't be aware of her reaction but she was very aware of him.

He'd grown even taller and he'd definitely filled out. He'd developed muscles where he hadn't had them before. He wore only a pair of black boardshorts with 'Lifeguard' emblazoned across his hips and she had plenty of opportunity to admire the view of sculpted muscles and smooth, tanned skin. His shoulders were broad, his biceps bulging, his waist narrow. He looked fit. He looked healthy. He looked magnificent.

She ran her gaze up the length of his spine and up his neck. She could see where the knobs of his vertebrae disappeared into his hair. He'd always had amazing hair, dark blond and thick, and at almost twenty-nine years of age it seemed he'd lost none of it.

Her gaze traced the line of his jaw. It was strong and square. He looked good, even better than she remembered, and she felt another rush of blood to her cheeks as her heart skittered in her chest.

Her hands gripped the edge of the desk as she observed him, keeping her fixed in place, and she wondered at the involuntary response. Was she stopping herself from crossing the room? While her rational mind might tell her that Ryder's unexpected appearance was of no consequence, it seemed her body had other ideas. Her palms were clammy and her mouth was dry and she suddenly felt like the sixteen-year-old schoolgirl she'd been when she'd last seen him.

When she had kissed him.

And he had kissed her back.

She knew from talking to her girlfriends that first kisses often weren't anywhere near as fabulous as they'd dreamed about but the kiss she and Ryder had shared had been everything she'd hoped for and more. It had been the biggest moment of her young life. It had *changed* her life.

She'd fallen in love.

First love.

She had only been a teenager but that hadn't made it any less real, any less all-encompassing, any less all-consuming.

And it hadn't made it any less painful when he'd walked out of her life.

CHAPTER TWO

Poppy knew it hadn't been Ryder's choice to leave but she'd spent many days—many months—waiting for him to acknowledge that he missed her as much as she missed him, but she'd heard nothing and the complete lack of contact had left her feeling foolish and embarrassed.

Their kiss had been everything she'd dreamt of but it obviously hadn't had the same impact on him. He'd probably forgotten all about it within days. But it had taken her much, much longer and now all those long-forgotten feelings came flooding back.

The anticipation, the joy and the delight. The spark, the excitement and the satisfaction. The pounding of her heart and the wobbling of her knees. Her nervousness and then her embarrassment over her teenage self and how she'd thrown herself at him. Unfortunately, her embarrassment had become her most powerful memory of the whole experience.

She hadn't been rejected as such but it had become fairly clear that she hadn't had the same lasting effect on him as he'd had on her.

She assumed he'd forgotten all about it. She could only hope so now. More than likely it was only seared into her memory. At least, if that was the case, maybe she'd get over her discomfiture. It would be difficult otherwise—especially as there was no denying he was now super-hot.

She stood in the corner of the tower, clutching the desk as if her life depended on it, and listened to the lifeguards' assessment of the patient as she brought her thoughts back to the present day.

The patient's English was far from fluent but even so it was obvious he was complaining of a headache and stomach pain. He was coughing intermittently. Poppy watched as Ryder slipped an oxygen mask over the man's nose and mouth and then took his blood pressure.

'BP one-forty over ninety. Pulse one hundred. I reckon we should keep him in the tower for observation,' Dutchy commented.

'Can you open your eyes for me, Tong?' Ryder asked. 'I think we should call the ambos just to be sure. He's drowsy and complaining of a headache. There's a good chance he's inhaled sea water and I reckon he's dehydrated and had a bit too much sun.' Ryder voiced his concerns about Tong's rapidly deteriorating condition.

'What do you think, Poppy?' Jet turned to Poppy.

Ryder turned too. 'Hey, Poppy, I didn't see you there.'

He smiled at her and she was grateful for the support of the desk. His smile was enough to fan the flames that were already racing through her and if it hadn't been for the furniture she suspected she'd be a messy puddle of oestrogen on the floor of the tower.

'Hello, Ryder.'

She did her best to hold his gaze even as she wondered why he was still able to affect her this way. This reaction was exactly why she steered clear of choosing boyfriends based on chemistry. She hated feeling out of control. Hated this feeling of losing control over her senses, her responses and her behaviour. Ever since she'd lost her heart to Ryder all those years ago she'd vowed not to let her emotions or her hormones carry her away again but, apparently, all it took was one smile from him and she felt like she was falling all over again.

Standing in the tower, clinging to the desk, an image of fairy-tale princesses trapped in castles, waiting for knights to rescue them, sprang to her mind before she told herself she was being ridiculous. She didn't need rescuing. She was perfectly content with her life. With Craig.

Yes, Craig. Remember Craig, she told herself. Safe, predictable Craig. He wouldn't distract her from her goals. He wouldn't let her down. He hadn't returned her calls yet but she knew he would. He was dependable. There were no great highs and lows. He was calm, and that was what she wanted. She knew where she was with Craig. She could remain focussed, protect her heart and keep control of her world. Her life was just how she liked it—simple, uncomplicated, safe.

She realised Jet was waiting with an expectant expression for her answer and she tried to remember what the question had been. 'Can you give me the history?' she asked.

'I pulled him out of Backpackers' Rip.' Poppy's question had been directed at Jet but the patient was Ryder's and he answered. 'He was completely submerged, not breathing initially, but he recovered spontaneously. He seemed to be okay and I left him with his friends but they came back to me and said he was complaining of a headache, dizziness and stomach pains. He's vomited a few times too. All typical symptoms of having inhaled water.'

His gaze was intense. She remembered that about

him. How he used to watch and listen and make her feel like what she said was important.

'How long ago did you get him out of the water?'

'About an hour ago.'

Poppy knew there was always a risk of secondary drowning if someone was suspected to have inhaled water. Even if the risk was slight, it couldn't be ignored. 'I think he should at least be rehydrated and it's important that he understands the potential dangers of getting water in his lungs. He should probably have an X-ray of his lungs and he should definitely be monitored. Leave the oxygen on and call the ambulance—they can put him on a drip, take him to hospital and keep an eye on him. Given that his English isn't great, I think it's better to be safe than sorry.'

'Okay. I'll call the ambos,' Jet replied. 'Dutchy, see if you can explain to Tong and his mates what we're going to do and, Easy, you'd better get back out on the beach.'

'I'll get out of the way, too,' Poppy said to Jet. She knew the lifeguards could cope without her, they did it every day. 'I'll go for a swim and see you at Lily's for dinner.'

He nodded as he picked up the phone.

Ryder held the door for Poppy, letting her leave the tower before him. They walked down the metal stairs to the beach as Poppy tried to work out what Ryder was doing in Sydney. And why she was so nervous.

It was a silly reaction. They weren't teenagers any more. She didn't need to be nervous but apparently the old feelings of a first crush, a first love still simmered beneath the surface and didn't need much stirring to rise to the top.

Her mind wandered, skittering from past to present at a million miles an hour, taking her attention away from the simple task of walking down a staircase. She missed the bottom step and stumbled as the soft sand gave way beneath her. Before she had a chance to right herself Ryder's arm was around her waist, holding her, supporting her. Her top was loose, skimming the waistband of her shorts, and his fingers rested lightly on her skin. Her body buzzed under his touch, her skin tingled and her nerves endings sprang to life.

She found her feet and stepped away, forcing him to drop his arm, and then she found herself missing the contact.

What was the matter with her? she chided herself. She was a grown woman, in a relationship with another man. It was ridiculous to let a schoolgirl crush from a dozen years ago affect her like this.

But she couldn't help but wonder what it meant that Ryder's touch could still make her buzz when Craig's touch had never set her pulse racing, had never made her skin feel like it was on fire. But was that Craig's fault or hers?

She knew she deliberately sought out relationships that weren't based on an overpowering sense of physical desire. She didn't want a relationship that created huge emotional fluctuations for her. She chose calm and measured deliberately. It made her feel safe. She had chosen Craig because he had been able to give her the things she'd needed at the time. Was it his fault that what she had needed had been a place to call home more than a person to share it with? Was it Craig's fault that she didn't want to fall in love?

Her experience with Ryder had taught her that.

Falling in love had left her exposed and vulnerable. Now she didn't want to be emotionally dependent on someone. She didn't want to be needy. She didn't want to rely on anyone but herself.

Ryder had been her first love. Her only love. She'd tried to convince herself it had been nothing but a teenage crush but she'd known she was lying to herself. Falling in love had left her feeling foolish and rejected. He'd broken her heart and she'd vowed not to let herself fall in love again. And she'd kept her word.

But now, twelve years later, her head and her heart were sending conflicting messages. One touch, one smile and she was transported back to her teenage years when Ryder had been her world. When she'd thought he'd been the answer to her prayers. When he'd been the shining star in her small galaxy.

'Hop in, I'll give you a ride down the beach.' Even if his muscles were new, his voice was deep and familiar and it brought her out of her reverie and back to the present.

The open-sided lifeguard buggy was parked at the bottom of the stairs and Ryder had walked around to the driver's side and was sliding into his seat, oblivious to the simmering tension that was coursing through Poppy's body.

Her head was still spinning, still recovering from his touch. Unable to make decisions of her own, she followed his instructions and clambered into the buggy, stepping over the rescue board that was slotted along the side.

She stared at Ryder, still trying to process the idea that, A: he was here in Bondi, and B: her hormones were going crazy.

'What?' he said as she continued to look at him. 'Have I got something stuck on my face?' He grinned at her and wiped a hand down his cheek.

'No.' Poppy smiled in return. 'I'm still trying to get my head around the fact that you're here. Last I heard you were on the other side of the country, in Perth. I wasn't expecting to see you but you don't seem surprised to see me.'

'I'm not,' he said as he steered the buggy around a group of young girls sunbathing on the sand.

'You knew I was coming?'

'Daisy mentioned it.'

'Daisy did? You've seen her?'

'Of course. I've seen her at the beach and I've been to dinner a few times with Jet at Lily and Daisy's.'

She wondered why no one had said anything to her. She knew she tended to get caught up in her own busy life but she was sure no one had mentioned anything. She was certain she would have remembered. Did they assume she wouldn't be interested?

'In fact, Jet invited me to dinner tonight too,' he continued.

'Are you coming?' she asked.

Ryder parked the buggy next to one of the yellow signs that the lifeguards had posted on the beach, warning swimmers of the dangerous currents. He shook his head as he hit the kill switch and shut off the engine. 'No.'

She didn't know whether to be relieved or disappointed. 'Are you busy?' She fished for more information, even as she tried to tell herself it didn't matter.

'No,' he explained. 'I thought you should have some time with just the four of you.'

'Oh.' Now she knew she was disappointed.

'Maybe we could have dinner another time. Catch up properly then.'

Her disappointment eased slightly. 'I'd like that,' she said as she hopped out of the buggy.

Ryder had always been good company. So often in her childhood she'd felt like she was lost amongst the noise and chaos of her surroundings and she knew she'd developed a boisterous personality in an effort to be seen, to be noticed, but it hadn't done much good. Their family living arrangements had been unusual, and added to that growing up so close in age to her siblings meant everyone around the Carlson siblings treated them as one entity.

But Ryder hadn't. He'd always had time for her. He'd always listened to her. She'd struggled to find her own identity but he'd always seemed to see her, to understand her. She'd like to spend time with him. Provided she could get her nerves under control.

'I've got a couple of orientation days scheduled with the ambulance service, starting tomorrow,' she told him. 'Once I get my roster sorted, we can sort something out.'

Poppy smiled at him and then stepped out of her shorts and dropped them on the sand. He tried not to look as she lifted the hem of her T-shirt and pulled it over her head in one smooth movement to reveal a black bikini and toned abdominal muscles. She dropped her T-shirt onto her shorts and walked north along the beach towards the safer stretch of water. Away from the rip. Away from him.

He tried not to stare as she made her way into the water but it was his job to keep an eye on the swimmers and the ocean. He couldn't help it if she was in his field of vision. He watched her wade into the water, watched her until she dived under a small wave and struck out away from the beach.

He turned his attention back to the rest of the ocean, keeping an eye on the swimmers who weren't as confident in the water but he kept her in the periphery of his vision as his mind stayed focussed on her.

She was still gorgeous. Long, toned, athletic limbs, big, green eyes that seemed to hold the secrets of the universe, thick, blonde hair that fell in waves past her shoulders and perfect heart-shaped lips. Thinking about her lips reminded him of their kiss. In truth, he'd never forgotten it.

He'd been a lanky, gawky seventeen-year-old virgin. He'd had a couple of girlfriends, nothing serious, but Poppy had captivated him. Since the age of fifteen he'd had a thing for her but he'd never been confident enough to tell her so.

And then, out of the blue, she had kissed him.

He had no idea who she had kissed before him but it had been an amazing kiss. Like nothing he'd ever experienced. It had been incredible and unexpected.

They had spent a lot of time together over the years. He'd turned up often at the Carlson house under the guise of being Jet's best friend, but Poppy had been the real attraction. But she'd never given any sign that she was interested in him as anything other than a friend.

Until she'd kissed him.

And there'd only been one problem. She'd just been saying goodbye. His family had been moving away, four thousand kilometres away to the opposite side of the country. Poppy had hugged him first. She'd wrapped her slim arms around his even skinnier shoulders and told him she would miss him.

He'd said nothing. He'd been a teenage boy—

he hadn't had the right words—and even if he had, the feeling of her embrace had left him speechless.

And then she'd kissed him and wiped all coherent thought from his young mind.

He'd been working on the courage to ask her out, finally deciding he needed to take the chance, before his world had imploded and the opportunity had been torn away from him by his mother's decision to pack up and move across the country. He'd figured he could have lived with that. It would have been a case of not knowing what he was missing but after she'd kissed him, after he'd had a taste of her, he'd known he would always rue the missed opportunity.

He hadn't wanted to leave. He hadn't wanted to leave *her*. But he'd had no choice. He'd had no valid reason to stay and his mother and his sister had needed him. Even as a teenage boy in love he'd been able to see that he had to go. Overnight he had become the man of the house and he'd had to do the right thing by his family. Especially considering that his father hadn't.

Eventually he'd got over the move. He'd got over the fact that he felt as if he'd been torn from Poppy's arms. And he'd got over the fact that his father's mid-life crisis—which had led him to run off with his much younger girlfriend—had instigated the change in his own circumstances. He'd even got over his parents' divorce, and eventually he'd got over the kiss too, but he'd never forgotten it.

He'd agonised over writing to Poppy, but he hadn't been any good with words. He'd been a seventeen-year-old boy who'd had no idea how to express what he'd been feeling, how *she* had made him feel, and so he'd said nothing, written nothing, and eventually the days had turned into weeks, which had turned into months, and all his thoughts had remained unspoken. And then it had been too late.

It had been the first kiss he'd had that had felt like it had had some meaning behind it, something shared, something emotional, rather than just something physical. It had become a moment in time, a moment in his history that had shaped him, and a moment he'd thought he'd put behind him, but now he was wondering what it would be like to kiss her again.

It was unlikely that he'd get that opportunity. He knew she had a partner, but it didn't mean he couldn't imagine what it would be like.

He kept his eyes on the water but his gaze kept drifting back to where Poppy was swimming.

He hadn't been surprised to see her as he'd been expecting her, but what he hadn't expected had been the sudden jolt of awareness when he'd seen her standing in the tower. He'd had the unsettling sensation of having the air knocked out of him. His pulse had been racing and it had felt as though his heart had suddenly got too big for his chest and had squeezed the air out of his lungs to make more room. He'd smiled and said hello and hoped he hadn't still sounded like the naïve, shy, tongue-tied teenager he'd been when he'd last seen her. But he suspected that he had.

She had become part of his past and he'd thought he'd got over her but seeing her again made it clear that there was still a connection. On his part at least.

He couldn't deny it was good to see her. Her clear green eyes still sparkled intensely, and when she looked at him, he felt as if he was the only person she was interested in seeing. He wondered if she made everyone feel that way.

Her smile still made the day brighter and her golden

blonde hair still begged to be wound around his fingers. But, of course, he'd never done that. He'd never had the courage.

And he wouldn't dare to dream of doing it now either. He figured she'd probably forgotten all about him in the past twelve years and she'd no doubt kissed dozens of boys—men—in that time. She would have moved on and he wasn't about to remind her of their shared history. That would be far too embarrassing.

He would have liked to have accepted Jet's invitation to dinner tonight but he'd been uncertain. He'd been unsure if Poppy would want him there but his uncertainty had stemmed more from the fact he'd imagined that her boyfriend would be with her and he hadn't wanted to deal with that. He'd been prepared for the fact that she would be different from the girl he remembered but he hadn't been prepared to see her with another man. He'd known it would mess with his memories.

Ryder shook his head as he tried to clear his thoughts. Those memories needed to stay locked away for now—he had a job to do and he couldn't afford distractions. He swivelled his gaze up and down the shoreline. The beach was starting to empty as families went home for dinner and to prepare for the week ahead, but his attention was diverted by a woman who wasn't heading for the promenade but was hurrying towards him. By her side was a young boy who was holding a beach towel against his head.

'Can you have a look at my son, please? He collided with a boogie-boarder. He got a knee to the head and he has a cut by his eye.'

'Okay.' Ryder squatted down in the sand. 'Keep holding that towel there for a minute,' he said as it looked like the mother was about to move her son's hand. 'What's your name?'

'Jackson.'

'All right, Jackson, I'll just ask you a couple of questions and then I'll have a look at your battle wounds.' The boy had walked up to Ryder so he didn't appear to have sustained a spinal injury but Ryder would do a quick check just for his own peace of mind. He knew that one of the lifeguards had sustained a fractured thoracic vertebra in a collision in the water and it had gone undetected for a couple of days.

'Have you got any pain anywhere else?'

'No.'

'Any tingling or numbness in your fingers or toes?'

Jackson wriggled his toes in the sand. 'No.'

'Take a deep breath for me.' The boy closed his eyes as he followed Ryder's instructions, making Ryder concerned. 'How does that feel?'

'I feel a bit dizzy.'

Ryder knew that could be shock or concussion. 'All right, let's put you up here on the back of the buggy and I'll have a look.' He unzipped the first-aid kit while he was talking and then lifted the boy up onto the tray of the ATV before pulling on a pair of surgical gloves. He opened a packet of gauze and a vial of saline.

'Can you take the towel?' he asked Jackson's mother.

Once the wound was exposed Ryder poured saline over the side of the boy's head to wash away the blood. Head wounds always bled a lot and often looked far worse than they actually were, but this cut had split the skin from the corner of Jackson's left eye halfway to his temple. There was a bruise forming already. He'd been knocked hard but the cut wasn't deep.

Ryder taped a wad of gauze over the wound. 'I think

we'll take you up to the tower to patch you up properly. You can hop up here with him,' he told the mother. 'I'll drive you back slowly.'

Ryder got Jackson back to the tower and up the stairs. He laid him on the treatment bed and slid the oxygen mask over the boy's nose and mouth, knowing that would help if he was in shock. He draped a space blanket over him to counteract the heat loss from his wet bathing shorts.

'Can you tell me what day it is, Jackson?' Ryder asked as he removed the wad of bloodied gauze.

'Sunday. Does this mean I can stay home from school tomorrow?'

'I reckon you deserve a day off,' Ryder told him. Jackson was going to look battered and bruised by tomorrow and would probably feel pretty tender.

Ryder managed to stem the flow of blood but Jackson was going to need more help than he was qualified to give him in order to close the wound.

'All right. The cut's not too deep but I reckon we'll get the ambos to have a look at it.' The cut was a couple of centimetres long and being close to the eye Ryder thought it was better to err on the side of caution.

'Will it need stitches?' Jackson's mother asked.

'I think they'll be able to glue the edges closed. That will mean no swimming for a week but he can have a quick shower in twenty-four hours.'

'So he's okay?'

'The ambos will do a more thorough check but it seems like he's come out of this without too much trouble, but if he gets a temperature in the next day or has any nausea or dizziness you'll need to take him to your local doctor.'

'Okay, thank you.'

Jet called the ambulance for the second time that day and Ryder left his patient in the care of the lifeguards in the tower. He needed to get back out onto the sand as it was time to start packing up.

The beach was patrolled from six in the morning until seven at night. The lifeguards worked staggered shifts with a maximum of eight on at a time, but because it wasn't yet peak season more than half had finished work, leaving skeleton staff to close the beach at the end of the day.

Ryder took the buggy and drove along the sand, pulling up the yellow warning signs, picking up cones and bringing in the flags. He pulled out the dangerous-current sign where Poppy had left her clothes.

Her clothes were gone.

He checked the beach but she was nowhere to be seen.

She hadn't said goodbye but, then, why would she? He consoled himself with the knowledge that at least it wouldn't be another twelve years until he saw her again.

Poppy towelled herself dry after a quick shower. The house had been empty when she'd got back from the beach but she could hear noise coming from the kitchen and she knew at least one of her sisters was home from the hospital. She rifled through her bag and found some clean underwear and a light cotton sundress. She got dressed and headed for the kitchen.

Her little sister, Daisy, was sliding a tray into the oven as Poppy walked in. She had her back to Poppy but when she straightened and turned, she had a big smile on her pretty face.

'I thought I'd be able to sneak up on you.' Poppy laughed before she stepped forward and hugged her tightly.

'You should know better than that. You've just got out of the shower. You smell fresh.'

'That's good to know.' Poppy smiled.

Daisy was completely deaf, having lost her hearing at the age of eight after contracting mumps. Because she had already been talking her speech was mostly unaffected by her hearing loss. She could lip read and sign, which gave her good communication options, provided she could see people's faces.

'What's for dinner?' Poppy asked.

'Baked snapper with baby potatoes. You can make a salad if you like.'

Poppy pulled a bottle of wine and salad ingredients from the fridge. She poured two glasses of wine, passing one to her sister, and then made sure she was standing at the kitchen bench, facing Daisy, before she continued their conversation.

'How was work?'

Daisy screwed up her nose. 'I don't think the nurse unit manager likes me.'

'Why not?' Poppy was flummoxed. *Everyone* liked Daisy.

Daisy was tiny, blonde, blue-eyed and beautiful—she reminded Poppy of a fairy—and people were naturally drawn to her. Almost everyone wanted to be her best friend, which was ironic as Daisy was quite happy with her own company. Daisy had been born a twin but the infection that had robbed her of her hearing had also claimed the life of her twin sister, Willow, and after that Daisy, who had only ever needed Willow's company, had retreated into her shell. She'd been mothered by her older siblings but because of the five-year age difference between Poppy and Daisy she had spent a lot of time on her own.

She was quiet and introverted but in the field of paediatric nursing she had found the place she felt comfortable. She loved working with kids—they were uncomplicated—and Daisy adored them and they her. Poppy knew Daisy would be completely happy if she could work with kids and never have to see an adult but even if Daisy didn't need adult company, it was rare for someone to take objection to her.

'What happened?' Poppy asked, wondering what could have gone wrong.

'It might have something to do with something she heard me say.'

Poppy didn't like to talk about her feelings but none of the Carlson siblings had any qualms about voicing their opinions on other matters. Even Lily and Daisy, the 'quiet' ones, weren't afraid to let people know their thoughts on general topics if it was something they felt strongly about. Along with their fair athletic looks the four of them shared determined natures and opinionated views.

'Which was?'

'We admitted a child today who has a serious case of chicken pox with several complications and I might have strongly suggested to her parents that there is a vaccine for this disease and they should consider vaccinating their children.'

'And what did the NUM say?'

'She told me it's not my place to lecture the parents.'

'She's probably right.'

Daisy sighed. 'I know. But I had no idea she was standing right behind me.'

'Would you have modified your lecture if you had known?'

'No. You know there are laws in New South Wales about vaccinating children unless there's a medical reason not to? If it's good enough for the government it's good enough for me.'

'That sounds like a serious discussion between two of my favourite sisters,' Jet said as he walked into the kitchen. 'What have I missed?'

'Daisy's been lecturing people about vaccinations again,' Poppy said with a smile.

'It's hard for me to keep quiet,' Daisy protested. 'I'm a walking advertisement for why vaccinations are so important.'

Jet gave her a quick hug on his way to the fridge. 'Yes, you are, Daise, stick to your guns.'

'I intend to.'

'Good for you,' he said as he helped himself to a beer and flipped the top off the bottle. He turned towards Poppy. 'How was your swim? Cleared the cobwebs out after your road trip?'

Poppy nodded.

'Craig didn't change his mind and come with you?' he asked.

'No. He was busy,' Poppy replied.

'Busy with what?'

Other than his work she wasn't exactly sure what he was busy doing. They hadn't spent a lot of time together lately. They never really did. Their relationship wasn't one where they spent every spare minute together and that was the way Poppy liked it. She suspected she'd grow tired of Craig if they lived in each other's pockets.

Craig didn't need to spend every second with her or hear how she felt about him constantly and the same went for her. They had a compatible partnership even if they didn't rely on each other emotionally.

They were working towards a common goal and that was enough for Poppy. With Craig's help she was going to achieve the financial and physical stability and security she craved much faster. With Craig's help she would pay off a mortgage and own a house.

For her part she'd been volunteering for any overtime shifts that had been offered, trying to save as much money as she could—working extra weekends and nights while Craig had worked days. 'Making money, I hope. We have to get our house finished.'

'I need to see this house. With the amount of money you seem to be throwing at it, I'm imagining something along the lines of the Taj Mahal by the time you're finished.'

Poppy laughed. 'It's nothing extravagant but I wanted to modernise it without losing the heritage feeling, and everything with a Queenslander seems to cost more.' The typical Queenslander house, built out of wood and raised off the ground on stilts, required a lot of TLC and a lot of cash if it had fallen into disrepair. Poppy and Craig had spent huge amounts on things that couldn't be seen—replacing beams and joists and panels in the frame, the walls and the floors, as well as rewiring the house, and they weren't done yet. The bathroom and laundry had recently been completed but the kitchen needed updating, the pool needed landscaping, and there was always wood that needed painting.

'Would you do it again? Renovate?'

'I don't know about "again,"' she said, as Lily joined them and Daisy took the snapper from the oven. 'It's not like we've even finished one yet. It's been a lot of effort.' On her part more than Craig's, she thought, but she didn't say that out loud. Craig put money into the house but she was the one who had the ideas, organised the tradesmen and picked up a paintbrush. To Craig the house was a sound investment but it was more than that to Poppy.

The house was her sanctuary and she loved the restoration process. She loved seeing her plans come to fruition, bringing the house back to life, but Craig had frequently reminded her not to get too attached. He looked at the house as an investment, his goal was purely financial. His aim was to renovate and sell for a profit and she knew she'd agreed to those plans in the beginning but the house had come to represent more than just dollars to her. It was her chance to have a home.

Initially she had seen the house as her path to financial security but during the renovation process it had come to represent physical security too. The house was a place she could call her own, and one that she had control over. She didn't want to pay someone else's mortgage. She didn't want to be at someone else's mercy. She didn't want to be a tenant, always hoping that she would be able to stay. She wanted a place of her own. One she couldn't be moved out of without her consent. She wanted security and stability and she was prepared to work hard to get it.

The house represented those things and she hoped that once the house was finished Craig would love it as much as she did and agree to keep it.

'I'd like to propose a toast,' Lily said as they sat down to dinner. 'To the four of us being together again.'

'It's been much too long,' Daisy added as they raised their glasses.

Poppy knew that was her fault. Her siblings had dinner together regularly, it was she who had been missing. She'd spent every spare minute on her goals. Every spare day either doing an extra shift or wielding a hammer, screwdriver or paintbrush. She hadn't wanted to spend the time or the money on trips to Sydney. Looking around the table now, she was sorry that she hadn't made more of an effort but she consoled herself with the knowledge that it would all be worth it in the end, once her house was finished.

'It's good to be here,' she said, 'and I'd like to think we'll be able to have family dinner at my house next year.'

'Maybe we could have Christmas in Brisbane,' Daisy suggested.

'Speaking of Christmas...' The others laughed as Lily spoke up. She never missed an opportunity to organise them. 'Will everyone be in Sydney this year?'

Christmas had only become an event for the Carlson siblings in the past half a dozen years. They had grown up in a commune in Byron Bay. They'd had an unusual childhood and traditions had been non-existent. Birthdays, graduations, Christmas, none of those had been considered remarkable or special in any way. No fuss had ever been made about an event, no child had ever been singled out as anything or anyone special, no achievement ever congratulated. It had only been when the four of them had begun to spread their wings and experienced how other families celebrated that they had begun to have more traditional celebrations, and that had included Christmas.

Lily organised Christmas get-togethers now. She had

adopted her husband's traditions with family gathered around the table for lunch followed by a swim at the beach or in the pool in the afternoon. But Otto had been in London last Christmas and Lily had spent the day with her own siblings. Poppy wondered where Otto would be this year.

'I'll be here,' Poppy said. 'I won't have any leave.'

She hadn't discussed Christmas plans with Craig. They'd spent last Christmas in Sydney on a brief visit, which meant it was probably her turn to spend Christmas with his family, but she knew she'd rather spend it with hers. She'd had one Christmas with his family and she'd felt like a fish out of water. It had been strange. Her discomfort hadn't been specifically related to Christmas, she had never felt like a good fit with them. She still felt like an outsider, always hovering on the edges. She knew she was to blame—she didn't want to get too involved. She didn't want to be rejected.

The dinner conversation was robust as they caught up on everything from work to books they'd enjoyed to Jet's love life and training schedule, but as the evening progressed Poppy found she was more interested in the topics that weren't being discussed—no one had mentioned Otto and no one had mentioned Ryder either.

She wondered where Ryder would be for Christmas. Was his move to Sydney permanent? Were his family still in Perth? But she didn't want to bring Ryder's name up in front of her sisters, she didn't want to draw attention to her interest. She knew her sisters would ask probing questions that she wouldn't have the answers to.

As the eldest sibling, Lily was the organiser. She was the writer of lists and the one who made sure they all kept in touch. Lily had a strong protective nature, an inherent desire to look out for her siblings. She would want to know all the details and Poppy wasn't ready to divulge anything just yet. If ever.

Daisy was the dreamer, seemingly content in her own world and, being deaf, it was too easy for her to ignore everyone and everything going on around her. But Daisy was also the romantic in the family and Poppy knew she would start to imagine all sorts of starry-eyed scenarios and Poppy wasn't sure that was where she wanted the conversation to head.

She decided to wait for a chance to speak to Jet alone, he'd be the least likely to wonder about her questions. He wouldn't analyse her comments, he'd take them at face value and answer in his usual straightforward manner with no additional cross-examination.

When Jet offered to do the dishes, Poppy saw her opportunity and volunteered to help.

'I didn't realise Ryder was in Bondi,' she said as she filled the sink with water. 'What's he doing here?' She asked the question that had been on the tip of her tongue all night.

'He's been travelling around Australia on a bit of a gap year.'

'How did he end up working with you? I thought it was pretty competitive to get work at Bondi.' Not to mention requiring a high skill level.

'We're down a couple of lifeguards because of injuries and Easy's been working as a lifeguard at Cottesloe Beach in Perth so the council offered him a casual position to fill the gaps over summer, just until the others are fit again.'

'He's a professional lifeguard?' Poppy knew that the paid lifeguard jobs were coveted. The job was demanding, challenging and rewarding but, in Poppy's opinion, not remunerated adequately given the level of responsibility the lifeguards had and the hours they worked, and she couldn't imagine that anyone would plan on being a lifeguard for ever. She knew there were plenty of lifeguards who had been in the job for years but she, privately, thought they should be aspiring to more. She thought *Ryder* should be aspiring to more but, for once, she kept her opinion to herself, knowing it said more about her than about Ryder.

As Poppy collapsed into bed at the end of a hectic but fabulous day her phone beeped, alerting her to a missed call from Craig. She crawled under the covers and rang him back.

'Hi, sorry I missed your call,' she said, even as she wondered why she was apologising. He was the one who had let her calls go unanswered. But she tried to rein in her irritation. It wasn't like Craig to be uncontactable. He was consistent. Safe. Predictable. He rarely turned his phone off. Doing so was out of character for him and she found it unsettling. 'Is everything okay?'

'Yes, everything's fine. I've just got home from golf.'

'At nine o'clock at night?'

'I stayed for dinner at the club.'

Her irritation rose to the surface again. There were a dozen tasks that that needed to be completed on the house and while some of those things required professional, skilled tradespeople, other jobs could be done by her and Craig. He could have been wielding a paintbrush instead of a golf club today. He could have been returning her calls instead of dining out.

'You didn't start the painting?' She was annoyed now and she could hear the abruptness in her tone but she couldn't temper it.

'No. I don't see much point when there's still work to

be done inside,' he replied. 'The kitchen, the deck, those bifold doors need to be installed. We can get painters in once everything is finished.'

Who was going to pay for that? Poppy wondered. She knew that some of the painting would have to be done by professionals, scaffolding would need to be set up to do the exterior, but they'd agreed that they would tackle some of the internal painting themselves to save money.

All Poppy could see was dollars. She'd been working overtime, taking every extra shift that was offered to her, in order to save the money needed to finish their house. Surely Craig could do his bit rather than take a day off to play golf?

CHAPTER THREE

RYDER SAT IN the lifeguard tower and monitored the beach. He alternated between peering through the binoculars, scanning the beach with his naked eyes and checking the monitors that displayed the feeds from the cameras installed along the promenade, looking for anything untoward.

He was currently volunteering for every available shift. He wanted to be busy, he wanted to keep his *mind* busy. He'd spent far too much time over the past several days thinking about Poppy and wondering how her first shifts had gone, and it was time he focussed on something else.

He hadn't seen her for twelve years and he'd managed to get through each day without thinking about her constantly but now that he had seen her again he couldn't get her out of his head.

It was ridiculous. He was ridiculous. Sitting here like a lovestruck teenager.

After a dozen years she couldn't possibly still be the same girl he'd once known. Once loved. But try telling his heart that. The minute he'd laid eyes on her again he'd been knocked for six. His heart had started racing, leaving him so short of breath he'd felt as if he'd just completed the physically torturous, gruelling life-guard challenge.

But it didn't matter how he felt or what he thought. She was dating another guy. In an adult world that didn't leave room for him.

They could only be friends. He knew they couldn't go back to their teenage years, back to their first kiss, but he couldn't stop himself from wishing for more.

A knock on the tower door brought him out of the past. He jumped up from his seat before anyone else had even moved, eager to answer the call, eager to have something to occupy his time and his mind.

He opened the door to find a couple of teenagers pacing on the threshold. He could tell they had come from the skate park. They weren't wearing boardshorts, they were wearing shoes and shirts with their shorts and were dressed predominantly in black despite the warm weather.

'Hey, boys, what's the problem?'

'Our friend came off his skateboard.'

Bingo.

'He hit his head. He seems pretty bad.'

Attending to incidents on the beach or in the ocean were only part of the lifeguards' duties. As council employees they also responded to incidents in other council areas like the skate park, the roads and footpaths or the area around the Bondi Pavilion building. Because the ambos had to come from the station near the hospital while the lifeguards were on location, on some days they seemed to spend just as much time assisting off the beach as they did on it. Mostly that wasn't an issue, only becoming problematic when there were several incidents at once that took multiple lifeguards away from the beach. Or when one incident required several lifeguards to attend.

Ryder grabbed a kit bag and a radio. 'I've got this one, Gibbo,' he said over his shoulder. 'Can you send someone with the spinal board to back me up?' It would be faster for the larger equipment to follow Ryder but he knew he needed it on hand. The risk of head or spinal injuries was high in the skate bowl.

The skate park was three hundred metres south of the tower, overlooking the beach. Ryder slung the kit bag over his shoulder and set out. The boys kept pace with him as he ran along the promenade.

The skate park was large with several different areas catering for differing levels of abilities. There were grommets on scooters and boards in the gentler areas but no one was skating in the bowl. Ryder looked over the edge and saw several boarders clustered around a prostrate figure on the ground. He stepped over the lip and down into the bowl.

The skate park was baking in the sun. The concrete bowl soaked up the heat and there was no shade to offer any protection. The blue-painted concrete was hot under his bare feet but he knew from experience that he wouldn't notice in a minute.

He slid the first-aid kit from his shoulder and squatted down beside the injured teenager. His eyes were closed. His face was ashen and a sheen of sweat coated his skin.

'What's his name?'

'Connor.'

'Connor, can you hear me? My name's Ryder, I'm a lifeguard, come to check you out.'

Connor opened his eyes. Ryder thought his pupils were a little sluggish to react to the light and the left one appeared slightly more dilated. But at least he was conscious.

Ryder surveyed their surroundings. A skateboard lay by Connor's side but Ryder couldn't see any protective equipment. 'Was he wearing a helmet?' he asked.

'No.'

He held back a sigh, wondering when these kids would learn. He'd seen the tricks they attempted, he'd seen how hard they fell and he'd seen the injuries they'd sustained and he knew they'd seen them too. But so many of them still seemed to think they were invincible. The delusions of youth, he thought. If he had a dollar for every young boy who needed help on the beach or in the skate park he'd be a rich man. Ryder wasn't sure if it was due to a lack of concentration, a lack of judgement, a lack of awareness of the consequences of their actions or just an increased attraction to risky activities, or all of them, but it was almost always the boys getting into strife.

He focussed on his patient. Connor had a suspected head injury and an obvious fracture of his left lower leg. His foot was at an awkward angle and Ryder knew he would be in immense pain. He wouldn't be climbing out of the bowl. But before he could be moved Ryder needed to check for any additional injuries, especially spinal. He radioed for the tower to request an ambulance and started his assessment while he waited for back-up.

'Other than your leg, does it hurt anywhere else?'

'My head.' Connor's voice was faint and Ryder suspected the pain was making him feel sick.

'Can you tell me what day it is?'

'Saturday?'

It was Wednesday. After school.

'Are you allergic to anything?' Ryder asked while

he checked Connor's wrist and neck, looking for any allergy alerts. He wasn't convinced he could take Connor's word for it given his condition but there was no sign of any medic alert necklace or bracelet or anything to indicate he had a pre-existing medical condition.

He opened his kit bag and prepared some pain relief. Getting Connor out of the skate bowl was going to hurt.

He handed him the little green inhaler. 'Breathe through the inhaler, mate. That'll settle the pain a bit before we get you out of here.'

Six or seven breaths would effectively kickstart the pain relief and make it possible to move him without causing too much more discomfort. By the time Gibbo and Dutchy arrived with the spinal board Ryder had satisfied himself that Connor hadn't sustained a spinal injury and the pain relief had begun to work.

'The ambos are on the way,' Dutchy said as he slid down into the bowl.

Ryder nodded in response before giving them a summary of Connor's history. 'We need to splint his leg, stabilise his neck as a precaution and get him out of the bowl and into the shade,' he said in conclusion.

He spoke to Connor. 'How are you feeling now, mate? Is that whistle doing the trick?'

Connor grinned and stuck up one thumb. The pain relief was having the desired effect but Ryder knew the move would still be uncomfortable.

'Good stuff. We're going to stabilise you and carry you out of here ready for the ambos. It'll probably hurt a bit. Just keep hold of that whistle and suck on it when you need to.'

The green whistle was good for about half an hour of pain relief, which would be enough to cover Connor until the paramedics arrived and could give him something stronger if needed.

Ryder and Dutchy wrapped a cervical collar around Connor's neck before sliding a splint made of thick cardboard onto the boy's leg. Ryder added some padding, filling in the gaps, before taping it in position. Once Connor's injuries were suitably protected, they rolled him while Gibbo positioned the stretcher. They secured Connor on the stretcher and lifted him gently. Ryder could hear the sirens of the approaching ambulance as the three lifeguards hoisted their patient carefully out of the bowl. They carried him over the hot pavement to a shady spot where the ambos would have access and laid him on the ground.

The ambulance pulled to a stop beside them. The siren was silenced, although the lights continued to flash. Ryder recognised Alex as he climbed out of the ambulance and went to open the rear doors. Poppy climbed out of the driver's seat and walked towards Ryder.

He couldn't help but notice how good she looked. The uniforms were not usually flattering but hers looked as though it had been custom fitted. Her pants were belted, showing off her narrow waist, and the fabric hugged her hips and thighs and drew his attention to the curve of her bottom. The normally unbecoming uniform did nothing to hide Poppy's sensational figure.

'Hey, what have we got?' she asked as she squatted beside him.

Ryder redirected his gaze and his mind and returned his focus to their patient. 'This is Connor, fifteen-year-old male, who came off second best in a battle with the bowl. He has a fractured left lower leg and he's a bit confused. He wasn't wearing a helmet so he's likely concussed and may possibly have a head injury.'

He was still in a lot of pain, gripping tightly to the green whistle.

Poppy nodded before speaking to Connor. 'Hi, Connor. I'm Poppy, a paramedic. I'm going to have a look at you and then I reckon we'll go for a ride to the hospital.'

'Can you close your eyes for me, Connor? Keep them closed,' she said as he followed her instructions, 'I'll open them for you, one at a time, okay?'

Poppy took a small torch from one of her many pockets and pointed it at Connor's cheek. She lifted one of his eyelids and flicked the torchlight over his eye, watching for a reaction, before repeating the test on the other eye.

She then repeated the tests Ryder had done for a possible spinal injury and once she agreed with his assessment and cleared him of anything serious they transferred him to the ambulance stretcher, still taking care to support his head.

'Do you want to change the splint on his leg?' Ryder asked.

Poppy shook her head. 'No. That seems secure and stable enough. It will just cause more discomfort if we change it. Bondi General is only a few minutes' drive away.'

Ryder watched as Poppy inserted a cannula into the back of Connor's hand, ready for more pain relief if needed, and slipped an oxygen mask over his nose and mouth to help with shock.

'Has his family been notified?' she asked as she and Alex raised the stretcher up on its legs.

'Not yet. I'll speak to his mates and sort that out. I'll get someone to meet him at the hospital.'

Poppy nodded as she loaded Connor into the back of the ambulance. She climbed into the driver's seat and Ryder watched as she drove away.

He returned to work but having seen Poppy he now found it harder than ever to keep his thoughts on track. He smiled. Maybe he was still more like those teenage boys than he wanted to admit. Lacking concentration and easily distracted. He didn't want to think he was attracted to risky activities but what else could he call being fixated on another man's girlfriend? He didn't need his degree in psychology to know it was a mistake. This was a situation that was never going to end well for him.

Poppy threw her sandwich wrapper in the bin and checked her watch. She and Alex were taking a late meal break on Campbell Parade but she had time to duck across to the tower. She knew the lifeguards liked to hear updates on their patients but she also knew it wasn't absolutely necessary and she was using Connor's accident as an excuse to see Ryder.

She knocked on the door.

The lifeguard who opened the door was halfway through pulling his shirt on but even though his face was obscured she knew it was Ryder. She was trained to be observant and after the other day she'd recognise his naked chest and ripped abdominal muscles anywhere. The image was permanently imprinted on her brain. She let go of her disappointment as his shirt covered up her view.

'Hey.' He smiled at her and her stomach fluttered.

'Hi,' she said. 'I was just grabbing something to eat across the road and thought I'd update you on Connor.'

'Any dramas?'

Poppy shook her head. 'Not really. He was lucky. He had a simple fracture of his left tib and fib, as you know, but they also picked up a hairline fracture of his skull. Nothing that he won't make a full recovery from, though, so that's a plus.'

Ryder grinned and said, 'Maybe next time he'll wear a helmet.'

'Maybe. But even if he does you and I both know there will be plenty more just like him. Plenty of kids who take risks. We see it every day.'

'I know. The invincibility of youth. But I don't suppose we can blame them really—we weren't so different. You were pretty wild.' Ryder laughed.

'I blame Jet.' She smiled. 'And you were a part of it, too.'

Life in the commune on the outskirts of Byron Bay had been largely unsupervised. The adults in the commune had professed not to believe in structured learning, firm discipline or strict supervision, and Poppy and Jet along with a band of mischievous childhood friends, including Ryder, had spent their time running wild in the bush, jumping off the rocks into the ocean with their surfboards and generally creating chaos.

Poppy's mother had worked in the general store and had dabbled in natural therapies and healing and her father had run a surf school, but while he had taught the children to surf they had mostly been left to their own devices and, to all intents and purposes, had virtually raised themselves. She hadn't minded as a teenager but as she'd matured she'd wondered if her parents' way of raising a family had been the best. She'd known they'd thought they were free from social norms but she actually would have liked some more attention and had probably needed a few more boundaries.

Lily had been the voice of reason, the one Poppy hadn't wanted to disappoint, the one she'd looked up to, who'd set an example for the rest of them. She often wondered where she would be today if she hadn't had Lily's sensible, calming influence. 'I'm not sure that my childhood should be held up as an example of what is desirable,' she said.

She had been in the thick of things but she hadn't really been a huge risk-taker. She'd only joined in because Ryder had been part of the group. Jumping into the ocean to go surfing had been no hardship, she would have walked over hot coals for him.

'Maybe not, but I think you turned out okay.'

He smiled and she felt the old, familiar sense of connection. The one she had only ever felt with him. It was strange that after almost a dozen years she still had the sense that they were close. The sense that he knew her, that he truly understood her.

He was leaning against the doorjamb, close enough to touch. She wanted to touch him. She wanted to slide her hand under his shirt and place her palm over his heart. She wanted to feel his skin under hers.

She clenched her hand into a fist at her side to stop herself from doing anything unwise. Maybe they could still be friends but she knew she couldn't hope for anything more.

To her right she saw Bluey jogging up the stairs from the beach. As Ryder moved to give him room to enter the tower, he stepped towards her and she caught her breath as his movement brought him even further into her space. His leg brushed against her hip and she waited for him to move away once Bluey had passed by, but he stayed in the doorway, connected to her.

She could smell him now. He smelt like the ocean,

salty and warm, and she realised he must have been into the sea since she'd seen him earlier in the afternoon.

She inhaled his scent as she tilted her head and looked up into his blue eyes.

He was watching her, his gaze intense.

All she had to do was reach for him.

She wanted to pull his head towards hers, pull his mouth to hers, press her lips against his and kiss him again. Like she'd done twelve years before.

But she couldn't.

Those days were gone.

They could only be friends.

She knew once upon a time she'd wanted more but they had both moved on.

She took a step back, a half-step really, just enough to break their physical connection, enough to break the spell he seemed to have cast over her, enough to let her breathe again.

'Have you got plans for tonight?' he asked. 'Do you want to grab a bite to eat?'

Her heart leapt before she remembered that she did have plans. Disappointment flooded through her. 'I can't. Daisy and I are going to see a movie at the Italian film festival.' Foreign films were Daisy's favourite, the subtitles made them the perfect choice for her. Poppy wondered briefly if he'd like to come with them but she didn't want to extend the invitation without checking with Daisy first.

'How about some time over the weekend, then?'

She shook her head. 'That's no good either. Craig is coming to town, we're looking at properties to rent.' As was her way, if she wasn't working, she had filled any gaps in her schedule with other activities. She liked to be busy and with Craig coming to Sydney as well she had no spare time. But she hoped he wouldn't think she was avoiding him. She wanted to make sure they kept or rekindled their friendship. He was still important to her. 'Can I take a rain check?'

Poppy and Daisy lay on their surfboards and let Backpackers' Rip carry them out past the breaking waves. The rip might create problems for unsuspecting swimmers and cause no end of headaches for the Bondi lifeguards but for the surfers it acted as a highway, carrying them out to sea and letting them save their energy. Using the power of the water meant there was no need to paddle hard to get out the back.

The Carlson siblings had surfed all their lives. Growing up in Byron Bay and having a father who was a surf instructor and ex-professional surfer had meant they had been put on boards almost the moment they could stand. Poppy hadn't surfed for almost a year, since the last time she'd been to Bondi. She hadn't even brought her board down with her on this trip but had borrowed one from Lily.

Lily hadn't used her board for months either and had declined to come with them today. Poppy was enjoying surfing with Daisy but next time she'd insist that Lily come too. There was no better way to free your mind than to paddle out into the ocean, thinking only about what the water was doing, about the next wave. The freedom of riding a wave into shore was exhilarating and Poppy was pretty sure Lily could use some time to clear her head. It was like riding a bike—she wouldn't have lost her skills, she just needed to commit the time.

Poppy needed to clear her mind too. She was irritated and she knew the ocean would help to calm her down. She had spent hours over the past couple of weeks looking at potential rental properties in anticipation of Craig's visit. She had lined up three properties to view only to find out—when she'd called him to check his flight details—that he'd cancelled his trip to Sydney for the weekend as he was snowed under at work.

Subsequently, she'd cancelled the appointments to view two of the potential rentals in Surry Hills, which was Craig's preferred suburb. She wasn't prepared to waste her time looking at properties she didn't want to live in. She justified the cancellations by telling herself that Craig was fussy and the rental property market was competitive. She knew the agent would want to meet both of them and that the properties were likely to be snapped up before Craig got to Sydney.

Poppy wanted to live near Bondi—she was the one who would be coming and going in the dark. She wanted to be close to work and near the beach, whereas Craig wanted to be closer to the city. He didn't want to tackle the rush-hour commute but given that he usually worked from eight in the morning until six she figured he'd miss the heaviest traffic. She'd gone alone to look at the one property she'd earmarked in Bondi but it was small and gloomy, a bit depressing really, and she'd reluctantly crossed it off her list.

Now, as she sat on her board out beyond the break, waiting for her turn on a wave, she tried to quash her irritation at Craig and her wasted afternoon. She wasn't annoyed about not seeing Craig but she was annoyed by the inconvenience and the time she'd wasted. What sort of person did that make her? That she wasn't upset about not seeing her boyfriend? What was wrong with her?

She knew exactly what was wrong.

Ryder.

She couldn't get him out of her head.

She wasn't missing Craig and she wasn't desperate to see him, they didn't have that sort of relationship. She didn't depend on him emotionally and she knew he didn't depend on her. Which was how she liked it. She didn't want to rely on Craig for love and affection. She could get hurt that way.

But she'd barely even thought about Craig over the past few days, she'd been too busy thinking about Ryder. And sex. Which was another unfamiliar pastime for her. Sex wasn't high on her list of priorities. Sure, she felt the need for it occasionally but since seeing Ryder again she'd found herself thinking about it constantly. Thinking about being in his arms, touching him, making love to him.

Her hormones had gone into overdrive—just like when she'd first fallen for him as a teenager.

Ryder was an idea that had remained trapped in the depths of her psyche. She had relegated him to her past and closed that part of herself off, the part that had loved him. She hadn't wanted to love again, it was too painful, but seeing him again had awoken those memories with a vengeance.

He was an itch that had never been scratched.

But she knew it was more than that. Something about him still made her heart sing. She felt a sense of anticipation and excitement when he was near. He still fascinated her. She needed to be careful.

The light was beginning to fade as the day drifted towards dusk and the last of the beachgoers started to make their way home. There were a few other surfers in the water but not many swimmers. The day had been overcast and a storm was threatening. Thunder rumbled in the distance. The storm was getting closer and Poppy knew they'd have to call it a day before the weather turned nasty. The ocean was not an ideal spot to be in an electrical storm.

Daisy was on her board beside her and she turned her head as a burst of lightning lit up the sky to the north. Daisy wouldn't have heard the thunder but the bright flash of light was enough to catch her attention.

Surfers around them began to catch waves in to the beach as another lightning bolt crackled to their right. It was close. Poppy signalled to Daisy that they should follow suit as a thunderclap crashed overhead. A set was rolling in and they waited their turn before catching a wave behind another pair of surfers.

Poppy could feel the static electricity in the air as they hit the shore and she had just picked her board up out of the water when lightning flashed in front of her. It was so bright she turned her head to block the light. She heard the damp sand sizzle where one fork of lightning struck the beach and the ground trembled beneath her feet.

A second fork arced between the sky and the earth but this one didn't reach the sand. Poppy watched in horror as it hit one of the men who had surfed in on the wave before Daisy and her. He was still in the shallow water and the strike knocked him off his feet and threw him through the air.

He landed on his back, facing the sky.

Poppy and Daisy ripped off their leg ropes, dropped their boards and sprinted towards the man.

The man's wetsuit had a hole just below his right shoulder, a couple of inches in from his armpit, and Poppy knew that was the point of contact. His eyes were closed and he wasn't breathing.

The smell of burnt flesh made bile rise up in her throat.

She crouched down beside him and put her fingers on his wrist, searching for a pulse. Nothing.

The man was lying on damp sand, surrounded by a few centimetres of water. Poppy knew the tide was turning and the air was still charged with electricity. She didn't want to administer first aid in the water during a thunderstorm. His mate was beside him, sitting completely still, doing nothing, obviously in shock, looking dazedly from Poppy and Daisy back to the unconscious surfer.

'Grab him under his arms,' she said to his mate, 'We need to drag him out of the water.'

She grabbed the man's feet and they pulled him out of the shallows and moved him higher up the beach onto drier sand.

'What's his name?' she asked as they'd got him to semi-safety and she knelt again in the sand.

'Scotty.' The man still looked dazed but at least he was able to respond to her questions and instructions. 'He's my brother. Is he going to be okay?'

'I don't know,' she said. There was no way of sugarcoating the facts. She held Scotty's wrist and felt again for a pulse as she watched for any slight rise and fall of his chest to indicate that he was breathing. 'Do you know how to do CPR?' she asked the patient's brother.

'Kind of.'

'I'm a paramedic. Follow my instructions and we'll do our best until the lifeguards get here, okay?'

Scotty still wasn't breathing. Out of habit she shook his shoulder gently to see if she could rouse him. 'Scotty? Can you hear me?'

There was no sign of life.

Daisy was kneeling next to Poppy. She opened Scotty's mouth and checked that his tongue wasn't blocking his airway. She gripped him under the chin.

'I need you to do the breaths for me,' she told the man. Daisy was a nurse, trained in CPR, but she didn't want to expose Daisy to any risk. If Scotty's brother was competent with the breaths, that was Poppy's preferred option. She would do the compressions—they were the most important thing at this stage. 'Hold his head back like Daisy is doing and breathe for him when I tell you,' she said.

The man nodded and Poppy signed instructions to Daisy, telling her to make sure the lifeguards were on their way, as she started chest compressions. 'I'll count to thirty and then stop while you give two breaths, okay?'

She'd started on the third round of compressions before she heard the lifeguard buggy pull up beside them. It felt like ten minutes, not one.

She turned her head and saw Ryder and Dutchy jump out of the buggy. She didn't think she'd ever been as pleased to see Ryder.

'Lightning strike,' she told them she continued counting in her head. 'We're going to need the defib.'

Ryder nodded and turned back to lift the defibrillator bag from the buggy as Dutchy dropped the kit bag in the sand and pulled a pair of scissors from it. Poppy sat back on the count of thirty and instructed Scotty's brother to give two breaths as Dutchy quickly cut open a flap in the front of Scotty's wetsuit, running the scissors down from one armpit, then across the chest and down the other side. He peeled back the front of the wetsuit and Poppy immediately resumed compressions. She was aware of Ryder preparing the defibrillator but she had no time to watch him. She trusted him to do his job as he would have to trust her to do hers.

Ryder knelt opposite her. He had a towel in his hand and wiped it over Scotty's chest, drying it off before attaching the sticky pads for the defibrillator. His presence was reassuring. He worked calmly and quickly. He knew what he was doing. Like all the lifeguards, he was well trained in the routine of pre-hospital care.

The defib charged and Poppy sat back, following the instructions from the mechanical voice. They all waited while the machine analysed the heart rhythm and then directed Ryder to apply a shock.

Scotty lifted off the ground as the machine delivered a charge, trying to shock his heart out of fibrillation and restore its normal rhythm.

They waited but there was no change.

'Continue CPR,' the machine instructed.

'Do you want me to swap places with you?' Ryder asked.

She lifted her head and looked into his eyes. She shook her head. 'I'm okay for another couple of rounds.' She was used to performing CPR. She resumed compressions while Dutchy fitted a face mask over Scotty's nose and mouth. A silicone bulb was attached to the mask, Dutchy would be able to take over from Scotty's brother and squeeze air into Scotty's lungs.

'Analysing rhythm.'

The defibrillator instructed them to stand clear.

'Delivering shock.'

Another jolt. But still no change. Poppy continued with a fifth round of compressions.

'The colour in his face is getting better,' Daisy said.

Poppy agreed. Even in the grey and overcast afternoon light she thought she could see some colour returning.

'Analysing rhythm.'

The defibrillator deliberated a possible third shock. The verdict came back.

'No shock advised. Check pulse.'

Poppy completed her compressions while Ryder checked for a pulse. 'I've got something!'

Dutchy still held the mask over Scotty's face but before he could give any more rescue breaths Scotty lifted a hand and pushed Dutchy away.

'We've got him!'

Poppy couldn't believe it as Scotty coughed and his eyelids fluttered.

Daisy had the oxygen mask ready. Dutchy swapped the face mask for the smaller oxygen mask and looped the elastic behind Scotty's head.

'Come up here, where he can see you,' Poppy directed his brother, who was kneeling down by Scotty's feet. She knew Scotty would be disoriented and thought he'd respond better if he could see a familiar face amongst the crowd of strangers.

She spoke quietly to Scotty as his brother moved into view. 'You're on Bondi Beach. You were struck by lightning. We resuscitated you and now we're going to take you to hospital.'

Poppy, Ryder, Dutchy and Daisy rolled Scotty onto the stretcher and with Scotty's brother's help lifted him onto the back of the lifeguard buggy. Poppy sat with Scotty as Ryder and Dutchy quickly threw their bags into the buggy. Ryder climbed in the back next to Poppy and helped her stabilise the stretcher as Dutchy drove them all back to the tower.

Adrenalin coursed through her. Was it due to the incident that had just taken place or because Ryder was sitting beside her? She wasn't sure.

Her paramedic's uniform gave her confidence but even without it she knew she'd done a good job and thanks to all their efforts, and the defibrillator, it was a good outcome for Scotty, but she still felt shaky and she suspected it was because of Ryder's proximity. She wanted to lean against him, lean on him, but she couldn't do it.

The ambulance was parked on the promenade, lights flashing, by the time they reached the steps to the tower.

Ryder reached for her hand to help her down from the buggy so they could offload Scotty. Even though she didn't really need his assistance, her body ached to touch him so she took the hand he offered her. His grip was gentle and warm and Poppy didn't want to let go but they needed to look after Scotty.

Alex was on duty and he came down the stairs and met them on the sand. Poppy briefed him while they transferred Scotty over, carrying him up to the promenade and loading him into the ambulance while his brother watched, still clearly dazed.

Poppy put her hand on his shoulder. 'Go with him,' she said.

Ryder added, 'We'll collect your boards and you can pick them up from here tomorrow.'

Poppy and Daisy were both shivering as the ambulance departed.

'You need to get warmed up,' Ryder said.

'I'll take the buggy and pick up the boards while I bring the flags and signs in,' Dutchy offered. The light was fading fast now and the beach had emptied of swimmers and people who had stayed to watch the drama unfolding, leaving just the lifeguards, Poppy and Daisy.

'Come on,' Ryder said as he opened the door to the tower. 'I'll put the kettle on. Are you okay?'

Poppy and Daisy both nodded. Neither of them were strangers when it came to emergencies, but a cup of tea was still welcome.

'Do you need to use the phone?' he asked Poppy as he filled the kettle.

'What for?'

'I thought you might want to let Craig know where you are. That you've been held up.'

Poppy shook her head. 'He didn't come down to Sydney in the end.' She had wondered whether or not she should tell Ryder that her plans had changed but had decided not to. Now she couldn't remember why she'd come to that decision. Had she thought going out to dinner with him might have been tempting fate? 'He got held up at work,' she explained.

'That's too bad,' he said without any trace of regret in his voice. 'Have you got plans for dinner? I could take you both out—as a thank you for doing my job for me?'

'I'm going out with friends from the hospital,' Daisy told him.

'I don't have plans,' Poppy said. Craig's cancellation had left her at a loose end.

Ryder grinned. 'How does Chinese and a couple of beers sound?' He paused, his brow furrowed as he asked, 'Do you drink beer?'

'I do.'

It was odd. She felt like she knew him so well still but the reality was that, after twelve years, they were strangers. But it didn't feel that way.

CHAPTER FOUR

POPPY WASHED AND dried her hair, letting it curl naturally over her shoulders. She had agonised over what to wear and in the end settled on black jeans, a black shirt and a scarf with a geometric print with traces of green. She knew the green highlighted the colour of her eyes and she hadn't been able to resist adding it in a slight touch of vanity, even though she knew she wasn't going on a date. She was simply having dinner with an old friend.

But old friends didn't normally make her feel giddy and excited.

She wasn't convinced it was a good idea to have dinner for two, not considering the way he still made her feel, but she wasn't going to cancel. She knew she shouldn't be so eager given she was irritated with Craig, but she knew her feelings for Ryder were bordering on dangerous. But maybe she was looking at Ryder through rose-coloured glasses. Perhaps catching up with him over dinner would give her a chance to make some new memories, let go of her embarrassment from years gone by and settle her nerves, she thought as she drove back to the Bondi lifeguard tower to meet him.

He'd showered and changed and was also casually dressed in jeans and a T-shirt. That was good, he wasn't dressed for a date, but unfortunately the T-shirt sculpted his chest and arms and showed off his new muscles. That wasn't helpful.

Now that their emergency was over she had time to look at him more closely and she couldn't resist.

His thick hair was still slightly damp and his square jaw was darkened by a five o'clock shadow. The muscles and the stubble were new. He had matured. He was a man now, no longer a boy. Definitely not a boy and she was very aware of him.

'If you don't mind where we eat, I thought I'd try an Asian restaurant that Dutchy recommended in Bondi Junction.'

He jumped into her car and directed her to the restaurant. Her car wasn't small but it suddenly felt that way. The thunderstorm had passed but she could still feel electricity humming in the air and she knew it was her reaction to Ryder. He looked good and smelt even better.

She forced herself to focus on her driving and pulled into a park. Once she got out of the car her head cleared a little. A bit of distance eased her tension. She couldn't think straight when he was sitting so close.

The restaurant, Lao Lao's Kitchen, was small and busy and the scent of garlic and chilli competed with Ryder's scent. The tables were tightly packed but they found a small, empty one against a wall.

A young girl greeted them as she brought the menu. Her dark hair was tied in two pigtails that stuck out from the side of her head and she was missing two front teeth. She was very cute and Poppy guessed her to be about seven or eight years old. She must be the daughter of the owners.

'My grandpa will come and take your order,' she said as she put the menus on the table.

Poppy revised her assessment. Granddaughter of the owners probably.

'Thank you,' Poppy said to the girl as she poured water into their glasses.

She smiled at Poppy and Poppy felt a jolt of familiarity. As if she'd met the girl before. 'What is your name?' Poppy asked before the girl could leave, even though she couldn't possibly know her.

'An Na.'

Ryder pulled his chair into the table as the girl walked away. His knees banged into Poppy's, sending a bolt of electricity through her and stirring up the familiar feelings of desire once more.

She kept her eyes down, studying the menu as if her life depended on it. She couldn't look at him, he'd always been able to tell what she was thinking and she did not want him to read her mind right now.

She found herself unusually tongue-tied. She was normally quite opinionated and vocal, perhaps it had been a mistake coming to dinner *à deux*. She should have given more consideration to how he made her feel. She'd been telling herself they could rekindle their friendship but when she sat opposite him, close enough to see the different shades of blue in his eyes, close enough to feel his breath of the back of her hands, she couldn't deny that she was still attracted to him.

The attraction hadn't diminished after all those years and she found it disconcerting. Acknowledging her feelings, even silently, made her feel vulnerable, which added to her sense of unease.

But feeling attracted to Ryder was okay, she reassured herself as an elderly gentleman came to take their order. She didn't have to talk about it and she definitely didn't intend to act on it.

'Do you know what you'd like?' their waiter asked.

The menu had been a blur before her eyes, she'd been looking at it but hadn't been able to focus or concentrate. 'I'm happy with anything,' she said.

'Chef's choice?' Ryder asked.

'Sure.'

'Why don't you bring us a few of the chef's favourites?' Ryder requested. 'Maybe three small and a couple of larger dishes for us to share, and two beers. Thanks.'

'So, catch me up on the last twelve years,' he said as the waiter left the two of them alone.

Poppy laughed. 'That will take all night.'

'Sounds like you've got a lot to tell me.' He was smiling. 'Luckily I have plenty of time. There's nowhere else I need to be.'

He sat back in his chair and looked at her like he'd looked at her on the day she'd kissed him and she knew for certain that there was nowhere else she *wanted* to be.

'It feels strange,' she said.

'What does? Being here with me?'

'No.' That felt surprisingly good. Normal. Like old times. And that was what was so strange. That she should so easily slip back into their relationship. His company was easy. She knew that wasn't how he'd got his nickname, which came from a movie, but it suited his personality perfectly. At least in her opinion. 'I feel like it's only been weeks, months since I've seen you but it's really been almost half my life, yet I feel like you should still know everything that's happened.'

'So tell me. Get me up to speed and it will seem like the old days,' he said, and, once again his words accurately reflected her thoughts. 'You left Byron as soon as you finished school and headed to Brisbane?'

Poppy nodded.

'And became a paramedic? I thought medicine was high on your list, like Lily?'

'I realised I wasn't cut out for years of studying and ultimately I didn't want to be cooped up in a hospital or clinic. I wanted to help people but I also wanted to be amongst the action. Paramedic seemed a better fit. No two days are the same.'

She'd also worked out that she would be able to hide behind the uniform. She wouldn't need to form relationships with patients. Most of them she would only deal with once. That suited her perfectly. She wouldn't get attached to them and they wouldn't become too familiar, dependent or attached to her either. She wasn't good at close relationships, she preferred to keep her distance, and being a paramedic allowed her to do that.

'Have you been in Brisbane ever since?'

She shook her head. 'No. After I graduated from uni I worked in Brisbane for a couple of years and then I went to London. There were good jobs there for paramedics and I thought I wanted adventure.'

'You thought you did?'

She smiled. 'Turns out when I left Byron I was looking for a change, not adventure. When I moved to Brisbane it gave me a chance to find out who I was. You know what it was like in the commune,' she said. Ryder had spent countless hours with Poppy and Jet in the surf and at the commune and Poppy knew he would remember the dynamics.

'Us kids were seen and treated as one entity, by everyone really, the members of the commune and the public. If I wasn't seen as one of the commune kids I was seen as just another one of the Carlson tribe. I needed to find my own identity. Once I graduated and got some experience I wanted to push myself a bit more, test myself a bit more, so I went to London. It was fun for a while, for a summer, but I missed the sky and the sun and the weather and my siblings. I wanted a place to call home. I needed a place to call home and London wasn't it. So I came back.'

Her goal as a teenager had been to escape the commune as quickly as possible and it had taken her a while to figure out that the change she'd been looking for was security and stability, not adventure.

'And you met Craig in Brisbane?'

Poppy shook her head. 'We met in the UK. I travelled to the other side of the world and ended up meeting someone from Brisbane. I was really homesick; he was coming home and I decided to come back with him. It felt like it was meant to be.'

'It's serious with him? You're happy?'

Poppy hesitated. 'I think so.' It wasn't about being happy with Craig but how did she explain that without making herself sound weird. In her mind she was responsible for her own happiness. Her relationship with Craig was about achieving other goals. Her twin goals of security and stability.

'That doesn't sound very convincing. What's wrong? Are you unhappy in Sydney? Are you missing Craig?'

'Not really.' She had been finding herself more annoyed with him over the past couple of weeks. She didn't feel like she was a priority for him and considering everything she was giving up to make this move she found herself irritated. 'I just need a bit of time to adjust to the move.'

'It wasn't your idea?'

'No. Craig got promoted at work and the promotion meant a move to Sydney.'

'So you're following someone else's plan? That doesn't sound like you.'

He was right. She'd always set goals and timelines for herself and there had always been something she'd been working towards. Her current plan was to own her house. She imagined that having a place to call her own would provide her with the security and stability she needed and she was on her way to achieving her goal—admittedly with Craig's help—but now she'd let Craig change her plans and uproot her from her house. Was that why she was feeling unsettled? Because she was following Craig's plan? She was here in Sydney and where was he? Still in Brisbane.

Her plans had been derailed by Craig and somehow Ryder had spotted the problem.

'You didn't want to move here?' Ryder asked when Poppy hadn't verbalised her thoughts.

'I was happy to move...' She'd been happy to make the move to Sydney because it meant she and Craig could maintain the status quo of their relationship. Moving together meant they hadn't needed to have a conversation about their relationship and where it was headed, and Poppy was always happy to avoid conversations that focussed on her feelings. It had been far easier to agree to the move except now she was here and he wasn't. If it hadn't been for her siblings—and Ryder, added the little voice in her head—she would be even more annoyed.

'But?'

'But the plan was that we move together but now I'm here and he's still in my house in Brisbane.'

'You have a house there?'

'Well, we do. Craig and I bought it together. I miss my house,' she admitted, choosing not to outline that she missed the house more than she missed Craig. She and Craig hadn't discussed how long the move to Sydney would be for but Poppy knew she had never imagined leaving her home permanently.

'You miss your house!' The surprise was evident in Ryder's voice. 'It's just a building.'

She shook her head. 'It's more than that. It's my sanctuary. Growing up in the commune, we never had any privacy and then I lived in a university college and that was the same. I want somewhere that is mine, somewhere that reflects me.' She knew that Ryder was one of the few people she knew, one of the *only* people she knew, who would understand her logic.

'And does it reflect you?'

'It needs a lot of work.' She laughed. 'It needs time and love and money. It might reflect me more than I realised.'

'So you're going to keep it? You're not planning on selling it?'

'No!' She had spent endless hours working on their house and working additional shifts to pay for it. The house was a labour of love and she hadn't contemplated selling it. She *wouldn't* contemplate that. 'I have put my heart and soul into that house. I'll get the renovations finished and then we'll have to rent it out but I'm not going to sell it.' She knew that wasn't the agreement she and Craig had made but she still hoped to be able to change his mind.

'And Craig. Does he love it as much as you do?'

'He's not as attached to it as I am,' she admitted. 'He sees it as a good investment. He's an accountant,' she added by way of explanation.

'I'm sure you'll be able to convince him to keep it if it means that much to you.'

She wasn't so certain.

'A man in love will do anything,' Ryder added.

'I don't think that's the case.'

'Really? It is in my experience.'

Poppy hadn't been disagreeing with Ryder's opinion but rather with the idea that Craig loved her. 'Have you been in love?' she asked.

He nodded. 'Twice.'

'Twice!' She wondered about the type of women Ryder had loved. What did he look for?

'What about you?'

'Once,' she said. 'And I got my heart broken. I don't want to feel like that again.' She had never forgotten the pain of her first heartbreak. Losing Ryder had had long-lasting repercussions on her impressionable teenage heart.

'So you're not in love now? You're not in love with Craig?'

'We're compatible.'

'That's not what I asked.'

'We have similar goals.'

'That doesn't sound very romantic.'

'Romance isn't a high priority.' She still wasn't sure what she expected from a relationship but she knew she wasn't in love with Craig. And she didn't want to be. Love was fickle. Love led to heartbreak.

'But it should be,' he said. 'You should be spoiled, adored, loved. Life is too short to miss out on all those things.'

Coming from Ryder's lips, those words sounded wonderful but Poppy couldn't imagine they applied to her. In her world love wasn't reciprocated. She'd never felt adored by her parents and Ryder had left before she'd ever had a chance to find out what might happen. And surely their teenage love wouldn't have lasted.

She was unlovable and it was better not to expect too much. It was better not to dream of love.

'Tell me. How does Craig make you feel?'

Ryder always used to ask how she was feeling. Was she okay? Was she happy? Was she sad? Craig never asked. And she didn't want him to. She didn't want to discuss her feelings.

She didn't want to feel.

She didn't want to hurt.

'Does he make you feel like you can't live without him?' Ryder asked her. 'Does he make you feel excited? Like the world is a better place, a brighter, more positive place?'

'Is that how love feels?'

He had just described exactly how she had felt as a teenager.

He nodded. 'You remember what it was like,' he said.

Was he reading her mind again? 'What *what* was like?' she asked, even though she was afraid of what his answer would be.

'How it felt to be seventeen. Or, in your case, sixteen.'

Poppy swallowed. She remembered every minute detail. How Ryder had tasted. How he'd felt. How her breath had caught in her throat. How her pulse had raced. How her heart had broken.

He held her captive with his gaze as he said, 'You remember that sense of excitement, of anticipation. Like nothing else in the world mattered. That first amazing teenage kiss.'

Poppy nodded. She remembered that kiss like it was yesterday. 'I thought you'd forgotten all about that. It was so long ago.'

'No,' he said, shaking his head. 'I've never forgotten. That was the best and worst day of my young life. Finding out we were leaving Byron Bay and then getting kissed by you. Mind you, the best and worst wasn't in that order,' he said with a smile.

'And then I never heard from you again,' she accused.

'I know. I'm sorry, I had no idea what to say.'

'I thought about coming to find you,' Poppy said. She'd been upset when he'd left but also envious that he'd managed to escape. She couldn't wait to get out of Byron. She'd thought she was destined for bigger and better things but, in hindsight, it hadn't been all bad. But once Ryder had left her life had felt drained of colour and she had fantasised about running away to be with him. By the end of the following year, when she'd finished high school and had been accepted into university in Brisbane, she had put him to the back of her mind.

'Why didn't you?'

She shrugged. 'It was just a teenage fantasy. I felt that you understood me in a way no one else did, especially my parents, and when you left I felt like I'd lost someone really important, but running away wasn't very realistic. I knew I had to finish school.'

'You stuck to your plan.'

'I guess I did. When I didn't hear from you, I realised how foolish the idea of running away was and getting an education and using that to get out of Byron seemed a bit more sensible. I guess I grew up.' And forgot about falling in love. She had seen from Lily's example that studying hard was the way to get out of Byron.

Despite the fact that she was being forced to remember those foolish teenage days and emotions, she was enjoying Ryder's company. Even if she didn't want to talk about her feelings he was happy to listen to her talk about her plans. He always had been and she had lapped up his attention. He had made her feel that her ideas were worth something. That they were important. That *she* was important.

'Have you been back to Byron recently?' Ryder asked. 'How are your mum and dad?'

'They're well, I guess.'

'You guess? You haven't seen them?'

'Not for a while,' she admitted. Some people might argue that a year was longer than 'a while' but Poppy was never in a hurry to return to Byron Bay. She accepted it was a beautiful place but she was quite happy to leave it to the hordes of tourists who flocked to the district.

'You must have driven through Byron on your way here. You didn't stop?'

'It wasn't the right spot to stop. I wanted to get closer to Sydney before I broke the journey.' Byron was only a two-hour drive from Brisbane on the direct route to Sydney but she'd deliberately driven for an extra hour before stretching her legs. 'They wouldn't have cared if I stopped or not. You know we're not close.' She shrugged. That was why she'd kept on driving. The reception she would have received would not have been the one she'd hoped for and so she'd decided it was better to keep driving and avoid the disappointment.

She knew she should get over herself. Plenty of people had grown up in worse environments than she had and she was fortunate to have her siblings, but it didn't change the fact that she had never felt valued or loved by her own parents.

Growing up in the commune, parenting had been a collective responsibility. Her father, Pete, had spent time with them in the surf but that had usually been a group activity with numerous children, not just the Carlson siblings. There had been very little time spent alone as a family unit. There had always been other people around and Poppy didn't feel she'd ever formed a close bond with either of her parents.

Neither of them were demonstrative or overly affectionate, her mother in particular, and Poppy often wondered if she had even wanted kids. She knew Goldie had fallen pregnant unexpectedly with Lily when she'd only been nineteen but she'd gone on to have four more children. Surely they hadn't all been mistakes?

'They're still your parents,' Ryder interrupted her thoughts.

'Don't judge me,' she said. Ryder might be a good listener but she did *not* want to talk about her parents. 'Why don't we talk about your family for a bit? They're not nearly as crazy as mine.'

'Maybe not as extraordinary as yours but we've had our fair share of drama and dysfunction, although thankfully we seem to be coming out the other side now.'

Poppy couldn't imagine Ryder creating drama. He'd always been her stabilising influence. Sure, he'd joined in on their wild, youthful escapades but he was far from dysfunctional. From her perspective he'd had a perfectly normal family.

'What drama did you have?'

'Aside from my dad's affair with a colleague, you mean?'

'Aside from that.' People had affairs all the time and while she disagreed with it in principle it was hardly unusual and, in her mind, it didn't make his family any more dysfunctional than many others. Particularly when compared to hers.

Ryder hadn't spoken to his father in years. His dad's affair had been the reason his mother had dragged him and his sister across the country to Perth. Ryder's parents had been teachers and they'd taught at the same school. Their marriage had broken down when his father had had an affair with another teacher and his mother had taken the children and left. Ryder blamed his father not only for breaking his mother's heart but for having the affair that had forced their move to Western Australia. The move that had ripped him away from Poppy.

'We lived with my grandmother when we first got to Perth, Mum's mum, but that didn't go so well. Mum was pretty fragile and I think she was hoping for some emotional support but my grandmother was more in favour of the "put on a brave face and get on with things" approach. Mum just seemed to give up. She spent a lot of time in her room, which didn't help Lucy. Lucy was only young and she needed her mother. Things were a bit of a mess for a while.'

That was an understatement but he didn't want to go into specifics tonight. It wasn't a cheerful subject. His mother had started drinking and his sister had stopped eating. It had been a cry for help but he hadn't recognised it at the time and he had blamed himself for some of his sister's suffering. For a long time he'd felt there was more he could have, should have, done. He'd felt like he failed both his mother and his sister. He'd tried to give them what they'd needed but he hadn't been able to. What they'd needed most had been his father and he'd let them all down.

'They're both doing better now,' he said. 'Mum has a new partner, he's a nice guy, and Lucy has turned the corner. That's why I could embark on my road trip.'

Steve was a good addition to their family and knowing his mum and his sister had someone to watch over them helped Ryder sleep at night.

'Are you running away from home?' Poppy teased.

'No.' A part of him wished he could stay in Bondi but that hadn't been his plan and he knew he was only thinking of it now because of Poppy. But it wasn't really on his agenda. 'I'll be going back. They still need me.'

'And what about what you need?' she asked. 'What about your hopes and dreams and plans? What do you want?'

He wanted Poppy.

Seeing her again had made him realise that he'd never truly got over her. It was crazy to think those old feelings were still there, as all-consuming as ever. He wondered if he should tell her but decided against it. What was the point? It was likely to make one of them feel uncomfortable and it was irrelevant now anyway—as long as she was in a relationship, she was off limits.

He wished he could be happy for her but in his opinion it didn't sound as though she had found the perfect guy. She should have romance and love. She might want security—who didn't?—but he suspected she still had more of her parents' free spirit in her than she cared to admit. And she needed to be given a chance to soar. He didn't think she should be constrained by finances and budgets. She had always had plans but that had been to escape Byron Bay. He'd thought she'd travel, see the world. Perhaps her idea of escape was different from his.

Despite that, he could understand her desire for a home to call her own. The commune had been chaotic but he had loved it. It had been a happy environment, although he could see how it might have been overwhelming if it was your home, but he'd never pictured her choosing to live in a city. He'd thought she'd feel stifled. She needed freedom. The surf. The sun. She was bound to the earth and the ocean and the sky.

But twelve years was a long time and the Poppy he'd known had changed. She'd grown up, taken on responsibility. He could understand her need for stability but he wondered whether the old Poppy was still in there somewhere. The one who'd run wild in the bush and surfed off the rocks.

He hoped so.

Ryder watched the ocean, double-checking every woman with blonde hair, wondering if he would see Poppy. He had tried to forget her, he had tried not to compare all other women to her, but after dinner last night he was finding it impossible not to think about her. Their connection had been special and he felt it still. It wasn't just because of shared history, it went deeper than that, yet he couldn't explain why he should feel this connection with her and only her. He didn't believe in soul mates. At least, not until he was around her.

His kept his mind on Poppy but his eyes on the sea. The ocean was calm for the moment but the day was warm and he knew people had a tendency to get complacent when the water was flat. It wasn't as threatening but the water was just as deep and the tides could still take you out of your depth or wash you off a sand bar. You could drown just as easily on a calm day if you weren't a confident swimmer.

Ryder felt like the ocean. One minute he'd been calm, rolling towards a life in Perth and a new career, when suddenly the wind had blown in and brought change. Seeing Poppy again made him rethink his vague plans.

He was flexible and returning to Perth was optional. He could go wherever his career, his life or love took him.

What if Poppy was still his perfect woman? Twelve years ago he'd thought that she was the one but teenage hormones didn't translate into everlasting love—did they?

He needed to find out who she had become. It sounded like she was focussed, she still had her goals set. That was the Poppy he'd known—full of plans. But her plans now were about security and stability. Her plans were all financial. What had happened to the Poppy who'd been eager to escape Byron Bay? What had happened to the Poppy who had planned to conquer the world? Who'd had such a zest for life? For living? What did she dream about? Was she happy?

Was Craig the love of her life?

It didn't sound like that to Ryder but what did he know? He'd been spectacularly unlucky in love.

Maybe Craig was exactly what Poppy wanted. What she needed.

She'd bought a house with Craig—that was a serious step, more serious than just living together in a rental. It smacked of something more permanent. She hadn't exactly been singing his praises but perhaps she'd just been trying to spare Ryder's feelings?

She wanted security and stability and Craig was giving her that.

Ryder knew he couldn't compete. Not at the moment. How was a mature age student, waiting to get his career started and who worked as a casual lifeguard with nothing to his name, going to be able to provide her with the things she wanted?

But what if Poppy was supposed to be with him? What if she was the one? Still the one.

But he was jumping ahead of himself. Way ahead. Indulging in his fantasies. He still had a memory in his head left over from twelve years ago about what life with Poppy would look like. But there was nothing to say he would get that chance.

He hoped he wouldn't have to be content with friendship, he thought as his attention was captured by the sight of a bikini-clad girl running up to the buggy.

'There's a man down the beach,' she said as she waved her arm towards the north end of the beach, 'having some sort of fit.'

'Jump in,' Ryder said, pushing his own thoughts aside. 'Can you take me to him?'

The girl nodded and climbed into the ATV, stepping over the rescue board that was stored on the passenger side of the buggy.

Ryder started the engine and headed north, driving along the wet, hard-packed sand. He picked up the radio as he drove and called the incident into the tower. 'Central, this is Easy. I've got a report of a man having a seizure on the beach. I'm checking it out and will update you.'

'Copy that. I'll send Bluey to assist.'

Ryder hit the siren on the buggy, clearing the crowds as he weaved his way up the beach.

'Over there.' The girl pointed to her left.

Ryder could see a large crowd gathering on the sand. He hit the kill switch on the ATV as he brought it to a stop several metres from the crowd. He knew he wasn't going to be able to drive any closer. He jumped out and grabbed the two-way radio and the medical kit and ran through the soft sand, pushing his way through the onlookers.

As the crowd parted Ryder saw an elderly gentleman

lying on a towel in full sun. He was convulsing, his eyes were rolled back in his head and he was frothing at the mouth. Ryder crouched down beside him. 'Sir, I'm a lifeguard. I'm here to help you.'

As he'd expected, there was no response.

He looked up at the crowd. 'Is there anyone here who knows this man?'

No one spoke up and then the girl who'd fetched him said, 'He seemed to be by himself. My friends and I were sitting nearby. There didn't seem to be anyone with him.'

'No one who has gone swimming perhaps?' Ryder asked. But there was only one towel, which the man was lying on, and no bags or any evidence that someone else had been there.

The girls shook her head.

Ryder called the tower again. 'Central, I'm going to need some help and an ambulance. I have an unidentified elderly male having a seizure. Unknown onset. Non-responsive but breathing.'

Jet's reply came back. 'Bluey is on his way. I'll call the ambos.'

There wasn't much Ryder could do. The man was possibly dehydrated but he had no way of getting fluids into him. He was lying in full sun and getting him into the shade was probably the best he could manage until help arrived. He looked around. There were dozens of beach umbrellas stuck into the sand.

'Could someone hold an umbrella over us for some shade?' he asked as he heard Bluey pushing his way through the mass of people that seemed to be growing by the second. As usual, a drama attracted spectators.

The seizure abated as Bluey arrived, carrying the oxygen and the defib unit.

The man had stopped thrashing and foaming at the mouth but his eyes were still glazed and Ryder could tell he wasn't aware of his surroundings. Far from it.

Ryder had no way of telling what had caused the seizure. Epilepsy would be his guess but it could be any number of things and whatever the cause the seizure had lasted several minutes making it a medical emergency.

He was able to take the man's pulse, his heart was racing, but when he tried to hook the oxygen mask over the man's mouth and nose the man lashed out, knocking the mask from Ryder's hands.

'Sir? Can you hear me? You're on Bondi Beach, and you've a had a seizure, I'm a lifeguard and I want to give you some oxygen.' Ryder spoke quietly and clearly as he tried again to position the mask but the man had the same reaction. He wondered what the man thought was happening.

He picked up the radio and called Jet. 'How far away are the ambos?' he asked. He needed their help. There was no way he and Bluey could get this patient onto a stretcher and back to the tower without assistance.

'Gibbo's bringing them over in a buggy. They're almost with you.'

The crowd parted as Jet finished speaking and Ryder could see Poppy coming towards him just as he managed to secure the oxygen mask in place. He breathed out a sigh of relief.

Poppy knelt in the sand beside him. 'Hey, what have we got?'

Ryder told her what he knew, which was very little. 'Elderly gentleman having a seizure that lasted several minutes. It took me a few minutes to reach him and the fit continued for more than five after I arrived on the scene. He was breathing but was non-responsive.

He's still non-responsive and agitated. Nil communication. Pulse ninety-six. No companions. No ID. No Medic Alert.'

Poppy was nodding. 'Was his whole body seizing or just his limbs?'

'His whole body. And quite violently. We've put the umbrella over him now but he was in full sun.'

'Does he have a bag with him?' Poppy asked. 'Any medication?'

'I haven't seen a bag. There was an empty water bottle beside him and the towel he's lying on, that seems to be it.' The man's eyes were closed now but Ryder could hear him breathing in the oxygen.

Poppy's colleague squatted beside them and spoke to the man. 'Sir, we're from the ambulance.' Alex put his hand on the man's shoulder but the man reacted violently again, just as he'd done with Ryder, but this time his fist connected with Alex, startling everyone.

The man's eyes opened as Alex kept talking. Clearly distressed, he continued to hit out, pushing Alex away. He pulled the oxygen mask from his face but still didn't speak. He pointed to his ears.

Ryder watched as Poppy nodded and said, 'It's okay, I understand.' She was signing as she spoke.

She turned around and looked at Ryder. 'He's deaf,' she explained.

CHAPTER FIVE

POPPY SAW RYDER'S expression clear as her words went
some way to explain the man's reaction. She turned
back to the patient. He had calmed down slightly but
still looked frightened. She knew that patients coming
out of a fit were often disoriented and scared and she
imagined it must be doubly frightening for someone
who was deaf or had an additional disability. Her hands
flew as she explained what had happened.

I'm a paramedic, she signed as she touched the sym-
bol on her uniform. *You are on Bondi Beach. You had
a seizure. Do you understand?*

She spoke quietly, her words accompanying her
hands, letting him choose to either read her lips or her
hands. Slowly, he calmed down.

*I'm going to put the oxygen mask back on for you.
Is that okay?*

Poppy kept her information as brief as possible,
knowing it would be easier for him if he could give her
yes or no answers.

What is your name?

Anthony, he signed.

*My name is Poppy. Have you had a fit before, An-
thony?*

He nodded his head.

My colleague and I are just going to check your condition. Is that okay?

She waited for him to nod before asking Alex to start taking his obs and speaking to the lifeguards. 'I'm just explaining to him what happened,' she said, as Alex slipped a pulse oximeter onto his finger. 'He's an epileptic. His name is Anthony.'

Anthony was signing to her.

That's okay, we understand, she signed back.

'He's apologising for striking out. He was confused when he woke up and with so many people surrounding him he thought he was being attacked,' she told the others as she wrapped the blood-pressure cuff around Anthony's arm.

She turned back to the patient. *Is there anyone with you? Family? A friend?*

He shook his head, signed, *My wife is at work.*

Poppy nodded. *We need to take you to hospital. Okay?*

He shook his head, surprising her. She hadn't thought he would refuse. His condition had stabilised so it was no longer an emergency but he still needed to be properly assessed.

You need to be assessed. You're probably dehydrated. It's a hot day so you will probably need a drip. That might be all and then you will be able to go home. I can call your wife for you and get her to meet us at the hospital.

He nodded and signed, *Okay.*

Will she be able to hear me? Poppy knew that there were a lot of deaf couples in society. She needed to make sure Anthony's wife would be able to hear her.

Anthony nodded and Poppy pulled her phone from a pocket in the side of her trousers.

'I'm just going to call Anthony's wife to let her know what has happened and to get her to meet us at Bondi General. Can you load him on a stretcher, and we'll get him to the ambulance?'

Poppy unloaded the stretcher in the emergency bay at Bondi General. She had travelled in the back with Anthony and he was quite stable and seemed much calmer now. She'd called ahead and asked for Lily to meet them, knowing it would help Anthony to be assessed by a doctor who could also sign.

This is Dr Carlson, Poppy told him. *She will take care of you. She can sign too.*

Poppy saw him do a double take when he saw Lily. *She looks like you.*

Poppy smiled. *She is my sister. You're in good hands. Your wife is on her way.*

Thank you.

My pleasure, she signed as they pushed the stretcher into the hospital before transferring him to a hospital barouche and leaving him with Lily.

'Was everything okay with Anthony?' Poppy asked as she stepped out onto the deck and handed Lily a glass of wine.

'Yes, poor man. He was pretty confused but he was okay. He had some IV fluids and then his wife took him home.'

Poppy's shift had been busy and halfway through she'd debated the wisdom of putting her hand up for the extra hours given that she'd got home late last night after dinner with Ryder, but Craig's no-show had left her with time on her hands and she was pleased she'd been there for Anthony. She'd hoped she'd helped him to negotiate what would have been a scary event. 'It would have been terrifying for him.'

'He was lucky that you were there, really.'

'I keep thinking what if that had been Daisy in that situation.' The idea made Poppy feel emotional. 'She'd be so vulnerable.'

'She doesn't have any underlying health problems.'

'I know, but if she was in an accident and alone, who would take care of her? Who's going to take care of any of us?'

Lily frowned and sipped her wine. 'What are you talking about?'

'Do you think there's something wrong with us? Do you think there's a reason we can't have successful relationships? Daisy's never had a serious boyfriend. Jet has had a million short-term flings and you and Otto aren't exactly living in marital bliss.'

'What about you and Craig? You're living together. That's a pretty serious relationship if you ask me.'

'I'm not living with him right now, I'm living with you. I put myself in the same category. We're all screwed up. I should be living with Craig and you should be living with Otto and yet, here we are, living here with Daisy like three spinsters.'

'I don't think it's as bad as all that.'

'Don't you?'

'No. You and Craig are only apart temporarily.'

Poppy knew that wasn't really at the core of her concerns. She and Craig didn't spend much time together anyway and she wasn't really missing him. And that was the problem. She wasn't missing Craig and she couldn't stop thinking about Ryder. If she and Craig were going to make it as a couple, should she be spending so much time thinking about another man?

'And what about you and Otto?' she asked, in an effort to get her mind off Ryder. 'What is happening with the two of you?'

Lily sighed. 'I don't know.'

'Do you miss him?'

'I try not to think about it.'

Poppy fell silent as she thought about Lily and Otto. In her opinion they were perfect together and if they weren't going to make it Poppy knew she would lose all faith in any of the Carlson siblings being able to sustain a serious relationship.

'What's bothering you? This isn't just about me and Otto, is it?' Lily asked. She always knew when something was troubling her siblings. It was part of her role in the family, to fix things.

Poppy wished she could fix things for Lily but she knew it wasn't that easy. For a start, Lily would have to *want* to fix things.

'I'm just thinking about missed opportunities,' she said.

In the few quiet moments she'd had during her shift today she'd found herself constantly reliving last night's dinner. Recalling how easily the conversation had flowed, how they had laughed and finished each other's sentences. How the twelve years apart had dissolved in the space of a few hours and how they had quickly re-established their easy camaraderie.

Dinner with Ryder had also made her examine her relationship with Craig.

She knew she was with Craig because he was a safe choice. They might not have amazing chemistry but she had convinced herself she didn't want that. She didn't want to feel out of control. She didn't want to feel vulnerable.

Her parents, her mother in particular, were not affectionate, not demonstrative with their feelings, and Poppy had never felt unconditionally loved by either of them. And then Ryder, her first love, had left her. She'd learned from experience that love was a painful emotion. It was better to learn to live without it. Wanting something you couldn't have was only going to lead to heartache.

She didn't want to look for love. She didn't want to risk rejection.

Or so she'd been telling herself.

She knew Craig wasn't going to break her heart but why then did she get the feeling she'd made a mistake? The buzz she got from being with Ryder—was it a mistake to never feel that with anyone else? Was she so afraid of rejection that she was willing to live in the shadows?

Being with Ryder made her feel as if she was in full sunshine, her world was right, happy. She was able to live in the moment. Ryder reminded her of the girl she used to be. The girl who had laughed and dreamed. Where had that girl gone?

She'd lost her sense of adventure. She'd replaced it with a good work ethic but were the two mutually exclusive?

She'd had a goal to own her own house and she hadn't achieved it yet but it wasn't far off—half a house with Craig still counted—and maybe once she'd ticked that box she could think about what she wanted next.

'Did something happen with Craig?'

'No.' Poppy shook her head as she topped up their wine glasses. 'With Ryder.'

'Ryder?'

Poppy nodded. 'I kissed him.'

'What!' Lily almost choked on a mouthful of wine. 'When? Last night?' Lily knew that Poppy and Ryder had caught up for dinner.

'No, not last night. Twelve years ago.'

'Oh.' Poppy heard the relief in Lily's voice and she knew her sister thought it was all water under the bridge and nothing to worry about. What she didn't know was that Poppy wanted to do it all over again. 'That was so long ago, why are you thinking about it now?'

'I can't *stop* thinking about it. I hadn't thought about him for years but since I've seen him again I can't get it out of my mind and it's making me wonder what I'm doing with Craig.' She didn't divulge that she wanted to kiss Ryder again. That information wasn't for sharing, not even with Lily. 'Isn't absence supposed to make the heart grow fonder?' Poppy asked, wondering if that was the case for Lily and Otto.

'Supposedly. That's not how you're feeling?'

'No.'

'Is Ryder your missed opportunity?'

'I think he might be,' Poppy admitted.

'And how does he fit into your plans?'

He didn't fit in with her plans. Not at all.

He stirred all sorts of emotions in her, simultaneously making her feel calm and nervous. Her soul was calm when she was with him, even if her heart was racing and her knees were shaky. When she was with Ryder she felt like she was where she was supposed to be, was who she was supposed to be, but she knew he didn't fit in with her plans.

But she couldn't bring herself to say that. Admitting that would mean he wouldn't be part of her life in the future and she wasn't ready to say goodbye to him again. Not yet.

She remained silent.

'I think you should go and see Craig,' Lily suggested. 'See how you feel after a weekend in Brisbane. Ryder is gorgeous and sort of familiar but perhaps seeing him is confusing your feelings for Craig.'

Poppy paid the cab driver and lifted her bag from the seat. She pushed open the front gate and saw Craig's car in the driveway. She hadn't told him she was coming. She'd had a feeling he'd try to talk her out of it and she knew she couldn't put it off.

She needed to get herself back on an even keel. Lily had been right. Spending some time with Craig would help to remind her of why they were together. Coming home would give her a chance to put Ryder out of her mind. A chance to focus on Craig and on their relationship.

She stood inside the front gate and took a moment to assess her feelings. She was restless and had a strange sense of foreboding. Was it just because Ryder had unsettled her equilibrium or was it due to something else? She had no idea but surely she should be feeling differently? She was about to see Craig for the first time in three weeks. Shouldn't she be excited, eager, happy?

But she was none of those things.

She was pleased to be home but she felt like something was missing. Someone.

She shook her head. She was being ridiculous. It was time to grow up and time to put Ryder out of her mind.

She shut the gate and climbed the steps leading to the front of the house.

The bottom step was loose and the paint on the wooden banister flaked off under her hand. She added those two jobs to the long list she already had. She breathed in the scent of the frangipani that grew in the corner between the house and the staircase. She loved that perfume and if she closed her eyes she could picture how the house would look, the fragrant flowers of the frangipani with its glossy green leaves contrasting with the freshly painted white woodwork of the façade. One day her house would be perfect.

She pushed open the wooden louvre doors on the small veranda and slid her key into the front door. The house was in darkness save for a sliver of light that spilled into the passage from the master bedroom, where the door was slightly ajar. She was about to push the bedroom door open when she heard water running in the bathroom at the back of the house. Was Craig in the shower?

She paused, waiting to feel a sense of expectation and eagerness over seeing Craig again, but there was nothing. Their relationship wasn't built on sexual chemistry, it was built on shared goals and mutual respect and that had been enough for her. Until now, a little voice in her head said.

She hoped Lily was right. She hoped this visit would give her what she needed. An opportunity to remind herself of the value of their relationship. Of the benefits.

She dropped her bag and walked the length of the passage. She'd surprise Craig in the shower, she thought as she heard the water shut off. Maybe she just needed to try harder to breathe some life into their relationship, she thought as she tried not to think about how differently she'd feel if it was Ryder in the shower.

The bathroom door swung open before she could reach it. Poppy had expected to see Craig emerge and she froze, momentarily confused, when she saw a woman coming towards her. Her first thought was they had an intruder but as her brain caught up with her eyes she realised the woman was almost naked, wearing nothing but an unbuttoned man's business shirt and a pair of bikini briefs. Poppy didn't recognise the woman but she recognised the shirt. It was one of Craig's. One she'd bought him.

'Who the hell are you?'

The woman looked a little startled but not as thrown by the situation as Poppy thought she should be. She recovered quickly. 'Dee.'

That told Poppy nothing. And why was she almost naked?

The picture gradually came into focus. It was surely only seconds but it felt like an eternity. Craig's car in the drive. A light on in the bedroom—*her* bedroom— a semi-naked woman coming out of the bathroom.

Craig was cheating on her.

She turned her back on the woman—Dee—and shoved the bedroom door open, taking some small delight in seeing the horrified expression on Craig's face when he saw her standing there instead of the woman he had been expecting.

She would have laughed at his expression except that she was furious and embarrassed. She hated being wrong-footed. She hated feeling like a fool.

She was the planner. The one who always knew how things would end. The one who had an end game. Or at least she had been until the last couple of weeks. Ryder had unsettled her life and now it looked as though Craig was adding to her confusion.

She hadn't told Craig she was coming so that he couldn't convince her not to. She'd wanted him be the one who was surprised. Turned out they were both surprised.

The trouble was, she hated surprises. She hated losing control.

'Poppy!' Craig was sitting on the edge of the bed, checking his phone. It didn't look so bad—if she ignored the fact that he was naked. 'I wasn't expecting you.'

'Evidently.'

She could feel Dee hovering behind her. She stretched her arm out, putting her hand on the doorframe, blocking her entry, shutting her out.

Craig grabbed a pillow and put it over his lap. Poppy wasn't sure why. She'd seen him naked plenty of times but he was obviously feeling uncomfortable. She hoped he was feeling guilty.

'Is there something you've forgotten to tell me?' She wasn't sure how she was managing to sound calm and rational. She'd caught Craig cheating on her so she should be throwing things, screaming at him or bursting into tears—all those things she'd seen in the movies—but although she felt like an idiot she was far from devastated.

If anything, it reinforced that she'd been sensible not to fall in love. If she'd loved Craig then his infidelity would hurt far more.

She felt foolish but not heartbroken.

She turned to Dee. 'I think you should leave.' Her voice was quiet but steely. She shot a glare in Dee's direction but knew she would save most of her anger for Craig. Just because she wasn't heartbroken it didn't mean he would escape without hearing her thoughts on his behaviour.

'I'll drive you home.'

Craig had pulled on a pair of shorts while she'd been glaring at Dee.

'No, you won't,' Poppy told him. She folded her

arms. 'She can take your car or you can call her a cab but you are staying here. I think there are some things we need to discuss.' She wasn't sure where she got the courage to speak to him like that. The shock made her bolshy.

Was this what he'd been getting up to? Was this why he hadn't come down to Sydney as planned? Was this a one-off or something more? Was Dee the reason he'd been hard to get hold of? Was she what was keeping him busy—not work and not golf?

She hated feeling like a fool and she hated being made a fool of even more. Was he taking her for one?

No more.

'What's going on?' she asked once Dee had left and she and Craig had moved their discussion to the living room. She wasn't comfortable having this conversation in their bedroom given the circumstances and that annoyed her. 'Was this your way of telling me it's over? You wanted me to catch you being unfaithful?'

'No! I would never do that. I wasn't expecting you. You didn't tell me you were coming back. I didn't want to hurt you.'

She had to believe him. He was safe, dependable, reliable, and she didn't think he would deliberately hurt her. That was one of the things she liked about him.

'I want you to be happy,' he continued. 'I want us both to be happy and I know I'm not. I haven't been happy for a long time and I don't think you're happy either.'

Was he right?

She knew he was.

A month ago she would have argued that she was happy but now she knew that wasn't true. She just hadn't realised that something was missing from her life.

'You spend all your time either at work or working on the house,' Craig said. 'We don't do anything together and I don't want to spend my life like that. We're like flatmates. We don't talk about anything other than this house and your plans for it. I thought moving to Sydney might give us a different purpose, something else to focus on, but I've been happier since you left.'

Poppy felt cut to the bone. 'With Dee?'

He nodded. 'I really did intend to speak to you. Life has to be better than what we had. I want passion, excitement. I want more.'

He wasn't apologising. He didn't sound sorry. She supposed no one should apologise for being happy. Or for being right.

There was no excitement in their relationship but that was what she'd thought she wanted. Right up until the moment Ryder had reappeared in her life.

She knew she'd been lying to herself. She wanted excitement. She wanted desire. She wanted that buzz.

But she also wanted stability and security. Could she have it all?

Stability, security and excitement?

Maybe not. But perhaps this was her chance to find out.

Could she explore things with Ryder without giving up her goals? Without giving up everything?

She knew that was impossible. There would be some risk. Was she brave enough?

Poppy turned her phone on as she walked off the plane, ready to let Lily know she'd arrived, but as she walked through the gate lounge she heard a familiar, but unexpected, voice.

'Hey, how are you doing?'

'Ryder!' Poppy's smile was wide and spontaneous. She'd been feeling like a complete fool but the unexpected sight of Ryder was enough to immediately cheer her up.

'What are you doing here?'

'Lily got called into work,' he said as he slung an arm around her shoulder as he walked beside her. Poppy almost missed a step as Ryder's touch triggered the now familiar buzz of excitement and anticipation to burst through her. It didn't escape her notice that this was the exact buzz that had been missing when she'd gone to see Craig. She'd tried to reason with herself as to why the buzz wasn't necessary but she knew she was kidding herself. The buzz was addictive and she wanted more. 'Jet and Daisy are working too,' he continued, 'so Lily asked me to collect you.'

Poppy wondered if that was true or if Lily was meddling. Her head was still spinning and she knew she didn't have the capacity to work out what was going on. Did Ryder know what had happened?'

'I could have taken a cab.'

'I wasn't sure if you'd want company. If you want to be alone I'll drop you home and take off.'

She was quiet throughout the car trip. Sorting through her thoughts. Wondering how much to tell Ryder. He had always been a good listener, a sounding board, and she supposed he would be no different now, but did she want to discuss the drama of her love life, the failings of her relationship with him? She wasn't sure.

She was still undecided when Ryder turned his car into Moore Street and pulled up in front of Lily's house.

'Thanks for the lift.'

'No worries. What are you going to do now?'

There was nothing she needed to do. She was home a day earlier than planned so her time was her own but she felt caged. Restless. 'I might go for a walk.' It was early evening, still light, and a walk might help her to relax.

'Would you like company?'

She nodded. 'I would.'

Ryder's company would be a good distraction. She was angry and upset but she didn't want to be alone with her thoughts. He might be able to keep her mind off her own shortcomings.

She knew she didn't love Craig so being rejected by him shouldn't hurt but that wasn't the case. She'd thought her heart was tougher than this. It wasn't his infidelity that hurt her but his rejection of her. Once again, she'd been found to be undeserving of someone's love.

'Did Lily tell you what happened?' Poppy asked as they headed along the cliff top walk towards Tamarama Beach.

'Not exactly. She just said you'd had a shock and were flying back early. I assumed it had something to do with Craig.'

'Craig and his boss.'

'It's a work thing?'

'I guess that's one way to look at it. Craig's new boss was at our house when I arrived on Friday night. I hadn't met her before and she wasn't expecting to meet me. She was wearing one of Craig's shirts and not much else. Turns out Craig is sleeping with his boss.'

'Shit.'

'It gets worse.' It was easier to talk when they were walking side by side, looking out at the ocean. Much easier than sitting opposite each other at a table. She didn't feel quite so foolish when she couldn't see his expression.

'What could be worse?'

'He's taken a new deal and he's staying in Brisbane. He's not coming to Sydney.' It was strange how easily she could talk to Ryder but had never been able to really open up with anyone else. He knew things about her that even her own siblings didn't.

'Why is that worse? You don't *want* him to move here now, do you?'

'But I'm already here. I transferred to Sydney for him. I didn't need to move.' Even though her siblings were in Sydney she hadn't really wanted to move. She hadn't wanted to leave her house.

'Being here isn't the end of the world. You have a good job and your family is here. You can stay.'

'But I had a life in Brisbane too and I gave it up for Craig. I thought I was giving it up for us, for our future together, but apparently I gave it up for nothing.'

'I understand the situation sucks and it wasn't what you expected but isn't it better to know now what sort of person he is?'

'What do you mean, "now"?'

'Before you found yourself married with a couple of kids. Being cheated on is tough but better now than after you are married. It's a lot harder to walk away then.'

'It's not that easy now.'

'Of course it is.'

'We have a house together,' she argued.

'It's just a house.'

But it was more than that to her. How did she explain that it was the thought that she might lose her house that was upsetting her more than Craig's actions? 'I can't believe that he took her home to *my* house.'

'You're more upset about *where* he cheated on you than over the fact he did cheat on you?'

Ryder's tone suggested there was something wrong with her emotionally if she was more attached to her house than to her boyfriend of almost two years. Was he right?

'He violated my privacy, my sanctuary. That's what hurts the most. I didn't want to rely on him and it turns out I shouldn't have.' By buying the house together she knew she had created a dependence on him financially but she'd thought they'd had the same end goal in sight. 'I didn't need him to love me, I just needed him to respect me.'

'Everyone needs to be loved, Poppy.'

She shook her head. 'No. Not me. I don't want to be in love. I don't want to be dependent on someone else for my emotional needs.'

She'd been right when she'd asked Lily what was wrong with them. Why they couldn't seem to have successful relationships. She blamed her parents, although she knew that was probably unfair. You needed to be brave to love because love could hurt and she suspected she wasn't brave enough.

As she tried to work out how to articulate her thoughts without making herself sound completely crazy, she felt a few spots of rain. They had turned for home but when she looked over her shoulder she could see a southerly storm front rolling in behind them. Before she could say anything the heavens opened and within seconds they were soaked to the skin by the deluge.

Ryder grabbed her hand and even though they were already drenched, they ran for home.

* * *

Poppy changed out of her wet clothes and by the time she came back into the kitchen Ryder had stripped off his shirt and hung it over the back of a chair to dry.

Poppy swallowed, suddenly nervous and unsure where to look. She'd seen him bare-chested and semi-naked plenty of times at work over the past couple of weeks but it seemed far more intimate now in this setting. There was just two of them with nothing else to focus on. No medical emergency to draw her attention, no crowds of beachgoers.

'Would you like me to see if Lily has some of Otto's clothes in her room? You could borrow a shirt?'

'No, it's okay, my shirt won't take long to dry,' he said as he opened the fridge and pulled out a block of cheese. He looked right at home in Lily's kitchen. Anyone walking in would assume he lived there but he'd always fitted in seamlessly into their lives. Why should things be any different now?

'What are you doing?'

'I thought you'd be hungry. I'm making cheesy treats. I assume you still eat them?'

Poppy smiled. Toasted cheese sandwiches had been their go-to after school, post-surfing snack. 'They're still my favourite,' she said.

Poppy opened beers for them both, pinching them from Jet's supply, before she sat down to enjoy the view as Ryder bent over to open the oven and turn on the grill. It had always been Ryder who had made this snack for them and sitting watching him and breathing in the scent of grilled cheese transported her back through the years. To when they'd had nothing to worry about other than catching a wave or whether there was bread and cheese in the kitchen.

It was funny how she had always thought of him as Jet's friend, but revisiting the memory of those months before his family had moved away she realised now that he had spent far more time with her than he had with Jet. There had been a time when Jet had been sidelined with glandular fever and while Ryder had visited him frequently, Jet's fatigue had meant those visits had been brief and Ryder had spent more time with Poppy. Had that been a conscious action on his part? One day she might find the courage to ask him.

'Can you cook anything else or is this still your go-to?'

'Are you complaining?' He grinned at her as he slid the sandwiches out of the grill.

'Not at all. Just curious.'

'I think I'm pretty handy in the kitchen,' he said as he piled the sandwiches on a plate and took them out to the deck.

They sat in silence, eating their way through the pile of sandwiches as they watched the storm roll over the ocean.

'Feeling better?' Ryder asked when the plate was almost empty.

'A little,' she admitted.

'I know it seems bad now and you're hurting but you *will* be okay.'

'I just hate being taken for a fool.'

'Look on the bright side. I know how much you love to make plans—this is a perfect chance to make some new ones.'

Despite herself, Poppy found herself laughing.

'The future is as bright as you want to make it,' he added.

What would her future look like now?

She had assumed she and Craig would continue on as they had, happily cohabiting. But apparently there hadn't been so much of the happy. She hadn't pictured herself getting married, making that sort of commitment, and Craig had never mentioned it either. She hadn't dreamed of marriage. It wasn't as if she'd seen many examples of happy marriages. Her parents had never married and Lily and Otto's marriage was strained, to say the least. Even Ryder's parents were divorced. Poppy hadn't expected or even wanted to be married but she had expected fidelity.

She finished the last sandwich and rested her head back on the chair.

'You look exhausted. Time for bed.'

Ryder stood and reached for her hand, pulling her to her feet. His hand was warm, his grip gentle and comforting, and Poppy didn't want to let go of him. Tears sprang to her eyes as she was suddenly overwhelmed. She wasn't sure if what she was feeling was affection for Ryder or if she was simply overcome with emotion after the events of the past twenty-four hours but she struggled to keep the tears from overflowing.

'Hey, it'll be okay, you'll be okay.' Ryder wrapped her in his embrace and Poppy leaned into him, taking solace in his strength. 'You'll get through this.'

She stood still for a long time. She didn't want to move, she could have stayed like that all night, wrapped in his arms, blocking out the world. She took a deep breath. His naked chest was warm under her cheek and she was suddenly aware of the intimacy of their posture.

If she turned her face a few millimetres she would be able to press her lips against his bare skin.

'I'm here for you, okay?' he said.

Poppy looked up at him to find him watching her. She nodded and placed her hands on his chest and he relaxed his arms, allowing her freedom to move, but she wasn't intending on pushing him away and he didn't let her go.

His blue eyes were dark and intense, his expression unreadable. She stood still and silent as she watched him dip his head towards her. Suddenly his expression was completely readable, his intention clear. He moved in slow motion and she knew she could stop him at any time. But she wasn't going to do that. She didn't want to stop him.

She spread her hands apart and ran them around his back as she stepped in closer again.

'What do you need, Poppy?'

'You.' She needed him like she needed oxygen. She'd wanted him for as long as she could remember and perhaps tonight her wish would be granted.

There was no room in her head for the thoughts of the past day, there was no room for anything other than the man who stood before her, who held her as if he never wanted to let her go and looked at her as if he couldn't live without her.

'Are you sure?'

Her reply was silent. She nodded and raised herself onto her toes and pressed her mouth to his.

She heard him moan and his hands moved down below her waist. He cupped her bottom and pulled her towards him until she was pressed against his groin. She could feel his erection, strong and hard between them. He teased her lips apart with his tongue and she opened her mouth willingly, offering herself to him. All her old fantasies returned. She had dreamed of this moment many times over the years and tonight she would take the moment a step further. She wasn't going to miss her opportunity again.

CHAPTER SIX

Ryder closed his eyes as Poppy's lips parted under his. He'd imagined having a second chance many times—was tonight it?

Her lips were soft, her mouth warm and moist. She felt good in his arms and she tasted even better.

He didn't stop to think about the wisdom of what they were doing. He didn't want to stop. Not unless she asked him to. He'd been waiting years for this moment and he'd given up thinking it would ever eventuate.

She'd had a traumatic twenty-four hours and he didn't want to take advantage of her but he did want to take her. To claim her. To have her. And if she didn't object he would have her right here, right now, on the cool tiles of the living-room floor.

He didn't want to let her go but they needed privacy as her sisters could walk in at any moment. He lifted her up and she wrapped her legs around his waist as she clung to him. Her arms went around his neck as he carried her to the bedroom.

Craig was an idiot, he thought as he took one, two, three steps across the room to reach the bed. Did Craig have any idea what he was throwing away?

But Ryder was grateful. Craig's actions had given Poppy back to him and he wasn't going to walk away again.

He stopped at the bed and Poppy slid her legs from around his waist and stood in front of him. He could see her pulse beating at the base of her throat, her lips were parted, her mouth pink and soft, her eyes gleaming.

Her fingers left his shoulders and held the hem of her T-shirt. She tugged it over her head, revealing creamy flesh and full, rounded breasts.

Ryder swallowed. There was only so much temptation he could stand. He forgot about everything that had happened over the past day, the past week, that past twelve years. He only had one thought. *Get her into bed before she comes to her senses.*

He brought his eyes back to her face. She pinned him with her gaze but as she dropped her T-shirt on the floor and her hands moved lower, and he couldn't help himself. His eyes followed the path of her movements.

Her fingers undid the button on her shorts and she pushed them to the floor and stepped out of them. She stood before him wearing nothing but a bra and a pair of very skimpy briefs.

Ryder was mesmerised. His eyes travelled upwards, up the length of her bare legs, long and tanned, to her slim hips, to the tiny triangle of fabric at the junction of her thighs that was barely preserving her modesty.

He couldn't speak. A severe lack of blood to his brain had robbed him of the power of speech. But he could admire. So he did.

She was gorgeous.

His gaze travelled higher, over her flat stomach and her round belly button to her full breasts that seemed to strain against the lace of her bra.

She was perfect.

He ran his fingers up her thigh, cupping the curve of her bottom. Poppy closed her eyes and arched her hips, letting him pull her closer to him. He bent his head and kissed her. She opened her mouth, joining them together. Ryder ran his hand over her hip and up across her ribs until his fingers grazed her breast. Through the lace of her bra he felt her nipple peak under his touch. She moaned softly and reached for him but he wasn't done yet.

Her eyes were still closed as he reached behind her back. His fingers found the clasp of her bra and with a flick of his thumb he undid the fastening. Her hair tumbled over her shoulders as her breasts spilled from the lace. He pushed her hair to one side and lowered his head. He flicked his tongue over one breast, sucking it into his mouth. He heard Poppy moan as he teased her nipple with his mouth. He had one hand wrapped behind her, holding her close, and he slid his other hand down her stomach, his fingers sliding under the fabric of her briefs. His fingers slid between her thighs. She was wet and warm and felt like heaven.

'Make love to me, Ryder.'

He dropped to his knees in front of her and gently pulled her underwear down. She was shaking, unsteady on her feet. She sat on the edge of the bed as he knelt before her.

He ran one hand up the smooth skin of the inside of her thigh. Her knees were spread wide and she moaned and thrust her hips towards him as his fingers found her centre. He put his head between her thighs, replacing his fingers with his tongue. His hands went under her bottom as he lifted her to his mouth, supporting her there as his tongue darted inside her. She was slick and sweet and she moaned as he explored her inner sanctum. He enjoyed oral sex, giving and receiving, and tonight was no exception.

Poppy thrust her hips towards him again, urging him deeper. Her legs wrapped around his chest, holding him in place, not that he had plans to go anywhere. She was wet and hot, her sex swollen with desire as he tasted her and teased her, making her pant, making her beg for him.

'Ryder, please. I want you naked. I want you inside me.'

'Patience, Poppy,' he said, his voice muffled against the soft skin of her hip bone. 'Relax and enjoy, we've got all night.' He wasn't ready to stop. Not yet. He knew she was close to climaxing and he wanted to bring her to orgasm like this. He wanted to taste it, to feel it.

He ignored her request as he continued to work his magic with his tongue, licking and sucking the swollen bud of her desire. He continued until Poppy had forgotten her request, until she had forgotten everything except her own satisfaction.

'Yes, yes... Oh, Ryder, don't stop.'

He had no intention of stopping. He heard her sharp little intake of breath and then she began to shudder.

'Yes. Oh, Ryder.'

She buried her fingers in his hair and clamped her thighs around his shoulders as she came. Shuddering and gasping before she collapsed, relaxed and spent.

'God, you're good at that,' she said, and he could hear the smile and contentment in her voice.

'Thank you.' He stood up from his knees and lay alongside her on the bed, his hand resting on her stomach as she cuddled into him.

'Now will you get naked?' she asked. He turned his head to look at her. 'It's your turn,' she said. 'I want to feel you inside me.'

Poppy watched as Ryder's blue eyes darkened. They

were a dark navy now, the brightness overcome with lust and desire. She felt a surge of power, knowing that he wanted her as much as she wanted him. She slipped her fingers under the waistband of his jeans. She could see he wanted to give in.

'Please?' she begged.

'Seeing as you asked so nicely,' he replied with a grin as he flicked open the button of his jeans.

Poppy took charge. She sat up and pushed him onto his back, tugging his jeans over his hips as she undressed him. His boxer shorts came off with his jeans and as his erection sprang free Poppy's groin flooded with heat. She straddled him, trapping him between her thighs. She cupped his testes and then encircled his shaft with her hand. It was thick and hard and warm and pulsed with a life of its own as she ran her hand up its length. She rolled her fingers over the end and coaxed the moisture from his body. Ryder gasped and his body shook with lust.

'In my wallet,' he panted. 'I have protection.'

Ryder's jeans were lying on the floor. Poppy stretched to her right and lifted them to the bed. She found his wallet in the front pocket. She flicked it open and pulled out a condom. She tore open the packet and rolled the sheath down over him.

She was still sitting across his thighs and Ryder's eyes darkened further as she brought herself forward and raised herself up onto her knees. She put her hands either side of his head and kept her eyes on his face as she lifted herself up and took his length inside her. He closed his eyes and she watched him breathe in deeply as her flesh encased him, joining them together.

She filled herself with his length before lifting her weight from him. She lifted herself up again, and down, as Ryder held onto her hips and started to time her thrusts, matching their rhythms together. Slow at first and then gradually faster. And faster. Poppy tried to stay in charge but she found it impossible to control her body. All she could think of was how good this felt and that she wanted more. And more.

She let him take control. His thumbs were on the front of her hips, his fingers behind her pelvis as he guided her up and down, matching her rhythm to his thrusts, each movement bringing her closer to climax.

She liked this position. She liked being able to watch him, she liked being able to see him getting closer and closer to release. His lips were parted, his breathing was rapid and shallow, his thrusts getting faster. She spread her knees, letting him deeper inside her until she had taken all of him. Her body was flooded with heat. Every nerve ending was crying out for his touch. 'Now, Ryder. Now.'

He opened his eyes and his gaze locked with hers as he took her to the top of the peak.

Her body started to quiver and just when she didn't think she could stand it any longer she felt Ryder shudder. She held her breath as he thrust into her and she could feel his release as he came inside her, claiming her as they climaxed together.

Completely spent and satisfied, she collapsed onto him, covering his body with hers. Their skin felt warm and flushed from their efforts and they were both panting as he wrapped his arms around her back, holding her to him. She could feel his heart beating under her chest. She could feel it as its rhythm slowed, gradually returning to normal.

She closed her eyes and lay quietly, listening to the sound of Ryder's breathing.

For once in her life she had completely let herself lose control and it felt good.

She had never given herself over so totally to someone else or to her desires. Tonight had been a long time coming and she didn't regret a second of it.

Maybe Craig had done her a favour. Ryder certainly had.

She smiled.

'What's that smile for?' Ryder asked.

She opened her eyes and found him watching her. 'I didn't know sex could be like that.'

When she'd been in relationships, more often than not she'd had sex because she'd known it was expected of her but she'd never felt a desperate burning desire for it. Unless, it seemed, Ryder was around.

'It was pretty amazing,' he agreed.

'It was incredible.' She'd had good sex but she'd never experienced mind-blowing sex. Until now.

'There's more where that came from,' he said as he pressed his lips against the soft skin at the base of her throat.

Poppy's smile widened as his fingers trailed over her hip bone and slid between her thighs and she forgot all about feeling obliged to have sex and focussed instead on the bliss of making love.

Poppy woke to the sound of a text message.

She opened her eyes, expecting to see Ryder in the bed next to her before remembering that he'd left in the early hours of the morning. She bit back her disappointment. She'd wanted him to stay but he hadn't wanted to run into her sisters.

She hoped that had been his only reason for leaving. She hoped he didn't think they'd made a mistake. Hoped he wasn't regretting what they'd done.

She scolded herself as she reached over to pick up her phone. As usual she was overthinking things and assuming the worst. Her mood lifted when she saw his message on the screen.

Are you awake?

She was smiling as she dialled his number. 'Good morning,' she said when he answered. 'I'm awake now. Where are you?'

'I'm out the front. Grab your board and your wetsuit. We're going surfing.'

Poppy's heart skipped a beat. He obviously wasn't having second thoughts.

She quickly pulled on her swimsuit, brushed her teeth and grabbed her gear. She closed the front door quietly. Ryder was waiting on the kerb. He greeted her with a kiss and took her surfboard, sliding it into the back of his car next to his.

'How did you sleep?' he asked her as he drove her down to Bronte Beach.

'Like a baby.' She'd expected to have a restless night, she'd expected that her mind would be spinning as she processed what had happened with Craig, but Ryder had managed to distract her completely in the most delightful of ways.

'No regrets?'

She smiled. 'None. Why?'

'I was worried you might be feeling like we rushed things a bit.'

'No.' She shook her head as she wondered if she should tell him that she'd been waiting twelve years for last night to happen. That could hardly be called rushing things. 'You?'

'Maybe.'

'Oh.' She didn't like the sound of that.

'Don't get me wrong, I enjoyed every minute of it but you have to admit we didn't really think things through. I didn't give you a chance to process what had happened with Craig. You haven't had a chance to decide if you want to work things out.'

'Trust me, I don't.' Her relationship with Craig was well and truly over. She couldn't forgive infidelity and after last night there was no way she was ever going to settle for average sex again.

It was a glorious morning. The beach was bathed in pink light and the ocean was warm. She didn't want to think about Craig. She knew they would have things to sort out but that could wait. She blocked all thoughts of Craig from her mind. 'Is that all that was bothering you?' she asked, as they paddled out past the break.

'No.'

What more could there be? she thought nervously. 'Oh? What else is there?'

'I need to know if last night was just a one-off.'

Poppy's heart plummeted in her chest. Was that what he wanted? She was almost afraid to ask but she had to know. She swallowed the lump in her throat and said, 'Is that what you thought? Is that all you wanted?'

'What! No, not at all. I just needed to know if last night was just a reaction to Craig's behaviour or if it was more serious. I don't want to get caught in the middle and I don't want to be your rebound guy.'

Poppy could breathe again. 'You're not.'

Ryder sat up on his board and the morning sun caught his hair, turning the tips golden. His skin was bronzed and the water droplets on his shoulders glistened in the morning light. He looked like a Greek god and Poppy's breath caught in her throat and her insides wobbled. He was divine, inside and out, and she couldn't believe she'd finally managed to fulfil her teenage fantasy. She had enjoyed every minute of it and fully intended to do it again.

'I have been waiting for last night for twelve years,' she told him as she pushed herself into a sitting position and let her legs dangle in the water. 'It definitely wasn't a rebound thing.'

'Good,' he said as he reached for her board. He pulled her closer until their knees were touching and leaned towards her. He lifted his hand and slid his fingers under her hair, cupping the back of her head. She lifted her chin and his lips brushed her mouth.

She closed her eyes and parted her lips as he kissed her. He tasted salty and warm. She kissed him back, savouring the feel of his hands on her skin, his mouth on hers.

A small wave rocked her board. She opened her eyes and grabbed his forearms for support as she regained her balance.

Ryder ran his thumb along her jaw to the edge of her mouth and Poppy would have sworn she could feel the zing of awareness spread right through her from her lips to her toes. She sighed and sucked his thumb into her mouth.

'Where do we go from here?' he asked.

She took his hand, holding it in both of hers. 'I'm not sure.' She hadn't thought about what would happen next. She'd only got as far as last night.

'You don't have a plan?' He was smiling. Teasing her.

She shook her head. 'I just want to enjoy this.' Whatever *this* was.

He was watching her closely and she wondered if he knew what she was thinking. He usually did, but she couldn't help her fears. It was too soon to tell him how she felt. She couldn't do it.

She was scared of verbalising her feelings but she knew she needed to try to explain her thoughts to him. 'Whenever I make relationship plans, things go awry. Can we just spend some time together and see what happens?'

He nodded. 'Sure. If that's what you want.'

She appreciated that he didn't push her for more. She didn't want to make promises neither of them might be able to keep. It was better not to expect too much. She didn't want to be disappointed.

He knew the conversation was done for now and she watched him as he caught a wave. He carved up the ocean, his powerful legs working the board. She almost blushed when she thought that just last night she'd been tangled up in his legs. Just last night those powerful thighs had been between hers, taking her to places she'd only ever dreamed of.

She would enjoy this, enjoy him, she decided, for as long as it lasted.

Ryder dropped Poppy home after a post-surfing breakfast before he headed to work. Lily was lying on the couch and she closed her laptop and sat up when Poppy came into the lounge.

'You're looking better than I expected given the nasty surprise you copped,' she said. 'How are you feeling?'

'Great.'

'Really?'

'Yep.' Poppy could feel the enormous grin she had plastered on her face but she couldn't help it.

'And would your good mood have anything to do with Ryder?'

'What makes you say that?'

'I thought I saw him leaving here in the early hours of the morning.'

'You saw him? He didn't say anything.'

'He looked like he had his mind on other things. Are you going to tell me what's going on?'

'You asked him to pick me up from the airport.' Poppy sat on the couch next to her sister.

'This was hours later.'

'We went for a walk, he made me dinner…'

'And then?'

'I slept with him.'

'Oh, my God! Poppy! You don't think it's a bit soon to be jumping into bed with someone else? You've only just broken up with Craig.'

Poppy hadn't meant to say anything, not just yet, but her excited mood made her accidentally verbose. 'I didn't realise there was a rule.'

'There's not a rule exactly but most people I know wait a few days, not hours.'

Again, she felt like she'd been waiting twelve years for last night. In her opinion she'd done her time and she hadn't been willing to wait one more minute for what had turned out to be the most amazing experience of her life. But she wasn't about to tell Lily all of that. It was a little too revealing. 'It was just a bit of fun,' she said instead.

Lily raised one eyebrow. 'A bit of fun is revenge sex with a hot stranger. Sex that makes you think you're still desirable after your boyfriend cheats on you. It is *not* having sex with a guy you've known for years. A guy who you had a teenage crush on but who is first and foremost a friend. Someone you'll still have to see if things go pear-shaped!'

'I can handle it.'

'Are you sure? What's your plan?'

'My plan? I don't have one.'

Lily looked at her like she didn't recognise her and Poppy could understand that. She always had a plan but she'd got carried away last night. She'd let her hormones get the better of her and she'd slept with Ryder because she'd wanted to and before she could think about what came next. Now she just wanted to enjoy herself. She didn't want to make plans.

She'd never experienced anything like last night and she couldn't have planned it better if she'd tried, so that was her lesson. No plans.

'You've had a crush on Ryder for years,' Lily said. 'Can you handle a casual fling? I don't want you to get your heart broken.'

Poppy hadn't said anything about a casual fling. That wasn't where her mind was at but she was keeping that to herself. 'I know you like to protect us all but you don't need to worry. I'll be fine.'

Her boyfriend of two years had just cheated on her and she felt fine. Better than fine. She felt great. Craig's infidelity hadn't broken her heart and she didn't think Ryder would either. She could handle this.

For the next week Poppy thought she was handling things perfectly. She was taking things one day at a time, no plans, no expectations. It was very unlike her, this casual approach, but she was happy just spending time with Ryder. She'd wanted this chance for as long as she could remember and she was determined to enjoy it.

Work and Ryder were keeping her busy, which was good. It meant there was no time to spend thinking about Craig and the things they had to sort out. Poppy wanted to ignore that for as long as possible. She wanted to think only happy thoughts. She wanted to think about Ryder.

They spent almost every minute together when they weren't working—surfing, sharing meals and making love. Poppy was still blown away by how amazing the sex was. How had she never known it could be like that?

Maybe letting go was the secret.

Maybe Ryder was the secret.

Her muscles were still aching from the last session just half an hour ago and she was smiling as Ryder found them an empty table at Lao Lao's Kitchen. Poppy had wanted to stay in bed and order takeaway, but Ryder had insisted they go out and this restaurant was quickly becoming their favourite.

'Thank you, An Na,' Poppy said as the young girl brought their final dish. She cleared their empty plates as Ryder waved at someone across the restaurant.

Poppy turned back towards the door and saw a fit, athletic-looking brunette walking towards them.

'Hi, Steph, what are you doing here?' Ryder greeted her.

'Picking up a takeaway.'

'Steph, this is Poppy Carlson, Jet's sister. Poppy, this is Steph, one of the injured lifeguards.'

Ryder's introduction left Poppy a little disheartened. Was that all she was to him still? Jet's sister? She realised she wanted him to see her as someone more, someone important. A girlfriend. A partner. But was that fair? She was the one who hadn't wanted to make plans, hadn't wanted commitment. She couldn't expect one thing from him if she wasn't prepared to give him the same. She was scared to commit to a relationship officially. Relationships never worked out for her. If she wasn't committing in public she could pretend she wasn't committing in private.

But she knew that was a lie.

Despite what she'd told Lily, she was scared Ryder would leave her and break her heart in the process. She was scared he wouldn't love her.

Realising her musings were making her appear rude, she dragged her focus back to the conversation. 'How's your recovery going?' she asked, just as Steph's name was called.

'Slowly,' Steph replied as she glanced back over her shoulder. 'That's my order,' she said. 'Ryder can fill you in. Enjoy your dinner.'

'Which one was she?' Poppy asked as Steph returned to the counter. 'The fractured scapula?' she guessed. The other lifeguard had undergone a knee reconstruction and given the time frame Poppy thought Steph was far too mobile to be the post-op knee patient.

Ryder nodded.

'How long has she been off for?'

'I'm not a hundred per cent sure but I know she's keen to come back. She had a fitness test today.'

'How did she go?'

'I gather she struggled with some of the strength components. She couldn't pull the dummy out of the water.'

Poppy knew one of the tests was retrieving a forty-kilogram dummy and wrangling it onto a rescue board.

Managing the dead weight was difficult at the best of times, let alone after a fractured shoulder blade.

'There was a bit of discussion about finding her some suitable light duties but until she can handle all the physical components of the job she's not going to be fully cleared. It'll be another few weeks at least.'

'So you'll be around for a bit longer?'

'You're not keen to get rid of me, are you?'

'Not yet. But when Steph is cleared? What will that mean for you? Will you continue on your gap year?'

She knew Ryder's contract was only temporary. He was covering sick leave and once those lifeguards returned to duty his contract would be over. She had no idea what his plans were after that. And suddenly her idea of going with the flow, of not planning for the future, seemed less solid. Ryder might be gone before she knew it. And what would she do then?

He was shaking his head. 'I've just about run out of time. I'll be heading home at the end of summer.'

'Back to Perth?' Poppy didn't want to think of him leaving her again, moving back across the country just like he had twelve years before.

He nodded.

'To do what? Work as a lifeguard?'

'Is there something wrong with that?'

Poppy could hear she'd offended him but surely that wasn't his career plan? 'You don't think you'll get bored?'

'Have you had the same conversation with Jet? Does he seem bored to you?'

'He's still competing in the Ironman series,' she countered. 'I don't think he's planning on being a lifeguard for ever.'

'You don't think. But it is possible. Several of the

guys have been full-time lifeguards for years. There's good job satisfaction.'

'But not great pay.'

'It's not all about the money for me, Poppy. Some things are more important.'

Poppy would disagree but she thought it was wiser to stay silent.

'Don't stress,' he said. 'I have a plan. Are you working tomorrow?'

'No.' It had become her habit to volunteer for any available overtime shifts as she'd been eager for the extra income to put towards her house in Brisbane, but for the past week she hadn't put her hand up for additional hours but had chosen to spend the time with Ryder instead.

'Meet me at the North Bondi lifeguard tower at four and I'll show you my plan,' he said.

Poppy could see Ryder sitting in the sand at the base of the tower at the northern end of the beach. He was surrounded by half a dozen teenagers and as many surfboards. He was dressed in a pair of boardshorts and a T-shirt. His knees were bent and he rested his elbow on his knees, the T-shirt pulled tight across his back and sculpted to his arms, showcasing his muscles. He looked good, almost as good with a shirt on as without, she decided, and the thought made her smile.

She wondered what he was doing here. He was dressed in casual clothes, not his lifeguard uniform, and he was obviously not on duty. Giving surfing lessons perhaps? Was that his plan—to become a surf instructor? In her opinion that showed even less ambition than being a professional lifeguard *and* had less job security. Having grown up with a father who was a surf instructor, she knew that from personal experience.

Ryder had so much to offer the world and she knew she'd be disappointed if she found out that he wasn't going to challenge himself. The teenage Ryder had never backed away from a challenge. He'd been determined, bold and confident. She hoped that was still the case but this time she wouldn't leap to conclusions. He had promised to tell her his plan and she would listen first. This time she wouldn't make assumptions and she wouldn't judge.

Ryder and the kids were sitting in a semi-circle around a pile of hot chips, which were spread out on a square of white butcher's paper. They were eating and chatting but Ryder stood up as she reached them. 'Hey.'

She thought he was going to greet her with a kiss but he simply gestured to the kids. 'Guys, this is Poppy. I thought she could join us for a surf today.'

They sat in the sand and he went around the group and introduced the kids to her. There was a mixture of girls and boys and Poppy guessed them to be aged between fifteen and eighteen. They were a disparate group and she couldn't quite work out what they were doing with Ryder.

'Are you hungry?' he asked. 'Help yourself.'

Poppy reached for a chip as the conversation continued around her. She enjoyed watching him interact with the kids. There was nothing stilted or forced about his demeanour, he was completely relaxed and the kids were obviously just as comfortable with him.

'How do you know Easy?' one of the boys asked as Poppy munched on a chip.

Poppy wasn't sure how to answer. Did she say they were old friends? Worked together? Were sleeping together? That last description, while true, probably wasn't an appropriate response.

'Poppy is a paramedic,' Ryder replied before she could decide what to say. 'She works here at Bondi.'

'Cool.'

She wondered why Ryder hadn't said they were dating. Had it just been a bit of casual fun in his mind? Something to pass the time until he went back to Perth? She wished she could tell what he was thinking as easily as he seemed to be able to read her mind.

She knew she was being contradictory. She was the one who had insisted on keeping things casual. On not making plans. She knew it wasn't fair of her to want Ryder to be more invested in things than she was. It wasn't fair to expect him to risk his heart but when was life ever fair? She didn't want him to be able to walk away from her easily. She didn't want to be rejected by him.

'I couldn't handle all that blood.' The kids all chimed in, commenting on her choice of career and bringing her mind back to the present.

'What's the grossest thing you've seen?' one asked.

'You, Jase!' one of the boys teased.

'Tyler!' Ryder's voice was quiet but firm and Poppy could tell he was not pleased.

Tyler could obviously tell too. 'I was just kidding,' he said with a sheepish expression.

'Kidding around is fine but it's not okay to make jokes at the expense of others. You know our rules, Tyler.'

'Sorry, Easy. Sorry, Jase,' he apologised.

Jase and Ryder both nodded in acknowledgement before Jase asked again. 'Will you tell us?'

'You know the thing that grosses me out the most?'

Poppy said. The boys all leaned in to hear her answer
while most of the girls looked a little more hesitant. 'I
can handle the broken bones and the blood but the worst
is when people vomit. Especially if they vomit on me.'

'Yuck.'

'That is *so* gross.'

'Told you.' She smiled. 'And that happens a lot.
Most of what I do isn't gross. There are some car accidents but there are more heart attacks and getting pregnant women in labour to hospital. Around here there
are skateboarding injuries, surfing injuries and near-
drownings.'

'It's kinda cool you get to save lives.'

'Yeah, it's pretty cool,' Poppy admitted. She loved
her job. It was everything she'd hoped for and one of her
favourite things was how confident she felt in herself
when she was in uniform. She felt strong and capable
but it seemed like the kids had heard enough from her.
They had devoured the food and were now getting to
their feet, ready to hit the water.

'Are you coming for a surf, Easy?' Jase asked.

'In a bit.'

'You don't want to surf?' she asked as the kids
grabbed their boards and ran down to the water.

'I'd rather sit here and talk to you,' he replied as he
reached for her hand. 'I can't do that out there.'

She looked down at their hands, at their intertwined
fingers. Her body sprang to life at the slightest touch
from Ryder and her reaction scared her. Being with him
felt right, it felt perfectly natural, and she knew she'd
been waiting for him all her life, but she was finding
herself constantly on edge too, waiting for him to walk
away. Waiting for him to leave. She hated that feeling

but she couldn't divest herself of it. She was trying her best to ignore it but it wasn't easy.

'Who are those kids?' she asked, trying to keep her mind occupied. She had a fair idea but what she didn't know was how and why Ryder was involved.

'They're a group of at-risk teenagers I've been volunteering with through the local council. I offered to teach them to surf.'

'Why?'

'They've all had, or are having, tough times. They've experienced bullying or abuse or have been diagnosed with depression or anxiety. Exercise benefits their mental health and builds confidence. Teaching them to surf was something I could do and it gives them an escape as well as a network, a social support group if you like, along with some fresh air and exercise. It's a win-win for everyone mostly. I reckon I get as much out of it as they do.'

'I didn't know that was something you were interested in.' He was a natural with the kids. He'd always been a good listener; she'd never found him to be judgemental and it seemed the kids recognised that too. 'Why did you get involved?'

'When I came to Bondi one of the first jobs I did as a lifeguard was dealing with the aftermath of a suicide. Back in Perth I had some experience with people who were battling anxiety and depression and I decided I wanted to make a difference. This was one way of doing that.'

'What happened in Perth?'

'Mum and Lucy both battled depression but they dealt with it in different ways. Lucy developed an eating disorder and Mum was too busy numbing her loss with alcohol to notice.'

'And now? How are they doing now?'

'Much better. It's taken a while, though, and it was hard initially, there was a lot of baggage to sort through. To be honest, I think Lucy's problems started before we'd even left Byron. It was a cry for attention but no one noticed. Mum and Dad were too busy fighting and I was too busy trying to stay out of the way. It was only later that I felt there was more I could have done to help Lucy. More I *should* have done. At the time I was too focussed on myself. I was seventeen, I just wanted to get out of the house and spend time with you.'

'With me?'

'I was happy at your house. There was no fighting, no arguing.'

Poppy agreed there had been few arguments but in her opinion it had been because no one had taken responsibility for anything in the commune, including responsibility for the children. Life had just drifted along and the kids had learned to organise themselves. The kids had been left to their own devices, no curfews, no supervision, no boundaries and very few disagreements. Any arguments had to be sorted out amongst themselves. They might not have been showered with love and affection but they learned resilience.

But Poppy felt dreadful. She'd had no idea what he'd been going through. She'd never thought about what it must have been like at home for him. 'Ryder, I had no idea. I'm so sorry. I should have listened.'

'I didn't want to talk about it. I just wanted to get away, to pretend it wasn't happening, and being at your place gave me the chance to do that. Until the day that my mother announced we were leaving. Then there was no escaping reality and it hit us with a vengeance once we got to Perth. It was only then, when I spent more time at home, that I saw what was going on with Lucy. Her anxiety escalated as Mum's depression worsened. It was a cry for attention from Lucy but Mum didn't notice. She was dealing with her own pain. It was up to me to figure out how to get them through that.'

'But who looked after you? You were only a teenager yourself.'

He shrugged, dismissing her concerns. 'I was okay. But that's why I know what these kids are dealing with. I figure I can make a difference. This is what I want to do. Work with disadvantaged or troubled kids. I told you I had a plan—this is it.'

'So what exactly are you going to do?'

'I've already done it. You're looking at a newly qualified psychologist.'

'What? Why didn't you tell me?'

'When you were telling me off for having no aspirations, you mean?'

He was smiling at her but Poppy was embarrassed. She felt remorseful but somewhat vindicated. 'Well, I was right, wasn't I? You *do* want more. But if you have a psychology degree…' She trailed off, not wanting to say the wrong thing again.

'Why am I goofing around in Bondi?' Ryder finished. He'd always known what she was thinking. 'I only finished my degree in the middle of the year. I had to work while I was studying so I could only study part time, but Mum and Lucy are both doing okay now. That's why I could take off. This was my time.'

'So what comes next?'

'I've got a job offer in Perth, a graduate psychologist position, working with kids. I start in February.'

'So you're definitely leaving.'

He nodded and Poppy realised her fears were real.

He had plans that didn't include her. He would leave her and she'd be alone again.

She had assumed this thing between them wouldn't, couldn't, last. She'd known it was only a matter of time before things went wrong, before Ryder would realise there was something wrong with her, that she wasn't worthy of love, but it looked like he might be gone sooner than she'd expected, and despite what she'd told Lily she knew her heart would crumble when he left.

CHAPTER SEVEN

RYDER CHECKED THE TIME. Four hours left of his shift. Four hours until he would be on his way to collect Poppy. He used to look forward to the end of his shift so that he could go for a surf. Now he looked forward to seeing Poppy.

They had spent years apart but he'd never forgotten her, and while she was still the girl of his teenage fantasies, time had marked her. She was still gorgeous, she still set his pulse racing, still made him lose his mind, but part of the girl he remembered had got lost in an adult world. He supposed the same could be said of all of them.

Was it unfair to compare teenage Poppy with adult Poppy? Probably. Life changed people. But Poppy had changed more than he would have expected.

She'd always had plans but her plans seemed a little one-dimensional to him. He knew she would argue that she was focussed but he would debate that she was ignoring her emotional needs in deference to her financial ones. While he understood her need for stability and security, he didn't think that fulfilment lay in material possessions.

In his opinion fulfilment came from personal connections, from having your emotional and physical needs met. And at the heart of all that was love. Not money. He was determined to convince her that financial security was not the be all and end all. Emotional security, happiness, trust and love were all far more important.

He knew Poppy's parents, and particularly her mother, hadn't been overly affectionate and that, as a consequence, she guarded her heart. He knew she loved her siblings, but could she love him?

Poppy never talked about her feelings. None of the Carlson siblings had ever spent much time talking about their feelings—their opinions, sure, but not their emotions. As a teenage boy he hadn't wanted to talk about feelings either, he'd been content just to have Poppy's company. Now he wanted her to open up to him. He knew she found it hard. He knew she was scared and vulnerable and Craig's infidelity hadn't helped. It had felt like a betrayal of the worst kind. Craig had rejected her. He hadn't loved her.

Poppy had told him she hadn't loved Craig either but that didn't take away her greatest fear. Her fear of not being loved. She'd never admitted that to him but he knew that was it. After all these years he still felt like he sometimes knew her better than she knew herself.

And he knew he had to convince her that there was more to life than a house and a healthy bank balance. He had to convince her that she needed more. Deserved more.

She needed love.

She deserved love.

His ego told him that he was the one who could give her that. He was the one who could make her happy. But was he kidding himself? Could she love him?

Ryder was starting to feel a sense of urgency. Poppy

was refusing to discuss the future with him and that worried him. She always had a plan. Was she refusing to discuss her plans because they didn't include him?

Did she want to be with him or was she deliberately putting up barriers? What if, after all these years, he was just her rebound guy?

It was a possibility. She'd said she'd imagined being with him since she was sixteen but what if, after all those years, it was simply a case of him being in the right place at the right time as her relationship with Craig had imploded. Was that all this was? A matter of convenience?

Did it matter if he was the rebound guy?

He knew it did. At least to him.

He wanted a lifetime. He wanted the dream.

But was it just that? A dream. Not a reality. Not *their* reality?

He had to convince her they were meant to be together. They'd lost twelve years. He couldn't let her go now.

His time in Bondi was drawing closer to an end but as his departure date loomed he realised he didn't want to leave. Not without Poppy.

He was hoping to convince her that she could come with him. That she could make a home with him.

He still loved her, had never *stopped* loving her. Could she love him?

He hated this feeling of insecurity, hated this feeling of the unknown. He had to get her to talk to him. He had to know what she was thinking. What she was feeling. Had to know if he could be the one for her.

He knew she needed stability and security. She wanted a house, a home, and he wanted to give her that. He doubted he'd be able to convince her to move away from her siblings, but he didn't have to go back to Western Australia. He could stay here, he would stay here, he'd do it for her. He would prove to her that she was worthy of being loved, of being adored. He wouldn't let her down.

She needed him to be mature. Dependable. Reliable. Stable. She needed him to be all those things. He knew it, even if she didn't.

He would show her he could be all those things. That he could be everything she needed. And if she wasn't going to make plans, he would. He'd give it everything he had.

Ryder took a deep breath as he parked outside Poppy's house after his shift. This was it. The moment of truth.

He had booked a weekend away for the two of them, and they were headed to a bed and breakfast at a Hunter Valley winery. They would go wine tasting and walking. They'd make love, sleep late and have breakfast in bed. They could spend time together, make new memories and see what their future held.

He was smiling as he knocked on the door but his smile didn't last long.

She answered the door dressed in her paramedic's uniform.

'Did you have a shift today?' he asked. He hadn't realised she'd been rostered on.

'No.'

She looked worried, distracted. He could always tell when she had something on her mind and knew he would probably need to prise it out of her. She never willingly disclosed her feelings.

'What's happened?'

'I just got off the phone from Craig,' she said as she headed for the kitchen.

Ryder's heart raced in his chest as he followed her through to the deck. He knew it was over between Poppy and Craig but he couldn't help the feeling of jealousy that flared up against his will whenever he thought of Poppy with Craig. The mention of his name reminded Ryder of all the time Poppy had wasted on someone who didn't appreciate her.

'He wants to put the house on the market,' Poppy continued.

'That's good.' Relief washed over him. Selling the house would sever their last connection. Poppy could be done with Craig and move on. It was a good thing in his opinion but Poppy's face suggested she didn't agree. 'Isn't it?'

She was shaking her head. 'No. I don't want to sell it.'

Ryder frowned. If she didn't want to sell it could only mean one thing. 'You want to keep it?'

She nodded.

That made no sense to him. Why would she want to keep a house she'd bought with Craig? There could only be one reason. 'Are you going back to Brisbane?'

'No. I'm not planning on going back but I worked hard for that house.'

'I understand that. But it's just a house.'

'It's more than that,' she said. 'It's the first house I ever owned. It's my home. I've never felt like I've had a home before.'

'What about where you grew up?'

'The commune!? You remember what that was like? People drifted in and out of the houses as they pleased. It never felt like our house belonged to us and I want a place that I *know* is mine. My parents never owned that house, they didn't even own the land it was on, and we could have been kicked off at any time and left with nothing. I need to know I have a roof over my head and I've worked hard to get that and I'm not going to give it up.'

'What are you saying?'

'I don't want to sell. I want to buy Craig out. Which means I need all the money I can get.'

Ryder finally caught up. 'You're taking an extra shift? Tonight?'

She nodded. 'Yes.'

'What about our weekend away?'

'I'm sorry, Ryder, I need the money. I want to keep my house.'

Ryder could see his plans evaporating before him bur perhaps he could salvage something, he thought as he quickly ran through his options.

They could leave later. It would mean they lost a day but that was better than nothing. He was prepared to compromise. That was what love was all about, wasn't it? And he loved her. He suspected he'd never stopped loving her.

'Do you want to leave tomorrow instead?' he asked.

She shook her head. 'I've taken a shift tomorrow, too.'

'You're going to work all weekend?' She wouldn't look at him and he knew the answer. 'So we're not going away.'

'Can I take a rain check?'

He was beginning to suspect that life with Poppy might be an endless series of rain checks. Love was about compromise, respect, trust and honesty but Ryder didn't want to always be the only one making sacrifices, he didn't want to be the one always waiting. 'What's more important?' he asked. 'Being happy or working yourself to the bone?'

'I've put hours and hours of my time into that house, not to mention blood, sweat and tears and thousands of dollars. I'm not giving it up.'

He knew Poppy needed security and stability but he'd hoped their relationship might have been a higher priority than a house, but he'd obviously been kidding himself. 'There's more to life than a big bank balance and a fancy house, Poppy.'

If she didn't realise that then he had nothing to offer her.

His heart was heavy in his chest, his hopes and dreams dashed. Had he made a mistake? Had he let his memories could his judgement? Had the girl he remembered changed that much?

No, the Poppy he remembered was still there. Still making plans. The only problem was her current plan was to save her house at the expense of everything else.

He had plans too but it seemed that while he was considering a future with her, she was on a different path. Did he even matter?

Ryder was nursing a mild hangover courtesy of Jet, but he knew his lack of focus was related more to Poppy than to the beers he'd had last night.

After Poppy had cancelled their plans he'd gone directly to Jet and put his hand up for any extra shifts that were available. Jet had known about his plans for the weekend but he hadn't questioned him. He'd taken one look at him and said he'd see what he could do and he'd managed to find additional shifts. Ryder appreciated the opportunity to stay busy but even though it was a glorious November day not even the brilliant sunshine could lift his mood.

Poppy had called him twice last night but he'd let the calls go through to his message service. He didn't know if he wanted to hear what she had to say. He didn't trust himself not to lose his temper. He had always prided himself on being impartial, on being able to listen to other's points of view without judgement, but Poppy was testing his patience.

He wanted to be there for her but he also wanted her to give him the same consideration. He wanted to be important to her. He didn't want to be a stopgap, something or someone to be discarded the moment another priority came along. He wanted to be her priority.

Was he being unfair?

He didn't think so. Their relationship was fledgling but that didn't mean it wasn't important. It didn't mean he wasn't important.

If it had been any other weekend he would probably have been more understanding but this weekend was supposed to have been special and it hurt to think that Poppy could so easily give it up. Give him up.

She'd told him that she'd thought about being with him for twelve years. Now that she'd ticked that box, was she moving on? Was he nothing but a curiosity? A teenage fantasy that hadn't lived up to her expectations?

He'd been watching the water at the south end of the beach as his mind turned over. In front of him was a group of teenage boys, tackling each other and doing somersaults over the waves. He could remember doing the same thing in his youth but now, with the wisdom of experience, seeing these antics worried him. What if one of them mistimed his landing? Misjudged the depth of the water? Landed on their head? He thought of all the things that could go wrong but knew they wouldn't listen to his warnings. Knew they would consider him to be worrying over nothing.

He redirected his gaze, looking towards Backpackers' Rip, looking for anything out of the ordinary. The late afternoon swell was picking up, the breeze was coming in. He could see a lone swimmer getting close to the rip. A man with dark hair. He disappeared briefly behind a wave and Ryder waited for his head to bob up again. He didn't look like a confident swimmer and he made a note to keep an eye on him.

'Would you mind if we took a photo with you?'

Ryder's attention was drawn away from the ocean by two tourists, two pretty girls in bikinis, who brandished a cellphone. The lifeguards were constantly being asked to pose for photographs. Ryder didn't usually mind, it was a pleasant part of the job—unless the tourists got a little too familiar, which happened on occasion. This time, though, it was a couple of quick selfies and he was happy to oblige.

The girls checked the photos and, as they requested 'just one more', Ryder thought he saw a hand raised in the ocean.

He checked for the lone swimmer.

He couldn't see him.

The afternoon sun was behind him, bright on the water, and he wasn't one hundred per cent certain of what he'd seen. Maybe the swimmer had got out of the water. Maybe he hadn't seen a hand. It could have been a trick of the light. The sea was getting rough and the swell and the sunlight made it difficult to get a clear visual. But he needed to check.

He excused himself from the tourists and grabbed the binoculars and the radio. He'd call it into the Tower. Jet had a better vantage point from up there, he'd be able to see over the waves.

'Central, this is Ryder.'

'Go ahead, Easy.'

'I'm down at Backpackers'. I've had my eye on a lone swimmer, just north of the rip, behind the first breakers. I've lost sight of him behind the waves. Can you see if you can spot him? Male, dark hair.'

Ryder waited several seconds, knowing that Jet would be taking his time, scanning the waves, giving himself time to see if the swimmer was moving or giving him time to surface if he'd gone under. Looking for anything untoward. Ryder kept his eyes on the water too but came up with nothing.

'Nothing,' came Jet's reply. 'I can't see anyone on their own or anyone who looks like they're in trouble.'

Despite Jet confirming that he hadn't seen anything either, Ryder still felt uneasy. He knew it was possible that the man had returned to shore or was swimming with friends but he had the distinct impression that the man wasn't a strong swimmer and his sudden disappearance had him worried.

'I reckon I'll go out for a look,' he told Jet. 'Just to be on the safe side.'

'Copy that,' came the reply.

He lifted the rescue board from the rack on the side of the buggy and jogged into the water. He threw the board in front of him and leapt on, paddling out, up and over the swell. He didn't see anyone who looked in need of help on his way out and when he got to the spot where he'd last seen the man there was nothing but empty water. He sat astride the board and scanned the sea again. Nothing.

He paddled a little further out to check with the surfers. He knew they often came to the aid of struggling swimmers, and even though he couldn't see anyone who looked like they were being a Good Samaritan, they might be able to shed some light on the man's whereabouts. But none of them had noticed anything untoward either.

He figured the swimmer must have left the water while he'd been busy with the tourists. Maybe he'd imagined the hand in the air. Maybe he hadn't seen anything at all, he thought as he returned to the beach.

He spent the next hour patrolling the beach, pulling people out of the water, reuniting kids with their distracted parents, and he'd almost forgotten about the lone swimmer when a young woman approached the buggy where he and Bluey were standing.

Ryder initially thought she was also after a photo but then he saw she wasn't smiling or holding a cellphone. She looked worried.

'Please, can you help me?' She spoke with what Ryder thought was an Eastern European accent. 'My boyfriend is missing.'

'What do you mean, missing?'

This woman was in her early twenties and he assumed the boyfriend would be a similar age. People that age didn't go missing on Bondi.

'He went for a swim. I fell asleep. He has not come back.'

'When was this? How long ago?'

The woman gave a little shrug as if she wasn't quite sure but her eyes filled with tears, her distress obvious. 'One hour?'

'Where were you sleeping?' Ryder asked.

She pointed to the southern end of the beach and

Ryder's heart plummeted. She was pointing towards Backpackers' Rip. 'Can he swim?'

'A little.'

That was not what he wanted to hear.

'What does he look like? Dark hair, blond? Tall, short?' Ryder accompanied his questions with hand gestures. Pointing at her hair, raising his hand high and low but she didn't seem to need his pantomime, her English was accented but good.

'Not as tall as you,' she said as she looked him up and down. 'Smaller. Dark hair.'

'What's his name?'

'Sergei.'

'And what is your name?'

'Mika.'

'Okay, Mika, I want you to take a look and see if you can see him in the water,' Ryder said as he handed her a pair of binoculars. Maybe with some additional magnification she would spot him.

He switched on the radio. 'Ryder to Central. We've got a report of a missing person who might have gone swimming. Possibly in Backpackers'.' His voice remained calm even though his gut was churning. Had he missed something? He knew Jet would be thinking the same as him.

He turned to Mika, who was standing next to Bluey, binoculars raised. 'Can you see him?'

She shook her head.

'Central, Bluey and I will head out but we need someone to check the beach, the foreshore, everywhere.' There was a possibility that Sergei wasn't in the water. It was a slim chance but there nonetheless. 'And can you send someone down here with the defib?'

'Copy that,' Jet replied. 'I'll send Dutchy down and get Gibbo to launch the jet-ski.'

There were eight lifeguards on duty and this search and rescue would stretch them thin on other parts of the beach but that was unavoidable. They needed all the manpower they could muster. Ryder knew Jet would call the police as well as the paramedics.

He grabbed one rescue board as Bluey dashed off to pick up one that was stored further along the beach. He ran into the water, threw the board down and leapt on. The swell had dropped, the tide had eased and the water was clear. It was getting late but there was still enough light to ensure good visibility. The lifeguards would have been thinking about packing up soon but that would change now, depending on the outcome of their search.

He looked over his shoulder as he paddled out. He could see Dutchy in one of the buggies, heading for Mika, and he could hear the whine of the jet-ski as Gibbo hit the water.

'Central.' He spoke out loudly, knowing the radio microphone in his armband would relay his words to the tower. 'Tell Gibbo to head out the back, he can check the rip.'

Backpackers' Rip could have carried an unsuspecting swimmer out to sea or Sergei could be stranded on the rocks past Icebergs. Ryder thought that second scenario was unlikely as someone would have alerted the tower, but if he'd been carried out to sea they might never find him.

He kept paddling as he searched the water, top and bottom, but he couldn't quieten the voice in his head, the one that told him that if the swimmer he'd thought he'd seen earlier had been Sergei then there was a good chance that it was going to be too late to save him now.

'What's going on, man?' He looked up to see one of the surfers he'd spoken to earlier paddling towards him.

'We've had a report of a missing person. It's possible he may have gone swimming.'

'Is it the guy you were looking for earlier?'

'Could be. Have any of you helped someone out today? Taken them out of the water?'

'Not me, man, but I'll check with the others. Who are we looking for?'

'A man, slight build, mid-twenties, dark hair.' It was important to know Ryder wasn't looking for a female, or a teenager, or an elderly swimmer, but Ryder knew, in reality, they were looking for a body. A poor swimmer wasn't going to last in the ocean in these conditions for an hour or more, and even a competent swimmer would have become fatigued. If Sergei was in the water they were looking at a recovery exercise and that knowledge weighed heavily on Ryder's conscience.

The surfer nodded and paddled off.

'Gibbo has got nothing.' Jet's voice came through the radio in Ryder's armband.

'We've got nothing either,' Ryder responded. Everyone seemed to be accounted for. Maybe Sergei hadn't gone swimming after all. 'Have you checked the toilet block and showers?'

'Yes, we're covering all bases,' Jet replied, and Ryder could hear what was unsaid. Sergei hadn't been found on dry land and, therefore, he must be in the water. His stomach sat like a stone in his belly.

'I've called Lifesaver One, they're on the way,' Jet added.

Ryder heard the chopper approaching as the surfer returned.

'Most of the guys have only been in the water for

about an hour,' the surfer told him, 'and there've been plenty of swimmers with dark hair.' Ryder knew that was always the case, it was like trying to pick a needle out of a haystack if that was his only defining feature. 'But no one has seen anyone in trouble or given anyone any assistance.'

The surfer's information sounded like good news but Ryder's antennae were twitching. He knew how quickly and silently people could drown. If Sergei had been swimming alone, which seemed like the case, he could easily have drowned without anyone noticing.

He thanked the surfer as Lifesaver One appeared over the headland. The helicopter hovered over the ocean, staying high enough above the waves so the wash from its rotors didn't disturb the water.

Ryder and Bluey waited as the chopper moved slowly overhead but there was nothing to indicate they'd spotted anything untoward.

'Do we keep looking?' Bluey asked.

Ryder nodded. He could see two ambulances and a quick response vehicle parked near the lifeguard tower plus several police cars. Police could be seen combing the beach but there was still no sign of Sergei. Ryder wouldn't give up until it got too dark to see. Or until Sergei was found.

He paddled towards Icebergs Surf Club and drifted over a bed of seaweed near the rocks. The rocks cast shadows on the water and the dark seaweed took on a slightly sinister appearance. Patches of pale sand broke through the blackness, providing some relief. His eyes skimmed the sea bed, looking without really seeing, but as he lifted his head to see if anyone else had had any success something caught his eye. Unsure if it was an irregular shape or an unexpected movement, he looked beneath the surface again.

He peered into the water.

Something pale was moving in the depths. It might have been weed or a stingray or a fish but as his eyes adjusted to the gloom he was filled with dread. Briefly he hoped his eyes were deceiving him but in reality he knew they were not.

He wasn't looking at a patch of sand. Or a fish.

It was a hand. And it was several feet under the surface.

CHAPTER EIGHT

'Blue! Over here,' he yelled over his shoulder as he slid off his board and dived down to the ocean floor.

The hand belonged to a dark-haired man. Ryder pulled on his arm but the man didn't move. His lungs were burning as he dived deeper. The man's eyes were open, staring lifelessly into the ocean.

He pulled on the man's shorts. This time he moved slightly but he still didn't come free. Ryder looked down. The man's foot was tangled in the seaweed. He was trapped, tethered to the ocean floor. He must have gone under and become stuck.

Ryder surfaced and breathed in deeply, preparing to dive again.

'Have you found him?' Bluey asked.

He nodded. He was certain it was Sergei. It *had* to be Sergei.

'I'll let everyone know.' Bluey's usual happy disposition was subdued by Ryder's expression. There was no need for further discussion, it was obvious the outcome was a tragic one.

Ryder submerged himself again, this time diving deeper to free Sergei's foot. The weed was thick and slippery and he had to work hard to free it. Sergei must have panicked when the weed had wrapped around his foot. Of course he would have panicked but somehow he had made the situation worse by thrashing about.

He pulled the weed from around Sergei's ankle and then grabbed him under the armpits and dragged him to the surface. He might be slight but he was a dead weight and Ryder's muscles and lungs were screaming by the time he broke through the waves.

Sergei was limp and unresponsive.

Bluey had called for the jet-ski and Ryder and Bluey wrangled the body onto the rescue sled that was towed behind the ski. Gibbo would get him back to shore as quickly as possible so resuscitation could be attempted. They could only assume how long he'd been submerged for and all efforts would have to be made to revive him.

Ryder and Bluey paddled into shore. Ryder was exhausted, mentally and physically drained, but he had to keep going. He hopped off his rescue board in the shallow water and dragged it back to the lifeguard buggy.

Gibbo had brought the jet-ski in nearby and Ryder could see dozens of first responders circling around. There were several paramedics in attendance, Poppy amongst them, as well as an intensive care doctor.

Poppy's blonde hair shone in the afternoon light and guided him up from the water like a beacon. Despite the fact that she had cancelled their plans, despite the fact that she had made it clear that he wasn't her priority, he couldn't prevent his heart rate from escalating when he saw her. He still wanted her, she still stirred him. He hadn't stopped loving her and he knew he wouldn't for a long time. It was possible he would always love her.

She was sitting with Mika, with one arm wrapped around the girl's shoulder. Poppy saw him coming up the beach and she smiled at him but her smile didn't reach her eyes. The afternoon had taken a toll on all of them, most of all Sergei and Mika.

It was getting late and Ryder could feel a slight chill in the air. Normally by this time the crowds on the beach would be starting to thin out but there was still a large number of people hanging around. They were attracted to the drama, wanting to know how the story ended.

In an attempt to give Sergei some privacy the police had erected a screen around him and the mass of first responders. Ryder couldn't get close but he didn't need to. He could hear the resuscitation efforts and while he understood the need for the medics to try their best, he knew, in his gut, it had been too long. Sergei's skin was grey and waxy. It would take a miracle to bring him back.

Ryder's knees were like jelly. Goosebumps covered his skin and he knew he should get warm but his legs weren't steady enough to support him. He knelt in the sand to give himself a minute to recover.

'How are you doing?'

He looked up to find Jet standing in front of him. He was holding out a beach towel and Ryder took it and wrapped it around himself as he tried to stop the shivering.

'I'm okay,' he said, even though he wasn't. He was far from okay, but he wasn't about to have that conversation here, now, on the sand in the midst of the crowd. He didn't want strangers hearing his thoughts. Hearing him confess his regrets. His guilt.

He felt responsible for the situation they found themselves in. Had it been Sergei he'd seen earlier? Had he raised a hand? Had he requested assistance? Had he been to blame? Was there more he could have done?

'You should go up to the tower and get warm,' Jet said.

'In a minute.' Like the rest of the crowd he couldn't make himself move away but he had more invested in the outcome. Not that he thought, for one minute, it would be anything but tragic, but he was going to force himself to stay until the end. He owed Sergei that much.

He got to his feet. There was nothing he could do for Sergei but perhaps there was something he could do for Mika.

He walked over to where Poppy and Mika were sitting and sat beside Poppy. She had Mika wrapped in a space blanket, trying to combat the cold and the shock. An oxygen cylinder stood at the ready. Just in case. He could tell Poppy wanted to shield Mika from the drama, wanted to protect her, but Mika was only half turned away and Ryder could understand her compulsion to watch. As if she could ward off the inevitable if she was brave enough to watch.

Mika looked across at Ryder. 'He is not going to be okay, is he?'

Her voice was flat. She wasn't asking a question but stating a fact.

'I'm sorry,' he said. 'No one saw him go under.'

Ryder sounded exhausted and Poppy knew he was trying to keep his emotions under control. She knew he would be struggling to make sense of the tragedy, knew his mind would be churning with questions, wondering if there was anything else he could have done.

She had seen him pull Sergei to the surface and she could imagine how he was feeling. She had seen plenty of dead bodies in her line of work and she knew Ryder would have seen his fair share too but you never became immune to the suffering, the loss, the effect that someone's passing had on family and loved ones. And with someone who was young, whose death had in all likelihood been avoidable, it was especially difficult to accept.

She could feel the tension in his shoulders, could see it in the set of his jaw, and knew he was fighting to hold himself together. She knew he wouldn't want to lose his composure in public.

She wished she could take him in her arms and make everything better, but for now all she could do was let him know she was there for him. She slid her free hand under the towel that was wrapped around his shoulders. Her fingers found his and she squeezed his hand gently, reassuring him, trying to comfort him with her presence, but there was no response from Ryder. His hand was cold and still. He didn't react, she got nothing back.

Was he upset with her?

She knew she'd ruined his plans but there would be other weekends. She'd thought he would understand. He always had. He always knew what she was thinking, how she was feeling, without her having to spell it out for him.

Perhaps it was just the stress of the day. Perhaps he wasn't upset with her but upset with the situation. That was understandable. She would make it up to him, she promised herself. This time she would be a shoulder for him to lean on.

To their credit the medics tried everything possible in difficult conditions but their resuscitation efforts were in vain. The defibrillator reported no shockable rhythm and the drugs didn't work. The intensive care specialist eventually called time of death and Sergei was covered with a sheet.

'I need to get Mika to the ambulance,' Poppy said to Ryder as the other paramedics, lifeguards and police moved Sergei to a stretcher and lifted it, preparing to carry him off the beach. 'I'll meet you at the tower.'

She was loath to leave him but she had a job to do. But the sooner she had Mika sorted the sooner she would be able to give Ryder her attention.

'Come with me, Mika.' She kept her arm wrapped around the woman's shoulders and led her across the sand. She doubted she would be able to walk across the beach without assistance. Without someone to gently encourage her to put one foot in front of the other.

News crews and beachgoers lined the promenade. They were being held back by the police but Poppy also wanted to shield Mika from curious spectators. She had enough to deal with. The emergency services workers were met with silence but Poppy could still feel hundreds of eyes watching them. It was an uncomfortable sensation. As quickly as she could she got Mika sorted, handing her over to a policewoman who would take care of her. Mika didn't need medical attention, the police would look after her, leaving Poppy and her colleague, Alex, free to check on the lifeguards. She passed Mika and Sergei's belongings over and went to tell Alex to meet her in the tower.

Ryder was sitting by the desk, leaning forward, his elbows on his knees, his head in his hands, staring at the floor. Poppy went to him without hesitation. She put her hand on his shoulder and he lifted his head. He looked wiped out, mentally and emotionally exhausted. She stepped closer, between his knees, and held his head against her. She didn't speak. What could she say?

She rubbed his back, her hand making small, firm circles, reassuring him through touch, but Ryder still didn't respond. He had dropped his hands but otherwise was motionless. It was almost as though he was completely unaware of her presence.

Jet had boiled the kettle and handed Ryder and Bluey each a mug of hot coffee. Poppy could smell something else. Whisky? Had he added a dash? It wouldn't hurt.

'What now?' she asked him.

'It's almost seven. Dutchy can close the beach and we'll have a debrief.'

'Ryder and Bluey need to get warm. They need to shower and change.'

Jet nodded. 'They can head to the shower block now, we'll manage the beach.'

Ryder still hadn't spoken and Poppy was worried. She bent down and kissed him gently, focussing his attention on her for a moment. 'I'll come back after my shift,' she said, 'and take you home with me.'

She would be his sounding board, she would give him someone to lean on, to talk to. It was her turn to listen and this time she would be there for him.

By the time Poppy returned to the lifeguard tower Ryder was showered and dressed. He had changed into jeans and a T-shirt and had thrown a thick, warm jacket over his top but he still felt cold and, if he was honest, he didn't really feel like company. In fact, he'd had deliberated long and hard about whether or not he'd wait for Poppy to come back.

His mind had been spinning in the shower and he'd had trouble sorting through one thought before another one would take over. Could he have done more? Could he have saved Sergei? Life was short, and today's tragedy reinforced that fact. What did he want from his life?

What did Poppy want? Did she want him? Did they have a future? Where would they go from here?

He was still trying to process his thoughts when Poppy walked in. If he'd wanted to escape he'd missed his opportunity.

'How's Mika doing?' he asked, forcing himself to say something.

'She's in good hands. She's with a social worker. She'll organise embassy assistance and a translator and whatever else Mika needs.'

Ryder nodded but couldn't find the energy to continue the conversation.

Poppy reached for his hands and tugged him out of the chair. 'Come on, time to go.'

He let her lead him outside. It was easier to stay silent and go with her than to explain how he was feeling. There were things they needed to sort out. Sergei's death had crystallised his thoughts in one respect. Life was tenuous and he wasn't prepared to sit around and wait for Poppy to decide if she wanted a relationship with him or not.

He needed to know how she felt.

He loved her and he needed to hear how she felt. He needed to know if she was going to take a chance on love. On him.

He didn't want to lose Poppy but if they didn't have a future he wanted to know.

Ryder hadn't said one word during the drive home and even though it was only a short distance Poppy's concern escalated. He was usually the first to make conversation but his responses to her attempts to talk were monosyllabic at best and once they were inside things didn't improve.

'Are you hungry?' she asked.

'No.'

'I think you should eat something. I'll make cheesy treats. Comfort food.'

He gave her a half-smile in reply but nothing more.

She fed him, hoping food would improve his state of mind. She waited until he had demolished the sandwiches before testing the waters again.

'Any better?'

'Not really.'

She nestled into his side and put her hand on his chest, connecting them together. 'It was a tragic accident,' she said, trying to reassure him. 'Everyone did their best.'

'Did I?' he sighed. 'Do you know I thought I'd seen a raised hand in Backpackers' earlier in the afternoon. I went out looking but didn't find anything. What if that was Sergei? What if I missed something?'

'Why would you think that? Sergei wasn't reported missing until late in the day and no one else saw anything. I was on the beach, listening, when you were searching. No one suspected anything untoward.'

'You know how silently and quickly people drown. What if I could have done more? What if this is my fault? There hasn't been a death from drowning at Bondi for several years.'

'But there have been deaths from other causes. As lifeguards, do you blame yourselves every time?'

'To a degree. Don't you?'

'As a paramedic I've learned that people die. Sometimes we are able to help, sometimes we aren't, but it's not helpful to dwell on the fatalities. We hope to learn from any mistakes but sometimes there is nothing that can be done. Doing our best is all that's possible.'

'I'm not sure that I did my best.'

'Bondi Beach isn't only your responsibility. No one else noticed Sergei in trouble. Not another lifeguard, not the tower, not a surfer. His girlfriend didn't even know. You can't blame yourself.'

'I'm sure Mika does.'

'Oh, Ryder. I don't think anyone will think this is your fault.' She hugged him tightly, wishing she could take his pain away or at least share it. She hated to see him hurting.

'I might not be totally to blame but I have to take some of the responsibility. One minute Mika and Sergei are enjoying a trip to Australia, a day at the beach, and the next Mika is dealing with her boyfriend's body. It made me think about my life. My mortality. My future. It made me think about what I want. Each of us has limited time and I want to make the most of my life. I want to be happy. I want to make a difference. I want to be someone's priority. I want to be *your* priority.'

Poppy went cold. Her hands trembled and her heart pounded and she knew it was fear.

She needed Ryder, she loved him, but she heard his unspoken words and she couldn't disagree. She hadn't put him first.

She had never told him how she felt. She hadn't told him or shown him. She'd just expected him to know—he'd always known what she was thinking. She'd thought he'd know how she felt, how important he was to her. 'You…'

'I what?' he prompted. 'I am your priority?' He shook his head. 'I don't think so. Your house, your career, your bank balance, you've chosen all of that over me. I shouldn't have been at work today. I was only there because you changed our plans. You chose to go to work instead of spending time with me. If I hadn't been at work maybe Sergei would have been someone else's responsibility. Maybe someone else would have saved him.'

'You're blaming me?'

'No.' He shook his head. 'Not for Sergei. That's my cross to bear. But I don't think you and I want the same things and it makes me wonder what I'm doing here. My job here is temporary and today I didn't even do it well. I've got a job waiting for me in Perth. You've got your house in Brisbane, your career. If we want different things then there's nothing to keep me here.'

'What are you saying?' Poppy was shaking now.

'You need to work out what you want. You need to decide if you have room for me in your life. I had to leave you twelve years ago and I don't want to leave you again but life is short. I don't want to always be waiting.'

'You're leaving?'

'I have a job waiting for me in Perth. It's time.'

'You're going back to Perth!?' He couldn't mean it. He couldn't be talking about leaving her again.

'I've been thinking about my options for a while, today's events just helped to clarify my future for me.'

'No.' She couldn't let him go. She couldn't lose him. Not again. She needed more time. 'You need to rest. Things won't seem so grim in the morning, they never do.'

'I don't see what will change. In the morning Sergei will still be dead and I'll still be waiting for you to choose me.'

She wasn't ready to let him go. 'Come to bed. Let me comfort you,' she said, but Ryder shook his head.

'No. I'm not going to be good company, I need to be alone.'

She stood in the passage and watched as he walked out the door. The words she knew she should have said stuck in her throat, threatening to choke her. She had lied to herself. Told herself that she didn't want anything serious, that she wouldn't fall in love, but the truth was she'd already been in love. She had always loved Ryder.

Why couldn't she tell him?

She sank to the floor as the door closed behind him. Her legs couldn't support her any longer.

Had that just happened? Had Ryder left her? Had she lost him again?

Tears ran down her face as she grappled with the thought that once more she'd been rejected. But she couldn't blame Ryder. This was all her fault.

He was right. She'd put her house before him. How stupid was she? What was the point of having a home if she didn't have Ryder?

She'd wanted a life that was safe and predictable but that wasn't realistic. Life wasn't safe and predictable and a life without Ryder would mean nothing. She couldn't let him go. She'd give up everything she had if she got to keep Ryder.

She had to let him know.

She thought about going after him but her legs wouldn't move and she knew she needed to work through this. She would only get one chance, she needed to make it count.

She needed a plan. She needed to prepare.

Tomorrow she would put the wheels in motion. She would show Ryder how she felt. She would speak to Craig and agree to put the house on the market, that would be the first step, and then she'd speak to Ryder. She had time. He wouldn't leave her tomorrow.

* * *

Ryder sat in the wooden lifeguard tower at Tamarama Beach and tried to concentrate on the ocean. It was a glorious day but even the early morning surf he'd had and the sight of the sun on the ocean couldn't lift his spirits. He was struggling to reconcile himself with Sergei's death and the part he'd had to play. A lot had gone wrong and he accepted that most of it was not his responsibility. Sergei shouldn't have been swimming at the southern end of the beach but if Mika hadn't fallen asleep it could have been different. If Sergei had been a stronger swimmer, if his foot hadn't got stuck, if someone else had seen something, the outcome could have been very different.

In hindsight he knew he'd done his best and he knew he couldn't change what had happened but next time he'd trust his instincts. But Sergei's death wasn't the only problem. He was in a bad mood and he knew it was because of his uncertainty over Poppy.

Sergei's death had reinforced for him that losing someone you loved had to be the worst pain imaginable and he was terrified he was going to lose Poppy. He'd given her a chance to tell him how she felt and she'd told him nothing.

He'd thought he understood her, sometimes he'd thought he knew her better than she knew herself, but in this case he was flying blind. He'd thought she loved him but he wondered now if he really knew her at all. He had no idea what she was thinking and he could go crazy trying to figure her out.

He didn't want to be without her but a relationship had to be a reciprocal agreement. If she didn't love him then he'd have to accept they were done. They had no future.

If she didn't want him, if she didn't need him, he'd go home. Back to Perth. He wasn't sure that his mother or sister needed him any more either but they were family. He didn't want to leave Poppy, but if she didn't want him he had no reason to stay in Bondi.

He loved her but he'd got over her once before.

He didn't want to do it again but the situation was out of his hands. It was up to Poppy.

He sighed and picked up the binoculars and scanned the surf. Jet had suggested that he take the day off but he'd insisted on keeping his shift. It was better to be busy. It gave him less time to think about Sergei. Less time to think about Poppy.

Tamarama had two permanent rips and was one of Sydney's most treacherous beaches. It was adjacent Bondi, one beach further south, and was staffed by the Bondi lifeguards during the busy summer period. Ryder could see many experienced surfers in the water but it was the inexperienced ones he was keeping under surveillance. He wished there was a way of discouraging novice surfers to avoid Tamarama but it was a popular surf spot with good consistent waves.

He had his eye trained on a lone surfer who appeared to be drifting south towards Bronte and the notorious rock formation called The Twins. Many surfers had come unstuck in that stretch of ocean. The two tall rocks, The Twins, were separated by a narrow channel of water and the tide created a vortex that, once it took hold of you, sucked you in between the rocks against your will. It was a skill to be able to escape the power of the ocean. Time the waves incorrectly and you'd find yourself thrown against the rocks, putting you at risk of abrasions, broken bones or worse.

He kept his binoculars focussed on the surfer, knowing he needed to paddle north, away from the rocks, back towards the beach. But unless he was a strong swimmer and also aware of the dangers, Ryder knew it would be difficult for him to make it.

Every second that passed saw him pulled closer and closer to the rocks. He saw him begin to paddle and he willed him on but his efforts were in vain. The rip was dragging him further from safety. Closer to danger.

Ryder knew he couldn't wait any longer. The surfer was in trouble.

He stood up and dropped the binoculars on the bench.

'Gibbo, call Central and tell them to send the jet-ski. There's a surfer headed for The Twins.'

He grabbed the rescue tube and flew down the stairs, leaving Gibbo in the tower, knowing that the outcome of this emergency was all up to him. If the surfer was sucked between the two massive rocks there was only one way he was coming out and that would be with Ryder and the rescue tube. The long rescue boards were useless in the narrow gap between the rocks, as were the jet-skis.

The jet-ski would take several minutes to arrive. It needed to travel one and a half kilometres from Bondi to Tamarama and Ryder had no idea if it had been launched today. If it was still on the trailer by the tower, that would add even more precious minutes before it could be of assistance. In any case, in this situation the jet-ski was only useful for transporting a patient back to shore. It was impossible to get near The Twins using the ski. The vortex created by the tide would simply suck the jet-ski in as well, smashing it against the rocks.

Ryder slung the strap of the rescue tube diagonally over his chest and one shoulder, tucked the bright yellow tube under his arm and sprinted down the beach.

He ran through the shallow water, threw the tube behind him and dived under the first wave break, surfacing and swimming strongly towards The Twins as the tube floated in his wake, pulled along by the rope.

He swam parallel to the beach, lifting his head every now and then to check his direction. He could see the surfer. He was still trying to paddle away from the rocks but he was making absolutely no progress. He had seconds before he would be sucked in between the rocks.

Ryder swam harder, knowing it was futile. There was no way he could reach him in time.

The next wave was his undoing. It picked the surfer up and swept him into the gap and Ryder lost sight of him.

'Bondi Fifteen, can you head to Tamarama Beach. Lifeguards have requested standby assistance for a water rescue.'

'Copy that,' Poppy said, as she swung the ambulance around and headed towards Tamarama. She parked on the road overlooking the beach. There was a crowd of people standing on the path that ran along the clifftop and stretched from Coogee Beach past Bronte and Tamarama to Bondi and was popular with joggers and walkers. The spectators were all looking to the right, at the southern end of the beach.

She and Alex climbed out of the ambulance and joined the spectators at the clifftop fence. People were pointing at a surfer who was paddling furiously but, despite his efforts, was getting dragged closer and closer to the rocks at the base of the cliff. A lifeguard was closing in on him, cutting through the water with strong strokes, a yellow rescue tube dragging along behind him. The swell was large today, good for surfing but not so good for rescues.

A flash of red in the water to her left caught her eye. She turned her head and could see the Bondi lifeguard jet-ski racing south. She recognised Jet on the back of the jet-ski, his blond curls streaming behind him in the wind. She turned back towards the rocks. She saw the lifeguard pause and lift his head to check on the surfer's location. Her stomach dropped. It looked like Ryder.

She strained her eyes but the distance and the breaking waves made it impossible to see for certain. He had broad shoulders, thick hair that could be either dark blonde or brown. She felt in her gut that it was Ryder, the tilt of his head, the shape of his jaw was familiar, but he shouldn't be working. After the drama of yesterday, after Sergei's drowning, surely Ryder should have been given the day off? What was he doing at work?

'Can I borrow the binos?' she asked. Alex passed the binoculars over and she lifted them to her face.

Her stomach lurched.

It *was* Ryder.

She lowered the binoculars, widening her field of vision. The tide was strong and the surfer was getting pulled further and further away from Ryder.

He was close to the rocks now.

In the blink of an eye he was sucked behind a large rock. Swept out of sight.

Her heart was in her mouth as she saw Ryder put his head down and swim towards the rocks. He followed the surfer, swimming directly into the path of danger until he too disappeared from view.

She held her breath, waiting, willing him to reappear.

It seemed to take for ever, but eventually she saw him, swimming strongly away from the massive rock formation. It was slow going as he dragged the surfer behind him. The yellow rescue tube was around the surfer's chest and the rope attached to the harness stretched tightly from Ryder's shoulders to the tube. The surfboard was nowhere to be seen as he swam towards the open water.

The jet-ski was stationary in the water. Jet was on the back, sitting behind another lifeguard, possibly Dutchy. Why weren't they moving?

She realised they couldn't risk going closer or they'd be putting themselves at risk of getting smashed on the rocks. Ryder was going to have to swim to them.

Poppy checked his progress. The surfer was conscious, floating on his back with one arm held across his chest. He was attempting a half-backstroke movement, trying to swim, but it was clear Ryder was doing the majority of the work. He towed the surfer away from the shore but it was slow going.

She heard the thump-thump-thump of a helicopter and looked up. Lifesaver One appeared, hovering above the ocean. Beneath the chopper the jet-ski was moving again. It had turned ninety degrees and was heading out to sea. Poppy frowned. Where were they going?

And then she saw it. A rogue wave was bearing down on them and the jet-ski was sitting in the impact zone.

Dutchy rode the jet-ski up the face of the wave, dropping down the other side, the rescue mat flying in his wake.

Poppy eyes followed the path of the wave.

It was heading straight for Ryder and he had absolutely nowhere to go.

Her heart skittered in her chest as she watched in horror as the wave picked him up, lifted him over the surfer and hurled him towards the rocks.

She heard someone scream as Ryder was slammed, head first, into the rock and then sucked into the chasm.

Alex grabbed her arm, squeezing her forearm tight, and she realised she was the one screaming.

The wave collected the surfer next and he disappeared too, into the seething mass of white water at the base of the rocks. Roped together, they were powerless, insignificant against the force of the massive wall of water.

Poppy gripped the fence that ran along the cliff edge, her knuckles white with tension, as she waited, helplessly, for the water to release them. After what seemed like a lifetime one of the men was spat out from its hold.

It was the surfer who reappeared first, easily identified by the yellow tube that was still strapped around his chest.

She waited for Ryder, knowing he'd be close as he'd still be attached via the rope. As long as it had held.

She was afraid to breathe, afraid to blink, afraid to look away. The wind blew off the ocean and her eyes were stinging but she didn't turn her head, didn't close her eyes.

The surfer bobbed in the water. He wasn't trying to swim but this time the current pulled him away from the shore and eventually Ryder came into view.

He floated in the water.

He wasn't moving.

Waves crashed over his face and still he was immobile. Surely it was only a matter of time before he started to sink?

Poppy's heart was racing in her chest, making her feel faint. She bent double as a wave of nausea overwhelmed her. Bile rose in her throat as she fought fear.

She wanted to yell out, to tell the surfer to look out for Ryder, but she couldn't breathe and she couldn't scream and she knew the surfer wouldn't be able to hear her anyway. She was helpless, completely helpless.

She could see the surfer looking around. Could he feel Ryder's weight dragging on the rope? She saw when he registered the situation. He pulled on the rope with one hand, pulling himself towards Ryder and grabbed him with his good arm and somehow managed to hold his head out of the water.

The jet-ski was coming back for them and Poppy willed them to hurry.

Jet dived off the back off the ski and swam strongly towards Ryder. Poppy raised the binoculars in time to see him hook his arm under Ryder, unclip the rope from the rescue tube and separate the two men. He threw the rope to Dutchy, who pulled it through the water, dragging the surfer to the jet-ski.

Jet was treading water and supporting Ryder. He was limp in the water, lifeless.

Tears streamed down Poppy's cheeks as she silently begged Jet to save him. But what could he do? The jet-ski couldn't manage all of them in these conditions. Not with Ryder unconscious. Or worse.

CHAPTER NINE

JET WAS LOOKING up at the helicopter. He stretched one arm above his head and waved his hand in a circular motion, indicating to the crew that he needed help.

Poppy saw one of the rescue crew drop from the chopper. He landed in the water, feet first, and swam over to Jet. She watched as he and Jet slipped a harness over Ryder. They attached cables and winched Ryder and the rescue operator up to Lifesaver One. Ryder hung limply in the harness, giving Poppy no clue as to his condition.

As the helicopter banked and headed inland, she thought she might be sick. She had never felt so afraid or so helpless in all her life.

This was all her fault.

'Poppy, we need to go.'

Alex prompted her and she turned her attention back to the beach as the chopper flew out of sight. All she could do now was pray that Ryder was okay. She still felt physically sick but she had a job to do.

Dutchy had the jet-ski idling past the breaking waves. Somehow he'd managed to get the surfer onto the rescue mat at the back of the ski and was now waiting for Jet, who was swimming towards him. They'd be bringing the patient into the beach and she and Alex had work to do.

She took a deep breath and tried to steady her nerves as she and Alex grabbed kitbags and a stretcher from the ambulance and headed down to the sand.

The surfer was able to get himself off the rescue mat and walk up the beach but Poppy and Alex went to him, ready to support him if necessary. Over the man's shoulder Poppy mouthed a silent question to Jet. *Ryder?*

She knew, even if her family wasn't as used to lip-reading as they were, that Jet would understand her question. He put the tips of his thumb and forefinger together to make a circle, extending his three other fingers.

Okay.

He continued to sign, relaying a silent message. *Took a knock to the head, unconscious but breathing.*

He was alive.

Poppy breathed out and the tightness in her chest dissipated ever so slightly. Injured, but alive. How badly injured, she didn't know, but alive was better than the alternative. So much better.

She turned her attention to the patient. He had several nasty abrasions and was in significant pain with a dislocated shoulder, but after administering pain relief they were able to stabilise him and get him from the beach to the ambulance.

As Poppy pulled the ambulance to a stop in the emergency bay at Bondi General she could see Lily waiting with the team. She opened the rear doors and, while Alex unloaded the stretcher, she signed to Lily. *Was Ryder brought here?* She didn't want to discuss Ryder in front of another patient but she was desperate for news. Sign language allowed them to have a conversation.

Lily nodded.

Had he regained consciousness?

No. He's been taken off for scans.

Poppy longed to see him but she knew that was impossible. For now. She felt sick, completely helpless and utterly powerless.

Will you let me know if you hear anything? Tell him I'll be back as soon as my shift ends.

There was nothing else she could do.

Poppy burst into the emergency department of Bondi General. She'd had one update from Lily to let her know that Ryder had been admitted for observation after having his scans and that he was stable but still hadn't regained consciousness.

She was frantic, beside herself with worry, and knew she wouldn't relax until she'd seen him with her own eyes. Her concern was tinged with a heavy dose of guilt too. She couldn't shake the thought that Ryder's injury was all her fault.

She knew it was true. If they'd gone away like Ryder had planned he wouldn't have been in the water. He wouldn't have been at risk.

He wasn't supposed to be at work—not yesterday or today. He was supposed to be away with her for the weekend.

There was no denying *she* had put him in that position. She couldn't believe she'd thought it was more important to take the extra shifts at work than to spend time with him. Now she just had to hope she'd have an opportunity to make amends.

She saw Lily standing at the triage desk, waiting for her. Poppy didn't break stride. 'How is he?'

'He's sedated. The scans showed some swelling of

his brain but we won't know the full extent of his injuries until he regains consciousness.'

'Can I see him?' She was desperate. Nothing was more important to her than Ryder. Not her mortgage or her job. She'd been a fool.

Lily nodded and led her to his bedside. His eyes were closed and he looked pale under his tan. Poppy could see bruises and abrasions on the right side of his face. He had oxygen tubing under his nose and a dressing on his right shoulder. He was hooked up to various monitors but was breathing on his own. Poppy automatically checked the monitors, making sure the numbers were reasonable as she pulled the solitary chair away from the wall and positioned it next to the bed.

She sat down and reached for his left hand, wrapping her hands around his. She kissed his fingers and squeezed gently, hoping for a reaction, but there was nothing. He was still and silent.

She stroked the back of his hand as tears ran down her face. 'Ryder, I'm so sorry. This is all my fault.'

What if he didn't regain consciousness?

Why hadn't she gone after him last night? Why hadn't she been able to tell him what he'd wanted to hear? Why hadn't she been able to tell him how she felt?

What if she *never* got the chance?

The machines beeped and lights flashed but Poppy ignored them. She was attuned to the sounds of normal rhythms and could block out anything that wasn't sinister.

She was an idiot. A complete idiot. She could have lost him but she refused to contemplate the fact that he might not recover. As long as he was alive she had time to make it up to him.

She rested her head on the bed and promised she

would make amends. He had no idea how important he was to her. She hadn't told him and she certainly hadn't shown him. 'Please, be okay. I need you.'

She closed her eyes and held his hand and imagined that they were lying in bed together. Imagined that he was sleeping peacefully and would wake up and make love to her. She wondered if they would have that chance again.

Poppy was stiff and her back was aching but she was afraid to move. It had been several hours but she was afraid to let go of Ryder's hand in case he could feel her touch. She didn't want him to think she had left him. She didn't intend to leave him again and would stay by his side until he woke up.

She stood up but didn't move away. She kept hold of his hand, keeping their connection, as she kissed his forehead. 'I love you, Ryder. I should have told you that.'

The words flowed easily off her tongue now but she knew she had to find the courage to tell him when he woke up.

'I've always loved you.' She hadn't loved anyone else the same way. No one had ever made her feel like Ryder had but she had convinced herself that those feelings weren't real. She'd been sixteen years old, what did a teenager know about real love? But now she understood. It had been real and she wouldn't feel that way about anyone else. Ryder was the only man for her. She loved him and always had.

'I'm scared, Ryder,' she whispered as she sat down again. 'Scared that you won't love me. Scared that you'll leave me.'

'What did you say?'

For a moment Poppy thought she'd imagined the

sound of his voice but when she lifted her head she saw his eyes were open and he was looking at her.

'Oh, my God.' He was awake! 'Are you okay?'

Even as the words popped out of her mouth she realised it was a stupid question but before she could say anything else one of the nurses hustled in, forcing her to move away from Ryder's side. She stepped back reluctantly as the nurse checked Ryder's vital signs and started asking questions.

A second nurse and a doctor arrived and Poppy was asked to wait outside as the room filled with hospital staff.

She stood in the corridor, watching through the window, feeling further and further removed from Ryder. She pressed her hand against the glass and rested her forehead on the window and waited and watched as the medical staff ran through their tests.

She waited, hoping he'd ask for her.

But what if he didn't?

She sat in a chair in the corridor as the minutes passed.

She had finally found her voice but what if she didn't get a chance to use it? What if he didn't want to hear what she had to say?

Time passed and still no one came to call her.

What if they really were over?

'Do you want to stop and grab dinner somewhere before we go home?' Poppy asked Lily as she reversed her car out of the car park.

'I thought you weren't feeling well?'

Poppy had been out of sorts all day. She'd cancelled a shift at work, called in sick, which was something she'd *never* done, because she knew she knew she wouldn't be able to concentrate. She wasn't ill but she did feel nauseous. She knew it was nerves, anxiety, and she knew she'd brought it on herself. She was worried she'd really mucked everything up with Ryder and that there was no way back.

She hadn't seen him since she'd left the hospital last night. When she'd *had* to leave. Ryder hadn't asked to see her and then he'd been taken off for more scans while she'd waited. Visiting hours had ended before he'd returned to his room and she'd had to leave. She had no excuse to stay. She wasn't family, she wasn't his next of kin, she was nothing.

And she'd heard nothing from him today. Nothing at all.

The best she could get had been updates from Lily when she had been at work.

Thanks to Lily, Poppy knew Ryder was okay. He had some bruising but he'd been cleared of any serious injuries and the swelling of his brain was reducing.

She had intended on going to the hospital once visiting hours started, only to receive a second phone call from Lily telling her that Ryder had discharged himself.

She'd waited, hoping for a call, but Ryder had disappeared.

After that, she hadn't been able to sit still. She'd gone for a surf and called into the lifeguard tower, pretending to visit Jet but really hoping that Ryder might have gone there, but all the activity had done nothing to ease her anxiety.

She'd been happy to collect Lily when she had called saying her car had a flat battery and she needed a lift home. Even the detour to the supermarket had been a welcome distraction.

'I'm fine,' Poppy said in reply to Lily's question. She

was still anxious but she didn't feel like going home to stare at the walls while praying that Ryder would get in touch with her.

'Can we drop the shopping off first?' Lily asked. 'That way I can get changed before dinner.'

Poppy nodded and headed home. She parked the car and checked her phone, hoping Ryder might have messaged her and she'd missed it, even though she knew that was unlikely as she'd been checking her phone every few minutes for the entire day.

She saw Lily watching her. 'I'm sure he'll be in touch, Poppy.'

Poppy wished she felt as confident.

'I'll take the shopping in,' Lily told her. 'Why don't you pour us both a drink while I get changed and I'll meet you on the deck and we can work out what to do about dinner.'

Poppy shoved her stubbornly silent phone in her pocket and locked the car. She followed Lily into the house and continued through the kitchen, grabbing two glasses and an open bottle of wine from the fridge, and stepped out onto the deck.

The sun had set and fairy lights glowed around the balcony railing. A nest of candles glowed on the table and soft music played through the outdoor speakers. Daisy must be home, she thought.

She turned to go back inside to grab a third glass and jumped as she heard a voice in the semi-darkness.

'Hello, Poppy.'

'Ryder!'

He stood up from his seat in the corner of the deck. Why was he here?

'Is everything okay?' she asked.

'Everything is fine.'

'You're okay?'

'I'm fine,' he said as he took two steps towards her, closing the gap while she stood, stunned and surprised and fixed to the spot.

As her eyes adjusted to the gloom she could see the bruises on his face but his blue eyes were clear and bright and if she ignored the cuts and bruises he looked like his old self. His face was bruised but he was still gorgeous and, best of all, he was here and he was smiling.

She studied him closely. She wanted to touch him, she wanted to feel his face, to make sure he was really real and in one piece, but she didn't want to hurt him and she didn't want to overstep any boundaries that she might not be aware of. 'Are you really all right?'

He nodded as he lifted the wine and the glasses from her hand and put them on the table beside the candles. Her heart skipped a beat as his fingers brushed against hers.

'I was so scared,' she said.

'I know.'

'How do you know?'

'I heard you. In the hospital.'

Oh, God, how much had he heard?

'I thought you were asleep.'

'I'm glad I wasn't. I wouldn't know what you were thinking if I hadn't woken up to the sound of your voice.'

'It was easy to talk to you when I thought you were asleep.'

'Do I frighten you that much?'

'No, but the way you make me feel scares me.'

'Why?'

She couldn't speak. She'd been desperate to see him

but now the old familiar fear that her love wouldn't be wanted haunted her and made her mute.

'Be brave, Poppy,' he said. 'Tell me how you're feeling.'

But she couldn't do it. Not yet.

'If you're scared, how about I go first?' As always, he knew exactly what thoughts were in her head. She still had no idea how he did that. 'Sit with me and I'll tell you what I'm thinking. How I'm feeling,' he said as he guided her to the seats. 'Do you want me to start off?'

She nodded.

'It hurt to know your house was more important to you than I was. I was upset that you chose to work instead of spending the weekend with me.'

Poppy's heart sank like a stone. That was not what she had hoped or expected to hear. 'Oh, Ryder, I never meant to hurt you.' She was distraught. Mortified. 'I wish I could take it all back.' But she knew she couldn't. It was too late for that. It was done.

'But what hurts the most is that you can't share your feelings with me.'

'I've ruined everything, haven't I?'

He smiled at her. 'I'm not going to give up on you that easily. Not after waiting twelve years. I fell in love with you when I was seventeen. Did you know that?'

'No.' Her heart lightened a little. 'I loved you too.' Past tense was easier. She could do this. 'Do you think how we felt was real?'

'I do. I think how I feel now is real too.'

'How do you know?'

'Take my hand, close your eyes and tell me what you feel.'

He held his hand out to her and she took it. She closed her eyes as he wrapped his fingers around hers and joined them together. 'I can't tell where I finish and you start.' They were one. 'I feel like this is where I belong. With you,' she said as she opened her eyes again.

'This is *exactly* where you belong. You're home. We've come home to each other. Home isn't always a house. It's a place where you are safe and loved. Where the people who matter to you are. Home is a feeling. I understand your need for security and stability but you can get that from things other than a house. There are other ways and there are things that are more important.'

'Like?'

'Like love. You need love, Poppy. You need someone to love you. And that someone is me. *I* love you.'

'You love me?'

'I do. With every last battered and bruised piece of me. And now it's your turn.'

He loved her! The idea made her heart sing with delight. The knowledge made her brave.

'I was scared that you wouldn't love me. That you would think I'm not worthy of love.'

'Why on earth would you think that?'

'My parents never seemed to love us and I never believed you would love me,' she admitted. 'No one seems to need me and I didn't want to need anyone either. I loved you before and you left me and broke my heart. I didn't want to be in love again, I didn't want to be vulnerable.'

'I'm not going to hurt you.'

'But you are going to leave me. You're going back to Perth.'

He shook his head, wincing slightly at the movement. 'I don't want to go anywhere without you. I've been waiting twelve years to find my way back to you.

What happens next is up to you. You said you loved me before. Do you think you could love me again?'

'You were my first love and I've always kept a piece of you, the idea of you in my heart.' She took a deep breath. This was it. The biggest moment in her life. 'I've never stopped loving you. I loved you then and I love you now.'

'That wasn't so hard, was it?'

Ryder was laughing and Poppy laughed with him. 'Not as hard as I thought. It might even get easier with practice.'

He tugged on her hand and pulled her close. 'I'm pleased to hear that and just so you know, I'm not going anywhere. I'm not going to hurt you, or leave you. Not ever. I promise.'

'But what about Perth?'

'There will be other jobs. It doesn't matter to me where I work or where I am as long as you are with me. Nothing matters as long as we're together.' He kissed her as if they'd been apart for months, not hours, and only let her go to say, 'So, where will we go? Here, Perth or Brisbane?'

'Brisbane?'

He nodded. 'If you have your heart set on going back to Brisbane, I could look for a job there instead. I don't want you to have to choose between me and your house again.'

Poppy laughed. 'Don't worry. I've learned my lesson. I've spoken to Craig and told him to put the house on the market.'

'You have?'

She nodded.

'Are you sure?'

'I'm positive. It's done. I had a moment of clarity the

other night, watching you walking out my front door. You were right. It's just a house. My home is with you, wherever you are. I know that.'

'So, we have a plan. Our plan. For now we will stay in Sydney and I will be yours. I will be the one who makes you happy. I will be the person you depend on. The one you turn to. The one who makes you smile and laugh. The one who loves you.'

'That sounds perfect.' She was grinning from ear to ear.

'Which leaves just one more thing,' he said as he stood up from the seat and got down on one knee.

'What are you doing!?'

'Something I had planned to do this weekend before you moved the goalposts. This isn't quite how I envisaged this would go but I don't want to wait. I need to prove to you that I am committed, that I am here for you, always, no matter what,' he said. 'Poppy Carlson, I have loved you for as long as I can remember. I have never loved anyone the way I love you and I want our love to last a lifetime. I want to be by your side for eternity. Will you marry me?'

Tears welled in Poppy's eyes but she was smiling as she pulled Ryder to his feet.

'I gave you my heart twelve years ago,' she said, 'and now I give you the rest of me. Everything I am, everything I have, I give to you. I give you my heart, my body and my soul, now and for ever.'

She took a deep breath. She was still scared but she knew she could do this. With his love she could be brave, she could be happy, she could be anything she wanted. She looked into his eyes and said, 'I love you, Ryder, and I always will. We belong together and I don't ever want to be apart again. I never thought I cared about being married but if I get to be married to you then I will gladly spend the rest of my life by your side. You have brought me home and so, my love, my answer is yes. Yes, I will marry you.'

She could hear people clapping as she kissed him and then they were both enveloped in the arms of her siblings. Daisy was crying, Lily was smiling and Jet was high-fiving Ryder.

'What are you all doing here?' Poppy hadn't realised they'd had an audience. She'd been aware of nothing except Ryder.

'I asked them to come,' Ryder told her. 'I was hoping you'd say yes and I thought you might want to celebrate with your family.'

'You all knew about this?'

All three of them nodded.

'Your car didn't have a flat battery, did it?' she said to Lily, realising her siblings had all had a hand in the evening's events.

Lily shook her head. 'I needed an excuse to get you out of the house to give Ryder time to get here and prepare the surprise.'

Ryde took her hand and said, 'I know you don't like surprises but I thought you'd be okay with this one.'

Poppy smiled through her tears as she gazed at him. 'I'm definitely okay with this one. It couldn't be any better. It's perfect,' she said as she wrapped her arms around him and whispered into his ear, '*You're* perfect and I love you. Now and always.'

* * * * *

MILLS & BOON

Coming next month

CONSEQUENCES OF THEIR NEW YORK NIGHT
Tina Beckett

Nicola's mind was wandering, and her thoughts slid in and out of places that were best left for another time. The hospital was huge and the names of people she'd been introduced to were starting to squish together inside the confines of her skull.

And as the space grew even tighter, something had to give. So squeezing between the cracks came the memory of a night five weeks ago. And the tall stranger she'd fallen into bed with.

She swallowed. She still couldn't believe she'd done that. What had she been thinking?

She hadn't been. And that had been the idea. She hadn't wanted to think, to talk…to remember. She'd just wanted to feel. And, God, had she ever. She'd…

"Kaleb, could you come over here for a moment?" Harvey Smith's voice shocked her back to reality, making her blink. "I want you to meet the newest member of our team: Nicola Bradley. Her specialty is internal medicine with an emphasis on diagnostics. She'll be helping us crack the tough cases."

As the hospital administrator continued to speak, she turned to greet the newcomer, and a wave of shock knocked her flat, setting off all kinds of sirens and alarms.

"Nicola, meet Kaleb Sabat. He's New York City Memorial's chief of reconstructive surgery."

She somehow met the man's cool blue eyes without flinching. How was this even possible? Was this some sort of cosmic joke? If so, the punch line was lost on her.

The man she'd shared a crazy, impulsive night of sex with was NYC Memorial's chief of reconstructive surgery? Oh, God. What should she do? What *could* she do?

Quit? Run down the hallway until she found the nearest exit? No. Nicola was no chicken. At least she hoped not.

She was going to pretend it never happened, that's what she'd do. And hope that he did the same. Or maybe he didn't even remember her.

Please, God...

"Nice to meet you, Dr. Sabat," she murmured, placing the slightest emphasis on his title.

The man's head tilted sideways for a second, his eyebrows coming together as a host of changes came over his face, the last of which was sardonic amusement.

Oh, no. He remembered. *Remembered!*

They'd both had a little too much to drink that night five weeks ago, and she'd hoped...

If she'd had any idea he'd worked at the hospital she was transferring to, she would have moved off that barstool quicker than anyone believed possible. But she'd been grieving and needed to forget.

Kaleb had given her a few hours of respite...and more.

Continue reading
CONSEQUENCES OF THEIR NEW YORK NIGHT
Tina Beckett

Available next month
www.millsandboon.co.uk

COMING SOON!

We really hope you enjoyed reading this book. If you're looking for more romance, be sure to head to the shops when new books are available on

Thursday 18th March

To see which titles are coming soon, please visit

millsandboon.co.uk/nextmonth

WE'RE LOOKING FOR NEW AUTHORS FOR THE MILLS & BOON MEDICAL SERIES!

Whether you're a published author or an aspiring one, our editors would love to read your story.

You can submit the synopsis and first three chapters of your novel online, and find out more about the series, at **harlequin.submittable.com/submit**

We read all submissions and you do not need to have an agent to submit.

IF YOU'RE INTERESTED, WHY NOT HAVE A GO?

Submit your story at:
harlequin.submittable.com/submit

MILLS & BOON

LET'S TALK

Romance

For exclusive extracts, competitions
and special offers, find us online: